Michael, Brother of Jerry by Jack London

John Griffith "Jack" London was born John Griffith Chaney on January 12th, 1876 in San Francisco.

His father, William Chaney, was living with his mother Flora Wellman when she became pregnant. Chaney insisted she have an abortion. Flora's response was to turn a gun on herself. Although her wounds were not severe the trauma made her temporarily deranged.

In late 1876 his mother married John London and the young child was brought to live with them as they moved around the Bay area, eventually settling in Oakland where Jack completed grade school.

Jack also worked hard at several jobs, sometimes 12-18 hours a day, but his dream was university. He was lent money for that and after intense studying enrolled in the summer of 1896 at the University of California in Berkeley.

In 1897, at 21 , Jack searched out newspaper accounts of his mother's suicide attempt and the name of his biological father. He wrote to William Chaney, then living in Chicago. Chaney said he could not be London's father because he was impotent; and casually asserted that London's mother had relations with other men. Jack, devastated by the response, quit Berkeley and went to the Klondike. Though equally because of his continuing dire finances Jack might have taken that as the excuse he needed to leave.

In the Klondike Jack began to gather material for his writing but also accumulated many health problems, including scurvy, hip and leg problems many of which he then carried for life.

By the late 1890's Jack was regularly publishing short stories and by the turn of the century full blown novels.

By 1904 Jack had married, fathered two children and was now in the process of divorcing. A stint as a reporter on the Russo-Japanese war of 1904 was equal amounts trouble and experience. But that experience was always put to good use in a remarkable output of work.

Twelve years later Jack had amassed a wealth of writings many of which remain world classics. He had a reputation as a social activist and a tireless friend of the workers. And yet on November 22nd 1916 Jack London died in a cottage on his ranch at the age of only 40.

Index Of Contents

FOREWORD

Very early in my life, possibly because of the insatiable curiosity that was born in me, I came to dislike the performances of trained animals. It was my curiosity that spoiled for me this form of amusement, for I was led to seek behind the performance in order to learn how the performance was achieved. And what I found behind the brave show and glitter of performance was not nice. It was a body of cruelty so horrible that I am confident no normal person exists who, once aware of it, could ever enjoy looking on at any trained-animal turn.

Now I am not a namby-pamby. By the book reviewers and the namby-pambys I am esteemed a sort of primitive beast that delights in the spilled blood of violence and horror. Without arguing this matter of my general reputation, accepting it at its current face value, let me add that I have indeed lived life in a very rough school and have seen more than the average man's share of inhumanity and cruelty, from the forecastle and the prison, the slum and the desert, the execution-chamber and the lazar- house, to the battlefield and the military hospital. I have seen horrible deaths and mutilations. I have seen imbeciles hanged, because, being imbeciles, they did not possess the hire of lawyers. I have seen the hearts and stamina of strong men broken, and I have seen other men, by ill-treatment, driven to permanent and howling madness. I have witnessed the deaths of old and young, and even infants, from sheer starvation. I have seen men and women beaten by whips and clubs and fists, and I have seen the rhinoceros-hide whips laid around the naked torsos of black boys so heartily that each stroke stripped away the skin in full circle. And yet, let me add finally, never have I been so appalled and shocked by the world's cruelty as have I been appalled and shocked in the midst of happy, laughing, and applauding audiences when trained-animal turns were being performed on the stage.

One with a strong stomach and a hard head may be able to tolerate much of the unconscious and undeliberate cruelty and torture of the world that is perpetrated in hot blood and stupidity. I have such a stomach and head. But what turns my head and makes my gorge rise, is the cold-blooded, conscious, deliberate cruelty and torment that is manifest behind ninety- nine of every hundred trained-animal turns. Cruelty, as a fine art, has attained its perfect flower in the trained-animal world.

Possessed myself of a strong stomach and a hard head, inured to hardship, cruelty, and brutality, nevertheless I found, as I came to manhood, that I unconsciously protected myself from the hurt of the trained-animal turn by getting up and leaving the theatre whenever such turns came on the stage. I say "unconsciously." By this I mean it never entered my mind that this was a programme by which the possible death-blow might be given to trained-animal turns. I was merely protecting myself from the pain of witnessing what it would hurt me to witness.

But of recent years my understanding of human nature has become such that I realize that no normal healthy human would tolerate such performances did he or she know the terrible cruelty that lies behind them and makes them possible. So I am emboldened to suggest, here and now, three things:

First, let all humans inform themselves of the inevitable and eternal cruelty by the means of which only can animals be compelled to perform before revenue-paying audiences. Second, I suggest that all men and women, and boys and girls, who have so acquainted themselves with the essentials of the fine art of animal-training, should become members of, and ally themselves with, the local and national organizations of humane societies and societies for the prevention of cruelty to animals.

And the third suggestion I cannot state until I have made a preamble. Like hundreds of thousands of others, I have worked in other fields, striving to organize the mass of mankind into movements for the purpose of ameliorating its own wretchedness and misery. Difficult as this is to accomplish, it is still more difficult to persuade the human into any organised effort to alleviate the ill conditions of the lesser animals.

Practically all of us will weep red tears and sweat bloody sweats as we come to knowledge of the unavoidable cruelty and brutality on which the trained-animal world rests and has its being. But not one-tenth of one per cent. of us will join any organization for the prevention of cruelty to animals, and by our words and acts and contributions work to prevent the perpetration of cruelties on animals. This is a weakness of our own human nature. We must recognize it as we recognize heat and cold, the opaqueness of the non-transparent, and the everlasting down-pull of gravity.

And still for us, for the ninety-nine and nine-tenths per cent. of us, under the easy circumstance of our own weakness, remains another way most easily to express ourselves for the purpose of eliminating from the world the cruelty that is practised by some few of us, for the entertainment of the rest of us, on the trained animals, who, after all, are only lesser animals than we on the round world's surface. It is so easy. We will not have to think of dues or corresponding secretaries. We will not have to think of anything, save when, in any theatre or place of entertainment, a trained-animal turn is presented before us. Then, without premeditation, we may express our disapproval of such a turn by getting up from our seats and leaving the theatre for a promenade and a breath of fresh air outside, coming back, when the turn is over, to enjoy the rest of the programme. All we have to do is just that to eliminate the trained-animal turn from all public places of entertainment. Show the management that such turns are unpopular, and in a day, in an instant, the management will cease catering such turns to its audiences.

JACK LONDON

GLEN ELLEN, SONOMA COUNTY, CALIFORNIA,

December 8, 1915

CHAPTER I

But Michael never sailed out of Tulagi, nigger-chaser on the Eugenie. Once in five weeks the steamer Makambo made Tulagi its port of call on the way from New Guinea and the Shortlands to Australia. And on the night of her belated arrival Captain Kellar forgot Michael on the beach. In itself, this was nothing, for, at midnight, Captain Kellar was back on the beach, himself climbing the high hill to the Commissioner's bungalow while the boat's crew vainly rummaged the landscape and canoe houses.

In fact, an hour earlier, as the Makambo's anchor was heaving out and while Captain Kellar was descending the port gang-plank, Michael was coming on board through a starboard port-hole. This was because Michael was inexperienced in the world, because he was expecting to meet Jerry on board this boat since the last he had seen of him was on a boat, and because he had made a friend.

Dag Daughtry was a steward on the Makambo, who should have known better and who would have known better and done better had he not been fascinated by his own particular and peculiar reputation. By luck of birth possessed of a genial but soft disposition and a splendid constitution, his reputation was that for twenty years he had never missed his day's work nor his six daily quarts of bottled beer, even, as he bragged, when in the German islands, where each bottle of beer carried ten grains of quinine in solution as a specific against malaria.

The captain of the Makambo (and, before that, the captains of the Moresby, the Masena, the Sir Edward Grace, and various others of the queerly named Burns Philp Company steamers had done the same) was used to pointing him out proudly to the passengers as a man-thing novel and unique in the annals of the sea. And at such times Dag Daughtry, below on the for'ard deck, feigning unawareness as he went about his work, would steal side-glances up at the bridge where the captain and his passengers stared down on him, and his breast would swell pridefully, because he knew that the captain was saying: "See him! that's Dag Daughtry, the human tank. Never's been drunk or sober in twenty years, and has never missed his six quarts of beer per diem. You wouldn't think it, to look at him, but I assure you it's so. I can't understand. Gets my admiration. Always does his time, his time-and-a-half and his double- time over time. Why, a single glass of beer would give me heartburn and spoil my next good meal. But he flourishes on it. Look at him! Look at him!"

And so, knowing his captain's speech, swollen with pride in his own prowess, Dag Daughtry would continue his ship-work with extra vigour and punish a seventh quart for the day in advertisement of his remarkable constitution. It was a queer sort of fame, as queer as some men are; and Dag Daughtry found in it his justification of existence.

Wherefore he devoted his energy and the soul of him to the maintenance of his reputation as a six-quart man. That was why he made, in odd moments of off-duty, turtle-shell combs and hair ornaments for profit, and was prettily crooked in such a matter as stealing another man's dog. Somebody had to pay for the six quarts, which, multiplied by thirty, amounted to a tidy sum in the course of the month; and, since that man was Dag Daughtry, he found it necessary to pass Michael inboard on the Makambo through a starboard port-hole.

On the beach, that night at Tulagi, vainly wondering what had become of the whaleboat, Michael had met the squat, thick, hair-grizzled ship's steward. The friendship between them was established almost instantly, for Michael, from a merry puppy, had matured into a merry dog. Far beyond Jerry, was he a sociable good fellow, and this, despite the fact that he had known very few white men. First, there had been Mister Haggin, Derby and Bob, of Meringe; next, Captain Kellar and Captain Kellar's mate of the Eugenie; and, finally, Harley Kennan and the officers of the Ariel. Without exception, he had found them all different, and delightfully different, from the hordes of blacks he had been taught to despise and to lord it over.

And Dag Daughtry had proved no exception from his first greeting of "Hello, you white man's dog, what 'r' you doin' herein nigger country?" Michael had responded coyly with an assumption of dignified aloofness that was given the lie by the eager tilt of his ears and the good-humour that shone in his eyes. Nothing of this was missed by Dag Daughtry, who knew a dog when he saw one, as he studied Michael in the light of the lanterns held by black boys where the whaleboats were landing cargo.

Two estimates the steward quickly made of Michael: he was a likable dog, genial-natured on the face of it, and he was a valuable dog. Because of those estimates Dag Daughtry glanced about him quickly. No one was observing. For the moment, only blacks stood about, and their eyes were turned seaward where the sound of oars out of the darkness warned them to stand ready to receive the next cargo-laden boat. Off to the right, under another lantern, he could make out the Resident Commissioner's clerk and the Makambo's super-cargo heatedly discussing some error in the bill of lading.

The steward flung another quick glance over Michael and made up his mind. He turned away casually and strolled along the beach out of the circle of lantern light. A hundred yards away he sat down in the sand and waited.

"Worth twenty pounds if a penny," he muttered to himself. "If I couldn't get ten pounds for him, just like that, with a thank-you-ma'am, I'm a sucker that don't know a terrier from a greyhound. Sure, ten pounds, in any pub on Sydney beach."

And ten pounds, metamorphosed into quart bottles of beer, reared an immense and radiant vision, very like a brewery, inside his head.

A scurry of feet in the sand, and low sniffings, stiffened him to alertness. It was as he had hoped. The dog had liked him from the start, and had followed him.

For Dag Daughtry had a way with him, as Michael was quickly to learn, when the man's hand reached out and clutched him, half by the jowl, half by the slack of the neck under the ear. There was no threat in that reach, nothing tentative nor timorous. It was hearty, all-confident, and it produced confidence in Michael. It was roughness without hurt, assertion without threat, surety without seduction. To him it was the most natural thing in the world thus to be familiarly seized and shaken about by a total stranger, while a jovial voice muttered: "That's right, dog. Stick around, stick around, and you'll wear diamonds, maybe."

Certainly, Michael had never met a man so immediately likable. Dag Daughtry knew, instinctively to be sure, how to get on with dogs. By nature there was no cruelty in him. He never exceeded in peremptoriness, nor in petting. He did not overbid for Michael's friendliness. He did bid, but in a manner that conveyed no sense of bidding. Scarcely had he given Michael that introductory jowl-shake, when he released him and apparently forgot all about him.

He proceeded to light his pipe, using several matches as if the wind blew them out. But while they burned close up to his fingers, and while he made a simulation of prodigious puffing, his keen little blue eyes, under shaggy, grizzled brows, intently studied Michael. And Michael, ears cocked and eyes intent, gazed at this stranger who seemed never to have been a stranger at all.

If anything, it was disappointment Michael experienced, in that this delightful, two-legged god took no further notice of him. He even challenged him to closer acquaintance with an invitation to play, with an abrupt movement lifting his paws from the ground and striking them down, stretched out well before, his body bent down from the rump in such a curve that almost his chest touched the sand, his stump of a tail waving signals of good nature while he uttered a sharp, inviting bark. And the man was uninterested, pulling stolidly away at his pipe, in the darkness following upon the third match.

Never was there a more consummate love-making, with all the base intent of betrayal, than this cavalier seduction of Michael by the elderly, six- quart ship's steward. When Michael, not entirely unwitting of the snub of the man's lack of interest, stirred restlessly with a threat to depart, he had flung at him gruffly:

"Stick around, dog, stick around."

Dag Daughtry chuckled to himself, as Michael, advancing, sniffed his trousers' legs long and earnestly. And the man took advantage of his nearness to study him some more, lighting his pipe and running over the dog's excellent lines.

"Some dog, some points," he said aloud approvingly. "Say, dog, you could pull down ribbons like a candy-kid in any bench show anywheres. Only thing against you is that ear, and I could almost iron it out myself. A vet. could do it."

Carelessly he dropped a hand to Michael's ear, and, with tips of fingers instinct with sensuous sympathy, began to manipulate the base of the ear where its roots bedded in the tightness of skin-stretch over the skull. And Michael liked it. Never had a man's hand been so intimate with his ear without hurting it. But these fingers were provocative only of physical pleasure so keen that he twisted and writhed his whole body in acknowledgment.

Next came a long, steady, upward pull of the ear, the ear slipping slowly through the fingers to the very tip of it while it tingled exquisitely down to its roots. Now to one ear, now to the other, this happened, and all the while the man uttered low words that Michael did not understand but which he accepted as addressed to him.

"Head all right, good 'n' flat," Dag Daughtry murmured, first sliding his fingers over it, and then lighting a match. "An' no wrinkles, 'n' some jaw, good 'n' punishing, an' not a shade too full in the cheek or too empty."

He ran his fingers inside Michael's mouth and noted the strength and evenness of the teeth, measured the breadth of shoulders and depth of chest, and picked up a foot. In the light of another match he examined all four feet.

"Black, all black, every nail of them," said Daughtry, "an' as clean feet as ever a dog walked on, straight-out toes with the proper arch 'n' small 'n' not too small. I bet your daddy and your mother cantered away with the ribbons in their day."

Michael was for growing restless at such searching examination, but Daughtry, in the midst of feeling out the lines and build of the thighs and hocks, paused and took Michael's tail in his magic fingers, exploring the muscles among which it rooted, pressing and prodding the adjacent spinal column from which it sprang, and twisting it about in a most daringly intimate way. And Michael was in an ecstasy, bracing his hindquarters to one side or the other against the caressing fingers. With open hands laid along his sides and partly under him, the man suddenly lifted him from the ground. But before he could feel alarm he was back on the ground again.

"Twenty-six or -seven, you're over twenty-five right now, I'll bet you on it, shillings to ha'pennies, and you'll make thirty when you get your full weight," Dag Daughtry told him. "But what of it? Lots of the judges fancy the thirty-mark. An' you could always train off a few ounces. You're all dog n' all correct conformation. You've got the racing build and the fighting weight, an' there ain't no feathers on your legs."

"No, sir, Mr. Dog, your weight's to the good, and that ear can be ironed out by any respectable dog, doctor. I bet there's a hundred men in Sydney right now that would fork over twenty quid for the right of calling you his."

And then, just that Michael should not make the mistake of thinking he was being much made over, Daughtry leaned back, relighted his pipe, and apparently forgot his existence. Instead of bidding for good will, he was bent on making Michael do the bidding.

And Michael did, bumping his flanks against Daughtry's knee; nudging his head against Daughtry's hand, in solicitation for more of the blissful ear-rubbing and tail-twisting. Daughtry caught him by the jowl instead and slowly moved his head back and forth as he addressed him:

"What man's dog are you? Maybe you're a nigger's dog, an' that ain't right. Maybe some nigger's stole you, an' that'd be awful. Think of the cruel fates that sometimes happens to dogs. It's a damn shame. No white man's stand for a nigger ownin' the likes of you, an' here's one white man that ain't goin' to stand for it. The idea! A nigger ownin' you an' not knowin' how to train you. Of course a nigger stole you. If I laid eyes on him right now I'd up and knock seven bells and the Saint Paul chimes out of 'm. Sure thing I would. Just show 'm to me, that's all, an' see what I'd do to him. The idea of you takin' orders from a nigger an' fetchin' 'n' carryin' for him! No, sir, dog, you ain't goin' to do it any more. You're comin' along of me, an' I reckon I won't have to urge you."

Dag Daughtry stood up and turned carelessly along the beach. Michael looked after him, but did not follow. He was eager to, but had received no invitation. At last Daughtry made a low kissing sound with his lips. So low was it that he scarcely heard it himself and almost took it on faith, or on the testimony of his lips rather than of his ears, that he had made it. No human being could have heard it across the distance to Michael; but Michael heard it, and sprang away after in a great delighted rush.

CHAPTER II

Dag Daughtry strolled along the beach, Michael at his heels or running circles of delight around him at every repetition of that strange low lip- noise, and paused just outside the circle of lantern light where dusky forms laboured with landing cargo from the whaleboats and where the Commissioner's clerk and the Makambo's super-cargo still wrangled over the bill of lading. When Michael would have gone forward, the man withstrained him with the same inarticulate, almost inaudible kiss.

For Daughtry did not care to be seen on such dog-stealing enterprises and was planning how to get on board the steamer unobserved. He edged around outside the lantern shine and went on along the beach to the native village. As he had foreseen, all the able-bodied men were down at the boat-landing working cargo. The grass houses seemed lifeless, but at last, from one of them, came a challenge in the querulous, high-pitched tones of age:

"What name?"

"Me walk about plenty too much," he replied in the beche-de-mer English of the west South Pacific. "Me belong along steamer. Suppose 'm you take 'm me along canoe, washee-washee, me give 'm you fella boy two stick tobacco."

"Suppose 'm you give 'm me ten stick, all right along me," came the reply.

"Me give 'm five stick," the six-quart steward bargained. "Suppose 'm you no like 'm five stick then you fella boy go to hell close up."

There was a silence.

"You like 'm five stick?" Daughtry insisted of the dark interior.

"Me like 'm," the darkness answered, and through the darkness the body that owned the voice approached with such strange sounds that the steward lighted a match to see.

A blear-eyed ancient stood before him, balancing on a single crutch. His eyes were half-filmed over by a growth of morbid membrane, and what was not yet covered shone red and irritated. His hair was mangy, standing out in isolated patches of wispy grey. His skin was scarred and wrinkled and mottled, and in colour was a purplish blue surfaced with a grey coating that might have been painted there had it not indubitably grown there and been part and parcel of him.

A blighted leper, was Daughtry's thought as his quick eyes leapt from hands to feet in quest of missing toe- and finger-joints. But in those items the ancient was intact, although one leg ceased midway between knee and thigh.

"My word! What place stop 'm that fella leg?" quoth Daughtry, pointing to the space which the member would have occupied had it not been absent.

"Big fella shark-fish, that fella leg stop 'm along him," the ancient grinned, exposing a horrible aperture of toothlessness for a mouth.

"Me old fella boy too much," the one-legged Methuselah quavered. "Long time too much no smoke 'm tobacco. Suppose 'm you big fella white marster give 'm me one fella stick, close up me washee-washee you that fella steamer."

"Suppose 'm me no give?" the steward impatiently temporized.

For reply, the old man half-turned, and, on his crutch, swinging his stump of leg in the air, began sidling hippity-hop into the grass hut.

"All right," Daughtry cried hastily. "Me give 'm you smoke 'm quick fella."

He dipped into a side coat-pocket for the mintage of the Solomons and stripped off a stick from the handful of pressed sticks. The old man was transfigured as he reached avidly for the stick and received it. He uttered little crooning noises, alternating with sharp cries akin to pain, half-ecstatic, half-petulant, as he drew a black clay pipe from a hole in his ear-lobe, and into the bowl of it, with trembling fingers, untwisted and crumbled the cheap leaf of spoiled Virginia crop.

Pressing down the contents of the full bowl with his thumb, he suddenly plumped upon the ground, the crutch beside him, the one limb under him so that he had the seeming of a legless torso. From a small bag of twisted coconut hanging from his neck upon his withered and sunken chest, he drew out flint and steel and tinder, and, even while the impatient steward was proffering him a box of matches, struck a spark, caught it in the tinder, blew it into strength and quantity, and lighted his pipe from it.

With the first full puff of the smoke he gave over his moans and yelps, the agitation began to fade out of him, and Daughtry, appreciatively waiting, saw the trembling go out of his hands, the pendulous lip-quivering cease, the saliva stop flowing from the corners of his mouth, and placidity come into the fiery remnants of his eyes.

What the old man visioned in the silence that fell, Daughtry did not try to guess. He was too occupied with his own vision, and vividly burned before him the sordid barrenness of a poor-house ward, where an ancient, very like what he himself would become, maundered and gibbered and drooled for a crumb of tobacco for his old clay pipe, and where, of all horrors, no sip of beer ever obtained, much less six quarts of it.

And Michael, by the dim glows of the pipe surveying the scene of the two old men, one squatted in the dark, the other standing, knew naught of the tragedy of age, and was only aware, and overwhelmingly aware, of the immense likableness of this two-legged white god, who, with fingers of magic, through ear-roots and tail-roots and spinal column, had won to the heart of him.

The clay pipe smoked utterly out, the old black, by aid of the crutch, with amazing celerity raised himself upstanding on his one leg and hobbled, with his hippity-hop, to the beach. Daughtry was compelled to lend his strength to the hauling down from the sand into the water of the tiny canoe. It was a dug-out, as ancient and dilapidated as its owner, and, in order to get into it without capsizing, Daughtry wet one leg to the ankle and the other leg to the knee. The old man contorted himself aboard, rolling his body across the gunwale so quickly, that, even while it started to capsize, his weight was across the danger-point and counterbalancing the canoe to its proper equilibrium.

Michael remained on the beach, waiting invitation, his mind not quite made up, but so nearly so that all that was required was that lip-noise. Dag Daughtry made the lip-noise so low that the old man did not hear, and Michael, springing clear from sand to canoe, was on board without wetting his feet.

Using Daughtry's shoulder for a stepping-place, he passed over him and down into the bottom of the canoe. Daughtry kissed with his lips again, and Michael turned around so as to face him, sat down, and rested his head on the steward's knees.

"I reckon I can take my affydavy on a stack of Bibles that the dog just up an' followed me," he grinned in Michael's ear.

"Washee-washee quick fella," he commanded.

The ancient obediently dipped his paddle and started pottering an erratic course in the general direction of the cluster of lights that marked the Makambo. But he was too feeble, panting and wheezing continually from the exertion and pausing to rest off strokes between strokes. The steward impatiently took the paddle away from him and bent to the work.

Half-way to the steamer the ancient ceased wheezing and spoke, nodding his head at Michael.

"That fella dog he belong big white marster along schooner . . . You give 'm me ten stick tobacco," he added after due pause to let the information sink in.

"I give 'm you bang alongside head," Daughtry assured him cheerfully. "White marster along schooner plenty friend along me too much. Just now he stop 'm along Makambo. Me take 'm dog along him along Makambo."

There was no further conversation from the ancient, and though he lived long years after, he never mentioned the midnight passenger in the canoe who carried Michael away with him. When he saw and heard the confusion and uproar on the beach later that night when Captain Kellar turned Tulagi upside-down in his search for Michael, the old one-legged one remained discreetly silent. Who was he to seek trouble with the strange ones, the white masters who came and went and roved and ruled?

In this the ancient was in nowise unlike the rest of his dark-skinned Melanesian race. The whites were possessed of unguessed and unthinkable ways and purposes. They constituted another world and were as a play of superior beings on an exalted stage where was no reality such as black men might know as reality, where, like the phantoms of a dream, the white men moved and were as shadows cast upon the vast and mysterious curtain of the Cosmos.

The gang-plank being on the port side, Dag Daughtry paddled around to the starboard and brought the canoe to a stop under a certain open port.

"Kwaque!" he called softly, once, and twice.

At the second call the light of the port was obscured apparently by a head that piped down in a thin squeak.

"Me stop 'm, marster."

"One fella dog stop 'm along you," the steward whispered up. "Keep 'm door shut. You wait along me. Stand by! Now!"

With a quick catch and lift, he passed Michael up and into unseen hands outstretched from the iron wall of the ship, and paddled ahead to an open cargo port. Dipping into his tobacco pocket, he thrust a loose handful of sticks into the ancient's hand and shoved the canoe adrift with no thought of how its helpless occupant would ever reach shore.

The old man did not touch the paddle, and he was unregardful of the lofty-sided steamer as the canoe slipped down the length of it into the darkness astern. He was too occupied in counting the wealth of tobacco showered upon him. No easy task, his counting. Five was the limit of his numerals. When he had counted five, he began over again and counted a second five. Three fives he found in all, and two sticks over; and thus, at the end of it, he possessed as definite a knowledge of the number of sticks as would be possessed by the average white man by means of the single number seventeen.

More it was, far more, than his avarice had demanded. Yet he was unsurprised. Nothing white men did could surprise. Had it been two sticks instead of seventeen, he would have been equally unsurprised. Since all acts of white men were surprises, the only surprise of action they could achieve for a black man would be the doing of an unsurprising thing.

Paddling, wheezing, resting, oblivious of the shadow-world of the white men, knowing only the reality of Tulagi Mountain cutting its crest-line blackly across the dim radiance of the star-sprinkled sky, the reality of the sea and of the canoe he so feebly urged across it, and the reality of his fading strength and of the death into which he would surely end, the ancient black man slowly made his shoreward way.

CHAPTER III

In the meanwhile, Michael. Lifted through the air, exchanged into invisible hands that drew him through a narrow diameter of brass into a lighted room, Michael looked about him in expectancy of Jerry. But Jerry, at that moment, lay cuddled beside Villa Kennan's sleeping-cot on the slant deck of the Ariel, as that trim craft, the Shortlands astern and New Guinea dead ahead, heeled her scuppers a-whisper and garrulous to the sea-welter alongside as she logged her eleven knots under the press of the freshening trades. Instead of Jerry, from whom he had last parted on board a boat, Michael saw Kwaque.

Kwaque? Well, Kwaque was Kwaque, an individual, more unlike all other men than most men are unlike one another. No queerer estray ever drifted along the stream of life. Seventeen years old he was, as men measure time; but a century was measured in his lean-lined face, his wrinkled forehead, his hollowed temples, and his deep-sunk eyes. From his thin legs, fragile-looking as windstraws, the bones of which were sheathed in withered skin with apparently no muscle padding in between, from such frail stems sprouted the torso of a fat man. The huge and protuberant stomach was amply supported by wide and massive hips, and the shoulders were broad as those of a Hercules. But, beheld sidewise, there was no depth to those shoulders and the top of the chest. Almost, at that part of his anatomy, he seemed builded in two dimensions. Thin his arms were as his legs, and, as Michael first beheld him, he had all the seeming of a big-bellied black spider.

He proceeded to dress, a matter of moments, slipping into duck trousers and blouse, dirty and frayed from long usage. Two fingers of his left hand were doubled into a permanent bend, and, to an expert, would have advertised that he was a leper. Although he belonged to Dag Daughtry just as much as if the steward possessed a chattel bill of sale of him, his owner did not know that his anaesthetic twist of ravaged nerves tokened the dread disease.

The manner of the ownership was simple. At King William Island, in the Admiralties, Kwaque had made, in the parlance of the South Pacific, a pier-head jump. So to speak, leprosy and all, he had jumped into Dag Daughtry's arms. Strolling along the native runways in the fringe of jungle just beyond the beach, as was his custom, to see whatever he might pick up, the steward had picked up Kwaque. And he had picked him up in extremity.

Pursued by two very active young men armed with fire-hardened spears, tottering along with incredible swiftness on his two spindle legs, Kwaque had fallen exhausted at Daughtry's feet and looked up at him with the beseeching eyes of a deer fleeing from the hounds. Daughtry had inquired into the matter, and the inquiry was violent; for he had a wholesome fear of germs and bacilli, and when the two active young men tried to run him through with their filth-corroded spears, he caught the spear of one young man under his arm and put the other young man to sleep with a left hook to the jaw. A moment later the young man whose spear he held had joined the other in slumber.

The elderly steward was not satisfied with the mere spears. While the rescued Kwaque continued to moan and slubber thankfulness at his feet, he proceeded to strip them that were naked. Nothing they wore in the way of clothing, but from around each of their necks he removed a necklace of porpoise teeth that was worth a gold sovereign in mere exchange value. From the kinky locks of one of the naked young men he drew a hand-carved, fine-toothed comb, the lofty back of which was inlaid with mother-of-pearl, which he later sold in Sydney to a curio shop for eight shillings. Nose and ear ornaments of bone and turtle-shell he also rifled, as well as a chest-crescent of pearl shell, fourteen inches across, worth fifteen shillings anywhere. The two spears ultimately fetched him five shillings each from the tourists at Port Moresby. Not lightly may a ship steward undertake to maintain a six-quart reputation.

When he turned to depart from the active young men, who, back to consciousness, were observing him with bright, quick, wild-animal eyes, Kwaque followed so close at his heels as to step upon them and make him stumble. Whereupon he loaded Kwaque with his trove and put him in front to lead along the runway to the beach. And for the rest of the way to the steamer, Dag Daughtry grinned and chuckled at sight of his plunder and at sight of Kwaque, who fantastically titubated and ambled along, barrel-like, on his pipe-stems.

On board the steamer, which happened to be the Cockspur, Daughtry persuaded the captain to enter Kwaque on the ship's articles as steward's helper with a rating of ten shillings a month. Also, he learned Kwaque's story.

It was all an account of a pig. The two active young men were brothers who lived in the next village to his, and the pig had been theirs, so Kwaque narrated in atrocious beche-de-mer English. He, Kwaque, had never seen the pig. He had never known of its existence until after it was dead. The two young men had loved the pig. But what of that? It did not concern Kwaque, who was as unaware of their love for the pig as he was unaware of the pig itself.

The first he knew, he averred, was the gossip of the village that the pig was dead, and that somebody would have to die for it. It was all right, he said, in reply to a query from the steward. It was the custom. Whenever a loved pig died its owners were in custom bound to go out and kill somebody, anybody. Of course, it was better if they killed the one whose magic had made the pig sick. But, failing that one, any one would do. Hence Kwaque was selected for the blood-atonement.

Dag Daughtry drank a seventh quart as he listened, so carried away was he by the sombre sense of romance of this dark jungle event wherein men killed even strangers because a pig was dead.

Scouts out on the runways, Kwaque continued, brought word of the coming of the two bereaved pig-owners, and the village had fled into the jungle and climbed trees, all except Kwaque, who was unable to climb trees.

"My word," Kwaque concluded, "me no make 'm that fella pig sick."

"My word," quoth Dag Daughtry, "you devil-devil along that fella pig too much. You look 'm like hell. You make 'm any fella thing sick look along you. You make 'm me sick too much."

It became quite a custom for the steward, as he finished his sixth bottle before turning in, to call upon Kwaque for his story. It carried him back to his boyhood when he had been excited by tales of wild cannibals in far lands and dreamed some day to see them for himself. And here he was, he would chuckle to himself, with a real true cannibal for a slave.

A slave Kwaque was, as much as if Daughtry had bought him on the auction- block. Whenever the steward transferred from ship to ship of the Burns Philp fleet, he always stipulated that Kwaque should accompany him and be duly rated at ten shillings. Kwaque had no say in the matter. Even had he desired to escape in Australian ports, there was no need for Daughtry to watch him. Australia, with her "all-white" policy, attended to that. No dark-skinned human, whether Malay, Japanese, or Polynesian, could land on her shore without putting into the Government's hand a cash security of one hundred pounds.

Nor at the other islands visited by the Makambo had Kwaque any desire to cut and run for it. King William Island, which was the only land he had ever trod, was his yard-stick by which he measured all other islands. And since King William Island was cannibalistic, he could only conclude that the other islands were given to similar dietary practice.

As for King William Island, the Makambo, on the former run of the Cockspur, stopped there every ten weeks; but the direst threat Daughtry ever held over him was the putting ashore of him at the place where the two active young men still mourned their pig. In fact, it was their regular programme, each trip, to paddle out and around the Makambo and make ferocious grimaces up at Kwaque, who grimaced back at them from over the rail. Daughtry even encouraged this exchange of facial amenities for the purpose of deterring him from ever hoping to win ashore to the village of his birth.

For that matter, Kwaque had little desire to leave his master, who, after all, was kindly and just, and never lifted a hand to him. Having survived sea-sickness at the first, and never setting foot upon the land so that he never again knew sea-sickness, Kwaque was certain he lived in an earthly paradise. He never had to regret his inability to climb trees, because danger never threatened him. He had food regularly, and all he wanted, and it was such food! No one in his village could have dreamed of any delicacy of the many delicacies which he consumed all the time. Because of these matters he even pulled through a light attack of home-sickness, and was as contented a human as ever sailed the seas.

And Kwaque it was who pulled Michael through the port-hole into Dag Daughtry's stateroom and waited for that worthy to arrive by the roundabout way of the door. After a quick look around the room and a sniff of the bunk and under the bunk which informed him that Jerry was not present, Michael turned his attention to Kwaque.

Kwaque tried to be friendly. He uttered a clucking noise in advertisement of his friendliness, and Michael snarled at this black who had dared to lay hands upon him, a contamination, according to Michael's training, and who now dared to address him who associated only with white gods.

Kwaque passed off the rebuff with a silly gibbering laugh and started to step nearer the door to be in readiness to open it at his master's coming. But at first lift of his leg, Michael flew at it. Kwaque immediately put it down, and Michael subsided, though he kept a watchful guard. What did he know of this strange black, save that he was a black and that, in the absence of a white master, all blacks required watching? Kwaque tried slowly sliding his foot along the floor, but Michael knew the trick and with bristle and growl put a stop to it.

It was upon this tableau that Daughtry entered, and, while he admired Michael much under the bright electric light, he realized the situation.

"Kwaque, you make 'm walk about leg belong you," he commanded, in order to make sure.

Kwaque's glance of apprehension at Michael was convincing enough, but the steward insisted. Kwaque gingerly obeyed, but scarcely had his foot moved an inch when Michael's was upon him. The foot and leg petrified, while Michael stiff-leggedly drew a half-circle of intimidation about him.

"Got you nailed to the floor, eh?" Daughtry chuckled. "Some nigger-chaser, my word, any amount."

"Hey, you, Kwaque, go fetch 'm two fella bottle of beer stop 'm along icey-chestis," he commanded in his most peremptory manner.

Kwaque looked beseechingly, but did not stir. Nor did he stir at a harsher repetition of the order.

"My word!" the steward bullied. "Suppose 'm you no fetch 'm beer close up, I knock 'm eight bells 'n 'a dog-watch onta you. Suppose 'm you no fetch 'm close up, me make 'm you go ashore 'n' walk about along King William Island."

"No can," Kwaque murmured timidly. "Eye belong dog look along me too much. Me no like 'm dog kai-kai along me."

"You fright along dog?" his master demanded.

"My word, me fright along dog any amount."

Dag Daughtry was delighted. Also, he was thirsty from his trip ashore and did not prolong the situation.

"Hey, you, dog," he addressed Michael. "This fella boy he all right. Savvee? He all right."

Michael bobbed his tail and flattened his ears in token that he was trying to understand. When the steward patted the black on the shoulder, Michael advanced and sniffed both the legs he had kept nailed to the floor.

"Walk about," Daughtry commanded. "Walk about slow fella," he cautioned, though there was little need.

Michael bristled, but permitted the first timid step. At the second he glanced up at Daughtry to make certain.

"That's right," he was reassured. "That fella boy belong me. He all right, you bet."

Michael smiled with his eyes that he understood, and turned casually aside to investigate an open box on the floor which contained plates of turtle-shell, hack-saws, and emery paper.

"And now," Dag Daughtry muttered weightily aloud, as, bottle in hand, he leaned back in his arm-chair while Kwaque knelt at his feet to unlace his shoes, "now to consider a name for you, Mister Dog, that will be just to your breeding and fair to my powers of invention."

CHAPTER IV

Irish terriers, when they have gained maturity, are notable, not alone for their courage, fidelity, and capacity for love, but for their cool- headedness and power of self-control and restraint. They are less easily excited off their balance; they can recognize and obey their master's voice in the scuffle and rage of battle; and they never fly into nervous hysterics such as are common, say, with fox-terriers.

Michael possessed no trace of hysteria, though he was more temperamentally excitable and explosive than his blood-brother Jerry, while his father and mother were a sedate old couple indeed compared with him. Far more than mature Jerry, was mature Michael playful and rowdyish. His ebullient spirits were always on tap to spill over on the slightest provocation, and, as he was afterwards to demonstrate, he could weary a puppy with play. In short, Michael was a merry soul.

"Soul" is used advisedly. Whatever the human soul may be, informing spirit, identity, personality, consciousness, that intangible thing Michael certainly possessed. His soul, differing only in degree, partook of the same attributes as the human soul. He knew love, sorrow, joy, wrath, pride, self-consciousness, humour. Three cardinal attributes of the human soul are memory, will, and understanding; and memory, will, and understanding were Michael's.

Just like a human, with his five senses he contacted with the world exterior to him. Just like a human, the results to him of these contacts were sensations. Just like a human, these sensations on occasion culminated in emotions. Still further, like a human, he could and did perceive, and such perceptions did flower in his brain as concepts, certainly not so wide and deep and recondite as those of humans, but concepts nevertheless.

Perhaps, to let the human down a trifle from such disgraceful identity of the highest life-attributes, it would be well to admit that Michael's sensations were not quite so poignant, say in the matter of a needle-thrust through his foot as compared with a needle-thrust through the palm of a hand. Also, it is admitted, when consciousness suffused his brain with a thought, that the thought was dimmer, vaguer than a similar thought in a human brain. Furthermore, it is admitted that never, never, in a million lifetimes, could Michael have demonstrated a proposition in Euclid or solved a quadratic equation. Yet he was capable of knowing beyond all peradventure of a doubt that three bones are more than two bones, and that ten dogs compose a more redoubtable host than do two dogs.

One admission, however, will not be made, namely, that Michael could not love as devotedly, as wholeheartedly, unselfishly, madly, self-sacrificingly as a human. He did so love, not because he was Michael, but because he was a dog.

Michael had loved Captain Kellar more than he loved his own life. No more than Jerry for Skipper, would he have hesitated to risk his life for Captain Kellar. And he was destined, as time went by and the conviction that Captain Kellar had passed into the inevitable nothingness along with Meringe and the Solomons, to love just as absolutely this six-quart steward with the understanding ways and the fascinating lip-caress. Kwaque, no; for Kwaque was black. Kwaque he merely accepted, as an appurtenance, as a part of the human landscape, as a chattel of Dag Daughtry.

But he did not know this new god as Dag Daughtry. Kwaque called him "marster"; but Michael heard other white men so addressed by the blacks. Many blacks had he heard call Captain Kellar "marster." It was Captain Duncan who called the steward "Steward." Michael came to hear him, and his officers, and all the passengers, so call him; and thus, to Michael, his god's name was Steward, and for ever after he was to know him and think of him as Steward.

There was the question of his own name. The next evening after he came on board, Dag Daughtry talked it over with him. Michael sat on his haunches, the length of his lower jaw resting on Daughtry's knee, the while his eyes dilated, contracted and glowed, his ears ever pricking and repricking to listen, his stump tail thumping ecstatically on the floor.

"It's this way, son," the steward told him. "Your father and mother were Irish. Now don't be denying it, you rascal -"

This, as Michael, encouraged by the unmistakable geniality and kindness in the voice, wriggled his whole body and thumped double knocks of delight with his tail. Not that he understood a word of it, but that he did understand the something behind the speech that informed the string of sounds with all the mysterious likeableness that white gods possessed.

"Never be ashamed of your ancestry. An' remember, God loves the Irish, Kwaque! Go fetch 'm two bottle beer fella stop 'm along icey-chestis! Why, the very mug of you, my lad, sticks out Irish all over it." (Michael's tail beat a tattoo.) "Now don't be blarneyin' me. 'Tis well I'm wise to your insidyous, snugglin', heart-stealin' ways. I'll have ye know my heart's impervious. 'Tis soaked too long this many a day in beer. I stole you to sell you, not to be lovin' you. I could've loved you once; but that was before me and beer was introduced. I'd sell you for twenty quid right now, coin down, if the chance offered. An' I ain't goin' to love you, so you can put that in your pipe 'n' smoke it."

"But as I was about to say when so rudely interrupted by your 'fectionate ways -"

Here he broke off to tilt to his mouth the opened bottle Kwaque handed him. He sighed, wiped his lips with the back of his hand, and proceeded.

"'Tis a strange thing, son, this silly matter of beer. Kwaque, the Methusalem-faced ape grinnin' there, belongs to me. But by my faith do I belong to beer, bottles 'n' bottles of it 'n' mountains of bottles of it enough to sink the ship. Dog, truly I envy you, settin' there comfortable-like inside your body that's untainted of alcohol. I may own you, and the man that gives me twenty quid will own you, but never will a mountain of bottles own you. You're a freer man than I am, Mister Dog, though I don't know your name. Which reminds me -"

He drained the bottle, tossed it to Kwaque, and made signs for him to open the remaining one.

"The namin' of you, son, is not lightly to be considered. Irish, of course, but what shall it be? Paddy? Well may you shake your head. There's no smack of distinction to it. Who'd mistake you for a hod-carrier? Ballymena might do, but it sounds much like a lady, my boy. Ay, boy you are. 'Tis an idea. Boy! Let's see. Banshee Boy? Rotten. Lad of Erin!"

He nodded approbation and reached for the second bottle. He drank and meditated, and drank again.

"I've got you," he announced solemnly. "Killeny is a lovely name, and it's Killeny Boy for you. How's that strike your honourableness? high-soundin', dignified as a earl or . . . or a retired brewer. Many's the one of that gentry I've helped to retire in my day."

He finished his bottle, caught Michael suddenly by both jowls, and, leaning forward, rubbed noses with him. As suddenly released, with thumping tail and dancing eyes, Michael gazed up into the god's face. A definite soul, or entity, or spirit-thing glimmered behind his dog's eyes, already fond with affection for this hair-grizzled god who talked with him he knew not what, but whose very talking carried delicious and unguessable messages to his heart.

"Hey! Kwaque, you!"

Kwaque, squatted on the floor, his hams on his heels, paused from the rough-polishing of a shell comb designed and cut out by his master, and looked up, eager to receive command and serve.

"Kwaque, you fella this time now savvee name stop along this fella dog. His name belong 'm him, Killeny Boy. You make 'm name stop 'm inside head belong you. All the time you speak 'm this fella dog, you speak 'm Killeny Boy. Savvee? Suppose 'm you no savvee, I knock 'm block off belong you. Killeny Boy, savvee! Killeny Boy. Killeny Boy."

As Kwaque removed his shoes and helped him undress, Daughtry regarded Michael with sleepy eyes.

"I've got you, laddy," he announced, as he stood up and swayed toward bed. "I've got your name, an' here's your number, I got that, too: high- strung but reasonable. It fits you like the paper on the wall.

"High-strung but reasonable, that's what you are, Killeny Boy, high-strung but reasonable," he continued to mumble as Kwaque helped to roll him into his bunk.

Kwaque returned to his polishing. His lips stammered and halted in the making of noiseless whispers, as, with corrugated brows of puzzlement, he addressed the steward:

"Marster, what name stop 'm along that fella dog?"

"Killeny Boy, you kinky-head man-eater, Killeny Boy, Killeny Boy," Dag Daughtry murmured drowsily. "Kwaque, you black blood-drinker, run n' fetch 'm one fella bottle stop 'm along icey-chestis."

"No stop 'm, marster," the black quavered, with eyes alert for something to be thrown at him. "Six fella bottle he finish altogether."

The steward's sole reply was a snore.

The black, with the twisted hand of leprosy and with a barely perceptible infiltration of the same disease thickening the skin of the forehead between the eyes, bent over his polishing, and ever his lips moved, repeating over and over, "Killeny Boy."

CHAPTER V

For a number of days Michael saw only Steward and Kwaque. This was because he was confined to the steward's stateroom. Nobody else knew that he was on board, and Dag Daughtry, thoroughly aware that he had stolen a white man's dog, hoped to keep his presence secret and smuggle him ashore when the Makambo docked in Sydney.

Quickly the steward learned Michael's pre-eminent teachableness. In the course of his careful feeding of him, he gave him an occasional chicken bone. Two lessons, which would scarcely be called lessons, since both of them occurred within five minutes and each was not over half a minute in duration, sufficed to teach Michael that only on the floor of the room in the corner nearest the door could he chew chicken bones. Thereafter, without prompting, as a matter of course when handed a bone, he carried it to the corner.

And why not? He had the wit to grasp what Steward desired of him; he had the heart that made it a happiness for him to serve. Steward was a god who was kind, who loved him with voice and lip, who loved him with touch of hand, rub of nose, or enfolding arm. As all service flourishes in the soil of love, so with Michael. Had Steward commanded him to forego the chicken bone after it was in the corner, he would have served him by foregoing. Which is the way of the dog, the only animal that will cheerfully and gladly, with leaping body of joy, leave its food uneaten in order to accompany or to serve its human master.

Practically all his waking time off duty, Dag Daughtry spent with the imprisoned Michael, who, at command, had quickly learned to refrain from whining and barking. And during these hours of companionship Michael learned many things. Daughtry found that he already understood and obeyed simple things such as "no," "yes," "get up," and "lie down," and he improved on them, teaching him, "Go into the bunk and lie down," "Go under the bunk," "Bring one shoe," "Bring two shoes." And almost without any work at all, he taught him to roll over, to say his prayers, to play dead, to sit up and smoke a pipe with a hat on his head, and not merely to stand up on his hind legs but to walk on them.

Then, too, was the trick of "no can and can do." Placing a savoury, nose- tantalising bit of meat or cheese on the edge of the bunk on a level with Michael's nose, Daughtry would simply say, "No can." Nor would Michael touch the food till he received the welcome, "Can do." Daughtry, with the "no can" still in force, would leave the stateroom, and, though he remained away half an hour or half a dozen hours, on his return he would find the food untouched and Michael, perhaps, asleep in the corner at the head of the bunk which had been allotted him for a bed. Early in this trick once when the steward had left the room and Michael's eager nose was within an inch of the prohibited morsel, Kwaque, playfully inclined, reached for the morsel himself and received a lacerated hand from the quick flash and clip of Michael's jaws.

None of the tricks that he was ever eager to do for Steward, would Michael do for Kwaque, despite the fact that Kwaque had no touch of meanness or viciousness in him. The point was that Michael had been trained, from his first dawn of consciousness, to differentiate between black men and white men. Black men were always the servants of white men, or such had been his experience; and always they were objects of suspicion, ever bent on wreaking mischief and requiring careful watching. The cardinal duty of a dog was to serve his white god by keeping a vigilant eye on all blacks that came about.

Yet Michael permitted Kwaque to serve him in matters of food, water, and other offices, at first in the absence of Steward attending to his ship duties, and, later, at any time. For he realized, without thinking about it at all, that whatever Kwaque did for him, whatever food Kwaque spread for him, really proceeded, not from Kwaque, but from Kwaque's master who was also his master. Yet Kwaque bore no grudge against Michael, and was himself so interested in his lord's welfare and comfort, this lord who had saved his life that terrible day on King William Island from the two grief-stricken pig-owners, that he cherished Michael for his lord's sake. Seeing the dog growing into his master's affection, Kwaque himself developed a genuine affection for Michael, much in the same way that he worshipped anything of the steward's, whether the shoes he polished for him, the clothes he brushed and cleaned for him, or the six bottles of beer he put into the ice-chest each day for him.

In truth, there was nothing of the master-quality in Kwaque, while Michael was a natural aristocrat. Michael, out of love, would serve Steward, but Michael lorded it over the kinky-head. Kwaque possessed overwhelmingly the slave-nature, while in Michael there was little more of the slave-nature than was found in the North American Indians when the vain attempt was made to make them into slaves on the plantations of Cuba. All of which was no personal vice of Kwaque or virtue of Michael. Michael's heredity, rigidly selected for ages by man, was chiefly composed of fierceness and faithfulness. And fierceness and faithfulness, together, invariably produce pride. And pride cannot exist without honour, nor can honour without poise.

Michael's crowning achievement, under Daughtry's tutelage, in the first days in the stateroom, was to learn to count up to five. Many hours of work were required, however, in spite of his unusual high endowment of intelligence. For he had to learn, first, the spoken numerals; second, to see with his eyes and in his brain differentiate between one object, and all other groups of objects up to and including the group of five; and, third, in his mind, to relate an object, or any group of objects, with its numerical name as uttered by Steward.

In the training Dag Daughtry used balls of paper tied about with twine. He would toss the five balls under the bunk and tell Michael to fetch three, and neither two, nor four, but three would Michael bring forth and deliver into his hand. When Daughtry threw three under the bunk and demanded four, Michael would deliver the three, search about vainly for the fourth, then dance pleadingly with bobs of tail and half-leaps about Steward, and finally leap into the bed and secure the fourth from under the pillow or among the blankets.

It was the same with other known objects. Up to five, whether shoes or shirts or pillow-slips, Michael would fetch the number requested. And between the mathematical mind of Michael, who counted to five, and the mind of the ancient black at Tulagi, who counted sticks of tobacco in units of five, was a distance shorter than that between Michael and Dag Daughtry who could do multiplication and long division. In the same manner, up the same ladder of mathematical ability, a still greater distance separated Dag Daughtry from Captain Duncan, who by mathematics navigated the Makambo. Greatest mathematical distance of all was that between Captain Duncan's mind and the mind of an astronomer who charted the heavens and navigated a thousand million miles away among the stars and who tossed, a mere morsel of his mathematical knowledge, the few shreds of information to Captain Duncan that enabled him to know from day to day the place of the Makambo on the sea.

In one thing only could Kwaque rule Michael. Kwaque possessed a jews' harp, and, whenever the world of the Makambo and the servitude to the steward grew wearisome, he could transport himself to King William Island by thrusting the primitive instrument between his jaws and fanning weird rhythms from it with his hand, and when he thus crossed space and time, Michael sang, or howled, rather, though his howl possessed the same soft mellowness as Jerry's. Michael did not want to howl, but the chemistry of his being was such that he reacted to music as compulsively as elements react on one another in the laboratory.

While he lay perdu in Steward's stateroom, his voice was the one thing that was not to be heard, so Kwaque was forced to seek the solace of his jews' harp in the sweltering heat of the gratings over the fire-room. But this did not continue long, for, either according to blind chance, or to the lines of fate written in the book of life ere ever the foundations of the world were laid, Michael was scheduled for an adventure that was profoundly to affect, not alone his own destiny, but the destinies of Kwaque and Dag Daughtry and determine the very place of their death and burial.

CHAPTER VI

The adventure that was so to alter the future occurred when Michael, in no uncertain manner, announced to all and sundry his presence on the Makambo. It was due to Kwaque's carelessness, to commence with, for Kwaque left the stateroom without tight-closing the door. As the Makambo rolled on an easy sea the door swung back and forth, remaining wide open for intervals and banging shut but not banging hard enough to latch itself.

Michael crossed the high threshold with the innocent intention of exploring no farther than the immediate vicinity. But scarcely was he through, when a heavier roll slammed the door and latched it. And immediately Michael wanted to get back. Obedience was strong in him, for it was his heart's desire to serve his lord's will, and from the few days' confinement he sensed, or guessed, or divined, without thinking about it, that it was Steward's will for him to stay in the stateroom.

For a long time he sat down before the closed door, regarding it wistfully but being too wise to bark or speak to such inanimate object. It had been part of his early puppyhood education to learn that only live things could be moved by plea or threat, and that while things not alive did move, as the door had moved, they never moved of themselves, and were deaf to anything life might have to say to them. Occasionally he trotted down the short cross-hall upon which the stateroom opened, and gazed up and down the long hall that ran fore and aft.

For the better part of an hour he did this, returning always to the door that would not open. Then he achieved a definite idea. Since the door would not open, and since Steward and Kwaque did not return, he would go in search of them. Once with this concept of action clear in his brain, without timidities of hesitation and irresolution, he trotted aft down the long hall. Going around the right angle in which it ended, he encountered a narrow flight of steps. Among many scents, he recognized those of Kwaque and Steward and knew they had passed that way.

Up the stairs and on the main deck, he began to meet passengers. Being white gods, he did not resent their addresses to him, though he did not linger and went out on the open deck where more of the favoured gods reclined in steamer-chairs. Still no Kwaque or Steward. Another flight of narrow, steep stairs invited, and he came out on the boat-deck. Here, under the wide awnings, were many more of the gods, many times more than he had that far seen in his life.

The for'ard end of the boat-deck terminated in the bridge, which, instead of being raised above it, was part of it. Trotting around the wheel-house to the shady lee-side of it, he came upon his fate; for be it known that Captain Duncan possessed on board in addition to two fox-terriers, a big Persian cat, and that cat possessed a litter of kittens. Her chosen nursery was the wheel-house, and Captain Duncan had humoured her, giving her a box for her kittens and threatening the quartermasters with all manner of dire fates did they so much as step on one of the kittens.

But Michael knew nothing of this. And the big Persian knew of his existence before he did of hers. In fact, the first he knew was when she launched herself upon him out of the open wheel-house doorway. Even as he glimpsed this abrupt danger, and before he could know what it was, he leaped sideways and saved himself. From his point of view, the assault was unprovoked. He was staring at her with bristling hair, recognizing her for what she was, a cat, when she sprang again, her tail the size of a large man's arm, all claws and spitting fury and vindictiveness.

This was too much for a self-respecting Irish terrier. His wrath was immediate with her second leap, and he sprang to the side to avoid her claws, and in from the side to meet her, his jaws clamping together on her spinal column with a jerk while she was still in mid-air. The next moment she lay sprawling and struggling on the deck with a broken back.

But for Michael this was only the beginning. A shrill yelling, rather than yelping, of more enemies made him whirl half about, but not quick enough. Struck in flank by two full-grown fox-terriers, he was slashed and rolled on the deck. The two, by the way, had long before made their first appearance on the Makambo as little puppies in Dag Daughtry's coat pockets, Daughtry, in his usual fashion, having appropriated them ashore in Sydney and sold them to Captain Duncan for a guinea apiece.

By this time, scrambling to his feet, Michael was really angry. In truth, it was raining cats and dogs, such belligerent shower all unprovoked by him who had picked no quarrels nor even been aware of his enemies until they assailed him. Brave the fox-terriers were, despite the hysterical rage they were in, and they were upon him as he got his legs under him. The fangs of one clashed with his, cutting the lips of both of them, and the lighter dog recoiled from the impact. The other succeeded in taking Michael in flank, fetching blood and hurt with his teeth. With an instant curve, that was almost spasmodic, of his body, Michael flung his flank clear, leaving the other's mouth full of his hair, and at the same moment drove his teeth through an ear till they met. The fox-terrier, with a shrill yelp of pain, sprang back so impetuously as to ribbon its ear as Michael's teeth combed through it.

The first terrier was back upon him, and he was whirling to meet it, when a new and equally unprovoked assault was made upon him. This time it was Captain Duncan, in a rage at sight of his slain cat. The instep of his foot caught Michael squarely under the chest, half knocking the breath out of him and wholly lifting him into the air, so that he fell heavily on his side. The two terriers were upon him, filling their mouths with his straight, wiry hair as they sank their teeth in. Still on his side, as he was beginning to struggle to his feet, he clipped his jaws together on a leg of one, who screamed with pain and retreated on three legs, holding up the fourth, a fore leg, the bone of which Michael's teeth had all but crushed.

Twice Michael slashed the other four-footed foe and then pursued him in a circle with Captain Duncan pursuing him in turn. Shortening the distance by leaping across a chord of the arc of the other's flight, Michael closed his jaws on the back and side of the neck. Such abrupt arrest in mid-flight by the heavier dog brought the fox-terrier down on deck with, a heavy thump. Simultaneous with this, Captain Duncan's second kick landed, communicating such propulsion to Michael as to tear his clenched teeth through the flesh and out of the flesh of the fox-terrier.

And Michael turned on the Captain. What if he were a white god? In his rage at so many assaults of so many enemies, Michael, who had been peacefully looking for Kwaque and Steward, did not stop to reckon. Besides, it was a strange white god upon whom he had never before laid eyes.

At the beginning he had snarled and growled. But it was a more serious affair to attack a god, and no sound came from him as he leaped to meet the leg flying toward him in another kick. As with the cat, he did not leap straight at it. To the side to avoid, and in with a curve of body as it passed, was his way. He had learned the trick with many blacks at Meringe and on board the Eugenie, so that as often he succeeded as failed at it. His teeth came together in the slack of the white duck trousers. The consequent jerk on Captain Duncan's leg made that infuriated mariner lose his balance. Almost he fell forward on his face, part recovered himself with a violent effort, stumbled over Michael who was in for another bite, tottered wildly around, and sat down on the deck.

How long he might have sat there to recover his breath is problematical, for he rose as rapidly as his stoutness would permit, spurred on by Michael's teeth already sunk into the fleshy part of his shoulder. Michael missed his calf as he uprose, but tore the other leg of the trousers to shreds and received a kick that lifted him a yard above the deck in a half-somersault and landed him on his back on deck.

Up to this time the Captain had been on the ferocious offensive, and he was in the act of following up the kick when Michael regained his feet and soared up in the air, not for leg or thigh, but for the throat. Too high it was for him to reach it, but his teeth closed on the flowing black scarf and tore it to tatters as his weight drew him back to deck.

It was not this so much that turned Captain Duncan to the pure defensive and started him retreating backward, as it was the silence of Michael. Ominous as death it was. There were no snarls nor throat-threats. With eyes straight-looking and unblinking, he sprang and sprang again. Neither did he growl when he attacked nor yelp when he was kicked. Fear of the blow was not in him. As Tom Haggin had so often bragged of Biddy and Terrence, they bred true in Jerry and Michael in the matter of not wincing at a blow. Always, they were so made, they sprang to meet the blow and to encounter the creature who delivered the blow. With a silence that was invested with the seriousness of death, they were wont to attack and to continue to attack.

And so Michael. As the Captain retreated kicking, he attacked, leaping and slashing. What saved Captain Duncan was a sailor with a deck mop on the end of a stick. Intervening, he managed to thrust it into Michael's mouth and shove him away. This first time his teeth closed automatically upon it. But, spitting it out, he declined thereafter to bite it, knowing it for what it was, an inanimate thing upon which his teeth could inflict no hurt.

Nor, beyond trying to avoid him, was he interested in the sailor. It was Captain Duncan, leaning his back against the rail, breathing heavily, and wiping the streaming sweat from his face, who was Michael's meat. Long as it has taken to tell the battle, beginning with the slaying of the Persian cat to the thrusting of the mop into Michael's jaws, so swift had been the rush of events that the passengers, springing from their deck-chairs and hurrying to the scene, were just arriving when Michael eluded the mop of the sailor by a successful dodge and plunged in on Captain Duncan, this time sinking his teeth so savagely into a rotund calf as to cause its owner to splutter an incoherent curse and howl of wrathful surprise.

A fortunate kick hurled Michael away and enabled the sailor to intervene once again with the mop. And upon the scene came Dag Daughtry, to behold his captain, frayed and bleeding and breathing apoplectically, Michael raging in ghastly silence at the end of a mop, and a large Persian mother- cat writhing with a broken back.

"Killeny Boy!" the steward cried imperatively.

Through no matter what indignation and rage that possessed him, his lord's voice penetrated his consciousness, so that, cooling almost instantly, Michael's ears flattened, his bristling hair lay down, and his lips covered his fangs as he turned his head to look acknowledgment.

"Come here, Killeny!"

Michael obeyed, not crouching cringingly, but trotting eagerly, gladly, to Steward's feet.

"Lie down, Boy."

He turned half around as he flumped himself down with a sigh of relief, and, with a red flash of tongue, kissed Steward's foot.

"Your dog, Steward?" Captain Duncan demanded in a smothered voice wherein struggled anger and shortness of breath.

"Yes, sir. My dog. What's he been up to, sir?"

The totality of what Michael had been up to choked the Captain completely. He could only gesture around from the dying cat to his torn clothes and bleeding wounds and the fox-terriers licking their injuries and whimpering at his feet.

"It's too bad, sir . . . " Daughtry began.

"Too bad, hell!" the captain shut him off. "Bo's'n! Throw that dog overboard."

"Throw the dog overboard, sir, yes, sir," the boatswain repeated, but hesitated.

Dag Daughtry's face hardened unconsciously with the stiffening of his will to dogged opposition, which, in its own slow quiet way, would go to any length to have its way. But he answered respectfully enough, his features, by a shrewd effort, relaxing into a seeming of his customary good-nature.

"He's a good dog, sir, and an unoffending dog. I can't imagine what could a-made 'm break loose this way. He must a-had cause, sir -"

"He had," one of the passengers, a coconut planter from the Shortlands, interjected.

The steward threw him a grateful glance and continued.

"He's a good dog, sir, a most obedient dog, sir, look at the way he minded me right in the thick of the scrap an' come 'n' lay down. He's smart as chain-lightnin', sir; do anything I tell him. I'll make him make friends. See. . ."

Stepping over to the two hysterical terriers, Daughtry called Michael to him.

"He's all right, savvee, Killeny, he all right," he crooned, at the same time resting one hand on a terrier and the other on Michael.

The terrier whimpered and backed solidly against Captain Duncan's legs, but Michael, with a slow bob of tail and unbelligerent ears, advanced to him, looked up to Steward to make sure, then sniffed his late antagonist, and even ran out his tongue in a caress to the side of the other's ear.

"See, sir, no bad feelings," Daughtry exulted. "He plays the game, sir. He's a proper dog, he's a man-dog. Here, Killeny! The other one. He all right. Kiss and make up. That's the stuff."

The other fox-terrier, the one with the injured foreleg, endured Michael's sniff with no more than hysterical growls deep in the throat; but the flipping out of Michael's tongue was too much. The wounded terrier exploded in a futile snap at Michael's tongue and nose.

"He all right, Killeny, he all right, sure," Steward warned quickly.

With a bob of his tail in token of understanding, without a shade of resentment, Michael lifted a paw and with a playful casual stroke, dab- like, brought its weight on the other's neck and rolled him, head-downward, over on the deck. Though he snarled wrathily, Michael turned away composedly and looked up into Steward's face for approval.

A roar of laughter from the passengers greeted the capsizing of the fox- terrier and the good-natured gravity of Michael. But not alone at this did they laugh, for at the moment of the snap and the turning over, Captain Duncan's unstrung nerves had exploded, causing him to jump as he tensed his whole body.

"Why, sir," the steward went on with growing confidence, "I bet I can make him friends with you, too, by this time to-morrow . . . "

"By this time five minutes he'll be overboard," the captain answered. "Bo's'n! Over with him!"

The boatswain advanced a tentative step, while murmurs of protest arose from the passengers.

"Look at my cat, and look at me," Captain Duncan defended his action.

The boatswain made another step, and Dag Daughtry glared a threat at him.

"Go on!" the Captain commanded.

"Hold on!" spoke up the Shortlands planter. "Give the dog a square deal. I saw the whole thing. He wasn't looking for trouble. First the cat jumped him. She had to jump twice before he turned loose. She'd have scratched his eyes out. Then the two dogs jumped him. He hadn't bothered them. Then you jumped him. He hadn't bothered you. And then came that sailor with the mop. And now you want the bo's'n to jump him and throw him overboard. Give him a square deal. He's only been defending himself. What do you expect any dog that is a dog to do? lie down and be walked over by every strange dog and cat that comes along? Play the game, Skipper. You gave him some mighty hard kicks. He only defended himself."

"He's some defender," Captain Duncan grinned, with a hint of the return of his ordinary geniality, at the same time tenderly pressing his bleeding shoulder and looking woefully down at his tattered duck trousers. "All right, Steward. If you can make him friends with me in five minutes, he stays on board. But you'll have to make it up to me with a new pair of trousers."

"And gladly, sir, thank you, sir," Daughtry cried. "And I'll make it up with a new cat as well, sir. Come on, Killeny Boy. This big fella marster he all right, you bet."

And Michael listened. Not with the smouldering, smothering, choking hysteria that still worked in the fox-terriers did he listen, nor with quivering of muscles and jumps of over-wrought nerves, but coolly, composedly, as if no battle royal had just taken place and no rips of teeth and kicks of feet still burned and ached his body.

He could not help bristling, however, when first he sniffed a trousers' leg into which his teeth had so recently torn.

"Put your hand down on him, sir," Daughtry begged.

And Captain Duncan, his own good self once more, bent and rested a firm, unhesitating hand on Michael's head. Nay, more; he even caressed the ears and rubbed about the roots of them. And Michael the merry-hearted, who fought like a lion and forgave and forgot like a man, laid his neck hair smoothly down, wagged his stump tail, smiled with his eyes and ears and mouth, and kissed with his tongue the hand with which a short time before he had been at war.

CHAPTER VII

For the rest of the voyage Michael had the run of the ship. Friendly to all, he reserved his love for Steward alone, though he was not above many an undignified romp with the fox-terriers.

"The most playful-minded dog, without being silly, I ever saw," was Dag Daughtry's verdict to the Shortlands planter, to whom he had just sold one of his turtle-shell combs. "You see, some dogs never get over the play-idea, an' they're never good for anything else. But not Killeny Boy. He can come down to seriousness in a second. I'll show you, and I'll show you he's got a brain that counts to five an' knows wireless telegraphy. You just watch."

At the moment the steward made his faint lip-noise, so faint that he could not hear it himself and was almost for wondering whether or not he had made it; so faint that the Shortlands planter did not dream that he was making it. At that moment Michael was lying squirming on his back a dozen feet away, his legs straight up in the air, both fox-terriers worrying with well-stimulated ferociousness. With a quick out-thrust of his four legs, he rolled over on his side and with questioning eyes and pricked ears looked and listened. Again Daughtry made the lip-noise; again the Shortlands planter did not hear nor guess; and Michael bounded to his feet and to his lord's side.

"Some dog, eh?" the steward boasted.

"But how did he know you wanted him?" the planter queried. "You never called him."

"Mental telepathy, the affinity of souls pitched in the same whatever-you- call-it harmony," the steward mystified. "You see, Killeny an' me are made of the same kind of stuff, only run into different moulds. He might a-been my full brother, or me his, only for some mistake in the creation factory somewhere. Now I'll show you he knows his bit of arithmetic."

And, drawing the paper balls from his pocket, Dag Daughtry demonstrated to the amazement and satisfaction of the ring of passengers Michael's ability to count to five.

"Why, sir," Daughtry concluded the performance, "if I was to order four glasses of beer in a public-house ashore, an' if I was absent-minded an' didn't notice the waiter 'd only brought three, Killeny Boy there 'd raise a row instanter."

Kwaque was no longer compelled to enjoy his jews' harp on the gratings over the fire-room, now that Michael's presence on the Makambo was known, and, in the stateroom, on stolen occasions, he made experiments of his own with Michael. Once the jews' harp began emitting its barbaric rhythms, Michael was helpless. He needs must open his mouth and pour forth an unwilling, gushing howl. But, as with Jerry, it was not mere howl. It was more akin to a mellow singing; and it was not long before Kwaque could lead his voice up and down, in rough time and tune, within a definite register.

Michael never liked these lessons, for, looking down upon Kwaque, he hated in any way to be under the black's compulsion. But all this was changed when Dag Daughtry surprised them at a singing lesson. He resurrected the harmonica with which it was his wont, ashore in public- houses, to while away the time between bottles. The quickest way to start Michael singing, he discovered, was with minors; and, once started, he would sing on and on for as long as the music played. Also, in the absence of an instrument, Michael would sing to the prompting and accompaniment of Steward's voice, who would begin by wailing "kow-kow" long and sadly, and then branch out on some old song or ballad. Michael had hated to sing with Kwaque, but he loved to do it with Steward, even when Steward brought him on deck to perform before the laughter-shrieking passengers.

Two serious conversations were held by the steward toward the close of the voyage: one with Captain Duncan and one with Michael.

"It's this way, Killeny," Daughtry began, one evening, Michael's head resting on his lord's knees as he gazed adoringly up into his lord's face, understanding no whit of what was spoken but loving the intimacy the sounds betokened. "I stole you for beer money, an' when I saw you there on the beach that night I knew you'd bring ten quid anywheres. Ten quid's a horrible lot of money. Fifty dollars in the way the Yankees reckon it, an' a hundred Mex in China fashion.

"Now, fifty dollars gold 'd buy beer to beat the band, enough to drown me if I fell in head first. Yet I want to ask you one question. Can you see me takin' ten quid for you? . . . Go on. Speak up. Can you?"

And Michael, with thumps of tail to the floor and a high sharp bark, showed that he was in entire agreement with whatever had been propounded.

"Or say twenty quid, now. That's a fair offer. Would I? Eh! Would I? Not on your life. What d'ye say to fifty quid? That might begin to interest me, but a hundred quid would interest me more. Why, a hundred quid all in beer 'd come pretty close to floatin' this old hooker. But who in Sam Hill'd offer a hundred quid? I'd like to clap eyes on him once, that's all, just once. D'ye want to know what for? All right. I'll whisper it. So as I could tell him to go to hell. Sure, Killeny Boy, just like that, oh, most polite, of course, just a kindly directin' of his steps where he'd never suffer from frigid extremities."

Michael's love for Steward was so profound as almost to be a mad but enduring infatuation. What the steward's regard for Michael was coming to be was best evidenced by his conversation with Captain Duncan.

"Sure, sir, he must 've followed me on board," Daughtry finished his unveracious recital. "An' I never knew it. Last I seen of 'm was on the beach. Next I seen of 'm there, he was fast asleep in my bunk. Now how'd he get there, sir? How'd he pick out my room? I leave it to you, sir. I call it marvellous, just plain marvellous."

"With a quartermaster at the head of the gangway!" Captain Duncan snorted. "As if I didn't know your tricks, Steward. There's nothing marvellous about it. Just a plain case of steal. Followed you on board? That dog never came over the side. He came through a port-hole, and he never came through by himself. That nigger of yours, I'll wager, had a hand in the helping. But let's have done with beating about the bush. Give me the dog, and I'll say no more about the cat."

"Seein' you believe what you believe, then you'd be for compoundin' the felony," Daughtry retorted, the habitual obstinate tightening of his brows showing which way his will set. "Me, sir, I'm only a ship's steward, an' it wouldn't mean nothin' at all bein' arrested for dog-stealin'; but you, sir, a captain of a fine steamer, how'd it sound for you, sir? No, sir; it'd be much wiser for me to keep the dog that followed me aboard."

"I'll give ten pounds in the bargain," the captain proffered.

"No, it wouldn't do, it wouldn't do at all, sir, an' you a captain," the steward continued to reiterate, rolling his head sombrely. "Besides, I know where's a peach of an Angora in Sydney. The owner is gone to the country an' has no further use of it, an' it'd be a kindness to the cat, air to give it a good regular home like the Makambo."

CHAPTER VIIII

Another trick Dag Daughtry succeeded in teaching Michael so enhanced him in Captain Duncan's eyes as to impel him to offer fifty pounds, "and never mind the cat." At first, Daughtry practised the trick in private with the chief engineer and the Shortlands planter. Not until thoroughly satisfied did he make a public performance of it.

"Now just suppose you're policemen, or detectives," Daughtry told the first and third officers, "an' suppose I'm guilty of some horrible crime. An' suppose Killeny is the only clue, an' you've got Killeny. When he recognizes his master, me, of course, you've got your man. You go down the deck with him, leadin' by the rope. Then you come back this way with him, makin' believe this is the street, an' when he recognizes me you arrest me. But if he don't realize me, you can't arrest me. See?"

The two officers led Michael away, and after several minutes returned along the deck, Michael stretched out ahead on the taut rope seeking Steward.

"What'll you take for the dog?" Daughtry demanded, as they drew near, this the cue he had trained Michael to know.

And Michael, straining at the rope, went by, without so much as a wag of tail to Steward or a glance of eye. The officers stopped before Daughtry and drew Michael back into the group.

"He's a lost dog," said the first officer.

"We're trying to find his owner," supplemented the third.

"Some dog that, what'll you take for 'm?" Daughtry asked, studying Michael with critical eyes of interest. "What kind of a temper's he got?"

"Try him," was the answer.

The steward put out his hand to pat him on the head, but withdrew it hastily as Michael, with bristle and growl, viciously bared his teeth.

"Go on, go on, he won't hurt you," the delighted passengers urged.

This time the steward's hand was barely missed by a snap, and he leaped back as Michael ferociously sprang the length of the rope at him.

"Take 'm away!" Dag Daughtry roared angrily. "The treacherous beast! I wouldn't take 'm for gift!"

And as they obeyed, Michael strained backward in a paroxysm of rage, making fierce short jumps to the end of the tether as he snarled and growled with utmost fierceness at the steward.

"Eh? Who'd say he ever seen me in his life?" Daughtry demanded triumphantly. "It's a trick I never seen played myself, but I've heard tell about it. The old-time poachers in England used to do it with their lurcher dogs. If they did get the dog of a strange poacher, no gamekeeper or constable could identify 'm by the dog, mum was the word."

"Tell you what, he knows things, that Killeny. He knows English. Right now, in my room, with the door open, an' so as he can find 'm, is shoes, slippers, cap, towel, hair-brush, an' tobacco pouch. What'll it be? Name it an' he'll fetch it."

So immediately and variously did the passengers respond that every article was called for.

"Just one of you choose," the steward advised. "The rest of you pick 'm out."

"Slipper," said Captain Duncan, selected by acclamation.

"One or both?" Daughtry asked.

"Both."

"Come here, Killeny," Daughtry began, bending toward him but leaping back from the snap of jaws that clipped together close to his nose.

"My mistake," he apologized. "I ain't told him the other game was over. Now just listen an, watch. 'n' see if you can catch on to the tip I'm goin' to give 'm."

No one saw anything, heard anything, yet Michael, with a whine of eagerness and joy, with laughing mouth and wriggling body, was upon the steward, licking his hands madly, squirming and twisting in the embrace of the loved hands he had so recently threatened, making attempts at short upward leaps as he flashed his tongue upward toward his lord's face. For hard it was on Michael, a nerve and mental strain of the severest for him so to control himself as to play-act anger and threat of hurt to his beloved Steward.

"Takes him a little time to get over a thing like that," Daughtry explained, as he soothed Michael down.

"Now, Killeny! Go fetch 'm slipper! Wait! Fetch 'm one slipper. Fetch 'm two slipper."

Michael looked up with pricked ears, and with eyes filled with query as all his intelligent consciousness suffused them.

"Two slipper! Fetch 'm quick!"

He was off and away in a scurry of speed that seemed to flatten him close to the deck, and that, as he turned the corner of the deck-house to the stairs, made his hind feet slip and slide across the smooth planks.

Almost in a trice he was back, both slippers in his mouth, which he deposited at the steward's feet.

"The more I know dogs the more amazin' marvellous they are to me," Dag Daughtry, after he had compassed his fourth bottle, confided in monologue to the Shortlands planter that night just before bedtime. "Take Killeny Boy. He don't do things for me mechanically, just because he's learned to do 'm. There's more to it. He does 'm because he likes me. I can't give you the hang of it, but I feel it, I know it.

"Maybe, this is what I'm drivin' at. Killeny can't talk, as you 'n' me talk, I mean; so he can't tell me how he loves me, an' he's all love, every last hair of 'm. An' actions speakin' louder 'n' words, he tells me how he loves me by doin' these things for me. Tricks? Sure. But they make human speeches of eloquence cheaper 'n dirt. Sure it's speech. Dog-talk that's tongue-tied. Don't I know? Sure as I'm a livin' man born to trouble as the sparks fly upward, just as sure am I that it makes 'm happy to do tricks for me . . . just as it makes a man happy to lend a hand to a pal in a ticklish place, or a lover happy to put his coat around the girl he loves to keep her warm. I tell you . . . "

Here, Dag Daughtry broke down from inability to express the concepts fluttering in his beer-excited, beer-sodden brain, and, with a stutter or two, made a fresh start.

"You know, it's all in the matter of talkin', an' Killeny can't talk. He's got thoughts inside that head of his, you can see 'm shinin' in his lovely brown eyes, but he can't get 'em across to me. Why, I see 'm tryin' to tell me sometimes so hard that he almost busts. There's a big hole between him an' me, an' language is about the only bridge, and he can't get over the hole, though he's got all kinds of ideas an' feelings just like mine.

"But, say! The time we get closest together is when I play the harmonica an' he yow-yows. Music comes closest to makin' the bridge. It's a regular song without words. And . . . I can't explain how . . . but just the same, when we've finished our song, I know we've passed a lot over to each other that don't need words for the passin'."

"Why, d'ye know, when I'm playin' an' he's singin', it's a regular duet of what the sky-pilots 'd call religion an' knowin' God. Sure, when we sing together I'm absorbin' religion an' gettin' pretty close up to God. An' it's big, I tell you. Big as the earth an' ocean an' sky an' all the stars. I just seem to get hold of a sense that we're all the same stuff after all, you, me, Killeny Boy, mountains, sand, salt water, worms, mosquitoes, suns, an' shootin' stars an' blazin comets . . . "

Day Daughtry left his flight as beyond his own grasp of speech, and concluded, his half embarrassment masked by braggadocio over Michael:

"Oh, believe me, they don't make dogs like him every day in the week. Sure, I stole 'm. He looked good to me. An' if I had it over, knowin' as I do known 'm now, I'd steal 'm again if I lost a leg doin' it. That's the kind of a dog he is."

CHAPTER IX

The morning the Makambo entered Sydney harbour, Captain Duncan had another try for Michael. The port doctor's launch was coming alongside, when he nodded up to Daughtry, who was passing along the deck:

"Steward, I'll give you twenty pounds."

"No, sir, thank you, sir," was Dag Daughtry's answer. "I couldn't bear to part with him."

"Twenty-five pounds, then. I can't go beyond that. Besides, there are plenty more Irish terriers in the world."

"That's what I'm thinkin', sir. An' I'll get one for you. Right here in Sydney. An' it won't cost you a penny, sir."

"But I want Killeny Boy," the captain persisted.

"An' so do I, which is the worst of it, sir. Besides, I got him first."

"Twenty-five sovereigns is a lot of money . . . for a dog," Captain Duncan said.

"An' Killeny Boy's a lot of dog . . . for the money," the steward retorted. "Why, sir, cuttin' out all sentiment, his tricks is worth more 'n that. Him not recognizing me when I don't want 'm to is worth fifty pounds of itself. An' there's his countin' an' his singin', an' all the rest of his tricks. Now, no matter how I got him, he didn't have them tricks. Them tricks are mine. I taught him them. He ain't the dog he was when he come on board. He's a whole lot of me now, an' sellin' him would be like sellin' a piece of myself."

"Thirty pounds," said the captain with finality.

"No, sir, thankin' you just the same, sir," was Daughtry's refusal.

And Captain Duncan was forced to turn away in order to greet the port doctor coming over the side.

Scarcely had the Makambo passed quarantine, and while on her way up harbour to dock, when a trim man-of-war launch darted in to her side and a trim lieutenant mounted the Makambo's boarding-ladder. His mission was quickly explained. The Albatross, British cruiser of the second class, of which he was fourth lieutenant, had called in at Tulagi with dispatches from the High Commissioner of the English South Seas. A scant twelve hours having intervened between her arrival and the Makambo's departure, the Commissioner of the Solomons and Captain Kellar had been of the opinion that the missing dog had been carried away on the steamer. Knowing that the Albatross would beat her to Sydney, the captain of the Albatross had undertaken to look up the dog. Was the dog, an Irish terrier answering to the name of Michael, on board?

Captain Duncan truthfully admitted that it was, though he most unveraciously shielded Dag Daughtry by repeating his yarn of the dog coming on board of itself. How to return the dog to Captain Kellar? was the next question; for the Albatross was bound on to New Zealand. Captain Duncan settled the matter.

"The Makambo will be back in Tulagi in eight weeks," he told the lieutenant, "and I'll undertake personally to deliver the dog to its owner. In the meantime we'll take good care of it. Our steward has sort of adopted it, so it will be in good hands."

"Seems we don't either of us get the dog," Daughtry commented resignedly, when Captain Duncan had explained the situation.

But when Daughtry turned his back and started off along the deck, his constitutional obstinacy tightened his brows so that the Shortlands planter, observing it, wondered what the captain had been rowing him about.

Despite his six quarts a day and all his easy-goingness of disposition, Dag Daughtry possessed certain integrities. Though he could steal a dog, or a cat, without a twinge of conscience, he could not but be faithful to his salt, being so made. He could not draw wages for being a ship steward without faithfully performing the functions of ship steward. Though his mind was firmly made up, during the several days of the Makambo in Sydney, lying alongside the Burns Philp Dock, he saw to every detail of the cleaning up after the last crowd of outgoing passengers, and to every detail of preparation for the next crowd of incoming passengers who had tickets bought for the passage far away to the coral seas and the cannibal isles.

In the midst of this devotion to his duty, he took a night off and part of two afternoons. The night off was devoted to the public-houses which sailors frequent, and where can be learned the latest gossip and news of ships and of men who sail upon the sea. Such information did he gather, over many bottles of beer, that the next afternoon, hiring a small launch at a cost of ten shillings, he journeyed up the harbour to Jackson Bay, where lay the lofty-poled, sweet-lined, three-topmast American schooner, the Mary Turner.

Once on board, explaining his errand, he was taken below into the main cabin, where he interviewed, and was interviewed by, a quartette of men whom Daughtry qualified to himself as "a rum bunch."

It was because he had talked long with the steward who had left the ship, that Dag Daughtry recognized and identified each of the four men. That, surely, was the "Ancient Mariner," sitting back and apart with washed eyes of such palest blue that they seemed a faded white. Long thin wisps of silvery, unkempt hair framed his face like an aureole. He was slender to emaciation, cavernously checked, roll after roll of skin, no longer encasing flesh or muscle, hanging grotesquely down his neck and swathing the Adam's apple so that only occasionally, with queer swallowing motions, did it peep out of the mummy-wrappings of skin and sink back again from view.

A proper ancient mariner, thought Daughtry. Might be seventy-five, might just as well be a hundred and five, or a hundred and seventy-five.

Beginning at the right temple, a ghastly scar split the cheek-bone, sank into the depths of the hollow cheek, notched across the lower jaw, and plunged to disappearance among the prodigious skin-folds of the neck. The withered lobes of both ears were perforated by tiny gypsy-like circles of gold. On the skeleton fingers of his right hand were no less than five rings, not men's rings, nor women's, but foppish rings, "that would fetch a price," Daughtry adjudged. On the left hand were no rings, for there were no fingers to wear them. Only was there a thumb; and, for that matter, most of the hand was missing as well, as if it had been cut off by the same slicing edge that had cleaved him from temple to jaw and heaven alone knew how far down that skin-draped neck.

The Ancient Mariner's washed eyes seemed to bore right through Daughtry (or at least so Daughtry felt), and rendered him so uncomfortable as to make him casually step to the side for the matter of a yard. This was possible, because, a servant seeking a servant's billet, he was expected to stand and face the four seated ones as if they were judges on the bench and he the felon in the dock. Nevertheless, the gaze of the ancient one pursued him, until, studying it more closely, he decided that it did not reach to him at all. He got the impression that those washed pale eyes were filmed with dreams, and that the intelligence, the thing, that dwelt within the skull, fluttered and beat against the dream-films and no farther.

"How much would you expect?" the captain was asking, a most unsealike captain, in Daughtry's opinion; rather, a spick-and-span, brisk little business-man or floor-walker just out of a bandbox.

"He shall not share," spoke up another of the four, huge, raw-boned, middle-aged, whom Daughtry identified by his ham-like hands as the California wheat-farmer described by the departed steward.

"Plenty for all," the Ancient Mariner startled Daughtry by cackling shrilly. "Oodles and oodles of it, my gentlemen, in cask and chest, in cask and chest, a fathom under the sand."

"Share what, sir?" Daughtry queried, though well he knew, the other steward having cursed to him the day he sailed from San Francisco on a blind lay instead of straight wages. "Not that it matters, sir," he hastened to add. "I spent a whalin' voyage once, three years of it, an' paid off with a dollar. Wages for mine, an' sixty gold a month, seein' there's only four of you."

"And a mate," the captain added.

"And a mate," Daughtry repeated. "Very good, sir. An' no share."

"But yourself?" spoke up the fourth man, a huge-bulking, colossal-bodied, greasy-seeming grossness of flesh, the Armenian Jew and San Francisco pawnbroker the previous steward had warned Daughtry about. "Have you papers, letters of recommendation, the documents you receive when you are paid off before the shipping commissioners?"

"I might ask, sir," Dag Daughtry brazened it, "for your own papers. This ain't no regular cargo-carrier or passenger-carrier, no more than you gentlemen are a regular company of ship-owners, with regular offices, doin' business in a regular way. How do I know if you own the ship even, or that the charter ain't busted long ago, or that you're being libelled ashore right now, or that you won't dump me on any old beach anywheres without a soo-markee of what's comin' to me? Howsoever", he anticipated by a bluff of his own the show of wrath from the Jew that he knew would be wind and bluff, "howsoever, here's my papers . . . "

With a swift dip of his hand into his inside coat-pocket he scattered out in a wealth of profusion on the cabin table all the papers, sealed and stamped, that he had collected in forty-five years of voyaging, the latest date of which was five years back.

"I don't ask your papers," he went on. "What I ask is, cash payment in full the first of each month, sixty dollars a month gold -"

"Oodles and oodles of it, gold and gold and better than gold, in cask and chest, in cask and chest, a fathom under the sand," the Ancient Mariner assured him in beneficent cackles. "Kings, principalities and powers! all of us, the least of us. And plenty more, my gentlemen, plenty more. The latitude and longitude are mine, and the bearings from the oak ribs on the shoal to Lion's Head, and the cross-bearings from the points unnamable, I only know. I only still live of all that brave, mad, scallywag ship's company . . ."

"Will you sign the articles to that?" the Jew demanded, cutting in on the ancient's maunderings.

"What port do you wind up the cruise in?" Daughtry asked.

"San Francisco."

"I'll sign the articles that I'm to sign off in San Francisco then."

The Jew, the captain, and the farmer nodded.

"But there's several other things to be agreed upon," Daughtry continued. "In the first place, I want my six quarts a day. I'm used to it, and I'm too old a stager to change my habits."

"Of spirits, I suppose?" the Jew asked sarcastically.

"No; of beer, good English beer. It must be understood beforehand, no matter what long stretches we may be at sea, that a sufficient supply is taken along."

"Anything else?" the captain queried.

"Yes, sir," Daughtry answered. "I got a dog that must come along."

"Anything else? a wife or family maybe?" the farmer asked.

"No wife or family, sir. But I got a nigger, a perfectly good nigger, that's got to come along. He can sign on for ten dollars a month if he works for the ship all his time. But if he works for me all the time, I'll let him sign on for two an' a half a month."

"Eighteen days in the longboat," the Ancient Mariner shrilled, to Daughtry's startlement. "Eighteen days in the longboat, eighteen days of scorching hell."

"My word," quoth Daughtry, "the old gentleman'd give one the jumps. There'll sure have to be plenty of beer."

"Sea stewards put on some style, I must say," commented the wheat-farmer, oblivious to the Ancient Mariner, who still declaimed of the heat of the longboat.

"Suppose we don't see our way to signing on a steward who travels in such style?" the Jew asked, mopping the inside of his collar-band with a coloured silk handkerchief.

"Then you'll never know what a good steward you've missed, sir," Daughtry responded airily.

"I guess there's plenty more stewards on Sydney beach," the captain said briskly. "And I guess I haven't forgotten old days, when I hired them like so much dirt, yes, by Jinks, so much dirt, there were so many of them."

"Thank you, Mr. Steward, for looking us up," the Jew took up the idea with insulting oiliness. "We very much regret our inability to meet your wishes in the matter -"

"And I saw it go under the sand, a fathom under the sand, on cross-bearings unnamable, where the mangroves fade away, and the coconuts grow, and the rise of land lifts from the beach to the Lion's Head."

"Hold your horses," the wheat-farmer said, with a flare of irritation, directed, not at the Ancient Mariner, but at the captain and the Jew. "Who's putting up for this expedition? Don't I get no say so? Ain't my opinion ever to be asked? I like this steward. Strikes me he's the real goods. I notice he's as polite as all get-out, and I can see he can take an order without arguing. And he ain't no fool by a long shot."

"That's the very point, Grimshaw," the Jew answered soothingly. "Considering the unusualness of our . . . of the expedition, we'd be better served by a steward who is more of a fool. Another point, which I'd esteem a real favour from you, is not to forget that you haven't put a red copper more into this trip than I have -"

"And where'd either of you be, if it wasn't for me with my knowledge of the sea?" the captain demanded aggrievedly. "To say nothing of the mortgage on my house and on the nicest little best paying flat building in San Francisco since the earthquake."

"But who's still putting up? all of you, I ask you." The wheat-farmer leaned forward, resting the heels of his hands on his knees so that the fingers hung down his long shins, in Daughtry's appraisal, half-way to his feet. "You, Captain Doane, can't raise another penny on your properties. My land still grows the wheat that brings the ready. You, Simon Nishikanta, won't put up another penny, yet your loan-shark offices are doing business at the same old stands at God knows what per cent. to drunken sailors. And you hang the expedition up here in this hole-in-the- wall waiting for my agent to cable more wheat-money. Well, I guess we'll just sign on this steward at sixty a month and all he asks, or I'll just naturally quit you cold on the next fast steamer to San Francisco."

He stood up abruptly, towering to such height that Daughtry looked to see the crown of his head collide with the deck above.

"I'm sick and tired of you all, yes, I am," he continued. "Get busy! Well, let's get busy. My money's coming. It'll be here by to-morrow. Let's be ready to start by hiring a steward that is a steward. I don't care if he brings two families along."

"I guess you're right, Grimshaw," Simon Nishikanta said appeasingly. "The trip is beginning to get on all our nerves. Forget it if I fly off the handle. Of course we'll take this steward if you want him. I thought he was too stylish for you."

He turned to Daughtry.

"Naturally, the least said ashore about us the better."

"That's all right, sir. I can keep my mouth shut, though I might as well tell you there's some pretty tales about you drifting around the beach right now."

"The object of our expedition?" the Jew queried quickly.

Daughtry nodded.

"Is that why you want to come?" was demanded equally quickly.

Daughtry shook his head.

"As long as you give me my beer each day, sir, I ain't goin' to be interested in your treasure-huntin'. It ain't no new tale to me. The South Seas is populous with treasure-hunters -" Almost could Daughtry have sworn that he had seen a flash of anxiety break through the dream- films that bleared the Ancient Mariner's eyes. "And I must say, sir," he went on easily, though saying what he would not have said had it not been for what he was almost certain he sensed of the ancient's anxiousness, "that the South Seas is just naturally lousy with buried treasure. There's Keeling-Cocos, millions 'n' millions of it, pounds sterling, I mean, waiting for the lucky one with the right steer."

This time Daughtry could have sworn to having sensed a change toward relief in the Ancient Mariner, whose eyes were again filmy with dreams.

"But I ain't interested in treasure, sir," Daughtry concluded. "It's beer I'm interested in. You can chase your treasure, an' I don't care how long, just as long as I've got six quarts to open each day. But I give you fair warning, sir, before I sign on: if the beer dries up, I'm goin' to get interested in what you're after. Fair play is my motto."

"Do you expect us to pay for your beer in addition?" Simon Nishikanta demanded.

To Daughtry it was too good to be true. Here, with the Jew healing the breach with the wheat-farmer whose agents still cabled money, was the time to take advantage.

"Sure, it's one of our agreements, sir. What time would it suit you, sir, to-morrow afternoon, for me to sign on at the shipping commissioner's?"

"Casks and chests of it, casks and chests of it, oodles and oodles, a fathom under the sand," chattered the Ancient Mariner.

"You're all touched up under the roof," Daughtry grinned. "Which ain't got nothing to do with me as long as you furnish the beer, pay me due an' proper what's comin' to me the first of each an' every month, an' pay me off final in San Francisco. As long as you keep up your end, I'll sail with you to the Pit 'n' back an' watch you sweatin' the casks 'n' chests out of the sand. What I want is to sail with you if you want me to sail with you enough to satisfy me."

Simon Nishikanta glanced about. Grimshaw and Captain Doane nodded.

"At three o'clock to-morrow afternoon, at the shipping commissioner's," the Jew agreed. "When will you report for duty?"

"When will you sail, sir?" Daughtry countered.

"Bright and early next morning."

"Then I'll be on board and on duty some time to-morrow night, sir."

And as he went up the cabin companion, he could hear the Ancient Mariner maundering: "Eighteen days in the longboat, eighteen days of scorching hell . . ."

CHAPTER X

Michael left the Makambo as he had come on board, through a port-hole. Likewise, the affair occurred at night, and it was Kwaque's hands that received him. It had been quick work, and daring, in the dark of early evening. From the boat-deck, with a bowline under Kwaque's arms and a turn of the rope around a pin, Dag Daughtry had lowered his leprous servitor into the waiting launch.

On his way below, he encountered Captain Duncan, who saw fit to warn him:

"No shannigan with Killeny Boy, Steward. He must go back to Tulagi with us."

"Yes, sir," the steward agreed. "An' I'm keepin' him tight in my room to make safe. Want to see him, sir?"

The very frankness of the invitation made the captain suspicious, and the thought flashed through his mind that perhaps Killeny Boy was already hidden ashore somewhere by the dog-stealing steward.

"Yes, indeed I'd like to say how-do-you-do to him," Captain Duncan answered.

And his was genuine surprise, on entering the steward's room, to behold Michael just rousing from his curled-up sleep on the floor. But when he left, his surprise would have been shocking could he have seen through the closed door what immediately began to take place. Out through the open port-hole, in a steady stream, Daughtry was passing the contents of the room. Everything went that belonged to him, including the turtle-shell and the photographs and calendars on the wall. Michael, with the command of silence laid upon him, went last. Remained only a sea-chest and two suit-cases, themselves too large for the port-hole but bare of contents.

When Daughtry sauntered along the main deck a few minutes later and paused for a gossip with the customs officer and a quartermaster at the head of the gang-plank, Captain Duncan little dreamed that his casual glance was resting on his steward for the last time. He watched him go down the gang-plank empty-handed, with no dog at his heels, and stroll off along the wharf under the electric lights.

Ten minutes after Captain Duncan saw the last of his broad back, Daughtry, in the launch with his belongings and heading for Jackson Bay, was hunched over Michael and caressing him, while Kwaque, crooning with joy under his breath that he was with all that was precious to him in the world, felt once again in the side-pocket of his flimsy coat to make sure that his beloved jews' harp had not been left behind.

Dag Daughtry was paying for Michael, and paying well. Among other things, he had not cared to arouse suspicion by drawing his wages from Burns Philp. The twenty pounds due him he had abandoned, and this was the very sum, that night on the beach at Tulagi, he had decided he could realize from the sale of Michael. He had stolen him to sell. He was paying for him the sales price that had tempted him.

For, as one has well said: the horse abases the base, ennobles the noble. Likewise the dog. The theft of a dog to sell for a price had been the abasement worked by Michael on Dag Daughtry. To pay the price out of sheer heart-love that could recognize no price too great to pay, had been the ennoblement of Dag Daughtry which Michael had worked. And as the launch chug-chugged across the quiet harbour under the southern stars, Dag Daughtry would have risked and tossed his life into the bargain in a battle to continue to have and to hold the dog he had originally conceived of as being interchangeable for so many dozens of beer.

The Mary Turner, towed out by a tug, sailed shortly after daybreak, and Daughtry, Kwaque, and Michael looked their last for ever on Sydney Harbour.

"Once again these old eyes have seen this fair haven," the Ancient Mariner, beside them gazing, babbled; and Daughtry could not help but notice the way the wheat-farmer and the pawnbroker pricked their ears to listen and glanced each to the other with scant eyes. "It was in '52, in 1852, on such a day as this, all drinking and singing along the decks, we cleared from Sydney in the Wide Awake. A pretty craft, oh sirs, a most clever and pretty craft. A crew, a brave crew, all youngsters, all of us, fore and aft, no man was forty, a mad, gay crew. The captain was an elderly gentleman of twenty-eight, the third officer another of eighteen, the down, untouched of steel, like so much young velvet on his cheek. He, too, died in the longboat. And the captain gasped out his last under the palm trees of the isle unnamable while the brown maidens wept about him and fanned the air to his parching lungs."

Dag Daughtry heard no more, for he turned below to take up his new routine of duty. But while he made up bunks with fresh linen and directed Kwaque's efforts to cleaning long-neglected floors, he shook his head to himself and muttered, "He's a keen 'un. He's a keen 'un. All ain't fools that look it."

The fine lines of the Mary Turner were explained by the fact that she had been built for seal-hunting; and for the same reason on board of her was room and to spare. The forecastle with bunk-space for twelve, bedded but eight Scandinavian seamen. The five staterooms of the cabin accommodated the three treasure-hunters, the Ancient Mariner, and the mate, the latter a large-bodied, gentle-souled Russian-Finn, known as Mr. Jackson through inability of his shipmates to pronounce the name he had signed on the ship's articles.

Remained the steerage, just for'ard of the cabin, separated from it by a stout bulkhead and entered by a companionway on the main deck. On this deck, between the break of the poop and the steerage companion, stood the galley. In the steerage itself, which possessed a far larger living-space than the cabin, were six capacious bunks, each double the width of the forecastle bunks, and each curtained and with no bunk above it.

"Some fella glory-hole, eh, Kwaque?" Daughtry told his seventeen-years- old brown-skinned Papuan with the withered ancient face of a centenarian, the legs of a living skeleton, and the huge-stomached torso of an elderly Japanese wrestler. "Eh, Kwaque! What you fella think?"

And Kwaque, too awed by the spaciousness to speak, eloquently rolled his eyes in agreement.

"You likee this piecee bunk?" the cook, a little old Chinaman, asked the steward with eager humility, inviting the white man's acceptance of his own bunk with a wave of arm.

Daughtry shook his head. He had early learned that it was wise to get along well with sea-cooks, since sea-cocks were notoriously given to going suddenly lunatic and slicing and hacking up their shipmates with butcher knives and meat cleavers on the slightest remembered provocation. Besides, there was an equally good bunk all the way across the width of the steerage from the Chinaman's. The bunk next on the port side to the cook's and abaft of it Daughtry allotted to Kwaque. Thus he retained for himself and Michael the entire starboard side with its three bunks. The next one abaft of his own he named "Killeny Boy's," and called on Kwaque and the cook to take notice. Daughtry had a sense that the cook, whose name had been quickly volunteered as Ah Moy, was not entirely satisfied with the arrangement; but it affected him no more than a momentary curiosity about a Chinaman who drew the line at a dog taking a bunk in the same apartment with him.

Half an hour later, returning, from setting the cabin aright, to the steerage for Kwaque to serve him with a bottle of beer, Daughtry observed that Ah Moy had moved his entire bunk belongings across the steerage to the third bunk on the starboard side. This had put him with Daughtry and Michael and left Kwaque with half the steerage to himself. Daughtry's curiosity recrudesced.

"What name along that fella Chink?" he demanded of Kwaque. "He no like 'm you fella boy stop 'm along same fella side along him. What for? My word! What name? That fella Chink make 'm me cross along him too much!"

"Suppose 'm that fella Chink maybe he think 'm me kai-kai along him," Kwaque grinned in one of his rare jokes.

"All right," the steward concluded. "We find out. You move 'm along my bunk, I move 'm along that fella Chink's bunk."

This accomplished, so that Kwaque, Michael, and Ah Moy occupied the starboard side and Daughtry alone bunked on the port side, he went on deck and aft to his duties. On his next return he found Ah Moy had transferred back to the port side, but this time into the last bunk aft.

"Seems the beggar's taken a fancy to me," the steward smiled to himself.

Nor was he capable of guessing Ah Moy's reason for bunking always on the opposite side from Kwaque.

"I changee," the little old cook explained, with anxious eyes to please and placate, in response to Daughtry's direct question. "All the time like that, changee, plentee changee. You savvee?"

Daughtry did not savvee, and shook his head, while Ah Moy's slant eyes betrayed none of the anxiety and fear with which he privily gazed on Kwaque's two permanently bent fingers of the left hand and on Kwaque's forehead, between the eyes, where the skin appeared a shade darker, a trifle thicker, and was marked by the first beginning of three short vertical lines or creases that were already giving him the lion-like appearance, the leonine face so named by the experts and technicians of the fell disease.

As the days passed, the steward took facetious occasions, when he had drunk five quarts of his daily allowance, to shift his and Kwaque's bunks about. And invariably Ah Moy shifted, though Daughtry failed to notice that he never shifted into a bunk which Kwaque had occupied. Nor did he notice that it was when the time came that Kwaque had variously occupied all the six bunks that Ah Moy made himself a canvas hammock, suspended it from the deck beams above and thereafter swung clear in space and unmolested.

Daughtry dismissed the matter from his thoughts as no more than a thing in keeping with the general inscrutability of the Chinese mind. He did notice, however, that Kwaque was never permitted to enter the galley. Another thing he noticed, which, expressed in his own words, was: "That's the all-dangdest cleanest Chink I've ever clapped my lamps on. Clean in galley, clean in steerage, clean in everything. He's always washing the dishes in boiling water, when he isn't washing himself or his clothes or bedding. My word, he actually boils his blankets once a week!"

For there were other things to occupy the steward's mind. Getting acquainted with the five men aft in the cabin, and lining up the whole situation and the relations of each of the five to that situation and to one another, consumed much time. Then there was the path of the Mary Turner across the sea. No old sailor breathes who does not desire to know the casual course of his ship and the next port-of-call.

"We ought to be moving along a line that'll cross somewhere northard of New Zealand," Daughtry guessed to himself, after a hundred stolen glances into the binnacle. But that was all the information concerning the ship's navigation he could steal; for Captain Doane took the observations and worked them out, to the exclusion of the mate, and Captain Doane always methodically locked up his chart and log. That there were heated discussions in the cabin, in which terms of latitude and longitude were bandied back and forth, Daughtry did know; but more than that he could not know, because it was early impressed upon him that the one place for him never to be, at such times of council, was the cabin. Also, he could not but conclude that these councils were real battles wherein Messrs. Doane, Nishikanta, and Grimshaw screamed at each other and pounded the table at each other, when they were not patiently and most politely interrogating the Ancient Mariner.

"He's got their goat," the steward early concluded to himself; but, thereafter, try as he would, he failed to get the Ancient Mariner's goat.

Charles Stough Greenleaf was the Ancient Mariner's name. This, Daughtry got from him, and nothing else did he get save maunderings and ravings about the heat of the longboat and the treasure a fathom deep under the sand.

"There's some of us plays games, an' some of us as looks on an' admires the games they see," the steward made his bid one day. "And I'm sure these days lookin' on at a pretty game. The more I see it the more I got to admire."

The Ancient Mariner dreamed back into the steward's eyes with a blank, unseeing gaze.

"On the Wide Awake all the stewards were young, mere boys," he murmured.

"Yes, sir," Daughtry agreed pleasantly. "From all you say, the Wide Awake, with all its youngsters, was sure some craft. Not like the crowd of old 'uns on this here hooker. But I doubt, sir, that them youngsters ever played as clever games as is being played aboard us right now. I just got to admire the fine way it's being done, sir."

"I'll tell you something," the Ancient Mariner replied, with such confidential air that almost Daughtry leaned to hear. "No steward on the Wide Awake could mix a highball in just the way I like, as well as you. We didn't know cocktails in those days, but we had sherry and bitters. A good appetizer, too, a most excellent appetizer."

"I'll tell you something more," he continued, just as it seemed he had finished, and just in time to interrupt Daughtry away from his third attempt to ferret out the true inwardness of the situation on the Mary Turner and of the Ancient Mariner's part in it. "It is mighty nigh five bells, and I should be very pleased to have one of your delicious cocktails ere I go down to dine."

More suspicious than ever of him was Daughtry after this episode. But, as the days went by, he came more and more to the conclusion that Charles Stough Greenleaf was a senile old man who sincerely believed in the abiding of a buried treasure somewhere in the South Seas.

Once, polishing the brass-work on the hand-rails of the cabin companionway, Daughtry overheard the ancient one explaining his terrible scar and missing fingers to Grimshaw and the Armenian Jew. The pair of them had plied him with extra drinks in the hope of getting more out of him by way of his loosened tongue.

"It was in the longboat," the aged voice cackled up the companion. "On the eleventh day it was that the mutiny broke. We in the sternsheets stood together against them. It was all a madness. We were starved sore, but we were mad for water. It was over the water it began. For, see you, it was our custom to lick the dew from the oar-blades, the gunwales, the thwarts, and the inside planking. And each man of us had developed property in the dew-collecting surfaces. Thus, the tiller and the rudder-head and half of the plank of the starboard stern-sheet had become the property of the second officer. No one of us lacked the honour to respect his property. The third officer was a lad, only eighteen, a brave and charming boy. He shared with the second officer the starboard stern-sheet plank. They drew a line to mark the division, and neither, lapping up what scant moisture fell during the night-hours, ever dreamed of trespassing across the line. They were too honourable.

"But the sailors, no. They squabbled amongst themselves over the dew- surfaces, and only the night before one of them was knifed because he so stole. But on this night, waiting for the dew, a little of it, to become more, on the surfaces that were mine, I heard the noises of a dew-lapper moving aft along the port-gunwale, which was my property aft of the stroke-thwart clear to the stern. I emerged from a nightmare dream of crystal springs and swollen rivers to listen to this night-drinker that I feared might encroach upon what was mine.

"Nearer he came to the line of my property, and I could hear him making little moaning, whimpering noises as he licked the damp wood. It was like listening to an animal grazing pasture-grass at night and ever grazing nearer.

"It chanced I was holding a boat-stretcher in my hand, to catch what little dew might fall upon it. I did not know who it was, but when he lapped across the line and moaned and whimpered as he licked up my precious drops of dew, I struck out. The boat-stretcher caught him fairly on the nose, it was the bo's'n, and the mutiny began. It was the bo's'n's knife that sliced down my face and sliced away my fingers. The third officer, the eighteen-year-old lad, fought well beside me, and saved me, so that, just before I fainted, he and I, between us, hove the bo's'n's carcass overside."

A shifting of feet and changing of positions of those in the cabin plunged Daughtry back into his polishing, which he had for the time forgotten. And, as he rubbed the brass-work, he told himself under his breath: "The old party's sure been through the mill. Such things just got to happen."

"No," the Ancient Mariner was continuing, in his thin falsetto, in reply to a query. "It wasn't the wounds that made me faint. It was the exertion I made in the struggle. I was too weak. No; so little moisture was there in my system that I didn't bleed much. And the amazing thing, under the circumstances, was the quickness with which I healed. The second officer sewed me up next day with a needle he'd made out of an ivory toothpick and with twine he twisted out of the threads from a frayed tarpaulin."

"Might I ask, Mr. Greenleaf, if there were rings at the time on the fingers that were cut off?" Daughtry heard Simon Nishikanta ask.

"Yes, and one beauty. I found it afterward in the boat bottom and presented it to the sandalwood trader who rescued me. It was a large diamond. I paid one hundred and eighty guineas for it to an English sailor in the Barbadoes. He'd stolen it, and of course it was worth more. It was a beautiful gem. The sandalwood man did not merely save my life for it. In addition, he spent fully a hundred pounds in outfitting me and buying me a passage from Thursday Island to Shanghai."

"There's no getting away from them rings he wears," Daughtry overheard Simon Nishikanta that evening telling Grimshaw in the dark on the weather poop. "You don't see that kind nowadays. They're old, real old. They're not men's rings so much as what you'd call, in the old-fashioned days, gentlemen's rings. Real gentlemen, I mean, grand gentlemen, wore rings like them. I wish collateral like them came into my loan offices these days. They're worth big money."

"I just want to tell you, Killeny Boy, that maybe I'll be wishin' before the voyage is over that I'd gone on a lay of the treasure instead of straight wages," Dag Daughtry confided to Michael that night at turning- in time as Kwaque removed his shoes and as he paused midway in the draining of his sixth bottle. "Take it from me, Killeny, that old gentleman knows what he's talkin' about, an' has been some hummer in his days. Men don't lose the fingers off their hands and get their faces chopped open just for nothing, nor sport rings that makes a Jew pawnbroker's mouth water."

CHAPTER XI

Before the voyage of the Mary Turner came to an end, Dag Daughtry, sitting down between the rows of water-casks in the main-hold, with a great laugh rechristened the schooner "the Ship of Fools." But that was some weeks after. In the meantime he so fulfilled his duties that not even Captain Doane could conjure a shadow of complaint.

Especially did the steward attend upon the Ancient Mariner, for whom he had come to conceive a strong admiration, if not affection. The old fellow was different from his cabin-mates. They were money-lovers; everything in them had narrowed down to the pursuit of dollars. Daughtry, himself moulded on generously careless lines, could not but appreciate the spaciousness of the Ancient Mariner, who had evidently lived spaciously and who was ever for sharing the treasure they sought.

"You'll get your whack, steward, if it comes out of my share," he frequently assured Daughtry at times of special kindness on the latter's part. "There's oodles of it, and oodles of it, and, without kith or kin, I have so little time longer to live that I shall not need it much or much of it."

And so the Ship of Fools sailed on, all aft fooling and befouling, from the guileless-eyed, gentle-souled Finnish mate, who, with the scent of treasure pungent in his nostrils, with a duplicate key stole the ship's daily position from Captain Doane's locked desk, to Ah Moy, the cook, who kept Kwaque at a distance and never whispered warning to the others of the risk they ran from continual contact with the carrier of the terrible disease.

Kwaque himself had neither thought nor worry of the matter. He knew the thing as a thing that occasionally happened to human creatures. It bothered him, from the pain standpoint, scarcely at all, and it never entered his kinky head that his master did not know about it. For the same reason he never suspected why Ah Moy kept him so at a distance. Nor had Kwaque other worries. His god, over all gods of sea and jungle, he worshipped, and, himself ever intimately allowed in the presence, paradise was wherever he and his god, the steward, might be.

And so Michael. Much in the same way that Kwaque loved and worshipped did he love and worship the six-quart man. To Michael and Kwaque, the daily, even hourly, recognition and consideration of Dag Daughtry was tantamount to resting continuously in the bosom of Abraham. The god of Messrs. Doane, Nishikanta, and Grimshaw was a graven god whose name was Gold. The god of Kwaque and Michael was a living god, whose voice could be always heard, whose arms could be always warm, the pulse of whose heart could be always felt throbbing in a myriad acts and touches.

No greater joy was Michael's than to sit by the hour with Steward and sing with him all songs and tunes he sang or hummed. With a quantity or pitch even more of genius or unusualness in him than in Jerry, Michael learned more quickly, and since the way of his education was singing, he came to sing far beyond the best Villa Kennan ever taught Jerry.

Michael could howl, or sing, rather (because his howling was so mellow and so controlled), any air that was not beyond his register that Steward elected to sing with him. In addition, he could sing by himself, and unmistakably, such simple airs as "Home, Sweet Home," "God save the King," and "The Sweet By and By." Even alone, prompted by Steward a score of feet away from him, could he lift up his muzzle and sing "Shenandoah" and "Roll me down to Rio."

Kwaque, on stolen occasions when Steward was not around, would get out his Jews' harp and by the sheer compellingness of the primitive instrument make Michael sing with him the barbaric and devil-devil rhythms of King William Island. Another master of song, but one in whom Michael delighted, came to rule over him. This master's name was Cocky. He so introduced himself to Michael at their first meeting.

"Cocky," he said bravely, without a quiver of fear or flight, when Michael had charged upon him at sight to destroy him. And the human voice, the voice of a god, issuing from the throat of the tiny, snow-white bird, had made Michael go back on his haunches, while, with eyes and nostrils, he quested the steerage for the human who had spoken. And there was no human . . . only a small cockatoo that twisted his head impudently and sidewise at him and repeated, "Cocky."

The taboo of the chicken Michael had been well taught in his earliest days at Meringe. Chickens, esteemed by Mister Haggin and his white-god fellows, were things that dogs must even defend instead of ever attack. But this thing, itself no chicken, with the seeming of a wild feathered thing of the jungle that was fair game for any dog, talked to him with the voice of a god.

"Get off your foot," it commanded so peremptorily, so humanly, as again to startle Michael and made him quest about the steerage for the god-throat that had uttered it.

"Get off your foot, or I'll throw the leg of Moses at you," was the next command from the tiny feathered thing.

After that came a farrago of Chinese, so like the voice of Ah Moy, that again, though for the last time, Michael sought about the steerage for the utterer.

At this Cocky burst into such wild and fantastic shrieks of laughter that Michael, ears pricked, head cocked to one side, identified in the fibres of the laughter the fibres of the various voices he had just previously heard.

And Cocky, only a few ounces in weight, less than half a pound, a tiny framework of fragile bone covered with a handful of feathers and incasing a heart that was as big in pluck as any heart on the Mary Turner, became almost immediately Michael's friend and comrade, as well as ruler. Minute morsel of daring and courage that Cocky was, he commanded Michael's respect from the first. And Michael, who with a single careless paw-stroke could have broken Cocky's slender neck and put out for ever the brave brightness of Cocky's eyes, was careful of him from the first. And he permitted him a myriad liberties that he would never have permitted Kwaque.

Ingrained in Michael's heredity, from the very beginning of four-legged dogs on earth, was the defence of the meat. He never reasoned it. Automatic and involuntary as his heart-beating and air-breathing, was his defence of his meat once he had his paw on it, his teeth in it. Only to Steward, by an extreme effort of will and control, could he accord the right to touch his meat once he had himself touched it. Even Kwaque, who most usually fed him under Steward's instructions, knew that the safety of fingers and flesh resided in having nothing further whatever to do with anything of food once in Michael's possession. But Cocky, a bit of feathery down, a morsel-flash of light and life with the throat of a god, violated with sheer impudence and daring Michael's taboo, the defence of the meat.

Perched on the rim of Michael's pannikin, this inconsiderable adventurer from out of the dark into the sun of life, a mere spark and mote between the darks, by a ruffing of his salmon-pink crest, a swift and enormous dilation of his bead-black pupils, and a raucous imperative cry, as of all the gods, in his throat, could make Michael give back and permit the fastidious selection of the choicest tidbits of his dish.

For Cocky had a way with him, and ways and ways. He, who was sheer bladed steel in the imperious flashing of his will, could swashbuckle and bully like any over-seas roisterer, or wheedle as wickedly winningly as the first woman out of Eden or the last woman of that descent. When Cocky, balanced on one leg, the other leg in the air as the foot of it held the scruff of Michael's neck, leaned to Michael's ear and wheedled, Michael could only lay down silkily the bristly hair-waves of his neck, and with silly half-idiotic eyes of bliss agree to whatever was Cocky's will or whimsey so delivered.

Cocky became more intimately Michael's because, very early, Ah Moy washed his hands of the bird. Ah Moy had bought him in Sydney from a sailor for eighteen shillings and chaffered an hour over the bargain. And when he saw Cocky, one day, perched and voluble, on the twisted fingers of Kwaque's left hand, Ah Moy discovered such instant distaste for the bird that not even eighteen shillings, coupled with possession of Cocky and possible contact, had any value to him.

"You likee him? You wanchee?" he proffered.

"Changee for changee!" Kwaque queried back, taking for granted that it was an offer to exchange and wondering whether the little old cook had become enamoured of his precious jews' harp.

"No changee for changee," Ah Moy answered. "You wanchee him, all right, can do."

"How fashion can do?" Kwaque demanded, who to his beche-de-mer English was already adding pidgin English. "Suppose 'm me fella no got 'm what you fella likee?"

"No fashion changee," Ah Moy reiterated. "You wanchee, you likee he stop along you fella all right, my word."

And so did pass the brave bit of feathered life with the heart of pluck, called of men, and of himself, "Cocky," who had been birthed in the jungle roof of the island of Santo, in the New Hebrides, who had been netted by a two-legged black man-eater and sold for six sticks of tobacco and a shingle hatchet to a Scotch trader dying of malaria, and in turn had been traded from hand to hand, for four shillings to a blackbirder, for a turtle-shell comb made by an English coal-passer after an old Spanish design, for the appraised value of six shillings and sixpence in a poker game in the firemen's forecastle, for a second-hand accordion worth at least twenty shillings, and on for eighteen shillings cash to a little old withered Chinaman, so did pass Cocky, as mortal or as immortal as any brave sparkle of life on the planet, from the possession of one, Ah Moy, a sea-cock who, forty years before, had slain his young wife in Macao for cause and fled away to sea, to Kwaque, a leprous Black Papuan who was slave to one, Dag Daughtry, himself a servant of other men to whom he humbly admitted "Yes, sir," and "No, sir," and "Thank you, sir."

One other comrade Michael found, although Cocky was no party to the friendship. This was Scraps, the awkward young Newfoundland puppy, who was the property of no one, unless of the schooner Mary Turner herself, for no man, fore or aft, claimed ownership, while every man disclaimed having brought him on board. So he was called Scraps, and, since he was nobody's dog, was everybody's dog, so much so, that Mr. Jackson promised to knock Ah Moy's block off if he did not feed the puppy well, while Sigurd Halvorsen, in the forecastle, did his best to knock off Henrik Gjertsen's block when the latter was guilty of kicking Scraps out of his way. Yea, even more. When Simon Nishikanta, huge and gross as in the flesh he was and for ever painting delicate, insipid, feministic water-colours, when he threw his deck-chair at Scraps for clumsily knocking over his easel, he found the ham-like hand of Grimshaw so instant and heavy on his shoulder as to whirl him half about, almost fling him to the deck, and leave him lame-muscled and black-and-blued for days.

Michael, full grown, mature, was so merry-hearted an individual that he found all delight in interminable romps with Scraps. So strong was the play-instinct in him, as well as was his constitution strong, that he continually outplayed Scraps to abject weariness, so that he could only lie on the deck and pant and laugh through air-draughty lips and dab futilely in the air with weak forepaws at Michael's continued ferocious- acted onslaughts. And this, despite the fact that Scraps out-bullied him and out-scaled him at least three times, and was as careless and unwitting of the weight of his legs or shoulders as a baby elephant on a lawn of daisies. Given his breath back again, Scraps was as ripe as ever for another frolic, and Michael was just as ripe to meet him. All of which was splendid training for Michael, keeping him in the tiptop of physical condition and mental wholesomeness.

CHAPTER XII

So sailed the Ship of Fools, Michael playing with Scraps, respecting Cocky and by Cocky being bullied and wheedled, singing with Steward and worshipping him; Daughtry drinking his six quarts of beer each day, collecting his wages the first of each month, and admiring Charles Stough Greenleaf as the finest man on board; Kwaque serving and loving his master and thickening and darkening and creasing his brow with the growing leprous infiltration; Ah Moy avoiding the Black Papuan as the very plague, washing himself continuously and boiling his blankets once a week; Captain Doane doing the navigating and worrying about his flat-building in San Francisco; Grimshaw resting his ham-hands on his colossal knees and girding at the pawnbroker to contribute as much to the adventure as he was contributing from his wheat-ranches; Simon Nishikanta wiping his sweaty neck with the greasy silk handkerchief and painting endless water-colours; the mate patiently stealing the ship's latitude and longitude with his duplicate key; and the Ancient Mariner, solacing himself with Scotch highballs, smoking fragrant three-for-a-dollar Havanas that were charged to the adventure, and for ever maundering about the hell of the longboat, the cross-bearings unnamable, and the treasure a fathom under the sand.

Came a stretch of ocean that to Daughtry was like all other stretches of ocean and unidentifiable from them. No land broke the sea-rim. The ship the centre, the horizon was the invariable and eternal circle of the world. The magnetic needle in the binnacle was the point on which the Mary Turner ever pivoted. The sun rose in the undoubted east and set in the undoubted west, corrected and proved, of course, by declination, deviation, and variation; and the nightly march of the stars and constellations proceeded across the sky.

And in this stretch of ocean, lookouts were mastheaded at day-dawn and kept mastheaded until twilight of evening, when the Mary Turner was hove-to, to hold her position through the night. As time went by, and the scent, according to the Ancient Mariner, grow hotter, all three of the investors in the adventure came to going aloft. Grimshaw contented himself with standing on the main crosstrees. Captain Doane climbed even higher, seating himself on the stump of the foremast with legs a-straddle of the butt of the fore-topmast. And Simon Nishikanta tore himself away from his everlasting painting of all colour-delicacies of sea and sky such as are painted by seminary maidens, to be helped and hoisted up the ratlines of the mizzen rigging, the huge bulk of him, by two grinning, slim-waisted sailors, until they lashed him squarely on the crosstrees and left him to stare with eyes of golden desire, across the sun-washed sea through the finest pair of unredeemed binoculars that had ever been pledged in his pawnshops.

"Strange," the Ancient Mariner would mutter, "strange, and most strange. This is the very place. There can be no mistake. I'd have trusted that youngster of a third officer anywhere. He was only eighteen, but he could navigate better than the captain. Didn't he fetch the atoll after eighteen days in the longboat? No standard compasses, and you know what a small-boat horizon is, with a big sea, for a sextant. He died, but the dying course he gave me held good, so that I fetched the atoll the very next day after I hove his body overboard."

Captain Doane would shrug his shoulders and defiantly meet the mistrustful eyes of the Armenian Jew.

"It cannot have sunk, surely," the Ancient Mariner would tactfully carry across the forbidding pause. "The island was no mere shoal or reef. The Lion's Head was thirty-eight hundred and thirty-five feet. I saw the captain and the third officer triangulate it."

"I've raked and combed the sea," Captain Doane would then break out, "and the teeth of my comb are not so wide apart as to let slip through a four- thousand-foot peak."

"Strange, strange," the Ancient Mariner would next mutter, half to his cogitating soul, half aloud to the treasure-seekers. Then, with a sudden brightening, he would add:

"But, of course, the variation has changed, Captain Doane. Have you allowed for the change in variation for half a century! That should make a grave difference. Why, as I understand it, who am no navigator, the variation was not so definitely and accurately known in those days as now."

"Latitude was latitude, and longitude was longitude," would be the captain's retort. "Variation and deviation are used in setting courses and estimating dead reckoning."

All of which was Greek to Simon Nishikanta, who would promptly take the Ancient Mariner's side of the discussion.

But the Ancient Mariner was fair-minded. What advantage he gave the Jew one moment, he balanced the next moment with an advantage to the skipper.

"It's a pity," he would suggest to Captain Doane, "that you have only one chronometer. The entire fault may be with the chronometer. Why did you sail with only one chronometer?"

"But I was willing for two," the Jew would defend. "You know that, Grimshaw?"

The wheat-farmer would nod reluctantly and Captain would snap:

"But not for three chronometers."

"But if two was no better than one, as you said so yourself and as Grimshaw will bear witness, then three was no better than two except for an expense."

"But if you only have two chronometers, how can you tell which has gone wrong?" Captain Doane would demand.

"Search me," would come the pawnbroker's retort, accompanied by an incredulous shrug of the shoulders. "If you can't tell which is wrong of two, then how much harder must it be to tell which is wrong of two dozen? With only two, it's a fifty-fifty split that one or the other is wrong."

"But don't you realize -"

"I realize that it's all a great foolishness, all this highbrow stuff about navigation. I've got clerks fourteen years old in my offices that can figure circles all around you and your navigation. Ask them that if two chronometers ain't better than one, then how can two thousand be better than one? And they'd answer quick, snap, like that, that if two dollars ain't any better than one dollar, then two thousand dollars ain't any better than one dollar. That's common sense."

"Just the same, you're wrong on general principle," Grimshaw would oar in. "I said at the time that the only reason we took Captain Doane in with us on the deal was because we needed a navigator and because you and me didn't know the first thing about it. You said, 'Yes, sure'; and right away knew more about it than him when you wouldn't stand for buying three chronometers. What was the matter with you was that the expense hurt you. That's about as big an idea as your mind ever had room for. You go around looking for to dig out ten million dollars with a second- hand spade you call buy for sixty-eight cents."

Dag Daughtry could not fail to overhear some of these conversations, which were altercations rather than councils. The invariable ending, for Simon Nishikanta, would be what sailors name "the sea-grouch." For hours afterward the sulky Jew would speak to no one nor acknowledge speech from any one. Vainly striving to paint, he would suddenly burst into violent rage, tear up his attempt, stamp it into the deck, then get out his large- calibred automatic rifle, perch himself on the forecastle-head, and try to shoot any stray porpoise, albacore, or dolphin. It seemed to give him great relief to send a bullet home into the body of some surging, gorgeous-hued fish, arrest its glorious flashing motion for ever, and turn it on its side slowly to sink down into the death and depth of the sea.

On occasion, when a school of blackfish disported by, each one of them a whale of respectable size, Nishikanta would be beside himself in the ecstasy of inflicting pain. Out of the school perhaps he would reach a score of the leviathans, his bullets biting into them like whip-lashes, so that each, like a colt surprised by the stock-whip, would leap in the air, or with a flirt of tail dive under the surface, and then charge madly across the ocean and away from sight in a foam-churn of speed.

The Ancient Mariner would shake his head sadly; and Daughtry, who likewise was hurt by the infliction of hurt on unoffending animals, would sympathize with him and fetch him unbidden another of the expensive three- for-a-dollar cigars so that his feelings might be soothed. Grimshaw would curl his lip in a sneer and mutter: "The cheap skate. The skunk. No man with half the backbone of a man would take it out of the harmless creatures. He's that kind that if he didn't like you, or if you criticised his grammar or arithmetic, he'd kick your dog to get even . . . or poison it. In the good old days up in Colusa we used to hang men like him just to keep the air we breathed clean and wholesome."

But it was Captain Doane who protested outright.

"Look at here, Nishikanta," he would say, his face white and his lips trembling with anger. "That's rough stuff, and all you can get back for it is rough stuff. I know what I'm talking about. You've got no right to risk our lives that way. Wasn't the pilot boat Annie Mine sunk by a whale right in the Golden Gate? Didn't I sail in as a youngster, second mate on the brig Berncastle, into Hakodate, pumping double watches to keep afloat just because a whale took a smash at us? Didn't the full-rigged ship, the whaler Essex, sink off the west coast of South America, twelve hundred miles from the nearest land for the small boats to cover, and all because of a big cow whale that butted her into kindling-wood?"

And Simon Nishikanta, in his grouch, disdaining to reply, would continue to pepper the last whale into flight beyond the circle of the sea their vision commanded.

"I remember the whaleship Essex," the Ancient Mariner told Dag Daughtry. "It was a cow with a calf that did for her. Her barrels were two-thirds full, too. She went down in less than an hour. One of the boats never was heard of."

"And didn't another one of her boats get to Hawaii, sir?" Daughtry queried with all due humility of respect. "Leastwise, thirty years ago, when I was in Honolulu, I met a man, an old geezer, who claimed he'd been a harpooner on a whaleship sunk by a whale off the coast of South America. That was the first and last I heard of it, until right now you speaking of it, sir. It must a-been the same ship, sir, don't you think?"

"Unless two different ships were whale-sunk off the west coast," the Ancient Mariner replied. "And of the one ship, the Essex, there is no discussion. It is historical. The chance is likely, steward, that the man you mentioned was from the Essex."

CHAPTER XIII

Captain Doane worked hard, pursuing the sun in its daily course through the sky, by the equation of time correcting its aberrations due to the earth's swinging around the great circle of its orbit, and charting Sumner lines innumerable, working assumed latitudes for position until his head grew dizzy.

Simon Nishikanta sneered openly at what he considered the captain's inefficient navigation, and continued to paint water-colours when he was serene, and to shoot at whales, sea-birds, and all things hurtable when he was downhearted and sea-sore with disappointment at not sighting the Lion's Head peak of the Ancient Mariner's treasure island.

"I'll show I ain't a pincher," Nishikanta announced one day, after having broiled at the mast-head for five hours of sea-searching. "Captain Doane, how much could we have bought extra chronometers for in San Francisco, good second-hand ones, I mean?"

"Say a hundred dollars," the captain answered.

"Very well. And this ain't a piker's proposition. The cost of such a chronometer would have been divided between the three of us. I stand for its total cost. You just tell the sailors that I, Simon Nishikanta, will pay one hundred dollars gold money for the first one that sights land on Mr. Greenleaf's latitude and longitude."

But the sailors who swarmed the mast-heads were doomed to disappointment, in that for only two days did they have opportunity to stare the ocean surface for the reward. Nor was this due entirely to Dag Daughtry, despite the fact that his own intention and act would have been sufficient to spoil their chance for longer staring.

Down in the lazarette, under the main-cabin floor, it chanced that he took toll of the cases of beer which had been shipped for his especial benefit. He counted the cases, doubted the verdict of his senses, lighted more matches, counted again, then vainly searched the entire lazarette in the hope of finding more cases of beer stored elsewhere.

He sat down under the trap door of the main-cabin floor and thought for a solid hour. It was the Jew again, he concluded, the Jew who had been willing to equip the Mary Turner with two chronometers, but not with three; the Jew who had ratified the agreement of a sufficient supply to permit Daughtry his daily six quarts. Once again the steward counted the cases to make sure. There were three. And since each case contained two dozen quarts, and since his whack each day was half a dozen quarts, it was patent that, the supply that stared him in the face would last him only twelve days. And twelve days were none too long to sail from this unidentifiable naked sea-stretch to the nearest possible port where beer could be purchased.

The steward, once his mind was made up, wasted no time. The clock marked a quarter before twelve when he climbed up out of the lazarette, replaced the trapdoor, and hurried to set the table. He served the company through the noon meal, although it was all he could do to refrain from capsizing the big tureen of split-pea soup over the head of Simon Nishikanta. What did effectually withstrain him was the knowledge of the act which in the lazarette he had already determined to perform that afternoon down in the main hold where the water-casks were stored.

At three o'clock, while the Ancient Mariner supposedly drowned in his room, and while Captain Doane, Grimshaw, and half the watch on deck clustered at the mast-heads to try to raise the Lion's Head from out the sapphire sea, Dag Daughtry dropped down the ladder of the open hatchway into the main hold. Here, in long tiers, with alleyways between, the water-casks were chocked safely on their sides.

From inside his shirt the steward drew a brace, and to it fitted a half- inch bit from his hip-pocket. On his knees, he bored through the head of the first cask until the water rushed out upon the deck and flowed down into the bilge. He worked quickly, boring cask after cask down the alleyway that led to deeper twilight. When he had reached the end of the first row of casks he paused a moment to listen to the gurglings of the many half-inch streams running to waste. His quick ears caught a similar gurgling from the right in the direction of the next alleyway. Listening closely, he could have sworn he heard the sounds of a bit biting into hard wood.

A minute later, his own brace and bit carefully secreted, his hand was descending on the shoulder of a man he could not recognize in the gloom, but who, on his knees and wheezing, was steadily boring into the head of a cask. The culprit made no effort to escape, and when Daughtry struck a match he gazed down into the upturned face of the Ancient Mariner.

"My word!" the steward muttered his amazement softly. "What in hell are you running water out for?"

He could feel the old man's form trembling with violent nervousness, and his own heart smote him for gentleness.

"It's all right," he whispered. "Don't mind me. How many have you bored?"

"All in this tier," came the whispered answer. "You will not inform on me to the . . . the others?"

"Inform?" Daughtry laughed softly. "I don't mind telling you that we're playing the same game, though I don't know why you should play it. I've just finished boring all of the starboard row. Now I tell you, sir, you skin out right now, quietly, while the goin' is good. Everybody's aloft, and you won't be noticed. I'll go ahead and finish this job . . . all but enough water to last us say a dozen days."

"I should like to talk with you . . . to explain matters," the Ancient Mariner whispered.

"Sure, sir, an' I don't mind sayin', sir, that I'm just plain mad curious to hear. I'll join you down in the cabin, say in ten minutes, and we can have a real gam. But anyway, whatever your game is, I'm with you. Because it happens to be my game to get quick into port, and because, sir, I have a great liking and respect for you. Now shoot along. I'll be with you inside ten minutes."

"I like you, steward, very much," the old man quavered.

"And I like you, sir, and a damn sight more than them money-sharks aft. But we'll just postpone this. You beat it out of here, while I finish scuppering the rest of the water."

A quarter of an hour later, with the three money-sharks still at the mast- heads, Charles Stough Greenleaf was seated in the cabin and sipping a highball, and Dag Daughtry was standing across the table from him, drinking directly from a quart bottle of beer.

"Maybe you haven't guessed it," the Ancient Mariner said; "but this is my fourth voyage after this treasure."

"You mean . . . ?" Daughtry asked.

"Just that. There isn't any treasure. There never was one, any more than the Lion's Head, the longboat, or the bearings unnamable."'

Daughtry rumpled his grizzled thatch of hair in his perplexity, as he admitted:

"Well, you got me, sir. You sure got me to believin' in that treasure."

"And I acknowledge, steward, that I am pleased to hear it. It shows that I have not lost my cunning when I can deceive a man like you. It is easy to deceive men whose souls know only money. But you are different. You don't live and breathe for money. I've watched you with your dog. I've watched you with your nigger boy. I've watched you with your beer. And just because your heart isn't set on a great buried treasure of gold, you are harder to deceive. Those whose hearts are set, are most astonishingly easy to fool. They are of cheap kidney. Offer them a proposition of one hundred dollars for one, and they are like hungry pike snapping at the bait. Offer a thousand dollars for one, or ten thousand for one, and they become sheer lunatic. I am an old man, a very old man. I like to live until I die, I mean, to live decently, comfortably, respectably."

"And you like the voyages long? I begin to see, sir. Just as they're getting near to where the treasure ain't, a little accident like the loss of their water-supply sends them into port and out again to start hunting all over."

The Ancient Mariner nodded, and his sun-washed eyes twinkled.

"There was the Emma Louisa. I kept her on the long voyage over eighteen months with water accidents and similar accidents. And, besides, they kept me in one of the best hotels in New Orleans for over four months before the voyage began, and advanced to me handsomely, yes, bravely, handsomely."

"But tell me more, sir; I am most interested," Dag Daughtry concluded his simple matter of the beer. "It's a good game. I might learn it for my old age, though I give you my word, sir, I won't butt in on your game. I wouldn't tackle it until you are gone, sir, good game that it is."

"First of all, you must pick out men with money, with plenty of money, so that any loss will not hurt them. Also, they are easier to interest -"

"Because they are more hoggish," the steward interrupted. "The more money they've got the more they want."

"Precisely," the Ancient Mariner continued. "And, at least, they are repaid. Such sea-voyages are excellent for their health. After all, I do them neither hurt nor harm, but only good, and add to their health."

"But them scars, that gouge out of your face, all them fingers missing on your hand? You never got them in the fight in the longboat when the bo's'n carved you up. Then where in Sam Hill did you get the them? Wait a minute, sir. Let me fill your glass first." And with a fresh-brimmed glass, Charles Stough Greanleaf narrated the history of his scars.

"First, you must know, steward, that I am, well, a gentleman. My name has its place in the pages of the history of the United States, even back before the time when they were the United States. I graduated second in my class in a university that it is not necessary to name. For that matter, the name I am known by is not my name. I carefully compounded it out of names of other families. I have had misfortunes. I trod the quarter-deck when I was a young man, though never the deck of the Wide Awake, which is the ship of my fancy, and of my livelihood in these latter days.

"The scars you asked about, and the missing fingers? Thus it chanced. It was the morning, at late getting-up times in a Pullman, when the accident happened. The car being crowded, I had been forced to accept an upper berth. It was only the other day. A few years ago. I was an old man then. We were coming up from Florida. It was a collision on a high trestle. The train crumpled up, and some of the cars fell over sideways and fell off, ninety feet into the bottom of a dry creek. It was dry, though there was a pool of water just ten feet in diameter and eighteen inches deep. All the rest was dry boulders, and I bull's-eyed that pool.

"This is the way it was. I had just got on my shoes and pants and shirt, and had started to get out of the bunk. There I was, sitting on the edge of the bunk, my legs dangling down, when the locomotives came together. The berths, upper and lower, on the opposite side had already been made up by the porter.

"And there I was, sitting, legs dangling, not knowing where I was, on a trestle or a flat, when the thing happened. I just naturally left that upper berth, soared like a bird across the aisle, went through the glass of the window on the opposite side clean head-first, turned over and over through the ninety feet of fall more times than I like to remember, and by some sort of miracle was mostly flat-out in the air when I bull's-eyed that pool of water. It was only eighteen inches deep. But I hit it flat, and I hit it so hard that it must have cushioned me. I was the only survivor of my car. It struck forty feet away from me, off to the side. And they took only the dead out of it. When they took me out of the pool I wasn't dead by any means. And when the surgeons got done with me, there were the fingers gone from my hand, that scar down the side of my face . . . and, though you'd never guess it, I've been three ribs short of the regular complement ever since.

"Oh, I had no complaint coming. Think of the others in that car, all dead. Unfortunately, I was riding on a pass, and so could not sue the railroad company. But here I am, the only man who ever dived ninety feet into eighteen inches of water and lived to tell the tale. Steward, if you don't mind replenishing my glass . . ."

Dag Daughtry complied and in his excitement of interest pulled off the top of another quart of beer for himself.

"Go on, go on, sir," he murmured huskily, wiping his lips, "and the treasure-hunting graft. I'm straight dying to hear. Sir, I salute you."

"I may say, steward," the Ancient Mariner resumed, "that I was born with a silver spoon that melted in my mouth and left me a proper prodigal son. Also, that I was born with a backbone of pride that would not melt. Not for a paltry railroad accident, but for things long before as well as after, my family let me die, and I . . . I let it live. That is the story. I let my family live. Furthermore, it was not my family's fault. I never whimpered. I never let on. I melted the last of my silver spoon, South Sea cotton, an' it please you, cacao in Tonga, rubber and mahogany in Yucatan. And do you know, at the end, I slept in Bowery lodging-houses and ate scrapple in East-Side feeding-dens, and, on more than one occasion, stood in the bread-line at midnight and pondered whether or not I should faint before I fed."

"And you never squealed to your family," Dag Daughtry murmured admiringly in the pause.

The Ancient Mariner straightened up his shoulders, threw his head back, then bowed it and repeated, "No, I never squealed. I went into the poor- house, or the county poor-farm as they call it. I lived sordidly. I lived like a beast. For six months I lived like a beast, and then I saw my way out. I set about building the Wide Awake. I built her plank by plank, and copper-fastened her, selected her masts and every timber of her, and personally signed on her full ship's complement fore-and-aft, and outfitted her amongst the Jews, and sailed with her to the South Seas and the treasure buried a fathom under the sand.

"You see," he explained, "all this I did in my mind, for all the time I was a hostage in the poor-farm of broken men."

The Ancient Mariner's face grew suddenly bleak and fierce, and his right hand flashed out to Daughtry's wrist, prisoning it in withered fingers of steel.

"It was a long, hard way to get out of the poor-farm and finance my miserable little, pitiful little, adventure of the Wide Awake. Do you know that I worked in the poor-farm laundry for two years, for one dollar and a half a week, with my one available hand and what little I could do with the other, sorting dirty clothes and folding sheets and pillow-slips until I thought a thousand times my poor old back would break in two, and until I knew a million times the location in my chest of every fraction of an inch of my missing ribs."

"You are a young man yet -"

Daughtry grinned denial as he rubbed his grizzled mat of hair.

"You are a young man yet, steward," the Ancient Mariner insisted with a show of irritation. "You have never been shut out from life. In the poor-farm one is shut out from life. There is no respect, no, not for age alone, but for human life in the poor-house. How shall I say it? One is not dead. Nor is one alive. One is what once was alive and is in process of becoming dead. Lepers are treated that way. So are the insane. I know it. When I was young and on the sea, a brother-lieutenant went mad. Sometimes he was violent, and we struggled with him, twisting his arms, bruising his flesh, tying him helpless while we sat and panted on him that he might not do harm to us, himself, or the ship. And he, who still lived, died to us. Don't you understand? He was no longer of us, like us. He was something other. That is it, other. And so, in the poor-farm, we, who are yet unburied, are other. You have heard me chatter about the hell of the longboat. That is a pleasant diversion in life compared with the poor-farm. The food, the filth, the abuse, the bullying, the, the sheer animalness of it!

"For two years I worked for a dollar and a half a week in the laundry. And imagine me, who had melted a silver spoon in my mouth, a sizable silver spoon steward, imagine me, my old sore bones, my old belly reminiscent of youth's delights, my old palate ticklish yet and not all withered of the deviltries of taste learned in younger days, as I say, steward, imagine me, who had ever been free-handed, lavish, saving that dollar and a half intact like a miser, never spending a penny of it on tobacco, never mitigating by purchase of any little delicacy the sad condition of my stomach that protested against the harshness and indigestibility of our poor fare. I cadged tobacco, poor cheap tobacco, from poor doddering old chaps trembling on the edge of dissolution. Ay, and when Samuel Merrivale I found dead in the morning, next cot to mine, I first rummaged his poor old trousers' pocket for the half-plug of tobacco I knew was the total estate he left, then announced the news.

"Oh, steward, I was careful of that dollar and a half. Don't you see? I was a prisoner sawing my way out with a tiny steel saw. And I sawed out!" His voice rose in a shrill cackle of triumph. "Steward, I sawed out!"

Dag Daughtry held forth and up his beer-bottle as he said gravely and sincerely:

"Sir, I salute you."

"And I thank you, sir, you understand," the Ancient Mariner replied with simple dignity to the toast, touching his glass to the bottle and drinking with the steward eyes to eyes.

"I should have had one hundred and fifty-six dollars when I left the poor- farm," the ancient one continued. "But there were the two weeks I lost, with influenza, and the one week from a confounded pleurisy, so that I emerged from that place of the living dead with but one hundred and fifty- one dollars and fifty cents."

"I see, sir," Daughtry interrupted with honest admiration. "The tiny saw had become a crowbar, and with it you were going back to break into life again."

All the scarred face and washed eyes of Charles Stough Greenleaf beamed as he held his glass up.

"Steward, I salute you. You understand. And you have said it well. I was going back to break into the house of life. It was a crowbar, that pitiful sum of money accumulated by two years of crucifixion. Think of it! A sum that in the days ere the silver spoon had melted, I staked in careless moods of an instant on a turn of the cards. But as you say, a burglar, I came back to break into life, and I came to Boston. You have a fine turn for a figure of speech, steward, and I salute you."

Again bottle and glass tinkled together, and both men drank eyes to eyes and each was aware that the eyes he gazed into were honest and understanding.

"But it was a thin crowbar, steward. I dared not put my weight on it for a proper pry. I took a room in a small but respectable hotel, European plan. It was in Boston, I think I said. Oh, how careful I was of my crowbar! I scarcely ate enough to keep my frame inhabited. But I bought drinks for others, most carefully selected, bought drinks with an air of prosperity that was as a credential to my story; and in my cups (my apparent cups, steward), spun an old man's yarn of the Wide Awake, the longboat, the bearings unnamable, and the treasure under the sand. A fathom under the sand; that was literary; it was psychological; it smacked of the salt sea, and daring rovers, and the loot of the Spanish Main.

"You have noticed this nugget I wear on my watch-chain, steward? I could not afford it at that time, but I talked golden instead, California gold, nuggets and nuggets, oodles and oodles, from the diggings of forty-nine and fifty. That was literary. That was colour. Later, after my first voyage out of Boston I was financially able to buy a nugget. It was so much bait to which men rose like fishes. And like fishes they nibbled. These rings, also, bait. You never see such rings now. After I got in funds, I purchased them, too. Take this nugget: I am talking. I toy with it absently as I am telling of the great gold treasure we buried under the sand. Suddenly the nugget flashes fresh recollection into my mind. I speak of the longboat, of our thirst and hunger, and of the third officer, the fair lad with cheeks virgin of the razor, and that he it was who used it as a sinker when we strove to catch fish.

"But back in Boston. Yarns and yarns, when seemingly I was gone in drink, I told my apparent cronies, men whom I despised, stupid dolts of creatures that they were. But the word spread, until one day, a young man, a reporter, tried to interview me about the treasure and the Wide Awake. I was indignant, angry. Oh, softly, steward, softly; in my heart was great joy as I denied that young reporter, knowing that from my cronies he already had a sufficiency of the details.

"And the morning paper gave two whole columns and headlines to the tale. I began to have callers. I studied them out well. Many were for adventuring after the treasure who themselves had no money. I baffled and avoided them, and waited on, eating even less as my little capital dwindled away.

"And then he came, my gay young doctor, doctor of philosophy he was, for he was very wealthy. My heart sang when I saw him. But twenty-eight dollars remained to me, after it was gone, the poor-house, or death. I had already resolved upon death as my choice rather than go back to be of that dolorous company, the living dead of the poor-farm. But I did not go back, nor did I die. The gay young doctor's blood ran warm at thought of the South Seas, and in his nostrils I distilled all the scents of the flower-drenched air of that far-off land, and in his eyes I built him the fairy visions of the tradewind clouds, the monsoon skies, the palm isles and the coral seas.

"He was a gay, mad young dog, grandly careless of his largess, fearless as a lion's whelp, lithe and beautiful as a leopard, and mad, a trifle mad of the deviltries and whimsies that tickled in that fine brain of his. Look you, steward. Before we sailed in the Gloucester fishing- schooner, purchased by the doctor, and that was like a yacht and showed her heels to most yachts, he had me to his house to advise about personal equipment. We were overhauling in a gear-room, when suddenly he spoke:

"'I wonder how my lady will take my long absence. What say you? Shall she go along?'

"And I had not known that he had any wife or lady. And I looked my surprise and incredulity.

"'Just that you do not believe I shall take her on the cruise,' he laughed, wickedly, madly, in my astonished face. 'Come, you shall meet her.'

"Straight to his bedroom and his bed he led me, and, turning down the covers, showed there to me, asleep as she had slept for many a thousand years, the mummy of a slender Egyptian maid.

"And she sailed with us on the long vain voyage to the South Seas and back again, and, steward, on my honour, I grew quite fond of the dear maid myself."

The Ancient Mariner gazed dreamily into his glass, and Dag Daughtry took advantage of the pause to ask:

"But the young doctor? How did he take the failure to find the treasure?"

The Ancient Mariner's face lighted with joy.

"He called me a delectable old fraud, with his arm on my shoulder while he did it. Why, steward, I had come to love that young man like a splendid son. And with his arm on my shoulder, and I know there was more than mere kindness in it, he told me we had barely reached the River Plate when he discovered me. With laughter, and with more than one slap of his hand on my shoulder that was more caress than jollity, he pointed out the discrepancies in my tale (which I have since amended, steward, thanks to him, and amended well), and told me that the voyage had been a grand success, making him eternally my debtor.

"What could I do? I told him the truth. To him even did I tell my family name, and the shame I had saved it from by forswearing it.

"He put his arm on my shoulder, I tell you, and . . ."

The Ancient Mariner ceased talking because of a huskiness in his throat, and a moisture from his eyes trickled down both cheeks.

Dag Daughtry pledged him silently, and in the draught from his glass he recovered himself.

"He told me that I should come and live with him, and, to his great lonely house he took me the very day we landed in Boston. Also, he told me he would make arrangements with his lawyers, the idea tickled his fancy, 'I shall adopt you,' he said. 'I shall adopt you along with Isthar', Isthar was the little maid's name, the little mummy's name.

"Here was I, back in life, steward, and legally to be adopted. But life is a fond betrayer. Eighteen hours afterward, in the morning, we found him dead in his bed, the little mummy maid beside him. Heart-failure, the burst of some blood-vessel in the brain, I never learned.

"I prayed and pleaded with them for the pair to be buried together. But they were a hard, cold, New England lot, his cousins and his aunts, and they presented Isthar to the museum, and me they gave a week to be quit of the house. I left in an hour, and they searched my small baggage before they would let me depart.

"I went to New York. It was the same game there, only that I had more money and could play it properly. It was the same in New Orleans, in Galveston. I came to California. This is my fifth voyage. I had a hard time getting these three interested, and spent all my little store of money before they signed the agreement. They were very mean. Advance any money to me! The very idea of it was preposterous. Though I bided my time, ran up a comfortable hotel bill, and, at the very last, ordered my own generous assortment of liquors and cigars and charged the bill to the schooner. Such a to-do! All three of them raged and all but tore their hair . . . and mime. They said it could not be. I fell promptly sick. I told them they got on my nerves and made me sick. The more they raged, the sicker I got. Then they gave in. As promptly I grew better. And here we are, out of water and heading soon most likely for the Marquesas to fill our barrels. Then they will return and try for it again!"

"You think so, sir?"

"I shall remember even more important data, steward," the Ancient Mariner smiled. "Without doubt they will return. Oh, I know them well. They are meagre, narrow, grasping fools."

"Fools! all fools! a ship of fools!" Dag Daughtry exulted; repeating what he had expressed in the hold, as he bored the last barrel, listened to the good water gurgling away into the bilge, and chuckled over his discovery of the Ancient Mariner on the same lay as his own.

CHAPTER XIV

Early next morning, the morning watch of sailors, whose custom was to fetch the day's supply of water for the galley and cabin, discovered that the barrels were empty. Mr. Jackson was so alarmed that he immediately called Captain Doane, and not many minutes elapsed ere Captain Doane had routed out Grimshaw and Nishikanta to tell them the disaster.

Breakfast was an excitement shared in peculiarly by the Ancient Mariner and Dag Daughtry, while the trio of partners raged and bewailed. Captain Doane particularly wailed. Simon Nishikanta was fiendish in his descriptions of whatever miscreant had done the deed and of how he should be made to suffer for it, while Grimshaw clenched and repeatedly clenched his great hands as if throttling some throat.

"I remember, it was in forty-seven, nay, forty-six, yes, forty-six," the Ancient Mariner chattered. "It was a similar and worse predicament. It was in the longboat, sixteen of us. We ran on Glister Reef. So named it was after our pretty little craft discovered it one dark night and left her bones upon it. The reef is on the Admiralty charts. Captain Doane will verify me . . ."

No one listened, save Dag Daughtry, serving hot cakes and admiring. But Simon Nishikanta, becoming suddenly aware that the old man was babbling, bellowed out ferociously:

"Oh, shut up! Close your jaw! You make me tired with your everlasting 'I remember.'"

The Ancient Mariner was guilelessly surprised, as if he had slipped somewhere in his narrative.

"No, I assure you," he continued. "It must have been some error of my poor old tongue. It was not the Wide Awake, but the brig Glister. Did I say Wide Awake? It was the Glister, a smart little brig, almost a toy brig in fact, copper-bottomed, lines like a dolphin, a sea- cutter and a wind-eater. Handled like a top. On my honour, gentlemen, it was lively work for both watches when she went about. I was super- cargo. We sailed out of New York, ostensibly for the north-west coast, with sealed orders -"

"In the name of God, peace, peace! You drive me mad with your drivel!" So Nishikanta cried out in nervous pain that was real and quivering. "Old man, have a heart. What do I care to know of your Glister and your sealed orders!"

"Ah, sealed orders," the Ancient Mariner went on beamingly. "A magic phrase, sealed orders." He rolled it off his tongue with unction. "Those were the days, gentlemen, when ships did sail with sealed orders. And as super-cargo, with my trifle invested in the adventure and my share in the gains, I commanded the captain. Not in him, but in me were reposed the sealed orders. I assure you I did not know myself what they were. Not until we were around old Cape Stiff, fifty to fifty, and in fifty in the Pacific, did I break the seal and learn we were bound for Van Dieman's Land. They called it Van Dieman's Land in those days . . . "

It was a day of discoveries. Captain Doane caught the mate stealing the ship's position from his desk with the duplicate key. There was a scene, but no more, for the Finn was too huge a man to invite personal encounter, and Captain Dome could only stigmatize his conduct to a running reiteration of "Yes, sir," and "No, sir," and "Sorry, sir."

Perhaps the most important discovery, although he did not know it at the time, was that of Dag Daughtry. It was after the course had been changed and all sail set, and after the Ancient Mariner had privily informed him that Taiohae, in the Marquesas, was their objective, that Daughtry gaily proceeded to shave. But one trouble was on his mind. He was not quite sure, in such an out-of-the-way place as Taiohae, that good beer could be procured.

As he prepared to make the first stroke of the razor, most of his face white with lather, he noticed a dark patch of skin on his forehead just between the eyebrows and above. When he had finished shaving he touched the dark patch, wondering how he had been sunburned in such a spot. But he did not know he had touched it in so far as there was any response of sensation. The dark place was numb.

"Curious," he thought, wiped his face, and forgot all about it.

No more than he knew what horror that dark spot represented, did he know that Ah Moy's slant eyes had long since noticed it and were continuing to notice it, day by day, with secret growing terror.

Close-hauled on the south-east trades, the Mary Turner began her long slant toward the Marquesas. For'ard, all were happy. Being only seamen, on seamen's wages, they hailed with delight the news that they were bound in for a tropic isle to fill their water-barrels. Aft, the three partners were in bad temper, and Nishikanta openly sneered at Captain Doane and doubted his ability to find the Marquesas. In the steerage everybody was happy, Dag Daughtry because his wages were running on and a further supply of beer was certain; Kwaque because he was happy whenever his master was happy; and Ah Moy because he would soon have opportunity to desert away from the schooner and the two lepers with whom he was domiciled.

Michael shared in the general happiness of the steerage, and joined eagerly with Steward in learning by heart a fifth song. This was "Lead, kindly Light." In his singing, which was no more than trained howling after all, Michael sought for something he knew not what. In truth, it was the lost pack, the pack of the primeval world before the dog ever came in to the fires of men, and, for that matter, before men built fires and before men were men.

He had been born only the other day and had lived but two years in the world, so that, of himself, he had no knowledge of the lost pack. For many thousands of generations he had been away from it; yet, deep down in the crypts of being, tied about and wrapped up in every muscle and nerve of him, was the indelible record of the days in the wild when dim ancestors had run with the pack and at the same time developed the pack and themselves. When Michael was asleep, then it was that pack-memories sometimes arose to the surface of his subconscious mind. These dreams were real while they lasted, but when he was awake he remembered them little if at all. But asleep, or singing with Steward, he sensed and yearned for the lost pack and was impelled to seek the forgotten way to it.

Waking, Michael had another and real pack. This was composed of Steward, Kwaque, Cocky, and Scraps, and he ran with it as ancient forbears had ran with their own kind in the hunting. The steerage was the lair of this pack, and, out of the steerage, it ranged the whole world, which was the Mary Turner ever rocking, heeling, reeling on the surface of the unstable sea.

But the steerage and its company meant more to Michael than the mere pack. It was heaven as well, where dwelt God. Man early invented God, often of stone, or clod, or fire, and placed him in trees and mountains and among the stars. This was because man observed that man passed and was lost out of the tribe, or family, or whatever name he gave to his group, which was, after all, the human pack. And man did not want to be lost out of the pack. So, of his imagination, he devised a new pack that would be eternal and with which he might for ever run. Fearing the dark, into which he observed all men passed, he built beyond the dark a fairer region, a happier hunting-ground, a jollier and robuster feasting-hall and wassailing-place, and called it variously "heaven."

Like some of the earliest and lowest of primitive men, Michael never dreamed of throwing the shadow of himself across his mind and worshipping it as God. He did not worship shadows. He worshipped a real and indubitable god, not fashioned in his own four-legged, hair-covered image, but in the flesh-and-blood image, two-legged, hairless, upstanding, of Steward.

CHAPTER XV

Had the trade wind not failed on the second day after laying the course for the Marquesas; had Captain Doane, at the mid-day meal, not grumbled once again at being equipped with only one chronometer; had Simon Nishikanta not become viciously angry thereat and gone on deck with his rifle to find some sea-denizen to kill; and had the sea-denizen that appeared close alongside been a bonita, a dolphin, a porpoise, an albacore, or anything else than a great, eighty-foot cow whale accompanied by her nursing calf, had any link been missing from this chain of events, the Mary Turner would have undoubtedly reached the Marquesas, filled her water-barrels, and returned to the treasure-hunting; and the destinies of Michael, Daughtry, Kwaque, and Cocky would have been quite different and possibly less terrible.

But every link was present for the occasion. The schooner, in a dead calm, was rolling over the huge, smooth seas, her boom sheets and tackles crashing to the hollow thunder of her great sails, when Simon Nishikanta put a bullet into the body of the little whale calf. By an almost miracle of chance, the shot killed the calf. It was equivalent to killing an elephant with a pea-rifle. Not at once did the calf die. It merely immediately ceased its gambols and for a while lay quivering on the surface of the ocean. The mother was beside it the moment after it was struck, and to those on board, looking almost directly down upon her, her dismay and alarm were very patent. She would nudge the calf with her huge shoulder, circle around and around it, then range up alongside and repeat her nudgings and shoulderings.

All on the Mary Turner, fore and aft, lined the rail and stared down apprehensively at the leviathan that was as long as the schooner.

"If she should do to us, sir, what that other one did to the Essex," Dag Daughtry observed to the Ancient Mariner.

"It would be no more than we deserve," was the response. "It was uncalled-for, a wanton, cruel act."

Michael, aware of the excitement overside but unable to see because of the rail, leaped on top of the cabin and at sight of the monster barked defiantly. Every eye turned on him in startlement and fear, and Steward hushed him with a whispered command.

"This is the last time," Grimshaw muttered in a low voice, tense with anger, to Nishikanta. "If ever again, on this voyage, you take a shot at a whale, I'll wring your dirty neck for you. Get me. I mean it. I'll choke your eye-balls out of you."

The Jew smiled in a sickly way and whined, "There ain't nothing going to happen. I don't believe that Essex ever was sunk by a whale."

Urged on by its mother, the dying calf made spasmodic efforts to swim that were futile and caused it to veer and wallow from side to side.

In the course of circling about it, the mother accidentally brushed her shoulder under the port quarter of the Mary Turner, and the Mary Turner listed to starboard as her stern was lifted a yard or more. Nor was this unintentional, gentle impact all. The instant after her shoulder had touched, startled by the contact, she flailed out with her tail. The blow smote the rail just for'ard of the fore-shrouds, splintering a gap through it as if it were no more than a cigar-box and cracking the covering board.

That was all, and an entire ship's company stared down in silence and fear at a sea-monster grief-stricken over its dying progeny.

Several times, in the course of an hour, during which the schooner and the two whales drifted farther and farther apart, the calf strove vainly to swim. Then it set up a great quivering, which culminated in a wild wallowing and lashing about of its tail.

"It is the death-flurry," said the Ancient Mariner softly.

"By damn, it's dead," was Captain Doane's comment five minutes later. "Who'd believe it? A rifle bullet! I wish to heaven we could get half an hour's breeze of wind to get us out of this neighbourhood."

"A close squeak," said Grimshaw,

Captain Doane shook his head, as his anxious eyes cast aloft to the empty canvas and quested on over the sea in the hope of wind-ruffles on the water. But all was glassy calm, each great sea, of all the orderly procession of great seas, heaving up, round-topped and mountainous, like so much quicksilver.

"It's all right," Grimahaw encouraged. "There she goes now, beating it away from us."

"Of course it's all right, always was all right," Nishikanta bragged, as he wiped the sweat from his face and neck and looked with the others after the departing whale. "You're a fine brave lot, you are, losing your goat to a fish."

"I noticed your face was less yellow than usual," Grimshaw sneered. "It must have gone to your heart."

Captain Doane breathed a great sigh. His relief was too strong to permit him to join in the squabbling.

"You're yellow," Grimshaw went on, "yellow clean through." He nodded his head toward the Ancient Mariner. "Now there's the real thing as a man. No yellow in him. He never batted an eye, and I reckon he knew more about the danger than you did. If I was to choose being wrecked on a desert island with him or you, I'd take him a thousand times first. If -"

But a cry from the sailors interrupted him.

"Merciful God!" Captain Doane breathed aloud.

The great cow whale had turned about, and, on the surface, was charging straight back at them. Such was her speed that a bore was raised by her nose like that which a Dreadnought or an Atlantic liner raises on the sea.

"Hold fast, all!" Captain Doane roared.

Every man braced himself for the shock. Henrik Gjertsen, the sailor at the wheel, spread his legs, crouched down, and stiffened his shoulders and arms to hand-grips on opposite spokes of the wheel. Several of the crew fled from the waist to the poop, and others of them sprang into the main-rigging. Daughtry, one hand on the rail, with his free arm clasped the Ancient Mariner around the waist.

All held. The whale struck the Mary Turner just aft of the fore-shroud. A score of things, which no eye could take in simultaneously, happened. A sailor, in the main rigging, carried away a ratline in both hands, fell head-downward, and was clutched by an ankle and saved head-downward by a comrade, as the schooner cracked and shuddered, uplifted on the port side, and was flung down on her starboard side till the ocean poured level over her rail. Michael, on the smooth roof of the cabin, slithered down the steep slope to starboard and disappeared, clawing and snarling, into the runway. The port shrouds of the foremast carried away at the chain-plates, and the fore-topmast leaned over drunkenly to starboard.

"My word," quoth the Ancient Mariner. "We certainly felt that."

"Mr. Jackson," Captain Doane commanded the mate, "will you sound the well."

The mate obeyed, although he kept an anxious eye on the whale, which had gone off at a tangent and was smoking away to the eastward.

"You see, that's what you get," Grimshaw snarled at Nishikanta.

Nishikanta nodded, as he wiped the sweat away, and muttered, "And I'm satisfied. I got all I want. I didn't think a whale had it in it. I'll never do it again."

"Maybe you'll never have the chance," the captain retorted. "We're not done with this one yet. The one that charged the Essex made charge after charge, and I guess whale nature hasn't changed any in the last few years."

"Dry as a bone, sir," Mr. Jackson reported the result of his sounding.

"There she turns," Daughtry called out.

Half a mile away, the whale circled about sharply and charged back.

"Stand from under for'ard there!" Captain Doane shouted to one of the sailors who had just emerged from the forecastle scuttle, sea-bag in hand, and over whom the fore-topmast was swaying giddily.

"He's packed for the get-away," Daughtry murmured to the Ancient Mariner. "Like a rat leaving a ship."

"We're all rats," was the reply. "I learned just that when I was a rat among the mangy rats of the poor-farm."

By this time, all men on board had communicated to Michael their contagion of excitement and fear. Back on top of the cabin so that he might see, he snarled at the cow whale when the men seized fresh grips against the impending shock and when he saw her close at hand and oncoming.

The Mary Turner was struck aft of the mizzen shrouds. As she was hurled down to starboard, whither Michael was ignominiously flung, the crack of shattered timbers was plainly heard. Henrik Gjertsen, at the wheel, clutching the wheel with all his strength, was spun through the air as the wheel was spun by the fling of the rudder. He fetched up against Captain Doane, whose grip had been torn loose from the rail. Both men crumpled down on deck with the wind knocked out of them. Nishikanta leaned cursing against the side of the cabin, the nails of both hands torn off at the quick by the breaking of his grip on the rail.

While Daughtry was passing a turn of rope around the Ancient Mariner and the mizzen rigging and giving the turn to him to hold, Captain Doane crawled gasping to the rail and dragged himself erect.

"That fetched her," he whispered huskily to the mate, hand pressed to his side to control his pain. "Sound the well again, and keep on sounding."

More of the sailors took advantage of the interval to rush for'ard under the toppling fore-topmast, dive into the forecastle, and hastily pack their sea-bags. As Ah Moy emerged from the steerage with his own rotund sea-bag, Daughtry dispatched Kwaque to pack the belongings of both of them.

"Dry as a bone, sir," came the mate's report.

"Keep on sounding, Mr. Jackson," the captain ordered, his voice already stronger as he recovered from the shock of his collision with the helmsman. "Keep right on sounding. Here she comes again, and the schooner ain't built that'd stand such hammering."

By this time Daughtry had Michael tucked under one arm, his free arm ready to anticipate the next crash by swinging on to the rigging.

In making its circle to come back, the cow lost her bearings sufficiently to miss the stern of the Mary Turner by twenty feet. Nevertheless, the bore of her displacement lifted the schooner's stern gently and made her dip her bow to the sea in a stately curtsey.

"If she'd a-hit . . ." Captain Doane murmured and ceased.

"It'd a-ben good night," Daughtry concluded for him. "She's a-knocked our stern clean off of us, sir."

Again wheeling, this time at no more than two hundred yards, the whale charged back, not completing her semi-circle sufficiently, so that she bore down upon the schooner's bow from starboard. Her back hit the stem and seemed just barely to scrape the martingale, yet the Mary Turner sat down till the sea washed level with her stern-rail. Nor was this all. Martingale, bob-stays and all parted, as well as all starboard stays to the bowsprit, so that the bowsprit swung out to port at right angles and uplifted to the drag of the remaining topmast stays. The topmast anticked high in the air for a space, then crashed down to deck, permitting the bowsprit to dip into the sea, go clear with the butt of it of the forecastle head, and drag alongside.

"Shut up that dog!" Nishikanta ordered Daughtry savagery. "If you don't . . ."

Michael, in Steward's arms, was snarling and growling intimidatingly, not merely at the cow whale but at all the hostile and menacing universe that had thrown panic into the two-legged gods of his floating world.

"Just for that," Daughtry snarled back, "I'll let 'm sing. You made this mess, and if you lift a hand to my dog you'll miss seeing the end of the mess you started, you dirty pawnbroker, you."

"Perfectly right, perfectly right," the Ancient Mariner nodded approbation. "Do you think, steward, you could get a width of canvas, or a blanket, or something soft and broad with which to replace this rope? It cuts me too sharply in the spot where my three ribs are missing."

Daughtry thrust Michael into the old man's arm.

"Hold him, sir," the steward said. "If that pawnbroker makes a move against Killeny Boy, spit in his face, bite him, anything. I'll be back in a jiffy, sir, before he can hurt you and before the whale can hit us again. And let Killeny Boy make all the noise he wants. One hair of him's worth more than a world-full of skunks of money-lenders."

Daughtry dashed into the cabin, came back with a pillow and three sheets, and, using the first as a pad and knotting the last together in swift weaver's knots, he left the Ancient Mariner safe and soft and took Michael back into his own arms.

"She's making water, sir," the mate called. "Six inches, no, seven inches, sir."

There was a rush of sailors across the wreckage of the fore-topmast to the forecastle to pack their bags.

"Swing out that starboard boat, Mr. Jackson," the captain commanded, staring after the foaming course of the cow as she surged away for a fresh onslaught. "But don't lower it. Hold it overside in the falls, or that damned fish'll smash it. Just swing it out, ready and waiting, let the men get their bags, then stow food and water aboard of her."

Lashings were cast off the boat and the falls attached, when the men fled to holding-vantage just ere the whale arrived. She struck the Mary Turner squarely amidships on the port beam, so that, from the poop, one saw, as well as heard, her long side bend and spring back like a limber fabric. The starboard rail buried under the sea as the schooner heeled to the blow, and, as she righted with a violent lurch, the water swashed across the deck to the knees of the sailors about the boat and spouted out of the port scuppers.

"Heave away!" Captain Doane ordered from the poop. "Up with her! Swing her out! Hold your turns! Make fast!"

The boat was outboard, its gunwale resting against the Mary Turner's rail.

"Ten inches, sir, and making fast," was the mate's information, as he gauged the sounding-rod.

"I'm going after my tools," Captain Doane announced, as he started for the cabin. Half into the scuttle, he paused to add with a sneer for Nishikanta's benefit, "And for my one chronometer."

"A foot and a half, and making," the mate shouted aft to him.

"We'd better do some packing ourselves," Grimshaw, following on the captain, said to Nishikanta.

"Steward," Nishikanta said, "go below and pack my bedding. I'll take care of the rest."

"Mr. Nishikanta, you can go to hell, sir, and all the rest as well," was Daughtry's quiet response, although in the same breath he was saying, respectfully and assuringly, to the Ancient Mariner: "You hold Killeny, sir. I'll take care of your dunnage. Is there anything special you want to save, sir?"

Jackson joined the four men below, and as the five of them, in haste and trepidation, packed articles of worth and comfort, the Mary Turner was struck again. Caught below without warning, all were flung fiercely to port and from Simon Nishikanta's room came wailing curses of announcement of the hurt to his ribs against his bunk-rail. But this was drowned by a prodigious smashing and crashing on deck.

"Kindling wood, there won't be anything else left of her," Captain Doane commented in the ensuing calm, as he crept gingerly up the companionway with his chronometer cuddled on an even keel to his breast.

Placing it in the custody of a sailor, he returned below and was helped up with his sea-chest by the steward. In turn, he helped the steward up with the Ancient Mariner's sea-chest. Next, aided by anxious sailors, he and Daughtry dropped into the lazarette through the cabin floor, and began breaking out and passing up a stream of supplies, cases of salmon and beef, of marmalade and biscuit, of butter and preserved milk, and of all sorts of the tinned, desiccated, evaporated, and condensed stuff that of modern times goes down to the sea in ships for the nourishment of men.

Daughtry and the captain emerged last from the cabin, and both stared upward for a moment at the gaps in the slender, sky-scraping top-hamper, where, only minutes before, the main- and mizzen-topmasts had been. A second moment they devoted to the wreckage of the same on deck, the mizzen-topmast, thrust through the spanker and supported vertically by the stout canvas, thrashing back and forth with each thrash of the sail, the main-topmast squarely across the ruined companionway to the steerage.

While the mother-whale expressing her bereavement in terms of violence and destruction, was withdrawing the necessary distance for another charge, all hands of the Mary Turner gathered about the starboard boat swung outboard ready for lowering. A respectable hill of case goods, water-kegs, and personal dunnage was piled on the deck alongside. A glance at this, and at the many men of fore and aft, demonstrated that it was to be a perilously overloaded boat.

"We want the sailors with us, at any rate, they can row," said Simon Nishikanta.

"But do we want you?" Grimshaw queried gloomily. "You take up too much room, for your size, and you're a beast anyway."

"I guess I'll be wanted," the pawnbroker observed, as he jerked open his shirt, tearing out the four buttons in his impetuousness and showing a Colt's .44 automatic, strapped in its holster against the bare skin of his side under his left arm, the butt of the weapon most readily accessible to any hasty dip of his right hand. "I guess I'll be wanted. But just the same we can dispense with the undesirables."

"If you will have your will," the wheat-farmer conceded sardonically, although his big hand clenched involuntarily as if throttling a throat. "Besides, if we should run short of food you will prove desirable, for the quantity of you, I mean, and not otherwise. Now just who would you consider undesirable? the black nigger? He ain't got a gun."

But his pleasantries were cut short by the whale's next attack, another smash at the stern that carried away the rudder and destroyed the steering gear.

"How much water?" Captain Doane queried of the mate.

"Three feet, sir, I just sounded," came the answer. "I think, sir, it would be advisable to part-load the boat; then, right after the next time the whale hits us, lower away on the run, chuck the rest of the dunnage in, and ourselves, and get clear."

Captain Doane nodded.

"It will be lively work," he said. "Stand ready, all of you. Steward, you jump aboard first and I'll pass the chronometer to you."

Nishikanta bellicosely shouldered his vast bulk up to the captain, opened his shirt, and exposed his revolver.

"There's too many for the boat," he said, "and the steward's one of 'em that don't go along. Get that. Hold it in your head. The steward's one of 'em that don't go along."

Captain Doane coolly surveyed the big automatic, while at the fore of his consciousness burned a vision of his flat buildings in San Francisco.

He shrugged his shoulders. "The boat would be overloaded, with all this truck, anyway. Go ahead, if you want to make it your party, but just bear in mind that I'm the navigator, and that, if you ever want to lay eyes on your string of pawnshops, you'd better see that gentle care is taken of me., Steward!"

Daughtry stepped close.

"There won't be room for you . . . and for one or two others, I'm sorry to say."

"Glory be!" said Daughtry. "I was just fearin' you'd be wantin' me along, sir. Kwaque, you take 'm my fella dunnage belong me, put 'm in other fella boat along other side."

While Kwaque obeyed, the mate sounded the well for the last time, reporting three feet and a half, and the lighter freightage of the starboard boat was tossed in by the sailors.

A rangy, gangly, Scandinavian youth of a sailor, droop-shouldered, six feet six and slender as a lath, with pallid eyes of palest blue and skin and hair attuned to the same colour scheme, joined Kwaque in his work.

"Here, you Big John," the mate interfered. "This is your boat. You work here."

The lanky one smiled in embarrassment as he haltingly explained: "I tank I lak go along cooky."

"Sure, let him go, the more the easier," Nishikanta took charge of the situation. "Anybody else?"

"Sure," Dag Daughtry sneered to his face. "I reckon what's left of the beer goes with my boat . . . unless you want to argue the matter."

"For two cents -" Nishikanta spluttered in affected rage.

"Not for two billion cents would you risk a scrap with me, you money-sweater, you," was Daughtry's retort. "You've got their goats, but I've got your number. Not for two billion billion cents would you excite me into callin' it right now. Big John! Just carry that case of beer across, an' that half case, and store in my boat. Nishikanta, just start something, if you've got the nerve."

Simon Nishikanta did not dare, nor did he know what to do; but he was saved from his perplexity by the shout:

"Here she comes!"

All rushed to holding-ground, and held, while the whale broke more timbers and the Mary Turner rolled sluggishly down and back again.

"Lower away! On the run! Lively!"

Captain Doane's orders were swiftly obeyed. The starboard boat, fended off by sailors, rose and fell in the water alongside while the remainder of the dunnage and provisions showered into her.

"Might as well lend a hand, sir, seein' you're bent on leaving in such a hurry," said Daughtry, taking the chronometer from Captain Doane's hand and standing ready to pass it down to him as soon as he was in the boat.

"Come on, Greenleaf," Grimshaw called up to the Ancient Mariner.

"No, thanking you very kindly, sir," came the reply. "I think there'll be more room in the other boat."

"We want the cook!" Nishikanta cried out from the stern sheets. "Come on, you yellow monkey! Jump in!"

Little old shrivelled Ah Moy debated. He visibly thought, although none knew the intrinsicness of his thinking as he stared at the gun of the fat pawnbroker and at the leprosy of Kwaque and Daughtry, and weighed the one against the other and tossed the light and heavy loads of the two boats into the balance.

"Me go other boat," said Ah Moy, starting to drag his bag away across the deck.

"Cast off," Captain Doane commanded.

Scraps, the big Newfoundland puppy, who had played and pranced about through all the excitement, seeing so many of the Mary Turner's humans in the boat alongside, sprang over the rail, low and close to the water, and landed sprawling on the mass of sea-bags and goods cases.

The boot rocked, and Nishikanta, his automatic in his hand, cried out:

"Back with him! Throw him on board!"

The sailors obeyed, and the astounded Scraps, after a brief flight through the air, found himself arriving on his back on the Mary Turner's deck. At any rate, he took it for no more than a rough joke, and rolled about ecstatically, squirming vermicularly, in anticipation of what new delights of play were to be visited upon him. He reached out, with an enticing growl of good fellowship, for Michael, who was now free on deck, and received in return a forbidding and crusty snarl.

"Guess we'll have to add him to our collection, eh, sir?" Daughtry observed, sparing a moment to pat reassurance on the big puppy's head and being rewarded with a caressing lick on his hand from the puppy's blissful tongue.

No first-class ship's steward can exist without possessing a more than average measure of executive ability. Dag Daughtry was a first-class ship's steward. Placing the Ancient Mariner in a nook of safety, and setting Big John to unlashing the remaining boat and hooking on the falls, he sent Kwaque into the hold to fill kegs of water from the scant remnant of supply, and Ah Moy to clear out the food in the galley.

The starboard boat, cluttered with men, provisions, and property and being rapidly rowed away from the danger centre, which was the Mary Turner, was scarcely a hundred yards away, when the whale, missing the schooner clean, turned at full speed and close range, churning the water, and all but collided with the boat. So near did she come that the rowers on the side next to her pulled in their oars. The surge she raised, heeled the loaded boat gunwale under, so that a degree of water was shipped ere it righted. Nishikanta, automatic still in hand, standing up in the sternsheets by the comfortable seat he had selected for himself, was staggered by the lurch of the boat. In his instinctive, spasmodic effort to maintain balance, he relaxed his clutch on the pistol, which fell into the sea.

"Ha-ah!" Daughtry girded. "What price Nishikanta? I got his number, and he's lost you fellows' goats. He's your meat now. Easy meat? I should say! And when it comes to the eating, eat him first. Sure, he's a skunk, and will taste like one, but many's the honest man that's eaten skunk and pulled through a tight place. But you'd better soak 'im all night in salt water, first."

Grimshaw, whose seat in the sternsheets was none of the best, grasped the situation simultaneously with Daughtry, and, with a quick upstanding, and hooking out-reach of hand, caught the fat pawnbroker around the back of the neck, and with anything but gentle suasion jerked him half into the air and flung him face downward on the bottom boards.

"Ha-ah!" said Daughtry across the hundred yards of ocean.

Next, and without hurry, Grimshaw took the more comfortable seat for himself.

"Want to come along?" he called to Daughtry.

"No, thank you, sir," was the latter's reply. "There's too many of us, an' we'll make out better in the other boat."

With some bailing, and with others bending to the oars, the boat rowed frantically away, while Daughtry took Ah Moy with him down into the lazarette beneath the cabin floor and broke out and passed up more provisions.

It was when he was thus below that the cow grazed the schooner just for'ard of amidships on the port side, lashed out with her mighty tail as she sounded, and ripped clean away the chain plates and rail of the mizzen-shrouds. In the next roll of the huge, glassy sea, the mizzen- mast fell overside.

"My word, some whale," Daughtry said to Ah Moy, as they emerged from the cabin companionway and gazed at this latest wreckage.

Ah Moy found need to get more food from the galley, when Daughtry, Kwaque, and Big John swung their weight on the falls, one at a time, and hoisted the port boat, one end at a time, over the rail and swung her out.

"We'll wait till the next smash, then lower away, throw everything in, an' get outa this," the steward told the Ancient Mariner. "Lots of time. The schooner'll sink no faster when she's awash than she's sinkin' now."

Even as he spoke, the scuppers were nearly level with the ocean, and her rolling in the big sea was sluggish.

"Hey!" he called with sudden forethought across the widening stretch of sea to Captain Doane. "What's the course to the Marquesas? Right now? And how far away, sir?"

"Nor'-nor'-east-quarter-east!" came the faint reply. "Will fetch Nuka- Hiva! About two hundred miles! Haul on the south-east trade with a good full and you'll make it!"

"Thank you, sir," was the steward's acknowledgment, ere he ran aft, disrupted the binnacle, and carried the steering compass back to the boat.

Almost, from the whale's delay in renewing her charging, did they think she had given over. And while they waited and watched her rolling on the sea an eighth of a mile away, the Mary Turner steadily sank.

"We might almost chance it," Daughtry was debating aloud to Big John, when a new voice entered the discussion.

"Cocky! Cocky!" came plaintive tones from below out of the steerage companion.

"Devil be damned!" was the next, uttered in irritation and anger. "Devil be damned! Devil be damned!"

"Of course not," was Daughtry's judgment, as he dashed across the deck, crawled through the confusion of the main-topmast and its many stays that blocked the way, and found the tiny, white morsel of life perched on a bunk-edge, ruffling its feathers, erecting and flattening its rosy crest, and cursing in honest human speech the waywardness of the world and of ships and humans upon the sea.

The cockatoo stepped upon Daughtry's inviting index finger, swiftly ascended his shirt sleeve, and, on his shoulder, claws sunk into the flimsy shirt fabric till they hurt the flesh beneath, leaned head to ear and uttered in gratitude and relief, and in self-identification: "Cocky. Cocky."

"You son of a gun," Daughtry crooned.

"Glory be!" Cooky replied, in tones so like Daughtry's as to startle him.

"You son of a gun," Daughtry repeated, cuddling his cheek and ear against the cockatoo's feathered and crested head. "And some folks thinks it's only folks that count in this world."

Still the whale delayed, and, with the ocean washing their toes on the level deck, Daughtry ordered the boat lowered away. Ah Moy was eager in his haste to leap into the bow. Nor was Daughtry's judgment correct that the little Chinaman's haste was due to fear of the sinking ship. What Ah Moy sought was the place in the boat remotest from Kwaque and the steward.

Shoving clear, they roughly stored the supplies and dunnage out of the way of the thwarts and took their places, Ah Moy pulling bow-oar, next in order Big John and Kwaque, with Daughtry (Cocky still perched on his shoulder) at stroke. On top of the dunnage, in the sternsheets, Michael gazed wistfully at the Mary Turner and continued to snarl crustily at Scraps who idiotically wanted to start a romp. The Ancient Mariner stood up at the steering sweep and gave the order, when all was ready, for the first dip of the oars.

A growl and a bristle from Michael warned them that the whale was not only coming but was close upon them. But it was not charging. Instead, it circled slowly about the schooner as if examining its antagonist.

"I'll bet it's head's sore from all that banging, an' it's beginnin' to feel it," Daughtry grinned, chiefly for the purpose of keeping his comrades unafraid.

Barely had they rowed a dozen strokes, when an exclamation from Big John led them to follow his gaze to the schooners forecastle-head, where the forecastle cat flashed across in pursuit of a big rat. Other rats they saw, evidently driven out of their lairs by the rising water.

"We just can't leave that cat behind," Daughtry soliloquized in suggestive tones.

"Certainly not," the Ancient Mariner responded swinging his weight on the steering-sweep and heading the boat back.

Twice the whale gently rolled them in the course of its leisurely circling, ere they bent to their oars again and pulled away. Of them the whale seemed to take no notice. It was from the huge thing, the schooner, that death had been wreaked upon her calf; and it was upon the schooner that she vented the wrath of her grief.

Even as they pulled away, the whale turned and headed across the ocean. At a half-mile distance she curved about and charged back.

"With all that water in her, the schooner'll have a real kick-back in her when she's hit," Daughtry said. "Lordy me, rest on your oars an' watch."

Delivered squarely amidships, it was the hardest blow the Mary Turner had received. Stays and splinters of rail flew in the air as she rolled so far over as to expose half her copper wet-glistening in the sun. As she righted sluggishly, the mainmast swayed drunkenly in the air but did not fall.

"A knock-out!" Daughtry cried, at sight of the whale flurrying the water with aimless, gigantic splashings. "It must a-smashed both of 'em."

"Schooner he finish close up altogether," Kwaque observed, as the Mary Turner's rail disappeared.

Swiftly she sank, and no more than a matter of moments was it when the stump of her mainmast was gone. Remained only the whale, floating and floundering, on the surface of the sea.

"It's nothing to brag about," Daughtry delivered himself of the Mary Turner's epitaph. "Nobody'd believe us. A stout little craft like that sunk, deliberately sunk, by an old cow-whale! No, sir. I never believed that old moss-back in Honolulu, when he claimed he was a survivor of the sinkin' of the Essex, an' no more will anybody believe me."

"The pretty schooner, the pretty clever craft," mourned the Ancient Mariner. "Never were there more dainty and lovable topmasts on a three- masted schooner, and never was there a three-masted schooner that worked like the witch she was to windward."

Dag Daughtry, who had kept always footloose and never married, surveyed the boat-load of his responsibilities to which he was anchored, Kwaque, the Black Papuan monstrosity whom he had saved from the bellies of his fellows; Ah Moy, the little old sea-cook whose age was problematical only by decades; the Ancient Mariner, the dignified, the beloved, and the respected; gangly Big John, the youthful Scandinavian with the inches of a giant and the mind of a child; Killeny Boy, the wonder of dogs; Scraps, the outrageously silly and fat-rolling puppy; Cocky, the white-feathered mite of life, imperious as a steel-blade and wheedlingly seductive as a charming child; and even the forecastle cat, the lithe and tawny slayer of rats, sheltering between the legs of Ah Moy. And the Marquesas were two hundred miles distant full-hauled on the tradewind which had ceased but which was as sure to live again as the morning sun in the sky.

The steward heaved a sigh, and whimsically shot into his mind the memory- picture in his nursery-book of the old woman who lived in a shoe. He wiped the sweat from his forehead with the back of his hand, and was dimly aware of the area of the numbness that bordered the centre that was sensationless between his eyebrows, as he said:

"Well, children, rowing won't fetch us to the Marquesas. We'll need a stretch of wind for that. But it's up to us, right now, to put a mile or so between us an' that peevish old cow. Maybe she'll revive, and maybe she won't, but just the same I can't help feelin' leary about her."

CHAPTER XVI

Two days later, as the steamer Mariposa plied her customary route between Tahiti and San Francisco, the passengers ceased playing deck quoits, abandoned their card games in the smoker, their novels and deck chairs, and crowded the rail to stare at the small boat that skimmed to them across the sea before a light following breeze. When Big John, aided by Ah Moy and Kwaque, lowered the sail and unstepped the mast, titters and laughter arose from the passengers. It was contrary to all their preconceptions of mid-ocean rescue of ship-wrecked mariners from the open boat.

It caught their fancy that this boat was the Ark, what of its freightage of bedding, dry goods boxes, beer-cases, a cat, two dogs, a white cockatoo, a Chinaman, a kinky-headed black, a gangly pallid-haired giant, a grizzled Dag Daughtry, and an Ancient Mariner who looked every inch the part. Him a facetious, vacationing architect's clerk dubbed Noah, and so greeted him.

"I say, Noah," he called. "Some flood, eh? Located Ararat yet?"

"Catch any fish?" bawled another youngster down over the rail.

"Gracious! Look at the beer! Good English beer! Put me down for a case!"

Never was a more popular wrecked crew more merrily rescued at sea. The young blades would have it that none other than old Noah himself had come on board with the remnants of the Lost Tribes, and to elderly female passengers spun hair-raising accounts of the sinking of an entire tropic island by volcanic and earthquake action.

"I'm a steward," Dag Daughtry told the Mariposa's captain, "and I'll be glad and grateful to berth along with your stewards in the glory-hole. Big John there's a sailorman, an' the fo'c's'le 'll do him. The Chink is a ship's cook, and the nigger belongs to me. But Mr. Greenleaf, sir, is a gentleman, and the best of cabin fare and staterooms'll be none too good for him, sir."

And when the news went around that these were part of the survivors of the three-masted schooner, Mary Turner, smashed into kindling wood and sunk by a whale, the elderly females no more believed than had they the yarn of the sunken island.

"Captain Hayward," one of them demanded of the steamer's skipper, "could a whale sink the Mariposa?"

"She has never been so sunk," was his reply.

"I knew it!" she declared emphatically. "It's not the way of ships to go around being sunk by whales, is it, captain?"

"No, madam, I assure you it is not," was his response. "Nevertheless, all the five men insist upon it."

"Sailors are notorious for their unveracity, are they not?" the lady voiced her flat conclusion in the form of a tentative query.

"Worst liars I ever saw, madam. Do you know, after forty years at sea, I couldn't believe myself under oath."

Nine days later the Mariposa threaded the Golden Gate and docked at San Francisco. Humorous half-columns in the local papers, written in the customary silly way by unlicked cub reporters just out of grammar school, tickled the fancy of San Francisco for a fleeting moment in that the steamship Mariposa had rescued some sea-waifs possessed of a cock-and- bull story that not even the reporters believed. Thus, silly reportorial unveracity usually proves extraordinary truth a liar. It is the way of cub reporters, city newspapers, and flat-floor populations which get their thrills from moving pictures and for which the real world and all its spaciousness does not exist.

"Sunk by a whale!" demanded the average flat-floor person. "Nonsense, that's all. Just plain rotten nonsense. Now, in the 'Adventures of Eleanor,' which is some film, believe me, I'll tell you what I saw happen . . . "

So Daughtry and his crew went ashore into 'Frisco Town uheralded and unsung, the second following morning's lucubrations of the sea reporters being varied disportations upon the attack on an Italian crab fisherman by an enormous jellyfish. Big John promptly sank out of sight in a sailors' boarding-house, and, within the week, joined the Sailors' Union and shipped on a steam schooner to load redwood ties at Bandon, Oregon. Ah Moy got no farther ashore than the detention sheds of the Federal Immigration Board, whence he was deported to China on the next Pacific Mail steamer. The Mary Turner's cat was adopted by the sailors' forecastle of the Mariposa, and on the Mariposa sailed away on the back trip to Tahiti. Scraps was taken ashore by a quartermaster and left in the bosom of his family.

And ashore went Dag Daughtry, with his small savings, to rent two cheap rooms for himself and his remaining responsibilities, namely, Charles Stough Greenleaf, Kwaque, Michael, and, not least, Cocky. But not for long did he permit the Ancient Mariner to live with him.

"It's not playing the game, sir," he told him. "What we need is capital. We've got to interest capital, and you've got to do the interesting. Now this very day you've got to buy a couple of suit-cases, hire a taxicab, go sailing up to the front door of the Bronx Hotel like good pay and be damned. She's a real stylish hotel, but reasonable if you want to make it so. A little room, an inside room, European plan, of course, and then you can economise by eatin' out."

"But, steward, I have no money," the Ancient Mariner protested.

"That's all right, sir; I'll back you for all I can."

"But, my dear man, you know I'm an old impostor. I can't stick you up like the others. You . . . why . . . why, you're a friend, don't you see?"

"Sure I do, and I thank you for sayin' it, sir. And that's why I'm with you. And when you've nailed another crowd of treasure-hunters and got the ship ready, you'll just ship me along as steward, with Kwaque, and Killeny Boy, and the rest of our family. You've adopted me, now, an' I'm your grown-up son, an' you've got to listen to me. The Bronx is the hotel for you, fine-soundin' name, ain't it? That's atmosphere. Folk'll listen half to you an' more to your hotel. I tell you, you leaning back in a big leather chair talkin' treasure with a two-bit cigar in your mouth an' a twenty-cent drink beside you, why that's like treasure. They just got to believe. An' if you'll come along now, sir, we'll trot out an' buy them suit-cases."

Right bravely the Ancient Mariner drove to the Bronx in a taxi, registered his "Charles Stough Greenleaf" in an old-fashioned hand, and took up anew the activities which for years had kept him free of the poor- farm. No less bravely did Dag Daughtry set out to seek work. This was most necessary, because he was a man of expensive luxuries. His family of Kwaque, Michael, and Cocky required food and shelter; more costly than that was maintenance of the Ancient Mariner in the high-class hotel; and, in addition, was his six-quart thirst.

But it was a time of industrial depression. The unemployed problem was bulking bigger than usual to the citizens of San Francisco. And, as regarded steamships and sailing vessels, there were three stewards for every Steward's position. Nothing steady could Daughtry procure, while his occasional odd jobs did not balance his various running expenses. Even did he do pick-and-shovel work, for the municipality, for three days, when he had to give way, according to the impartial procedure, to another needy one whom three days' work would keep afloat a little longer.

Daughtry would have put Kwaque to work, except that Kwaque was impossible. The black, who had only seen Sydney from steamers' decks, had never been in a city in his life. All he knew of the world was steamers, far-outlying south-sea isles, and his own island of King William in Melanesia. So Kwaque remained in the two rooms, cooking and housekeeping for his master and caring for Michael and Cocky. All of which was prison for Michael, who had been used to the run of ships, of coral beaches and plantations.

But in the evenings, sometimes accompanied a few steps in the rear by Kwaque, Michael strolled out with Steward. The multiplicity of man-gods on the teeming sidewalks became a real bore to Michael, so that man-gods, in general, underwent a sharp depreciation. But Steward, the particular god of his fealty and worship, appreciated. Amongst so many gods Michael felt bewildered, while Steward's Abrahamic bosom became more than ever the one sure haven where harshness and danger never troubled.

"Mind your step," is the last word and warning of twentieth-century city life. Michael was not slow to learn it, as he conserved his own feet among the countless thousands of leather-shod feet of men, ever hurrying, always unregarding of the existence and right of way of a lowly, four- legged Irish terrier.

The evening outings with Steward invariably led from saloon to saloon, where, at long bars, standing on sawdust floors, or seated at tables, men drank and talked. Much of both did men do, and also did Steward do, ere, his daily six-quart stint accomplished, he turned homeward for bed. Many were the acquaintances he made, and Michael with him. Coasting seamen and bay sailors they mostly were, although there were many 'longshoremen and waterfront workmen among them.

From one of these, a scow-schooner captain who plied up and down the bay and the San Joaquin and Sacramento rivers, Daughtry had the promise of being engaged as cook and sailor on the schooner Howard. Eighty tons of freight, including deckload, she carried, and in all democracy Captain Jorgensen, the cook, and the two other sailors, loaded and unloaded her at all hours, and sailed her night and day on all times and tides, one man steering while three slept and recuperated. It was time, and double- time, and over-time beyond that, but the feeding was generous and the wages ran from forty-five to sixty dollars a month.

"Sure, you bet," said Captain Jorgensen. "This cook-feller, Hanson, pretty quick I smash him up an' fire him, then you can come along . . . and the bow-wow, too." Here he dropped a hearty, wholesome hand of toil down to a caress of Michael's head. "That's one fine bow-wow. A bow-wow is good on a scow when all hands sleep alongside the dock or in an anchor watch."

"Fire Hanson now," Dag Daughtry urged.

But Captain Jorgensen shook his slow head slowly. "First I smash him up."

"Then smash him now and fire him," Daughtry persisted. "There he is right now at the corner of the bar."

"No. He must give me reason. I got plenty of reason. But I want reason all hands can see. I want him make me smash him, so that all hands say, 'Hurrah, Captain, you done right.' Then you get the job, Daughtry."

Had Captain Jorgensen not been dilatory in his contemplated smashing, and had not Hanson delayed in giving sufficient provocation for a smashing, Michael would have accompanied Steward upon the schooner, Howard, and all Michael's subsequent experiences would have been totally different from what they were destined to be. But destined they were, by chance and by combinations of chance events over which Michael had no control and of which he had no more awareness than had Steward himself. At that period, the subsequent stage career and nightmare of cruelty for Michael was beyond any wildest forecast or apprehension. And as to forecasting Dag Daughtry's fate, along with Kwaque, no maddest drug-dream could have approximated it.

CHAPTER XVII

One night Dag Daughtry sat at a table in the saloon called the Pile-drivers' Home. He was in a parlous predicament. Harder than ever had it been to secure odd jobs, and he had reached the end of his savings. Earlier in the evening he had had a telephone conference with the Ancient Mariner, who had reported only progress with an exceptionally strong nibble that very day from a retired quack doctor.

"Let me pawn my rings," the Ancient Mariner had urged, not for the first time, over the telephone.

"No, sir," had been Daughtry's reply. "We need them in the business. They're stock in trade. They're atmosphere. They're what you call a figure of speech. I'll do some thinking to-night an' see you in the morning, sir. Hold on to them rings an' don't be no more than casual in playin' that doctor. Make 'm come to you. It's the only way. Now you're all right, an' everything's hunkydory an' the goose hangs high. Don't you worry, sir. Dag Daughtry never fell down yet."

But, as he sat in the Pile-drivers' Home, it looked as if his fall-down was very near. In his pocket was precisely the room-rent for the following week, the advance payment of which was already three days overdue and clamorously demanded by the hard-faced landlady. In the rooms, with care, was enough food with which to pinch through for another day. The Ancient Mariner's modest hotel bill had not been paid for two weeks, a prodigious sum under the circumstances, being a first-class hotel; while the Ancient Mariner had no more than a couple of dollars in his pocket with which to make a sound like prosperity in the ears of the retired doctor who wanted to go a-treasuring.

Most catastrophic of all, however, was the fact that Dag Daughtry was three quarts short of his daily allowance and did not dare break into the rent money which was all that stood between him and his family and the street. This was why he sat at the beer table with Captain Jorgensen, who was just returned with a schooner-load of hay from the Petaluma Flats. He had already bought beer twice, and evinced no further show of thirst. Instead, he was yawning from long hours of work and waking and looking at his watch. And Daughtry was three quarts short! Besides, Hanson had not yet been smashed, so that the cook-job on the schooner still lay ahead an unknown distance in the future.

In his desperation, Daughtry hit upon an idea with which to get another schooner of steam beer. He did not like steam beer, but it was cheaper than lager.

"Look here, Captain," he said. "You don't know how smart that Killeny Boy is. Why, he can count just like you and me."

"Hoh!" rumbled Captain Jorgensen. "I seen 'em do it in side shows. It's all tricks. Dogs an' horses can't count."

"This dog can," Daughtry continued quietly. "You can't fool 'm. I bet you, right now, I can order two beers, loud so he can hear and notice, and then whisper to the waiter to bring one, an', when the one comes, Killeny Boy'll raise a roar with the waiter."

"Hoh! Hoh! How much will you bet?"

The steward fingered a dime in his pocket. If Killeny failed him it meant that the rent-money would be broken in upon. But Killeny couldn't and wouldn't fail him, he reasoned, as he answered:

"I'll bet you the price of two beers."

The waiter was summoned, and, when he had received his secret instructions, Michael was called over from where he lay at Kwaque's feet in a corner. When Steward placed a chair for him at the table and invited him into it, he began to key up. Steward expected something of him, wanted him to show off. And it was not because of the showing off that he was eager, but because of his love for Steward. Love and service were one in the simple processes of Michael's mind. Just as he would have leaped into fire for Steward's sake, so would he now serve Steward in any way Steward desired. That was what love meant to him. It was all love meant to him, service.

"Waiter!" Steward called; and, when the waiter stood close at hand: "Two beers. Did you get that, Killeny? Two beers."

Michael squirmed in his chair, placed an impulsive paw on the table, and impulsively flashed out his ribbon of tongue to Steward's close-bending face.

"He will remember," Daughtry told the scow-schooner captain.

"Not if we talk," was the reply. "Now we will fool your bow-wow. I will say that the job is yours when I smash Hanson. And you will say it is for me to smash Hanson now. And I will say Hanson must give me reason first to smash him. And then we will argue like two fools with mouths full of much noise. Are you ready?"

Daughtry nodded, and thereupon ensued a loud-voiced discussion that drew Michael's earnest attention from one talker to the other.

"I got you," Captain Jorgensen announced, as he saw the waiter approaching with but a single schooner of beer. "The bow-wow has forgot, if he ever remembered. He thinks you an' me is fighting. The place in his mind for one beer, and two, is wiped out, like a wave on the beach wipes out the writing in the sand."

"I guess he ain't goin' to forget arithmetic no matter how much noise you shouts," Daughtry argued aloud against his sinking spirits. "An' I ain't goin' to butt in," he added hopefully. "You just watch 'm for himself."

The tall, schooner-glass of beer was placed before the captain, who laid a swift, containing hand around it. And Michael, strung as a taut string, knowing that something was expected of him, on his toes to serve, remembered his ancient lessons on the Makambo, vainly looked into the impassive face of Steward for a sign, then looked about and saw, not two glasses, but one glass. So well had he learned the difference between one and two that it came to him, how the profoundest psychologist can no more state than can he state what thought is in itself, that there was one glass only when two glasses had been commanded. With an abrupt upspring, his throat half harsh with anger, he placed both forepaws on the table and barked at the waiter.

Captain Jorgensen crashed his fist down.

"You win!" he roared. "I pay for the beer! Waiter, bring one more."

Michael looked to Steward for verification, and Steward's hand on his head gave adequate reply.

"We try again," said the captain, very much awake and interested, with the back of his hand wiping the beer-foam from his moustache. "Maybe he knows one an' two. How about three? And four?"

"Just the same, Skipper. He counts up to five, and knows more than five when it is more than five, though he don't know the figures by name after five."

"Oh, Hanson!" Captain Jorgensen bellowed across the bar-room to the cook of the Howard. "Hey, you square-head! Come and have a drink!"

Hanson came over and pulled up a chair.

"I pay for the drinks," said the captain; "but you order, Daughtry. See, now, Hanson, this is a trick bow-wow. He can count better than you. We are three. Daughtry is ordering three beers. The bow-wow hears three. I hold up two fingers like this to the waiter. He brings two. The bow-wow raises hell with the waiter. You see."

All of which came to pass, Michael blissfully unappeasable until the order was filled properly.

"He can't count," was Hanson's conclusion. "He sees one man without beer. That's all. He knows every man should ought to have a glass. That's why he barks."

"Better than that," Daughtry boasted. "There are three of us. We will order four. Then each man will have his glass, but Killeny will talk to the waiter just the same."

True enough, now thoroughly aware of the game, Michael made outcry to the waiter till the fourth glass was brought. By this time many men were about the table, all wanting to buy beer and test Michael.

"Glory be," Dag Daughtry solloquized. "A funny world. Thirsty one moment. The next moment they'd fair drown you in beer."

Several even wanted to buy Michael, offering ridiculous sums like fifteen and twenty dollars.

"I tell you what," Captain Jorgensen muttered to Daughtry, whom he had drawn away into a corner. "You give me that bow-wow, and I'll smash Hanson right now, and you got the job right away, come to work in the morning."

Into another corner the proprietor of the Pile-drivers' Home drew Daughtry to whisper to him:

"You stick around here every night with that dog of yourn. It makes trade. I'll give you free beer any time and fifty cents cash money a night."

It was this proposition that started the big idea in Daughtry's mind. As he told Michael, back in the room, while Kwaque was unlacing his shoes:

"It's this way Killeny. If you're worth fifty cents a night and free beer to that saloon keeper, then you're worth that to me . . . and more, my son, more. 'Cause he's lookin' for a profit. That's why he sells beer instead of buyin' it. An', Killeny, you won't mind workin' for me, I know. We need the money. There's Kwaque, an' Mr. Greenleaf, an' Cocky, not even mentioning you an' me, an' we eat an awful lot. An' room- rent's hard to get, an' jobs is harder. What d'ye say, son, to-morrow night you an' me hustle around an' see how much coin we can gather?"

And Michael, seated on Steward's knees, eyes to eyes and nose to nose, his jowls held in Steward's hand's wriggled and squirmed with delight, flipping out his tongue and bobbing his tail in the air. Whatever it was, it was good, for it was Steward who spoke.

CHAPTER XVIII

The grizzled ship's steward and the rough-coated Irish terrier quickly became conspicuous figures in the night life of the Barbary Coast of San Francisco. Daughtry elaborated on the counting trick by bringing Cocky along. Thus, when a waiter did not fetch the right number of glasses, Michael would remain quite still, until Cocky, at a privy signal from Steward, standing on one leg, with the free claw would clutch Michael's neck and apparently talk into Michael's ear. Whereupon Michael would look about the glasses on the table and begin his usual expostulation with the waiter.

But it was when Daughtry and Michael first sang "Roll me Down to Rio" together, that the ten-strike was made. It occurred in a sailors' dance- hall on Pacific Street, and all dancing stopped while the sailors clamoured for more of the singing dog. Nor did the place lose money, for no one left, and the crowd increased to standing room as Michael went through his repertoire of "God Save the King," "Sweet Bye and Bye," "Lead, Kindly Light," "Home, Sweet Home," and "Shenandoah."

It meant more than free beer to Daughtry, for, when he started to leave, the proprietor of the place thrust three silver dollars into his hand and begged him to come around with the dog next night.

"For that?" Daughtry demanded, looking at the money as if it were contemptible.

Hastily the proprietor added two more dollars, and Daughtry promised.

"Just the same, Killeny, my son," he told Michael as they went to bed, "I think you an' me are worth more than five dollars a turn. Why, the like of you has never been seen before. A real singing dog that can carry 'most any air with me, and that can carry half a dozen by himself. An' they say Caruso gets a thousand a night. Well, you ain't Caruso, but you're the dog-Caruso of the entire world. Son, I'm goin' to be your business manager. If we can't make a twenty-dollar gold-piece a night, say, son, we're goin' to move into better quarters. An' the old gent up at the Hotel de Bronx is goin' to move into an outside room. An' Kwaque's goin' to get a real outfit of clothes. Killeny, my boy, we're goin' to get so rich that if he can't snare a sucker we'll put up the cash ourselves 'n' buy a schooner for 'm, 'n' send him out a-treasure-huntin' on his own. We'll be the suckers, eh, just you an' me, an' love to."

The Barbary Coast of San Francisco, once the old-time sailor-town in the days when San Francisco was reckoned the toughest port of the Seven Seas, had evolved with the city until it depended for at least half of its earnings on the slumming parties that visited it and spent liberally. It was quite the custom, after dinner, for many of the better classes of society, especially when entertaining curious Easterners, to spend an hour or several in motoring from dance-hall to dance-hall and cheap cabaret to cheap cabaret. In short, the "Coast" was as much a sight-seeing place as was Chinatown and the Cliff House.

It was not long before Dag Daughtry was getting his twenty dollars a night for two twenty-minute turns, and was declining more beer than a dozen men with thirsts equal to his could have accommodated. Never had he been so prosperous; nor can it be denied that Michael enjoyed it. Enjoy it he did, but principally for Steward's sake. He was serving Steward, and so to serve was his highest heart's desire.

In truth, Michael was the bread-winner for quite a family, each member of which fared well. Kwaque blossomed out resplendent in russet-brown shoes, a derby hat, and a gray suit with trousers immaculately creased. Also, he became a devotee of the moving-picture shows, spending as much as twenty and thirty cents a day and resolutely sitting out every repetition of programme. Little time was required of him in caring for Daughtry, for they had come to eating in restaurants. Not only had the Ancient Mariner moved into a more expensive outside room at the Bronx; but Daughtry insisted on thrusting upon him more spending money, so that, on occasion, he could invite a likely acquaintance to the theatre or a concert and bring him home in a taxi.

"We won't keep this up for ever, Killeny," Steward told Michael. "For just as long as it takes the old gent to land another bunch of gold-pouched, retriever-snouted treasure-hunters, and no longer. Then it's hey for the ocean blue, my son, an' the roll of a good craft under our feet, an' smash of wet on the deck, an' a spout now an' again of the scuppers.

"We got to go rollin' down to Rio as well as sing about it to a lot of cheap skates. They can take their rotten cities. The sea's the life for us, you an' me, Killeny, son, an' the old gent an' Kwaque, an' Cocky, too. We ain't made for city ways. It ain't healthy. Why, son, though you maybe won't believe it, I'm losin' my spring. The rubber's goin' outa me. I'm kind o' languid, with all night in an' nothin' to do but sit around. It makes me fair sick at the thought of hearin' the old gent say once again, 'I think, steward, one of those prime cocktails would be just the thing before dinner.' We'll take a little ice-machine along next voyage, an' give 'm the best.

"An' look at Kwaque, Killeny, my boy. This ain't his climate. He's positively ailin'. If he sits around them picture-shows much more he'll develop the T.B. For the good of his health, an' mine an' yours, an' all of us, we got to get up anchor pretty soon an' hit out for the home of the trade winds that kiss you through an' through with the salt an' the life of the sea."

In truth, Kwaque, who never complained, was ailing fast. A swelling, slow and sensationless at first, under his right arm-pit, had become a mild and unceasing pain. No longer could he sleep a night through. Although he lay on his left side, never less than twice, and often three and four times, the hurt of the swelling woke him. Ah Moy, had he not long since been delivered back to China by the immigration authorities, could have told him the meaning of that swelling, just as he could have told Dag Daughtry the meaning of the increasing area of numbness between his eyes where the tiny, vertical, lion-lines were cutting more conspicuously. Also, could he have told him what was wrong with the little finger on his left hand. Daughtry had first diagnosed it as a sprain of a tendon. Later, he had decided it was chronic rheumatism brought on by the damp and foggy Sun Francisco climate. It was one of his reasons for desiring to get away again to sea where the tropic sun would warm the rheumatism out of him.

As a steward, Daughtry had been accustomed to contact with men and women of the upper world. But for the first time in his life, here in the underworld of San Francisco, in all equality he met such persons from above. Nay, more, they were eager to meet him. They sought him. They fawned upon him for an invitation to sit at his table and buy beer for him in whatever garish cabaret Michael was performing. They would have bought wine for him, at enormous expense, had he not stubbornly stuck to his beer. They were, some of them, for inviting him to their homes, "An' bring the wonderful dog along for a sing-song"; but Daughtry, proud of Michael for being the cause of such invitations, explained that the professional life was too arduous to permit of such diversions. To Michael he explained that when they proffered a fee of fifty dollars, the pair of them would "come a-runnin'."

Among the host of acquaintances made in their cabaret-life, two were destined, very immediately, to play important parts in the lives of Daughtry and Michael. The first, a politician and a doctor, by name Emory, Walter Merritt Emory, was several times at Daughtry's table, where Michael sat with them on a chair according to custom. Among other things, in gratitude for such kindnesses from Daughtry, Doctor Emory gave his office card and begged for the privilege of treating, free of charge, either master or dog should they ever become sick. In Daughtry's opinion, Dr. Walter Merritt Emory was a keen, clever man, undoubtedly able in his profession, but passionately selfish as a hungry tiger. As he told him, in the brutal candour he could afford under such changed conditions: "Doc, you're a wonder. Anybody can see it with half an eye. What you want you just go and get. Nothing'd stop you except . . . "

"Except?"

"Oh, except that it was nailed down, or locked up, or had a policeman standing guard over it. I'd sure hate to have anything you wanted."

"Well, you have," Doctor assured him, with a significant nod at Michael on the chair between them.

"Br-r-r!" Daughtry shivered. "You give me the creeps. If I thought you really meant it, San Francisco couldn't hold me two minutes." He meditated into his beer-glass a moment, then laughed with reassurance. "No man could get that dog away from me. You see, I'd kill the man first. I'd just up an' tell 'm, as I'm tellin' you now, I'd kill 'm first. An' he'd believe me, as you're believin' me now. You know I mean it. So'd he know I meant it. Why, that dog . . . "

In sheer inability to express the profundity of his emotion, Dag Daughtry broke off the sentence and drowned it in his beer-glass.

Of quite different type was the other person of destiny. Harry Del Mar, he called himself; and Harry Del Mar was the name that appeared on the programmes when he was doing Orpheum "time." Although Daughtry did not know it, because Del Mar was laying off for a vacation, the man did trained-animal turns for a living. He, too, bought drinks at Daughtry's table. Young, not over thirty, dark of complexion with large, long-lashed brown eyes that he fondly believed were magnetic, cherubic of lip and feature, he belied all his appearance by talking business in direct business fashion.

"But you ain't got the money to buy 'm," Daughtry replied, when the other had increased his first offer of five hundred dollars for Michael to a thousand.

"I've got the thousand, if that's what you mean."

"No," Daughtry shook his head. "I mean he ain't for sale at any price. Besides, what do you want 'm for?"

"I like him," Del Mar answered. "Why do I come to this joint? Why does the crowd come here? Why do men buy wine, run horses, sport actresses, become priests or bookworms? Because they like to. That's the answer. We all do what we like when we can, go after the thing we want whether we can get it or not. Now I like your dog, I want him. I want him a thousand dollars' worth. See that big diamond on that woman's hand over there. I guess she just liked it, and wanted it, and got it, never mind the price. The price didn't mean as much to her as the diamond. Now that dog of yours -"

"Don't like you," Dag Daughtry broke in. "Which is strange. He likes most everybody without fussin' about it. But he bristled at you from the first. No man'd want a dog that don't like him."

"Which isn't the question," Del Mar stated quietly. "I like him. As for him liking or not liking me, that's my look-out, and I guess I can attend to that all right."

It seemed to Daughtry that he glimpsed or sensed under the other's unfaltering cherubicness of expression a steelness of cruelty that was abysmal in that it was of controlled intelligence. Not in such terms did Daughtry think his impression. At the most, it was a feeling, and feelings do not require words in order to be experienced or comprehended.

"There's an all-night bank," the other went on. "We can stroll over, I'll cash a cheque, and in half an hour the cash will be in your hand."

Daughtry shook his head.

"Even as a business proposition, nothing doing," he said. "Look you. Here's the dog earnin' twenty dollars a night. Say he works twenty-five days in the month. That's five hundred a month, or six thousand a year. Now say that's five per cent., because it's easier to count, it represents the interest on a capital value of one hundred an' twenty thousand-dollars. Then we'll suppose expenses and salary for me is twenty thousand. That leaves the dog worth a hundred thousand. Just to be fair, cut it in half, a fifty-thousand dog. And you're offerin' a thousand for him."

"I suppose you think he'll last for ever, like so much land'," Del Mar smiled quietly.

Daughtry saw the point instantly.

"Give 'm five years of work, that's thirty thousand. Give 'm one year of work, it's six thousand. An' you're offerin' me one thousand for six thousand. That ain't no kind of business, for me . . . an' him. Besides, when he can't work any more, an' ain't worth a cent, he'll be worth just a plumb million to me, an' if anybody offered it, I'd raise the price."

CHAPTER XIX

"I'll see you again," Harry Del Mar told Daughtry, at the end of his fourth conversation on the matter of Michael's sale.

Wherein Harry Del Mar was mistaken. He never saw Daughtry again, because Daughtry saw Doctor Emory first.

Kwaque's increasing restlessness at night, due to the swelling under his right arm-pit, had began to wake Daughtry up. After several such experiences, he had investigated and decided that Kwaque was sufficiently sick to require a doctor. For which reason, one morning at eleven, taking Kwaque along, he called at Walter Merritt Emory's office and waited his turn in the crowded reception-room.

"I think he's got cancer, Doc.," Daughtry said, while Kwaque was pulling off his shirt and undershirt. "He never squealed, you know, never peeped. That's the way of niggers. I didn't find our till he got to wakin' me up nights with his tossin' about an' groanin' in his sleep. There! What'd you call it? Cancer or tumour, no two ways about it, eh?"

But the quick eye of Walter Merritt Emory had not missed, in passing, the twisted fingers of Kwaque's left hand. Not only was his eye quick, but it was a "leper eye." A volunteer surgeon in the first days out in the Philippines, he had made a particular study of leprosy, and had observed so many lepers that infallibly, except in the incipient beginnings of the disease, he could pick out a leper at a glance. From the twisted fingers, which was the anaesthetic form, produced by nerve-disintegration, to the corrugated lion forehead (again anaesthetic), his eyes flashed to the swelling under the right arm-pit and his brain diagnosed it as the tubercular form.

Just as swiftly flashed through his brain two thoughts: the first, the axiom, whenever and wherever you find a leper, look for the other leper; the second, the desired Irish terrier, who was owned by Daughtry, with whom Kwaque had been long associated. And here all swiftness of eye- flashing ceased on the part of Walter Merritt Emory. He did not know how much, if anything, the steward knew about leprosy, and he did not care to arouse any suspicions. Casually drawing his watch to see the time, he turned and addressed Daughtry.

"I should say his blood is out of order. He's run down. He's not used to the recent life he's been living, nor to the food. To make certain, I shall examine for cancer and tumour, although there's little chance of anything like that."

And as he talked, with just a waver for a moment, his gaze lifted above Daughtry's eyes to the area of forehead just above and between the eyes. It was sufficient. His "leper-eye" had seen the "lion" mark of the leper.

"You're run down yourself," he continued smoothly. "You're not up to snuff, I'll wager. Eh?"

"Can't say that I am," Daughtry agreed. "I guess I got to get back to the sea an' the tropics and warm the rheumatics outa me."

"Where?" queried Doctor Emory, almost absently, so well did he feign it, as if apparently on the verge of returning to a closer examination, of Kwaque's swelling.

Daughtry extended his left hand, with a little wiggle of the little finger advertising the seat of the affliction. Walter Merritt Emory saw, with seeming careless look out from under careless-drooping eyelids, the little finger slightly swollen, slightly twisted, with a smooth, almost shiny, silkiness of skin-texture. Again, in the course of turning to look at Kwaque, his eyes rested an instant on the lion-lines of Daughtry's brow.

"Rheumatism is still the great mystery," Doctor Emory said, returning to Daughtry as if deflected by the thought. "It's almost individual, there are so many varieties of it. Each man has a kind of his own. Any numbness?"

Daughtry laboriously wiggled his little finger.

"Yes, sir," he answered. "It ain't as lively as it used to was."

"Ah," Walter Merritt Emory murmured, with a vastitude of confidence and assurance. "Please sit down in that chair there. Maybe I won't be able to cure you, but I promise you I can direct you to the best place to live for what's the matter with you. Miss Judson!"

And while the trained-nurse-apparelled young woman seated Dag Daughtry in the enamelled surgeon's chair and leaned him back under direction, and while Doctor Emory dipped his finger-tips into the strongest antiseptic his office possessed, behind Doctor Emory's eyes, in the midst of his brain, burned the image of a desired Irish terrier who did turns in sailor-town cabarets, was rough-coated, and answered to the full name of Killeny Boy.

"You've got rheumatism in more places than your little finger," he assured Daughtry. "There's a touch right here, I'll wager, on your forehead. One moment, please. Move if I hurt you, Otherwise sit still, because I don't intend to hurt you. I merely want to see if my diagnosis is correct. There, that's it. Move when you feel anything. Rheumatism has strange freaks. Watch this, Miss Judson, and I'll wager this form of rheumatism is new to you. See. He does not resent. He thinks I have not begun yet . . ."

And as he talked, steadily, interestingly, he was doing what Dag Daughtry never dreamed he was doing, and what made Kwaque, looking on, almost dream he was seeing because of the unrealness and impossibleness of it. For, with a large needle, Doctor Emory was probing the dark spot in the midst of the vertical lion-lines. Nor did he merely probe the area. Thrusting into it from one side, under the skin and parallel to it, he buried the length of the needle from sight through the insensate infiltration. This Kwaque beheld with bulging eyes; for his master betrayed no sign that the thing was being done.

"Why don't you begin?" Dag Daughtry questioned impatiently. "Besides, my rheumatism don't count. It's the nigger-boy's swelling."

"You need a course of treatment," Doctor Emory assured him. "Rheumatism is a tough proposition. It should never be let grow chronic. I'll fix up a course of treatment for you. Now, if you'll get out of the chair, we'll look at your black servant."

But first, before Kwaque was leaned back, Doctor Emory threw over the chair a sheet that smelled of having been roasted almost to the scorching point. As he was about to examine Kwaque, he looked with a slight start of recollection at his watch. When he saw the time he startled more, and turned a reproachful face upon his assistant.

"Miss Judson," he said, coldly emphatic, "you have failed me. Here it is, twenty before twelve, and you knew I was to confer with Doctor Hadley over that case at eleven-thirty sharp. How he must be cursing me! You know how peevish he is."

Miss Judson nodded, with a perfect expression of contrition and humility, as if she knew all about it, although, in reality, she knew only all about her employer and had never heard till that moment of his engagement at eleven-thirty.

"Doctor Hadley's just across the hall," Doctor Emory explained to Daughtry. "It won't take me five minutes. He and I have a disagreement. He has diagnosed the case as chronic appendicitis and wants to operate. I have diagnosed it as pyorrhea which has infected the stomach from the mouth, and have suggested emetine treatment of the mouth as a cure for the stomach disorder. Of course, you don't understand, but the point is that I've persuaded Doctor Hadley to bring in Doctor Granville, who is a dentist and a pyorrhea expert. And they're all waiting for me these ten minutes! I must run.

"I'll return inside five minutes," he called back as the door to the hall was closing upon him. "Miss Judson, please tell those people in the reception-room to be patient."

He did enter Doctor Hadley's office, although no sufferer from pyorrhea or appendicitis awaited him. Instead, he used the telephone for two calls: one to the president of the board of health; the other to the chief of police. Fortunately, he caught both at their offices, addressing them familiarly by their first names and talking to them most emphatically and confidentially.

Back in his own quarters, he was patently elated.

"I told him so," he assured Miss Judson, but embracing Daughtry in the happy confidence. "Doctor Granville backed me up. Straight pyorrhea, of course. That knocks the operation. And right now they're jolting his gums and the pus-sacs with emetine. Whew! A fellow likes to be right. I deserve a smoke. Do you mind, Mr. Daughtry?"

And while the steward shook his head, Doctor Emory lighted a big Havana and continued audibly to luxuriate in his fictitious triumph over the other doctor. As he talked, he forgot to smoke, and, leaning quite casually against the chair, with arrant carelessness allowed the live coal at the end of his cigar to rest against the tip of one of Kwaque's twisted fingers. A privy wink to Miss Judson, who was the only one who observed his action, warned her against anything that might happen.

"You know, Mr. Daughtry," Walter Merritt Emory went on enthusiastically, while he held the steward's eyes with his and while all the time the live end of the cigar continued to rest against Kwaque's finger, "the older I get the more convinced I am that there are too many ill-advised and hasty operations."

Still fire and flesh pressed together, and a tiny spiral of smoke began to arise from Kwaque's finger-end that was different in colour from the smoke of a cigar-end.

"Now take that patient of Doctor Hadley's. I've saved him, not merely the risk of an operation for appendicitis, but the cost of it, and the hospital expenses. I shall charge him nothing for what I did. Hadley's charge will be merely nominal. Doctor Granville, at the outside, will cure his pyorrhea with emetine for no more than a paltry fifty dollars. Yes, by George, besides the risk to his life, and the discomfort, I've saved that man, all told, a cold thousand dollars to surgeon, hospital, and nurses."

And while he talked on, holding Daughtry's eyes, a smell of roast meat began to pervade the air. Doctor Emory smelled it eagerly. So did Miss Judson smell it, but she had been warned and gave no notice. Nor did she look at the juxtaposition of cigar and finger, although she knew by the evidence of her nose that it still obtained.

"What's burning?" Daughtry demanded suddenly, sniffing the air and glancing around.

"Pretty rotten cigar," Doctor Emory observed, having removed it from contact with Kwaque's finger and now examining it with critical disapproval. He held it close to his nose, and his face portrayed disgust. "I won't say cabbage leaves. I'll merely say it's something I don't know and don't care to know. That's the trouble. They get out a good, new brand of cigar, advertise it, put the best of tobacco into it, and, when it has taken with the public, put in inferior tobacco and ride the popularity of it. No more in mine, thank you. This day I change my brand."

So speaking, he tossed the cigar into a cuspidor. And Kwaque, leaning back in the queerest chair in which he had ever sat, was unaware that the end of his finger had been burned and roasted half an inch deep, and merely wondered when the medicine doctor would cease talking and begin looking at the swelling that hurt his side under his arm.

And for the first time in his life, and for the ultimate time, Dag Daughtry fell down. It was an irretrievable fall-down. Life, in its freedom of come and go, by heaving sea and reeling deck, through the home of the trade-winds, back and forth between the ports, ceased there for him in Walter Merritt Emory's office, while the calm-browed Miss Judson looked on and marvelled that a man's flesh should roast and the man wince not from the roasting of it.

Doctor Emory continued to talk, and tried a fresh cigar, and, despite the fact that his reception-room was overflowing, delivered, not merely a long, but a live and interesting, dissertation on the subject of cigars and of the tobacco leaf and filler as grown and prepared for cigars in the tobacco-favoured regions of the earth.

"Now, as regards this swelling," he was saying, as he began a belated and distant examination of Kwaque's affliction, "I should say, at a glance, that it is neither tumour nor cancer, nor is it even a boil. I should say . . . "

A knock at the private door into the hall made him straighten up with an eagerness that he did not attempt to mask. A nod to Miss Judson sent her to open the door, and entered two policemen, a police sergeant, and a professionally whiskered person in a business suit with a carnation in his button-hole.

"Good morning, Doctor Masters," Emory greeted the professional one, and, to the others: "Howdy, Sergeant;" "Hello, Tim;" "Hello, Johnson, when did they shift you off the Chinatown squad?"

And then, continuing his suspended sentence, Walter Merritt Emory held on, looking intently at Kwaque's swelling:

"I should say, as I was saying, that it is the finest, ripest, perforating ulcer of the bacillus leprae order, that any San Francisco doctor has had the honour of presenting to the board of health."

"Leprosy!" exclaimed Doctor Masters.

And all started at his pronouncement of the word. The sergeant and the two policemen shied away from Kwaque; Miss Judson, with a smothered cry, clapped her two hands over her heart; and Dag Daughtry, shocked but sceptical, demanded:

"What are you givin' us, Doc.?"

"Stand still! don't move!" Walter Merritt Emory said peremptorily to Daughtry. "I want you to take notice," he added to the others, as he gently touched the live-end of his fresh cigar to the area of dark skin above and between the steward's eyes. "Don't move," he commanded Daughtry. "Wait a moment. I am not ready yet."

And while Daughtry waited, perplexed, confused, wondering why Doctor Emory did not proceed, the coal of fire burned his skin and flesh, till the smoke of it was apparent to all, as was the smell of it. With a sharp laugh of triumph, Doctor Emory stepped back.

"Well, go ahead with what you was goin' to do," Daughtry grumbled, the rush of events too swift and too hidden for him to comprehend. "An' when you're done with that, I just want you to explain what you said about leprosy an' that nigger-boy there. He's my boy, an' you can't pull anything like that off on him . . . or me."

"Gentlemen, you have seen," Doctor Emory said. "Two undoubted cases of it, master and man, the man more advanced, with the combination of both forms, the master with only the anaesthetic form, he has a touch of it, too, on his little finger. Take them away. I strongly advise, Doctor Masters, a thorough fumigation of the ambulance afterward."

"Look here . . ." Dag Daughtry began belligerently.

Doctor Emory glanced warningly to Doctor Masters, and Doctor Masters glanced authoritatively at the sergeant who glanced commandingly at his two policemen. But they did not spring upon Daughtry. Instead, they backed farther away, drew their clubs, and glared intimidatingly at him. More convincing than anything else to Daughtry was the conduct of the policemen. They were manifestly afraid of contact with him. As he started forward, they poked the ends of their extended clubs towards his ribs to ward him off.

"Don't you come any closer," one warned him, flourishing his club with the advertisement of braining him. "You stay right where you are until you get your orders."

"Put on your shirt and stand over there alongside your master," Doctor Emory commanded Kwaque, having suddenly elevated the chair and spilled him out on his feet on the floor.

"But what under the sun . . ." Daughtry began, but was ignored by his quondam friend, who was saying to Doctor Masters:

"The pest-house has been vacant since that Japanese died. I know the gang of cowards in your department so I'd advise you to give the dope to these here so that they can disinfect the premises when they go in."

"For the love of Mike," Daughtry pleaded, all of stunned belligerence gone from him in his state of stunned conviction that the dread disease possessed him. He touched his finger to his sensationless forehead, then smelled it and recognized the burnt flesh he had not felt burning. "For the love of Mike, don't be in such a rush. If I've got it, I've got it. But that ain't no reason we can't deal with each other like white men. Give me two hours an' I'll get outa the city. An' in twenty-four I'll be outa the country. I'll take ship -"

"And continue to be a menace to the public health wherever you are," Doctor Masters broke in, already visioning a column in the evening papers, with scare-heads, in which he would appear the hero, the St. George of San Francisco standing with poised lance between the people and the dragon of leprosy.

"Take them away," said Waiter Merritt Emory, avoiding looking Daughtry in the eyes.

"Ready! March!" commanded the sergeant.

The two policemen advanced on Daughtry and Kwaque with extended clubs.

"Keep away, an' keep movin'," one of the policemen growled fiercely. "An' do what we say, or get your head cracked. Out you go, now. Out the door with you. Better tell that coon to stick right alongside you."

"Doc., won't you let me talk a moment?" Daughtry begged of Emory.

"The time for talking is past," was the reply. "This is the time for segregation. Doctor Masters, don't forget that ambulance when you're quit of the load."

So the procession, led by the board-of-heath doctor and the sergeant, and brought up in the rear by the policemen with their protectively extended clubs, started through the doorway.

Whirling about on the threshold, at the imminent risk of having his skull cracked, Dag Daughtry called back:

"Doc! My dog! You know 'm."

"I'll get him for you," Doctor Emory consented quickly. "What's the address?"

"Room eight-seven, Clay street, the Bowhead Lodging House, you know the place, entrance just around the corner from the Bowhead Saloon. Have 'm sent out to me wherever they put me, will you?"

"Certainly I will," said Doctor Emory, "and you've got a cockatoo, too?"

"You bet, Cocky! Send 'm both along, please, sir."

"My!" said Miss Judson, that evening, at dinner with a certain young interne of St. Joseph's Hospital. "That Doctor Emory is a wizard. No wonder he's successful. Think of it! Two filthy lepers in our office to- day! One was a coon. And he knew what was the matter the moment he laid eyes on them. He's a caution. When I tell you what he did to them with his cigar! And he was cute about it! He gave me the wink first. And they never dreamed what he was doing. He took his cigar and . . . "

CHAPTER XX

The dog, like the horse, abases the base. Being base, Waiter Merritt Emory was abased by his desire for the possession of Michael. Had there been no Michael, his conduct would have been quite different. He would have dealt with Daughtry as Daughtry had described, as between white men. He would have warned Daughtry of his disease and enabled him to take ship to the South Seas or to Japan, or to other countries where lepers are not segregated. This would have worked no hardship on those countries, since such was their law and procedure, while it would have enabled Daughtry and Kwaque to escape the hell of the San Francisco pest-house, to which, because of his baseness, he condemned them for the rest of their lives.

Furthermore, when the expense of the maintenance of armed guards over the pest-house, day and night, throughout the years, is considered, Walter Merritt Emory could have saved many thousands of dollars to the tax-payers of the city and county of San Francisco, which thousands of dollars, had they been spent otherwise, could have been diverted to the reduction of the notorious crowding in school-rooms, to purer milk for the babies of the poor, or to an increase of breathing-space in the park system for the people of the stifling ghetto. But had Walter Merritt Emory been thus considerate, not only would Daughtry and Kwaque have sailed out and away over the sea, but with them would have sailed Michael.

Never was a reception-roomful of patients rushed through more expeditiously than was Doctor Emory's the moment the door had closed upon the two policemen who brought up Daughtry's rear. And before he went to his late lunch, Doctor Emory was away in his machine and down into the Barbary Coast to the door of the Bowhead Lodging House. On the way, by virtue of his political affiliations, he had been able to pick up a captain of detectives. The addition of the captain proved necessary, for the landlady put up a stout argument against the taking of the dog of her lodger. But Milliken, captain of detectives, was too well known to her, and she yielded to the law of which he was the symbol and of which she was credulously ignorant.

As Michael started out of the room on the end of a rope, a plaintive call of reminder came from the window-sill, where perched a tiny, snow-white cockatoo.

"Cocky," he called. "Cocky."

Walter Merritt Emory glanced back and for no more than a moment hesitated. "We'll send for the bird later," he told the landlady, who, still mildly expostulating as she followed them downstairs, failed to notice that the captain of the detectives had carelessly left the door to Daughtry's rooms ajar.

But Walter Merritt Emory was not the only base one abased by desire of possession of Michael. In a deep leather chair, his feet resting in another deep leather chair, at the Indoor Yacht Club, Harry Del Mar yielded to the somniferous digestion of lunch, which was for him breakfast as well, and glanced through the first of the early editions of the afternoon papers. His eyes lighted on a big headline, with a brief five lines under it. His feet were instantly drawn down off the chair and under him as he stood up erect upon them. On swift second thought, he sat down again, pressed the electric button, and, while waiting for the club steward, reread the headline and the brief five lines.

In a taxi, and away, heading for the Barbary Coast, Harry Del Mar saw visions that were golden. They took on the semblance of yellow, twenty- dollar gold pieces, of yellow-backed paper bills of the government stamping of the United States, of bank books, and of rich coupons ripe for the clipping, and all shot through the flashings of the form of a rough-coated Irish terrier, on a galaxy of brilliantly-lighted stages, mouth open, nose upward to the drops, singing, ever singing, as no dog had ever been known to sing in the world before.

Cocky himself was the first to discover that the door was ajar, and was looking at it with speculation (if by "speculation" may be described the mental processes of a bird, in some mysterious way absorbing into its consciousness a fresh impression of its environment and preparing to act, or not act, according to which way the fresh impression modifies its conduct). Humans do this very thing, and some of them call it "free will." Cocky, staring at the open door, was in just the stage of determining whether or not he should more closely inspect that crack of exit to the wider world, which inspection, in turn, would determine whether or not he should venture out through the crack, when his eyes beheld the eyes of the second discoverer staring in.

The eyes were bestial, yellow-green, the pupils dilating and narrowing with sharp swiftness as they sought about among the lights and glooms of the room. Cocky knew danger at the first glimpse, danger to the uttermost of violent death. Yet Cocky did nothing. No panic stirred his heart. Motionless, one eye only turned upon the crack, he focused that one eye upon the head and eyes of the gaunt gutter-cat whose head had erupted into the crack like an apparition.

Alert, dilating and contracting, as swift as cautious, and infinitely apprehensive, the pupils vertically slitted in jet into the midmost of amazing opals of greenish yellow, the eyes roved the room. They alighted on Cocky. Instantly the head portrayed that the cat had stiffened, crouched, and frozen. Almost imperceptibly the eyes settled into a watching that was like to the stony stare of a sphinx across aching and eternal desert sands. The eyes were as if they had so stared for centuries and millenniums.

No less frozen was Cocky. He drew no film across his one eye that showed his head cocked sideways, nor did the passion of apprehension that whelmed him manifest itself in the quiver of a single feather. Both creatures were petrified into the mutual stare that is of the hunter and the hunted, the preyer and the prey, the meat-eater and the meat.

It was a matter of long minutes, that stare, until the head in the doorway, with a slight turn, disappeared. Could a bird sigh, Cocky would have sighed. But he made no movement as he listened to the slow, dragging steps of a man go by and fade away down the hall.

Several minutes passed, and, just as abruptly the apparition reappeared, not alone the head this time, but the entire sinuous form as it glided into the room and came to rest in the middle of the floor. The eyes brooded on Cocky, and the entire body was still save for the long tail, which lashed from one side to the other and back again in an abrupt, angry, but monotonous manner.

Never removing its eyes from Cocky, the cat advanced slowly until it paused not six feet away. Only the tail lashed back and forth, and only the eyes gleamed like jewels in the full light of the window they faced, the vertical pupils contracting to scarcely perceptible black slits.

And Cocky, who could not know death with the clearness of concept of a human, nevertheless was not altogether unaware that the end of all things was terribly impending. As he watched the cat deliberately crouch for the spring, Cocky, gallant mote of life that he was, betrayed his one and forgivable panic.

"Cocky! Cocky!" he called plaintively to the blind, insensate walls.

It was his call to all the world, and all powers and things and two-legged men-creatures, and Steward in particular, and Kwaque, and Michael. The burden of his call was: "It is I, Cocky. I am very small and very frail, and this is a monster to destroy me, and I love the light, bright world, and I want to live and to continue to live in the brightness, and I am so very small, and I'm a good little fellow, with a good little heart, and I cannot battle with this huge, furry, hungry thing that is going to devour me, and I want help, help, help. I am Cocky. Everybody knows me. I am Cocky."

This, and much more, was contained in his two calls of: "Cocky! Cocky!"

And there was no answer from the blind walls, from the hall outside, nor from all the world, and, his moment of panic over, Cocky was his brave little self again. He sat motionless on the window-sill, his head cocked to the side, with one unwavering eye regarding on the floor, so perilously near, the eternal enemy of all his kind.

The human quality of his voice had startled the gutter-cat, causing her to forgo her spring as she flattened down her ears and bellied closer to the floor.

And in the silence that followed, a blue-bottle fly buzzed rowdily against an adjacent window-pane, with occasional loud bumps against the glass tokening that he too had his tragedy, a prisoner pent by baffling transparency from the bright world that blazed so immediately beyond.

Nor was the gutter-cat without her ill and hurt of life. Hunger hurt her, and hurt her meagre breasts that should have been full for the seven feeble and mewing little ones, replicas of her save that their eyes were not yet open and that they were grotesquely unsteady on their soft, young legs. She remembered them by the hurt of her breasts and the prod of her instinct; also she remembered them by vision, so that, by the subtle chemistry of her brain, she could see them, by way of the broken screen across the ventilator hole, down into the cellar in the dark rubbish-corner under the stairway, where she had stolen her lair and birthed her litter.

And the vision of them, and the hurt of her hunger stirred her afresh, so that she gathered her body and measured the distance for the leap. But Cocky was himself again.

"Devil be damned! Devil be damned!" he shouted his loudest and most belligerent, as he ruffled like a bravo at the gutter-cat beneath him, so that he sent her crouching, with startlement, lower to the floor, her ears wilting rigidly flat and down, her tail lashing, her head turning about the room so that her eyes might penetrate its obscurest corners in quest of the human whose voice had so cried out.

All of which the gutter-cat did, despite the positive evidence of her senses that this human noise had proceeded from the white bird itself on the window-sill.

The bottle fly bumped once again against its invisible prison wall in the silence that ensued. The gutter-cat prepared and sprang with sudden decision, landing where Cocky had perched the fraction of a second before. Cocky had darted to the side, but, even as he darted, and as the cat landed on the sill, the cat's paw flashed out sidewise and Cocky leaped straight up, beating the air with his wings so little used to flying. The gutter-cat reared on her hind-legs, smote upward with one paw as a child might strike with its hat at a butterfly. But there was weight in the cat's paw, and the claws of it were outspread like so many hooks.

Struck in mid-air, a trifle of a flying machine, all its delicate gears tangled and disrupted, Cocky fell to the floor in a shower of white feathers, which, like snowflakes, eddied slowly down after, and after the plummet-like descent of the cat, so that some of them came to rest on her back, startling her tense nerves with their gentle impact and making her crouch closer while she shot a swift glance around and overhead for any danger that might threaten.

CHAPTER XXI

Harry Del Mar found only a few white feathers on the floor of Dag Daughtry's room in the Bowhead Lodging House, and from the landlady learned what had happened to Michael. The first thing Harry Del Mar did, still retaining his taxi, was to locate the residence of Doctor Emory and make sure that Michael was confined in an outhouse in the back yard. Next he engaged passage on the steamship Umatilla, sailing for Seattle and Puget Sound ports at daylight. And next he packed his luggage and paid his bills.

In the meantime, a wordy war was occurring in Walter Merritt Emory's office.

"The man's yelling his head off," Doctor Masters was contending. "The police had to rap him with their clubs in the ambulance. He was violent. He wanted his dog. It can't be done. It's too raw. You can't steal his dog this way. He'll make a howl in the papers."

"Huh!" quoth Walter Merritt Emory. "I'd like to see a reporter with backbone enough to go within talking distance of a leper in the pest-house. And I'd like to see the editor who wouldn't send a pest-house letter (granting it'd been smuggled past the guards) out to be burned the very second he became aware of its source. Don't you worry, Doc. There won't be any noise in the papers."

"But leprosy! Public health! The dog has been exposed to his master. The dog itself is a peripatetic source of infection."

"Contagion is the better and more technical word, Doc.," Walter Merritt Emory soothed with the sting of superior knowledge.

"Contagion, then," Doctor Masters took him up. "The public must be considered. It must not run the risk of being infected -"

"Of contracting the contagion," the other corrected smoothly.

"Call it what you will. The public -"

"Poppycock," said Walter Merritt Emory. "What you don't know about leprosy, and what the rest of the board of health doesn't know about leprosy, would fill more books than have been compiled by the men who have expertly studied the disease. The one thing they have eternally tried, and are eternally trying, is to inoculate one animal outside man with the leprosy that is peculiar to man. Horses, rabbits, rats, donkeys, monkeys, mice, and dogs, heavens, they have tried it on them all, tens of thousands of times and a hundred thousand times ten thousand times, and never a successful inoculation! They have never succeeded in inoculating it on one man from another. Here, let me show you."

And from his shelves Waiter Merritt Emory began pulling down his authorities.

"Amazing . . . most interesting . . ." Doctor Masters continued to emit from time to time as he followed the expert guidance of the other through the books. "I never dreamed . . . the amount of work they have done is astounding . . ."

"But," he said in conclusion, "there is no convincing a layman of the matter contained on your shelves. Nor can I so convince my public. Nor will I try to. Besides, the man is consigned to the living death of life- long imprisonment in the pest-house. You know the beastly hole it is. He loves the dog. He's mad over it. Let him have it. I tell you it's rotten unfair and cruel, and I won't stand for it."

"Yes, you will," Walter Merritt Emory assured him coolly. "And I'll tell you why."

He told him. He said things that no doctor should say to another, but which a politician may well say, and has often said, to another politician, things which cannot bear repeating, if, for no other reason, because they are too humiliating and too little conducive to pride for the average American citizen to know; things of the inside, secret governments of imperial municipalities which the average American citizen, voting free as a king at the polls, fondly thinks he manages; things which are, on rare occasion, partly unburied and promptly reburied in the tomes of reports of Lexow Committees and Federal Commissions.

And Walter Merritt Emory won his desire of Michael against Doctor Masters; had his wife dine with him at Jules' that evening and took her to see Margaret Anglin in celebration of the victory; returned home at one in the morning, in his pyjamas went out to take a last look at Michael, and found no Michael.

The pest-house of San Francisco, as is naturally the case with pest-houses in all American cities, was situated on the bleakest, remotest, forlornest, cheapest space of land owned by the city. Poorly protected from the Pacific Ocean, chill winds and dense fog-banks whistled and swirled sadly across the sand-dunes. Picnicking parties never came there, nor did small boys hunting birds' nests or playing at being wild Indians. The only class of frequenters was the suicides, who, sad of life, sought the saddest landscape as a fitting scene in which to end. And, because they so ended, they never repeated their visits.

The outlook from the windows was not inspiriting. A quarter of a mile in either direction, looking out along the shallow canyon of the sand-hills, Dag Daughtry could see the sentry-boxes of the guards, themselves armed and more prone to kill than to lay hands on any escaping pest-man, much less persuavively discuss with him the advisability of his return to the prison house.

On the opposing sides of the prospect from the windows of the four walls of the pest-house were trees. Eucalyptus they were, but not the royal monarchs that their brothers are in native habitats. Poorly planted, by politics, illy attended, by politics, decimated and many times repeatedly decimated by the hostile forces of their environment, a straggling corporal's guard of survivors, they thrust their branches, twisted and distorted, as if writhing in agony, into the air. Scrub of growth they were, expending the major portion of their meagre nourishment in their roots that crawled seaward through the insufficient sand for anchorage against the prevailing gales.

Not even so far as the sentry-boxes were Daughtry and Kwaque permitted to stroll. A hundred yards inside was the dead-line. Here, the guards came hastily to deposit food-supplies, medicines, and written doctors' instructions, retreating as hastily as they came. Here, also, was a blackboard upon which Daughtry was instructed to chalk up his needs and requests in letters of such size that they could be read from a distance. And on this board, for many days, he wrote, not demands for beer, although the six-quart daily custom had been broken sharply off, but demands like:

WHERE IS MY DOG?

HE IS AN IRISH TERRIER.

HE IS ROUGH-COATED.

HIS NAME IS KILLENY BOY.

I WANT MY DOG.

I WANT TO TALK TO DOC. EMORY.

TELL DOC. EMORY TO WRITE TO ME ABOUT MY DOG.

One day, Dag Daughtry wrote:

IF I DON'T GET MY DOG I WILL KILL DOC. EMORY.

Whereupon the newspapers informed the public that the sad case of the two lepers at the pest-house had become tragic, because the white one had gone insane. Public-spirited citizens wrote to the papers, declaiming against the maintenance of such a danger to the community, and demanding that the United States government build a national leprosarium on some remote island or isolated mountain peak. But this tiny ripple of interest faded out in seventy-two hours, and the reporter-cubs proceeded variously to interest the public in the Alaskan husky dog that was half a bear, in the question whether or not Crispi Angelotti was guilty of having cut the carcass of Giuseppe Bartholdi into small portions and thrown it into the bay in a grain-sack off Fisherman's Wharf, and in the overt designs of Japan upon Hawaii, the Philippines, and the Pacific Coast of North America.

And, outside of imprisonment, nothing happened of interest to Dag Daughtry and Kwaque at the pest-house until one night in the late fall. A gale was not merely brewing. It was coming on to blow. Because, in a basket of fruit, stated to have been sent by the young ladies of Miss Foote's Seminary, Daughtry had read a note artfully concealed in the heart of an apple, telling him on the forthcoming Friday night to keep a light burning in his window. Daughtry received a visitor at five in the morning.

It was Charles Stough Greenleaf, the Ancient Mariner himself. Having wallowed for two hours through the deep sand of the eucalyptus forest, he fell exhausted against the penthouse door. When Daughtry opened it, the ancient one blew in upon him along with a gusty wet splatter of the freshening gale. Daughtry caught him first and supported him toward a chair. But, remembering his own affliction, he released the old man so abruptly as to drop him violently into the chair.

"My word, sir," said Daughtry. "You must 'a' ben havin' a time of it. Here, you fella Kwaque, this fella wringin' wet. You fella take 'm off shoe stop along him."

But before Kwaque, immediately kneeling, could touch hand to the shoelaces, Daughtry, remembering that Kwaque was likewise unclean, had thrust him away.

"My word, I don't know what to do," Daughtry murmured, staring about helplessly as he realised that it was a leper-house, that the very chair in which the old man sat was a leper-chair, that the very floor on which his exhausted feet rested was a leper-floor.

"I'm glad to see you, most exceeding glad," the Ancient Mariner panted, extending his hand in greeting.

Dag Daughtry avoided it.

"How goes the treasure-hunting?" he queried lightly. "Any prospects in sight?"

The Ancient Mariner nodded, and with returning breath, at first whispering, gasped out:

"We're all cleared to sail on the first of the ebb at seven this morning. She's out in the stream now, a tidy bit of a schooner, the Bethlehem, with good lines and hull and large cabin accommodations. She used to be in the Tahiti trade, before the steamers ran her out. Provisions are good. Everything is most excellent. I saw to that. I cannot say I like the captain. I've seen his type before. A splendid seaman, I am certain, but a Bully Hayes grown old. A natural born pirate, a very wicked old man indeed. Nor is the backer any better. He is middle-aged, has a bad record, and is not in any sense of the word a gentleman, but he has plenty of money, made it first in California oil, then grub-staked a prospector in British Columbia, cheated him out of his share of the big lode he discovered and doubled his own wealth half a dozen times over. A very undesirable, unlikeable sort of a man. But he believes in luck, and is confident that he'll make at least fifty millions out of our adventure and cheat me out of my share. He's as much a pirate as is the captain he's engaged."

"Mr. Greenleaf, I congratulate you, sir," Daughtry said. "And you have touched me, sir, touched me to the heart, coming all the way out here on such a night, and running such risks, just to say good-bye to poor Dag Daughtry, who always meant somewhat well but had bad luck."

But while he talked so heartily, Daughtry saw, in a resplendent visioning, all the freedom of a schooner in the great South Seas, and felt his heart sink in realisation that remained for him only the pest- house, the sand-dunes, and the sad eucalyptus trees.

The Ancient Mariner sat stiffly upright.

"Sir, you have hurt me. You have hurt me to the heart."

"No offence, sir, no offence," Daughtry stammered in apology, although he wondered in what way he could have hurt the old gentleman's feelings.

"You are my friend, sir," the other went on, gravely censorious. "I am your friend, sir. And you give me to understand that you think I have come out here to this hell-hole to say good-bye. I came out here to get you, sir, and your nigger, sir. The schooner is waiting for you. All is arranged. You are signed on the articles before the shipping commissioner. Both of you. Signed on yesterday by proxies I arranged for myself. One was a Barbadoes nigger. I got him and the white man out of a sailors' boarding-house on Commercial Street and paid them five dollars each to appear before the Commissioner and sign on."

"But, my God, Mr. Greenleaf, you don't seem to grasp it that he and I are lepers."

Almost with a galvanic spring, the Ancient Mariner was out of the chair and on his feet, the anger of age and of a generous soul in his face as he cried:

"My God, sir, what you don't seem to grasp is that you are my friend, and that I am your friend."

Abruptly, still under the pressure of his wrath, he thrust out his hand.

"Steward, Daughtry. Mr. Daughtry, friend, sir, or whatever I may name you, this is no fairy-story of the open boat, the cross-bearings unnamable, and the treasure a fathom under the sand. This is real. I have a heart. That, sir", here he waved his extended hand under Daughtry's nose -"is my hand. There is only one thing you may do, must do, right now. You must take that hand in your hand, and shake it, with your heart in your hand as mine is in my hand."

"But . . . but. . ." Daughtry faltered.

"If you don't, then I shall not depart from this place. I shall remain here, die here. I know you are a leper. You can't tell me anything about that. There's my hand. Are you going to take it? My heart is there in the palm of it, in the pulse in every finger-end of it. If you don't take it, I warn you I'll sit right down here in this chair and die. I want you to understand I am a man, sir, a gentleman. I am a friend, a comrade. I am no poltroon of the flesh. I live in my heart and in my head, sir, not in this feeble carcass I cursorily inhabit. Take that hand. I want to talk with you afterward."

Dag Daughtry extended his hand hesitantly, but the Ancient Mariner seized it and pressed it so fiercely with his age-lean fingers as to hurt.

"Now we can talk," he said. "I have thought the whole matter over. We sail on the Bethlehem. When the wicked man discovers that he can never get a penny of my fabulous treasure, we will leave him. He will be glad to be quit of us. We, you and I and your nigger, will go ashore in the Marquesas. Lepers roam about free there. There are no regulations. I have seen them. We will be free. The land is a paradise. And you and I will set up housekeeping. A thatched hut, no more is needed. The work is trifling. The freedom of beach and sea and mountain will be ours. For you there will be sailing, swimming, fishing, hunting. There are mountain goats, wild chickens and wild cattle. Bananas and plantains will ripen over our heads, avocados and custard apples, also. The red peppers grow by the door, and there will be fowls, and the eggs of fowls. Kwaque shall do the cooking. And there will be beer. I have long noted your thirst unquenchable. There will be beer, six quarts of it a day, and more, more.

"Quick. We must start now. I am sorry to tell you that I have vainly sought your dog. I have even paid detectives who were robbers. Doctor Emory stole Killeny Boy from you, but within a dozen hours he was stolen from Doctor Emory. I have left no stone unturned. Killeny Boy is gone, as we shall be gone from this detestable hole of a city.

"I have a machine waiting. The driver is paid well. Also, I have promised to kill him if he defaults on me. It bears just a bit north of east over the sandhill on the road that runs along the other side of the funny forest . . . That is right. We will start now. We can discuss afterward. Look! Daylight is beginning to break. The guards must not see us . . . "

Out into the storm they passed, Kwaque, with a heart wild with gladness, bringing up the rear. At the beginning Daughtry strove to walk aloof, but in a trice, in the first heavy gust that threatened to whisk the frail old man away, Dag Daughtry's hand was grasping the other's arm, his own weight behind and under, supporting and impelling forward and up the hill through the heavy sand.

"Thank you, steward, thank you, my friend," the Ancient Mariner murmured in the first lull between the gusts.

CHAPTER XXII

Not altogether unwillingly, in the darkness of night, despite that he disliked the man, did Michael go with Harry Del Mar. Like a burglar the man came, with infinite caution of silence, to the outhouse in Doctor Emory's back yard where Michael was a prisoner. Del Mar knew the theatre too well to venture any hackneyed melodramatic effect such as an electric torch. He felt his way in the darkness to the door of the outhouse, unlatched it, and entered softly, feeling with his hands for the wire- haired coat.

And Michael, a man-dog and a lion-dog in all the stuff of him, bristled at the instant of intrusion, but made no outcry. Instead, he smelled out the intruder and recognised him. Disliking the man, nevertheless he permitted the tying of the rope around his neck and silently followed him out to the sidewalk, down to the corner, and into the waiting taxi.

His reasoning, unless reason be denied him, was simple. This man he had met, more than once, in the company of Steward. Amity had existed between him and Steward, for they had sat at table, and drunk together. Steward was lost. Michael knew not where to find him, and was himself a prisoner in the back yard of a strange place. What had once happened, could again happen. It had happened that Steward, Del Mar, and Michael had sat at table together on divers occasions. It was probable that such a combination would happen again, was going to happen now, and, once more, in the bright-lighted cabaret, he would sit on a chair, Del Mar on one side, and on the other side beloved Steward with a glass of beer before him, all of which might be called "leaping to a conclusion"; for conclusion there was, and upon the conclusion Michael acted.

Now Michael could not reason to this conclusion nor think to this conclusion, in words. "Amity," as an instance, was no word in his consciousness. Whether or not he thought to the conclusion in swift-related images and pictures and swift-welded composites of images and pictures, is a problem that still waits human solution. The point is: he did think. If this be denied him, then must he have acted wholly by instinct, which would seem more marvellous on the face of it than if, in dim ways, he had performed a vague thought-process.

However, into the taxi and away through the maze of San Francisco's streets, Michael lay alertly on the floor near Del Mar's feet, making no overtures of friendliness, by the same token making no demonstration of the repulsion of the man's personality engendered in him. For Harry Del Mar, who was base, and who had been further abased by his money-making desire for the possession of Michael, had had his baseness sensed by Michael from the beginning. That first meeting in the Barbary Coast cabaret, Michael had bristled at him, and stiffened belligerently, when he laid his hand on Michael's head. Nor had Michael thought about the man at all, much less attempted any analysis of him. Something had been wrong with that hand, the perfunctory way in which it had touched him under a show of heartiness that could well deceive the onlooker. The feel of it had not been right. There had been no warmth in it, no heart, no communication of genuine good approach from the brain and the soul of the man of which it was the telegraphic tentacle and transmitter. In short, the message or feel had not been a good message or feel, and Michael had bristled and stiffened without thinking, but by mere knowing, which is what men call "intuition."

Electric lights, a shed-covered wharf, mountains of luggage and freight, the noisy toil of 'longshoremen and sailors, the staccato snorts of donkey engines and the whining sheaves as running lines ran through the blocks, a crowd of white-coated stewards carrying hand-baggage, the quartermaster at the gangway foot, the gangway sloping steeply up to the Umatilla's promenade deck, more quartermasters and gold-laced ship's officers at the head of the gangway, and more crowd and confusion blocking the narrow deck, thus Michael knew, beyond all peradventure, that he had come back to the sea and its ships, where he had first met Steward, where he had been always with Steward, save for the recent nightmare period in the great city. Nor was there absent from the flashing visions of his consciousness the images and memories of Kwaque and Cocky. Whining eagerly, he strained at the leash, risking his tender toes among the many inconsiderate, restless, leather-shod feet of the humans, as he quested and scented for Cocky and Kwaque, and, most of all, for Steward.

Michael accepted his disappointment in not immediately meeting them, for from the dawn of consciousness, the limitations and restrictions of dogs in relation to humans had been hammered into him in the form of concepts of patience. The patience of waiting, when he wanted to go home and when Steward continued to sit at table and talk and drink beer, was his, as was the patience of the rope around the neck, the fence too high to scale, the narrowed-walled room with the closed door which he could never unlatch but which humans unlatched so easily. So that he permitted himself to be led away by the ship's butcher, who on the Umatilla had the charge of all dog passengers. Immured in a tiny between-decks cubby which was filled mostly with boxes and bales, tied as well by the rope around his neck, he waited from moment to moment for the door to open and admit, realised in the flesh, the resplendent vision of Steward which blazed through the totality of his consciousness.

Instead, although Michael did not guess it then, and, only later, divined it as a vague manifestation of power on the part of Del Mar, the well-tipped ship's butcher opened the door, untied him, and turned him over to the well-tipped stateroom steward who led him to Del Mar's stateroom. Up to the last, Michael was convinced that he was being led to Steward. Instead, in the stateroom, he found only Del Mar. "No Steward," might be described as Michael's thought; but by patience, as his mood and key, might be described his acceptance of further delay in meeting up with his god, his best beloved, his Steward who was his own human god amidst the multitude of human gods he was encountering.

Michael wagged his tail, flattened his ears, even his crinkled ear, a trifle, and smiled, all in a casual way of recognition, smelled out the room to make doubly sure that there was no scent of Steward, and lay down on the floor. When Del Mar spoke to him, he looked up and gazed at him.

"Now, my boy, times have changed," Del Mar addressed him in cold, brittle tones. "I'm going to make an actor out of you, and teach you what's what. First of all, come here . . . COME HERE!"

Michael obeyed, without haste, without lagging, and patently without eagerness.

"You'll get over that, my lad, and put pep into your motions when I talk to you," Del Mar assured him; and the very manner of his utterance was a threat that Michael could not fail to recognise. "Now we'll just see if I can pull off the trick. You listen to me, and sing like you did for that leper guy."

Drawing a harmonica from his vest pocket, he put it to his lips and began to play "Marching through Georgia."

"Sit down!" he commanded.

Again Michael obeyed, although all that was Michael was in protest. He quivered as the shrill-sweet strains from the silver reeds ran through him. All his throat and chest was in the impulse to sing; but he mastered it, for he did not care to sing for this man. All he wanted of him was Steward.

"Oh, you're stubborn, eh?" Del Mar sneered at him. "The matter with you is you're thoroughbred. Well, my boy, it just happens I know your kind and I reckon I can make you get busy and work for me just as much as you did for that other guy. Now get busy."

He shifted the tune on into "Georgia Camp Meeting." But Michael was obdurate. Not until the melting strains of "Old Kentucky Home" poured through him did he lose his self-control and lift his mellow-throated howl that was the call for the lost pack of the ancient millenniums. Under the prodding hypnosis of this music he could not but yearn and burn for the vague, forgotten life of the pack when the world was young and the pack was the pack ere it was lost for ever through the endless centuries of domestication.

"Ah, ha," Del Mar chuckled coldly, unaware of the profound history and vast past he evoked by his silver reeds.

A loud knock on the partition wall warned him that some sleepy passenger was objecting.

"That will do!" he said sharply, taking the harmonica from his lips. And Michael ceased, and hated him. "I guess I've got your number all right. And you needn't think you're going to sleep here scratching fleas and disturbing my sleep."

He pressed the call-button, and, when his room-steward answered, turned Michael over to him to be taken down below and tied up in the crowded cubby-hole.

During the several days and nights on the Umatilla, Michael learned much of what manner of man Harry Del Mar was. Almost, might it be said, he learned Del Mar's pedigree without knowing anything of his history. For instance he did not know that Del Mar's real name was Percival Grunsky, and that at grammar school he had been called "Brownie" by the girls and "Blackie" by the boys. No more did he know that he had gone from half-way-through grammar school directly into the industrial reform school; nor that, after serving two years, he had been paroled out by Harris Collins, who made a living, and an excellent one, by training animals for the stage. Much less could he know the training that for six years Del Mar, as assistant, had been taught to give the animals, and, thereby, had received for himself.

What Michael did know was that Del Mar had no pedigree and was a scrub as compared with thoroughbreds such as Steward, Captain Kellar, and Mister Haggin of Meringe. And he learned it swiftly and simply. In the day-time, fetched by a steward, Michael would be brought on deck to Del Mar, who was always surrounded by effusive young ladies and matrons who lavished caresses and endearments upon Michael. This he stood, although much bored; but what irked him almost beyond standing were the feigned caresses and endearments Del Mar lavished on him. He knew the cold-blooded insincerity of them, for, at night, when he was brought to Del Mar's room, he heard only the cold brittle tones, sensed only the threat and the menace of the other's personality, felt, when touched by the other's hand, only a stiffness and sharpness of contact that was like to so much steel or wood in so far as all subtle tenderness of heart and spirit was absent.

This man was two-faced, two-mannered. No thoroughbred was anything but single-faced and single-mannered. A thoroughbred, hot-blooded as it might be, was always sincere. But in this scrub was no sincerity, only a positive insincerity. A thoroughbred had passion, because of its hot blood; but this scrub had no passion. Its blood was cold as its deliberateness, and it did nothing save deliberately. These things he did not think. He merely realized them, as any creature realizes itself in liking and in not liking.

To cap it all, the last night on board, Michael lost his thoroughbred temper with this man who had no temper. It came to a fight. And Michael had no chance. He raged royally and fought royally, leaping to the attack, after being knocked over twice by open-handed blows under his ear. Quick as Michael was, slashing South Sea niggers by virtue of his quickness and cleverness, he could not touch his teeth to the flesh of this man, who had been trained for six years with animals by Harris Collins. So that, when he leaped, open-mouthed, for the bite, Del Mar's right hand shot out, gripped his under-jaw as he was in the air, and flipped him over in a somersaulting fall to the floor on his back. Once again he leapt open-mouthed to the attack, and was filliped to the floor so hard that almost the last particle of breath was knocked out of him. The next leap was nearly his last. He was clutched by the throat. Two thumbs pressed into his neck on either side of the windpipe directly on the carotid arteries, shutting off the blood to his brain and giving him most exquisite agony, at the same time rendering him unconscious far more swiftly than the swiftest anaesthetic. Darkness thrust itself upon him; and, quivering on the floor, glimmeringly he came back to the light of the room and to the man who was casually touching a match to a cigarette and cautiously keeping an observant eye on him.

"Come on," Del Mar challenged. "I know your kind. You can't get my goat, and maybe I can't get yours entirely, but I can keep you under my thumb to work for me. Come on, you!"

And Michael came. Being a thoroughbred, despite that he knew he was beaten by this two-legged thing which was not warm human but was so alien and hard that he might as well attack the wall of a room with his teeth, or a tree-trunk, or a cliff of rock, Michael leapt bare-fanged for the throat. And all that he leapt against was training, formula. The experience was repeated. His throat was gripped, the thumbs shut off the blood from his brain, and darkness smote him. Had he been more than a normal thoroughbred dog, he would have continued to assail his impregnable enemy until he burst his heart or fell in a fit. But he was normal. Here was something unassailable, adamantine. As little might he win victory from it, as from the cement-paved sidewalk of a city. The thing was a devil, with the hardness and coldness, the wickedness and wisdom, of a devil. It was as bad as Steward was good. Both were two- legged. Both were gods. But this one was an evil god.

He did not reason all this, nor any of it. Yet, transmuted into human terms of thought and understanding, it adequately describes the fulness of his state of mind toward Del Mar. Had Michael been entangled in a fight with a warm god, he could have raged and battled blindly, inflicting and receiving hurt in the chaos of conflict, as such a god, being warm, would have likewise received and given hurt, being only a flesh-and-blood, living, breathing entity after all. But this two-legged god-devil did not rage blindly and was incapable of passional heat. He was like so much cunning, massive steel machinery, and he did what Michael could never dream he did, and, for that matter, which few humans do and which all animal trainers do: he kept one thought ahead of Michael's thought all the time, and therefore, was able to have ready one action always in anticipation of Michael's next action. This was the training he had received from Harris Collins, who, withal he was a sentimental and doting husband and father, was the arch-devil when it came to animals other than human ones, and who reigned in an animal hell which he had created and made lucrative.

Michael went ashore in Seattle all eagerness, straining at his leash until he choked and coughed and was coldly cursed by Del Mar. For Michael was mastered by his expectation that he would meet Steward, and he looked for him around the first corner, and around all corners with undiminished zeal. But amongst the multitudes of men there was no Steward. Instead, down in the basement of the New Washington Hotel, where electric lights burned always, under the care of the baggage porter, he was tied securely by the neck in the midst of Alpine ranges of trunks which were for ever being heaped up, sought over, taken down, carried away, or added to.

Three days of this dolorous existence he passed. The porters made friends with him and offered him prodigious quantities of cooked meats from the leavings of the dining-room. Michael was too disappointed and grief-stricken over Steward to overeat himself, while Del Mar, accompanied by the manager of the hotel, raised a great row with the porters for violating the feeding instructions.

"That guy's no good," said the head porter to assistant, when Del Mar had departed. "He's greasy. I never liked greasy brunettes anyway. My wife's a brunette, but thank the Lord she ain't greasy."

"Sure," agreed the assistant. "I know his kind. Why, if you'd stick a knife into him he wouldn't bleed blood. It'd be straight liquid lard."

Whereupon the pair of them immediately presented Michael with vaster quantities of meat which he could not eat because the desire for Steward was too much with him.

In the meantime Del Mar sent off two telegrams to New York, the first to Harris Collins' animal training school, where his troupe of dogs was boarding through his vacation:

"Sell my dogs. You know what they can do and what they are worth. Am   done with them. Deduct the board and hold the balance for me until I   see you. I have the limit here of a dog. Every turn I ever pulled is   put in the shade by this one. He's a ten strike. Wait till you see   him."

The second, to his booking agent:

"Get busy. Book me over the best. Talk it up. I have the turn. A   winner. Nothing like it. Don't talk up top price but way over top   price. Prepare them for the dog when I give them the chance for the   once over. You know me. I am giving it straight. This will head the   bill anywhere all the time."

CHAPTER XXIII

Came the crate. Because Del Mar brought it into the baggage-room, Michael was suspicious of it. A minute later his suspicion was justified. Del Mar invited him to go into the crate, and he declined. With a quick deft clutch on the collar at the back of his neck, Del Mar jerked him off his footing and thrust him in, or partly in, rather, because he had managed to get a hold on the edge of the crate with his two forepaws. The animal trainer wasted no time. He brought the clenched fist of his free hand down in two blows, rat-tat, on Michael's paws. And Michael, at the pain, relaxed both holds. The next instant he was thrust inside, snarling his indignation and rage as he vainly flung himself at the open bars, while Del Mar was locking the stout door.

Next, the crate was carried out to an express wagon and loaded in along with a number of trunks. Del Mar had disappeared the moment he had locked the door, and the two men in the wagon, which was now bouncing along over the cobblestones, were strangers. There was just room in the crate for Michael to stand upright, although he could not lift his head above the level of his shoulders. And so standing, his head pressed against the top, a rut in the road, jolting the wagon and its contents, caused his head to bump violently.

The crate was not quite so long as Michael, so that he was compelled to stand with the end of his nose pressing against the end of the crate. An automobile, darting out from a cross-street, caused the driver of the wagon to pull in abruptly and apply the brake. With the crate thus suddenly arrested, Michael's body was precipitated forward. There was no brake to stop him, unless the soft end of his nose be considered the brake, for it was his nose that brought his body to rest inside the crate.

He tried lying down, confined as the space was, and made out better, although his lips were cut and bleeding by having been forced so sharply against his teeth. But the worst was to come. One of his forepaws slipped out through the slats or bars and rested on the bottom of the wagon where the trunks were squeaking, screeching, and jigging. A rut in the roadway made the nearest trunk tilt one edge in the air and shift position, so that when it tilted back again it rested on Michael's paw. The unexpectedness of the crushing hurt of it caused him to yelp and at the same time instinctively and spasmodically to pull back with all his strength. This wrenched his shoulder and added to the agony of the imprisoned foot.

And blind fear descended upon Michael, the fear that is implanted in all animals and in man himself, the fear of the trap. Utterly beside himself, though he no longer yelped, he flung himself madly about, straining the tendons and muscles of his shoulder and leg and further and severely injuring the crushed foot. He even attacked the bars with his teeth in his agony to get at the monster thing outside that had laid hold of him and would not let him go. Another rut saved him, however, tilting the trunk just sufficiently to enable his violent struggling to drag the foot clear.

At the railroad station, the crate was handled, not with deliberate roughness, but with such carelessness that it half-slipped out of a baggageman's hands, capsized sidewise, and was caught when it was past the man's knees but before it struck the cement floor. But, Michael, sliding helplessly down the perpendicular bottom of the crate, fetched up with his full weight on the injured paw.

"Huh!" said Del Mar a little later to Michael, having strolled down the platform to where the crate was piled on a truck with other baggage destined for the train. "Got your foot smashed. Well, it'll teach you a lesson to keep your feet inside."

"That claw is a goner," one of the station baggage-men said, straightening up from an examination of Michael through the bars.

Del Mar bent to a closer scrutiny.

"So's the whole toe," he said, drawing his pocket-knife and opening a blade. "I'll fix it in half a jiffy if you'll lend a hand."

He unlocked the box and dipped Michael out with the customary strangle- hold on the neck. He squirmed and struggled, dabbing at the air with the injured as well as the uninjured forepaw and increasing his pain.

"You hold the leg," Del Mar commanded. "He's safe with that grip. It won't take a second."

Nor did it take longer. And Michael, back in the box and raging, was one toe short of the number which he had brought into the world. The blood ran freely from the crude but effective surgery, and he lay and licked the wound and was depressed with apprehension of he knew not what terrible fate awaited him and was close at hand. Never, in his experience of men, had he been so treated, while the confinement of the box was maddening with its suggestion of the trap. Trapped he was, and helpless, and the ultimate evil of life had happened to Steward, who had evidently been swallowed up by the Nothingness which had swallowed up Meringe, the Eugenie, the Solomon Islands, the Makambo, Australia, and the Mary Turner.

Suddenly, from a distance, came a bedlam of noise that made Michael prick up his ears and bristle with premonition of fresh disaster. It was a confused yelping, howling, and barking of many dogs.

"Holy Smoke! It's them damned acting dogs," growled the baggageman to his mate. "There ought to be a law against dog-acts. It ain't decent."

"It's Peterson's Troupe," said the other. "I was on when they come in last week. One of 'em was dead in his box, and from what I could see of him it looked mighty like he'd had the tar knocked outa him."

"Got a wollopin' from Peterson most likely in the last town and then was shipped along with the bunch and left to die in the baggage car."

The bedlam increased as the animals were transferred from the wagon to a platform truck, and when the truck rolled up and stopped alongside Michael's he made out that it was piled high with crated dogs. In truth, there were thirty-five dogs, of every sort of breed and mostly mongrel, and that they were far from happy was attested by their actions. Some howled, some whimpered, others growled and raged at one another through the slots, and many maintained a silence of misery. Several licked and nursed bruised feet. Smaller dogs that did not fight much were crammed two or more into single crates. Half a dozen greyhounds were crammed into larger crates that were anything save large enough.

"Them's the high-jumpers," said the first baggageman. "An' look at the way they're packed. Peterson ain't going to pay any more excess baggage than he has to. Not half room enough for them to stand up. It must be hell for them from the time they leave one town till they arrive at the next."

But what the baggageman did not know was that in the towns the hell was not mitigated, that the dogs were still confined in their too-narrow prisons, that, in fact, they were life-prisoners. Rarely, except for their acts, were they taken out from their cages. From a business standpoint, good care did not pay. Since mongrel dogs were cheap, it was cheaper to replace them when they died than so to care for them as to keep them from dying.

What the baggageman did not know, and what Peterson did know, was that of these thirty-five dogs not one was a surviving original of the troupe when it first started out four years before. Nor had there been any originals discarded. The only way they left the troupe and its cages was by dying. Nor did Michael know even as little as the baggageman knew. He knew nothing save that here reigned pain and woe and that it seemed he was destined to share the same fate.

Into the midst of them, when with more howlings and yelpings they were loaded into the baggage car, was Michael's cage piled. And for a day and a part of two nights, travelling eastward, he remained in the dog inferno. Then they were loaded off in some large city, and Michael continued on in greater quietness and comfort, although his injured foot still hurt and was bruised afresh whenever his crate was moved about in the car.

What it was all about, why he was kept in his cramped prison in the cramped car, he did not ask himself. He accepted it as unhappiness and misery, and had no more explanation for it than for the crushing of the paw. Such things happened. It was life, and life had many evils. The why of things never entered his head. He knew things and some small bit of the how of things. What was, was. Water was wet, fire hot, iron hard, meat good. He accepted such things as he accepted the everlasting miracles of the light and of the dark, which were no miracles to him any more than was his wire coat a miracle, or his beating heart, or his thinking brain.

In Chicago, he was loaded upon a track, carted through the roaring streets of the vast city, and put into another baggage-car which was quickly in motion in continuation of the eastward journey. It meant more strange men who handled baggage, as it meant in New York, where, from railroad baggage-room to express wagon he was exchanged, for ever a crated prisoner and dispatched to one, Harris Collins, on Long Island.

First of all came Harris Collins and the animal hell over which he ruled. But the second event must be stated first. Michael never saw Harry Del Mar again. As the other men he had known had stepped out of life, which was a way they had, so Harry Del Mar stepped out of Michael's purview of life as well as out of life itself. And his stepping out was literal. A collision on the elevated, a panic scramble of the uninjured out upon the trestle over the street, a step on the third rail, and Harry Del Mar was engulfed in the Nothingness which men know as death and which is nothingness in so far as such engulfed ones never reappear nor walk the ways of life again.

CHAPTER XXIV

Harris Collins was fifty-two years of age. He was slender and dapper, and in appearance and comportment was so sweet- and gentle-spirited that the impression he radiated was almost of sissyness. He might have taught a Sunday-school, presided over a girls' seminary, or been a president of a humane society.

His complexion was pink and white, his hands were as soft as the hands of his daughters, and he weighed a hundred and twelve pounds. Moreover, he was afraid of his wife, afraid of a policeman, afraid of physical violence, and lived in constant dread of burglars. But the one thing he was not afraid of was wild animals of the most ferocious sorts, such as lions, tigers, leopards, and jaguars. He knew the game, and could conquer the most refractory lion with a broom-handle, not outside the cage, but inside and locked in.

It was because he knew the game and had learned it from his father before him, a man even smaller than himself and more fearful of all things except animals. This father, Noel Collins, had been a successful animal trainer in England, before emigrating to America, and in America he had continued the success and laid the foundation of the big animal training school at Cedarwild, which his son had developed and built up after him. So well had Harris Collins built on his father's foundation that the place was considered a model of sanitation and kindness. It entertained many visitors, who invariably went away with their souls filled with ecstasy over the atmosphere of sweetness and light that pervaded the place. Never, however, were they permitted to see the actual training. On occasion, performances were given them by the finished products which verified all their other delightful and charming conclusions about the school. But had they seen the training of raw novices, it would have been a different story. It might even have been a riot. As it was, the place was a zoo, and free at that; for, in addition to the animals he owned and trained and bought and sold, a large portion of the business was devoted to boarding trained animals and troupes of animals for owners who were out of engagements, or for estates of such owners which were in process of settlement. From mice and rats to camels and elephants, and even, on occasion, to a rhinoceros or a pair of hippopotamuses, he could supply any animal on demand.

When the Circling Brothers' big three-ring show on a hard winter went into the hands of the receivers, he boarded the menagerie and the horses and in three months turned a profit of fifteen thousand dollars. More, he mortgaged all he possessed against the day of the auction, bought in the trained horses and ponies, the giraffe herd and the performing elephants, and, in six months more was quit of an of them, save the pony Repeater who turned air-springs, at another profit of fifteen thousand dollars. As for Repeater, he sold the pony several months later for a sheer profit of two thousand. While this bankruptcy of the Circling Brothers had been the greatest financial achievement of Harris Collin's life, nevertheless he enjoyed no mean permanent income from his plant, and, in addition, split fees with the owners of his board animals when he sent them to the winter Hippodrome shows, and, more often than not, failed to split any fee at all when he rented the animals to moving-picture companies.

Animal men, the country over, acknowledged him to be, not only the richest in the business, but the king of trainers and the grittiest man who ever went into a cage. And those who from the inside had seen him work were agreed that he had no soul. Yet his wife and children, and those in his small social circle, thought otherwise. They, never seeing him at work, were convinced that no softer-hearted, more sentimental man had ever been born. His voice was low and gentle, his gestures were delicate, his views on life, the world, religion and politics, the mildest. A kind word melted him. A plea won him. He gave to all local charities, and was gravely depressed for a week when the Titanic went down. And yet, the men in the trained-animal game acknowledged him the nerviest and most nerveless of the profession. And yet, his greatest fear in the world was that his large, stout wife, at table, should crown him with a plate of hot soup. Twice, in a tantrum, she had done this during their earlier married life. In addition to his fear that she might do it again, he loved her sincerely and devotedly, as he loved his children, seven of them, for whom nothing was too good or too expensive.

So well did he love them, that the four boys from the beginning he forbade from seeing him work, and planned gentler careers for them. John, the oldest, in Yale, had elected to become a man of letters, and, in the meantime, ran his own automobile with the corresponding standard of living such ownership connoted in the college town of New Haven. Harold and Frederick were down at a millionaires' sons' academy in Pennsylvania; and Clarence, the youngest, at a prep. school in Massachusetts, was divided in his choice of career between becoming a doctor or an aviator. The three girls, two of them twins, were pledged to be cultured into ladies. Elsie was on the verge of graduating from Vassar. Mary and Madeline, the twins, in the most select and most expensive of seminaries, were preparing for Vassar. All of which required money which Harris Collins did not grudge, but which strained the earning capacity of his animal-training school. It compelled him to work the harder, although his wife and the four sons and three daughters did not dream that he actually worked at all. Their idea was that by virtue of superior wisdom he merely superintended, and they would have been terribly shocked could they have seen him, club in hand, thrashing forty mongrel dogs, in the process of training, which had become excited and out of hand.

A great deal of the work was done by his assistants, but it was Harris Collins who taught them continually what to do and how to do it, and who himself, on more important animals, did the work and showed them how. His assistants were almost invariably youths from the reform schools, and he picked them with skilful eye and intuition. Control of them, under their paroles, with intelligence and coldness on their part, were the conditions and qualities he sought, and such combination, as a matter of course, carried with it cruelty. Hot blood, generous impulses, sentimentality, were qualities he did not want for his business; and the Cedarwild Animal School was business from the first tick of the clock to the last bite of the lash. In short, Harris Collins, in the totality of results, was guilty of causing more misery and pain to animals than all laboratories of vivisection in Christendom.

And into this animal hell Michael descended, although his arrival was horizontal, across three thousand five hundred miles, in the same crate in which he had been placed at the New Washington Hotel in Seattle. Never once had he been out of the crate during the entire journey, and filthiness, as well as wretchedness, characterized his condition. Thanks to his general good health, the wound of the amputated toe was in the process of uneventful healing. But dirt clung to him, and he was infested with fleas.

Cedarwild, to look at, was anything save a hell. Velvet lawns, gravelled walks and drives, and flowers formally growing, led up to the group of long low buildings, some of frame and some of concrete. But Michael was not received by Harris Collins, who, at the moment, sat in his private office, Harry Del Mar's last telegram on his desk, writing a memorandum to his secretary to query the railroad and the express companies for the whereabouts of a dog, crated and shipped by one, Harry Del Mar, from Seattle and consigned to Cedarwild. It was a pallid-eyed youth of eighteen in overalls who received Michael, receipted for him to the expressman, and carried his crate into a slope-floored concrete room that smelled offensively and chemically clean.

Michael was impressed by his surroundings but not attracted by the youth, who rolled up his sleeves and encased himself in large oilskin apron before he opened the crate. Michael sprang out and staggered about on legs which had not walked for days. This particular two-legged god was uninteresting. He was as cold as the concrete floor, as methodical as a machine; and in such fashion he went about the washing, scrubbing, and disinfecting of Michael. For Harris Collins was scientific and antiseptic to the last word in his handling of animals, and Michael was scientifically made clean, without deliberate harshness, but without any slightest hint of gentleness or consideration.

Naturally, he did not understand. On top of all he had already experienced, not even knowing executioners and execution chambers, for all he knew this bare room of cement and chemical smell might well be the place of the ultimate life-disaster and this youth the god who was to send him into the dark which had engulfed all he had known and loved. What Michael did know beyond the shadow of any doubt was that it was all coldly ominous and terribly strange. He endured the hand of the youth- god on the scruff of his neck, after the collar had been unbuckled; but when the hose was turned on him, he resented and resisted. The youth, merely working by formula, tightened the safe grip on the scruff of Michael's neck and lifted him clear of the floor, at the same time, with the other hand, directing the stream of water into his mouth and increasing it to full force by the nozzle control. Michael fought, and was well drowned for his pains, until he gasped and strangled helplessly.

After that he resisted no more, and was washed out and scrubbed out and cleansed out with the hose, a big bristly brush, and much carbolic soap, the lather of which got into and stung his eyes and nose, causing him to weep copiously and sneeze violently. Apprehensive of what might at any moment happen to him, but by this time aware that the youth was neither positive nor negative for kindness or harm, Michael continued to endure without further battling, until, clean and comfortable, he was put away into a pen, sweet and wholesome, where he slept and for the time being forgot. The place was the hospital, or segregation ward, and a week of imprisonment was spent therein, in which nothing happened in the way of development of germ diseases, and nothing happened to him except regular good food, pure drinking-water, and absolute isolation from contact with all life save the youth-god who, like an automaton, attended on him.

Michael had yet to meet Harris Collins, although, from a distance, often he heard his voice, not loud, but very imperative. That the owner of this voice was a high god, Michael knew from the first sound of it. Only a high god, a master over ordinary gods, could be so imperative. Will was in that voice, and accustomedness to command. Any dog would have so decided as quickly as Michael did. And any dog would have decided that there was no love nor lovableness in the god behind the voice, nothing to warm one's heart nor to adore.

CHAPTER XXV

It was at eleven in the morning that the pale youth-god put collar and chain on Michael, led him out of the segregation ward, and turned him over to a dark youth-god who wasted no time of greeting on him and manifested no friendliness. A captive at the end of a chain, on the way Michael quickly encountered other captives going in his direction. There were three of them, and never had he seen the like. Three slouching, ambling monsters of bears they were, and at sight of them Michael bristled and uttered the lowest of growls; for he knew them, out of his heredity (as a domestic cow knows her first wolf), as immemorial enemies from the wild. But he had travelled too far, seen too much, and was altogether too sensible, to attack them. Instead, walking stiff-legged and circumspectly, but smelling with all his nose the strange scent of the creatures, he followed at the end of his chain his own captor god.

Continually a multitude of strange scents invaded his nostrils. Although he could not see through walls, he got the smells he was later to identify of lions, leopards, monkeys, baboons, and seals and sea-lions. All of which might have stunned an ordinary dog; but the effect on him was to make him very alert and at the same time very subdued. It was as if he walked in a new and monstrously populous jungle and was unacquainted with its ways and denizens.

As he was entering the arena, he shied off to the side more stiff-leggedly than ever, bristled all along his neck and back, and growled deep and low in his throat. For, emerging from the arena, came five elephants. Small elephants they were, but to him they were the hugest of monsters, in his mind comparable only with the cow-whale of which he had caught fleeting glimpses when she destroyed the schooner Mary Turner. But the elephants took no notice of him, each with its trunk clutching the tail of the one in front of it as it had been taught to do in making an exit.

Into the arena, he came, the bears following on his heels. It was a sawdust circle the size of a circus ring, contained inside a square building that was roofed over with glass. But there were no seats about the ring, since spectators were not tolerated. Only Harris Collins and his assistants, and buyers and sellers of animals and men in the profession, were ever permitted to behold how animals were tormented into the performance of tricks to make the public open its mouth in astonishment or laughter.

Michael forgot about the bears, who were quickly at work on the other side of the circle from that to which he was taken. Some men, rolling out stout bright-painted barrels which elephants could not crush by sitting on, attracted his attention for a moment. Next, in a pause on the part of the man who led him, he regarded with huge interest a piebald Shetland pony. It lay on the ground. A man sat on it. And ever and anon it lifted its head from the sawdust and kissed the man. This was all Michael saw, yet he sensed something wrong about it. He knew not why, had no evidence why, but he felt cruelty and power and unfairness. What he did not see was the long pin in the man's hand. Each time he thrust this in the pony's shoulder, the pony, stung by the pain and reflex action, lifted its head, and the man was deftly ready to meet the pony's mouth with his own mouth. To an audience the impression would be that in such fashion the pony was expressing its affection for the master.

Not a dozen feet away another Shetland, a coal-black one, was behaving as peculiarly as it was being treated. Ropes were attached to its forelegs, each rope held by an assistant, who jerked on the same stoutly when a third man, standing in front of the pony, tapped it on the knees with a short, stiff whip of rattan. Whereupon the pony went down on its knees in the sawdust in a genuflection to the man with the whip. The pony did not like it, sometimes so successfully resisting with spread, taut legs and mutinous head-tossings, as to overcome the jerk of the ropes, and, at the same time wheeling, to fall heavily on its side or to uprear as the pull on the ropes was relaxed. But always it was lined up again to face the man who rapped its knees with the rattan. It was being taught merely how to kneel in the way that is ever a delight to the audiences who see only the results of the schooling and never dream of the manner of the schooling. For, as Michael was quickly sensing, knowledge was here learned by pain. In short, this was the college of pain, this Cedarwild Animal School.

Harris Collins himself nodded the dark youth-god up to him, and turned an inquiring and estimating gaze on Michael.

"The Del Mar dog, sir," said the youth-god.

Collins's eyes brightened, and he looked Michael over more carefully.

"Do you know what he can do?" he queried.

The youth shook his head.

"Harry was a keen one," Collins went on, apparently to the youth-god but mostly for his own benefit, being given to thinking aloud. "He picked this dog as a winner. And now what can he do? That's the question. Poor Harry's gone, and we don't know what he can do. Take off the chain."

Released Michael regarded the master-god and waited for what might happen. A squall of pain from one of the bears across the ring hinted to him what he might expect.

"Come here," Collins commanded in his cold, hard tones.

Michael came and stood before him.

"Lie down!"

Michael lay down, although he did it slowly, with advertised reluctance.

"Damned thoroughbred!" Collins sneered at him. "Won't put any pep into your motions, eh? Well, we'll take care of that. Get up! Lie down! Get up! Lie down! Get up!"

His commands were staccato, like revolver shots or the cracks of whips, and Michael obeyed them in his same slow, reluctant way.

"Understands English, at any rate," said Collins.

"Wonder if he can turn the double flip," he added, expressing the golden dream of all dog-trainers. "Come on, we'll try him for a flip. Put the chain on him. Come over here, Jimmy. Put another lead on him."

Another reform-school graduate youth obeyed, snapping a girth about Michael's loins, to which was attached a thin rope.

"Line him up," Collins commanded. "Ready? Go!"

And the most amazing, astounding indignity was wreaked upon Michael. At the word "Go!", simultaneously, the chain on his collar jerked him up and back in the air, the rope on his hindquarters jerked that portion of him under, forward, and up, and the still short stick in Collins's hand hit him under the lower jaw. Had he had any previous experience with the manoeuvre, he would have saved himself part of the pain at least by springing and whirling backward in the air. As it was, he felt as if being torn and wrenched apart while at the same time the blow under his jaw stung him and almost dazed him. And, at the same time, whirled violently into the air, he fell on the back of his head in the sawdust.

Out of the sawdust he soared in rage, neck-hair erect, throat a-snarl, teeth bared to bite, and he would have sunk his teeth into the flesh of the master-god had he not been the slave of cunning formula. The two youths knew their work. One tightened the lead ahead, the other to the rear, and Michael snarled and bristled his impotent wrath. Nothing could he do, neither advance, nor retreat, nor whirl sideways. The youth in front by the chain prevented him from attacking the youth behind, and the youth behind, with the rope, prevented him from attacking the youth in front, and both prevented him from attacking Collins, whom he knew incontrovertibly to be the master of evil and hurt.

Michael's wrath was as superlative as was his helplessness. He could only bristle and tear his vocal chords with his rage. But it was a very ancient and boresome experience to Collins. He was even taking advantage of the moment to glance across the arena and size up what the bears were doing.

"Oh, you thoroughbred," he sneered at Michael, returning his attention to him. "Slack him! Let go!"

The instant his bonds were released, Michael soared at Collins, and Collins, timing and distancing with the accuracy of long years, kicked him under the jaw and whirled him back and down into the sawdust.

"Hold him!" Collins ordered. "Line him out!"

And the two youths, pulling in opposite directions with chain and rope, stretched him into helplessness.

Collins glanced across the ring to the entrance, where two teams of heavy draft-horses were entering, followed by a woman dressed to over-dressedness in the last word of a stylish street-costume.

"I fancy he's never done any flipping," Collins remarked, coming back to the problem of Michael for a moment. "Take off your lead, Jimmy, and go over and help Smith. Johnny, hold him to one side there and mind your legs. Here comes Miss Marie for her first lesson, and that mutt of a husband of hers can't handle her."

Michael did not understand the scene that followed, which he witnessed, for the youth led him over to look on at the arranging of the woman and the four horses. Yet, from her conduct, he sensed that she, too, was captive and ill-treated. In truth, she was herself being trained unwillingly to do a trick. She had carried herself bravely right to the moment of the ordeal, but the sight of the four horses, ranged two and two opposing her, with the thing patent that she was to hold in her hands the hooks on the double-trees and form the link that connected the two spans which were to pull in opposite directions, at the sight of this her courage failed her and she shrank back, drooping and cowering, her face buried in her hands.

"No, no, Billikens," she pleaded to the stout though youthful man who was her husband. "I can't do it. I'm afraid. I'm afraid."

"Nonsense, madam," Collins interposed. "The trick is absolutely safe. And it's a good one, a money-maker. Straighten up a moment." With his hands he began feeling out her shoulders and back under her jacket. "The apparatus is all right." He ran his hands down her arms. "Now! Drop the hooks." He shook each arm, and from under each of the fluffy lace cuffs fell out an iron hook fast to a thin cable of steel that evidently ran up her sleeves. "Not that way! Nobody must see. Put them back. Try it again. They must come down hidden in your palms. Like this. See. That's it. That's the idea."

She controlled herself and strove to obey, though ever and anon she cast appealing glances to Billikens, who stood remote and aloof, his brows wrinkled with displeasure.

Each of the men driving the harnessed spans lifted up the double-trees so that the girl could grasp the hooks. She tried to take hold, but broke down again.

"If anything breaks, my arms will be torn out of me," she protested.

"On the contrary," Collins reassured her. "You will lose merely most of your jacket. The worst that can happen will be the exposure of the trick and the laugh on you. But the apparatus isn't going to break. Let me explain again. The horses do not pull against you. They pull against each other. The audience thinks that they are pulling against you. Now try once more. Take hold the double-trees, and at the same moment slip down the hooks and connect. Now!"

He spoke sharply. She shook the hooks down out of her sleeves, but drew back from grasping the double-trees. Collins did not betray his vexation. Instead, he glanced aside to where the kissing pony and the kneeling pony were leaving the ring. But the husband raged at her:

"By God, Julia, if you throw me down this way!"

"Oh, I'll try, Billikens," she whimpered. "Honestly, I'll try. See! I'm not afraid now."

She extended her hands and clasped the double-trees. With a thin writhe of a smile, Collins investigated the insides of her clenched hands to make sure that the hooks were connected.

"Now brace yourself! Spread your legs. And straighten out." With his hands he manipulated her arms and shoulders into position. "Remember, you've got to meet the first of the strain with your arms straight out. After the strain is on, you couldn't bend 'em if you wanted to. But if the strain catches them bent, the wire'll rip the hide off of you. Remember, straight out, extended, so that they form a straight line with each other and with the flat of your back and shoulders. That's it. Ready now."

"Oh, wait a minute," she begged, forsaking the position. "I'll do it, oh, I will do it, but, Billikens, kiss me first, and then I won't care if my arms are pulled out."

The dark youth who held Michael, and others looking on, grinned. Collins dissembled whatever grin might have troubled for expression, and murmured:

"All the time in the world, madam. The point is, the first time must come off right. After that you'll have the confidence. Bill, you'd better love her up before she tackles it."

And Billikens, very angry, very disgusted, very embarrassed, obeyed, putting his arms around his wife and kissing her neither too perfunctorily nor very long. She was a pretty young thing of a woman, perhaps twenty years old, with an exceedingly childish, girlish face and a slender-waisted, generously moulded body of fully a hundred and forty pounds.

The embrace and kiss of her husband put courage into her. She stiffened and steeled herself, and with compressed lips, as he stepped clear of her, muttered, "Ready."

"Go!" Collins commanded.

The four horses, under the urge of the drivers, pressed lazily into their collars and began pulling.

"Give 'em the whip!" Collins barked, his eyes on the girl and noting that the pull of the apparatus was straight across her.

The lashes fell on the horses' rumps, and they leaped, and surged, and plunged, with their huge steel-shod hoofs, the size of soup-plates, tearing up the sawdust into smoke.

And Billikens forgot himself. The terribleness of the sight painted the honest anxiety for the woman on his face. And her face was a kaleidoscope. At the first, tense and fearful, it was like that of a Christian martyr meeting the lions, or of a felon falling through the trap. Next, and quickly, came surprise and relief in that there was no hurt. And, finally, her face was proudly happy with a smile of triumph. She even smiled to Billikens her pride at making good her love to him. And Billikens relaxed and looked love and pride back, until, on the spur of the second, Harris Collins broke in:

"This ain't a smiling act! Get that smile off your face. The audience has got to think you're carrying the pull. Show that you are. Make your face stiff till it cracks. Show determination, will-power. Show great muscular effort. Spread your legs more. Bring up the muscles through your skirt just as if you was really working. Let 'em pull you this way a bit and that way a bit. Give 'em to. Spread your legs more. Make a noise on your face as if you was being pulled to pieces an' that all that holds you is will-power. That's the idea! That's the stuff! It's a winner, Bill! It's a winner! Throw the leather into 'em! Make 'm jump! Make 'm get right down and pull the daylights out of each other!"

The whips fell on the horses, and the horses struggled in all their hugeness and might to pull away from the pain of the punishment. It was a spectacle to win approval from any audience. Each horse averaged eighteen hundredweight; thus, to the eye of the onlooker, seven thousand two hundred pounds of straining horse-flesh seemed wrenching and dragging apart the slim-waisted, delicately bodied, hundred-and-forty pound woman in her fancy street costume. It was a sight to make women in circus audiences scream with terror and turn their faces away.

"Slack down!" Collins commanded the drivers.

"The lady wins," he announced, after the manner of a ringmaster. "Bill, you've got a mint in that turn. Unhook, madam, unhook!"

Marie obeyed, and, the hooks still dangling from her sleeves, made a short run to Billikens, into whose arms she threw herself, her own arms folding him about the neck as she exclaimed before she kissed him:

"Oh, Billikens, I knew I could do it all the time! I was brave, wasn't I!"

"A give-away," Collins's dry voice broke in on her ecstasy. "Letting all the audience see the hooks. They must go up your sleeves the moment you let go. Try it again. And another thing. When you finish the turn, no chestiness. No making out how easy it was. Make out it was the very devil. Show yourself weak, just about to collapse from the strain. Give at the knees. Make your shoulders cave in. The ringmaster will half step forward to catch you before you faint. That's your cue. Beat him to it. Stiffen up and straighten up with an effort of will-power, will- power's the idea, gameness, and all that, and kiss your hands to the audience and make a weak, pitiful sort of a smile, as though your heart's been pulled 'most out of you and you'll have to go to the hospital, but for right then that you're game an' smiling and kissing your hands to the audience that's riping the seats up and loving you. Get me, madam? You, Bill, get the idea! And see she does it. Now, ready! Be a bit wistful as you look at the horses. That's it! Nobody'd guess you'd palmed the hooks and connected them. Straight out! Let her go!"

And again the thirty-six-hundredweight of horses on either side pitted its strength against the similar weight on the other side, and the seeming was that Marie was the link of woman-flesh being torn asunder.

A third and a fourth time the turn was rehearsed, and, between turns, Collins sent a man to his office, for the Del Mar telegram.

"You take her now, Bill," he told Marie's husband, as, telegram in hand, he returned to the problem of Michael. "Give her half a dozen tries more. And don't forget, any time any jay farmer thinks he's got a span that can pull, bet him on the side your best span can beat him. That means advance advertising and some paper. It'll be worth it. The ringmaster'll favour you, and your span can get the first jump. If I was young and footloose, I'd ask nothing better than to go out with your turn."

Harris Collins, in the pauses gazing down at Michael, read Del Mar's Seattle telegram:

"Sell my dogs. You know what they can do and what they are worth. Am   done with them. Deduct the board and hold the balance until I see   you. I have the limit of a dog. Every turn I ever pulled is put in   the shade by this one. He's a ten strike. Wait till you see him."

Over to one side in the busy arena, Collins contemplated Michael.

"Del Mar was the limit himself," he told Johnny, who held Michael by the chain. "When he wired me to sell his dogs it meant he had a better turn, and here's only one dog to show for it, a damned thoroughbred at that. He says it's the limit. It must be, but in heaven's name, what is its turn? It's never done a flip in its life, much less a double flip. What do you think, Johnny? Use your head. Suggest something."

"Maybe it can count," Johnny advanced.

"And counting-dogs are a drug on the market. Well, anyway, let's try."

And Michael, who knew unerringly how to count, refused to perform.

"If he was a regular dog, he could walk anyway," was Collins' next idea. "We'll try him."

And Michael went through the humiliating ordeal of being jerked erect on his hind legs by Johnny while Collins with the stick cracked him under the jaw and across the knees. In his wrath, Michael tried to bite the master-god, and was jerked away by the chain. When he strove to retaliate on Johnny, that imperturbable youth, with extended arm, merely lifted him into the air on his chain and strangled him.

"That's off," quoth Collins wearily. "If he can't stand on his hind legs he can't barrel-jump, you've heard about Ruth, Johnny. She was a winner. Jump in and out of nail-kegs, on her hind legs, without ever touching with her front ones. She used to do eight kegs, in one and out into the next. Remember when she was boarded here and rehearsed. She was a gold- mine, but Carson didn't know how to treat her, and she croaked off with penumonia at Cripple Creek."

"Wonder if he can spin plates on his nose," Johnny volunteered.

"Can't stand up on hind legs," Collins negatived. "Besides, nothing like the limit in a turn like that. This dog's got a specially. He ain't ordinary. He does some unusual thing unusually well, and it's up to us to locate it. That comes of Harry dying so inconsiderately and leaving this puzzle-box on my hands. I see I just got to devote myself to him. Take him away, Johnny. Number Eighteen for him. Later on we can put him in the single compartments."

CHAPTER XXVI

Number Eighteen was a big compartment or cage in the dog row, large enough with due comfort for a dozen Irish terriers like Michael. For Harris Collins was scientific. Dogs on vacation, boarding at the Cedarwild Animal School, were given every opportunity to recuperate from the hardships and wear and tear of from six months to a year and more on the road. It was for this reason that the school was so popular a boarding-place for performing animals when the owners were on vacation or out of "time." Harris Collins kept his animals clean and comfortable and guarded from germ diseases. In short, he renovated them against their next trips out on vaudeville time or circus engagement.

To the left of Michael, in Number Seventeen, were five grotesquely clipped French poodles. Michael could not see them, save when he was being taken out or brought back, but he could smell them and hear them, and, in his loneliness, he even started a feud of snarling bickeringness with Pedro, the biggest of them who acted as clown in their turn. They were aristocrats among performing animals, and Michael's feud with Pedro was not so much real as play-acted. Had he and Pedro been brought together they would have made friends in no time. But through the slow monotonous drag of the hours they developed a fictitious excitement and interest in mouthing their quarrel which each knew in his heart of hearts was no quarrel at all.

In Number Nineteen, on Michael's right, was a sad and tragic company. They were mongrels, kept spotlessly and germicidally clean, who were unattached and untrained. They composed a sort of reserve of raw material, to be worked into established troupes when an extra one or a substitute was needed. This meant the hell of the arena where the training went on. Also, in spare moments, Collins, or his assistants, were for ever trying them out with all manner of tricks in the quest of special aptitudes on their parts. Thus, a mongrel semblance to a cooker spaniel of a dog was tried out for several days as a pony-rider who would leap through paper hoops from the pony's back, and return upon the back again. After several falls and painful injuries, it was rejected for the feat and tried out as a plate-balancer. Failing in this, it was made into a see-saw dog who, for the rest of the turn, filled into the background of a troupe of twenty dogs.

Number Nineteen was a place of perpetual quarrelling and pain. Dogs, hurt in the training, licked their wounds, and moaned, or howled, or were irritable to excess on the slightest provocation. Always, when a new dog entered, and this was a regular happening, for others were continually being taken away to hit the road, the cage was vexed with quarrels and battles, until the new dog, by fighting or by non resistance, had commanded or been taught its proper place.

Michael ignored the denizens of Number Nineteen. They could sniff and snarl belligerently across at him, but he took no notice, reserving his companionship for the play-acted and perennial quarrel with Pedro. Also, Michael was out in the arena more often and far longer hours than any of them.

"Trust Harry not to make a mistake on a dog," was Collins's judgment; and constantly he strove to find in Michael what had made Del Mar declare him a ten strike and the limit.

Every indignity, in the attempt to find out, was wreaked upon Michael. They tried him at hurdle-jumping, at walking on forelegs, at pony-riding, at forward flips, and at clowning with other dogs. They tried him at waltzing, all his legs cord-fastened and dragged and jerked and slacked under him. They spiked his collar in some of the attempted tricks to keep him from lurching from side to side or from falling forward or backward. They used the whip and the rattan stick; and twisted his nose.

They attempted to make a goal-keeper of him in a football game between two teams of pain-driven and pain-bitten mongrels. And they dragged him up ladders to make him dive into a tank of water.

Even they essayed to make him "loop the loop", rushing him down an inclined trough at so high speed of his legs, accelerated by the slash of whips on his hindquarters, that, with such initial momentum, had he put his heart and will into it, he could have successfully run up the inside of the loop, and across the inside of the top of it, back-downward, like a fly on the ceiling, and on and down and around and out of the loop. But he refused the will and the heart, and every time, when he was unable at the beginning to leap sideways out of the inclined trough, he fell grievously from the inside of the loop, bruising and injuring himself.

"It isn't that I expect these things are what Harry had in mind," Collins would say, for always he was training his assistants; "but that through them I may get a cue to his specially, whatever in God's name it is, that poor Harry must have known."

Out of love, at the wish of his love-god, Steward, Michael would have striven to learn these tricks and in most of them would have succeeded. But here at Cedarwild was no love, and his own thoroughbred nature made him stubbornly refuse to do under compulsion what he would gladly have done out of love. As a result, since Collins was no thoroughbred of a man, the clashes between them were for a time frequent and savage. In this fighting Michael quickly learned he had no chance. He was always doomed to defeat. He was beaten by stereotyped formula before he began. Never once could he get his teeth into Collins or Johnny. He was too common-sensed to keep up the battling in which he would surely have broken his heart and his body and gone dumb mad. Instead, he retired into himself, became sullen, undemonstrative, and, though he never cowered in defeat, and though he was always ready to snarl and bristle his hair in advertisement that inside he was himself and unconquered, he no longer burst out in furious anger.

After a time, scarcely ever trying him out on a new trick, the chain and Johnny were dispensed with, and with Collins he spent all Collins's hours in the arena. He learned, by bitter lessons, that he must follow Collins around; and follow him he did, hating him perpetually and in his own body slowly and subtly poisoning himself by the juices of his glands that did not secrete and flow in quite their normal way because of the pressure put upon them by his hatred.

The effect of this, on his body, was not perceptible. This was because of his splendid constitution and health. Wherefore, since the effect must be produced somewhere, it was his mind, or spirit, or nature, or brain, or processes of consciousness, that received it. He drew more and more within himself, became morose, and brooded much. All of which was spiritually unhealthful. He, who had been so merry-hearted, even merrier-hearted than his brother Jerry, began to grow saturnine, and peevish, and ill-tempered. He no longer experienced impulses to play, to romp around, to run about. His body became as quiet and controlled as his brain. Human convicts, in prisons, attain this quietude. He could stand by the hour, to heel to Collins, uninterested, infinitely bored, while Collins tortured some mongrel creature into the performance of a trick.

And much of this torturing Michael witnessed. There were the greyhounds, the high-jumpers and wide-leapers. They were willing to do their best, but Collins and his assistants achieved the miracle, if miracle it may be called, of making them do better than their best. Their best was natural. Their better than best was unnatural, and it killed some and shortened the lives of all. Rushed to the springboard and the leap, always, after the take-off, in mid-air, they had to encounter an assistant who stood underneath, an extraordinarily long buggy-whip in hand, and lashed them vigorously. This made them leap from the springboard beyond their normal powers, hurting and straining and injuring them in their desperate attempt to escape the whip-lash, to beat the whip-lash in the air and be past ere it could catch their flying flanks and sting them like a scorpion.

"Never will a jumping dog jump his hardest," Collins told his assistants, "unless he's made to. That's your job. That's the difference between the jumpers I turn out and some of these dub amateur-jumping outfits that fail to make good even on the bush circuits."

Collins continually taught. A graduate from his school, an assistant who received from him a letter of recommendation, carried a high credential of a sheepskin into the trained-animal world.

"No dog walks naturally on its hind legs, much less on its forelegs," Collins would say. "Dogs ain't built that way. They have to be made to, that's all. That's the secret of all animal training. They have to. You've got to make them. That's your job. Make them. Anybody who can't, can't make good in this factory. Put that in your pipe and smoke it, and get busy."

Michael saw, without fully appreciating, the use of the spiked saddle on the bucking mule. The mule was fat and good-natured the first day of its appearance in the arena. It had been a pet mule in a family of children until Collins's keen eyes rested on it; and it had known only love and kindness and much laughter for its foolish mulishness. But Collins's eyes had read health, vigour, and long life, as well as laughableness of appearance and action in the long-eared hybrid.

Barney Barnato he was renamed that first day in the arena, when, also, he received the surprise of his life. He did not dream of the spike in the saddle, nor, while the saddle was empty, did it press against him. But the moment Samuel Bacon, a negro tumbler, got into the saddle, the spike sank home. He knew about it and was prepared. But Barney, taken by surprise, arched his back in the first buck he had ever made. It was so prodigious a buck that Collins eyes snapped with satisfaction, while Sam landed a dozen feet away in the sawdust.

"Make good like that," Collins approved, "and when I sell the mule you'll go along as part of the turn, or I miss my guess. And it will be some turn. There'll be at least two more like you, who'll have to be nervy and know how to fall. Get busy. Try him again."

And Barney entered into the hell of education that later won his purchaser more time than he could deliver over the best vaudeville circuits in Canada and the United States. Day after day Barney took his torture. Not for long did he carry the spiked saddle. Instead, bare- back, he received the negro on his back, and was spiked and set bucking just the same; for the spike was now attached to Sam's palm by means of leather straps. In the end, Barney became so "touchy" about his back that he almost began bucking if a person as much as looked at it. Certainly, aware of the stab of pain, he started bucking, whirling, and kicking whenever the first signal was given of some one trying to mount him.

At the end of the fourth week, two other tumblers, white youths, being secured, the complete, builded turn was performed for the benefit of a slender, French-looking gentleman, with waxed moustaches. In the end he bought Barney, without haggling, at Collins's own terms and engaged Sammy and the other two tumblers as well. Collins staged the trick properly, as it would be staged in the theatre, even had ready and set up all the necessary apparatus, and himself acted as ringmaster while the prospective purchaser looked on.

Barney, fat as butter, humorous-looking, was led into the square of cloth- covered steel cables and cloth-covered steel uprights. The halter was removed and he was turned loose. Immediately he became restless, the ears were laid back, and he was a picture of viciousness.

"Remember one thing," Collins told the man who might buy. "If you buy him, you'll be ringmaster, and you must never, never spike him. When he comes to know that, you can always put your hands on him any time and control him. He's good-natured at heart, and he's the gratefullest mule I've ever seen in the business. He's just got to love you, and hate the other three. And one warning: if he goes real bad and starts biting, you'll have to pull out his teeth and feed him soft mashes and crushed grain that's steamed. I'll give you the recipe for the digestive dope you'll have to put in. Now, watch!"

Collins stopped into the ring and caressed Barney, who responded in the best of tempers and tried affectionately to nudge and shove past on the way out of the ropes to escape what he knew was coming.

"See," Collins exposited. "He's got confidence in me. He trusts me. He knows I've never spiked him and that I always save him in the end. I'm his good Samaritan, and you'll have to be the same to him if you buy him. Now I'll give you your spiel. Of course, you can improve on it to suit yourself."

The master-trainer walked out of the rope square, stepped forward to an imaginary line, and looked down and out and up as if he were gazing at the pit of the orchestra beneath him, across at the body of the house, and up into the galleries.

"Ladies and gentlemen," he addressed the sawdust emptiness before him as if it were a packed audience, "this is Barney Barnato, the biggest joker of a mule ever born. He's as affectionate as a Newfoundland puppy, just watch -"

Stepping back to the ropes, Collins extended his hand across them, saying: "Come here, Barney, and show all these people who you love best."

And Barney twinkled forward on his small hoofs, nozzled the open hand, and came closer, nozzling up the arm, nudging Collins's shoulders with his nose, half-rearing as if to get across the ropes and embrace him. What he was really doing was begging and entreating Collins to take him away out of the squared ring from the torment he knew awaited him.

"That's what it means by never spiking him," Collins shot at the man with the waxed moustaches, as he stepped forward to the imaginary line in the sawdust, above the imaginary pit of the orchestra, and addressed the imaginary house.

"Ladies and gentlemen, Barney Barnato is a josher. He's got forty tricks up each of his four legs, and the man don't live that he'll let stick on big back for sixty seconds. I'm telling you this in fair warning, before I make my proposition. Looks easy, doesn't it? one minute, the sixtieth part of an hour, to be precise, sixty seconds, to stick on the back of an affectionate josher mule like Barney. Well, come on you boys and broncho riders. To anybody who sticks on for one minute I shall immediately pay the sum of fifty dollars; for two whole, entire minutes, the sum of five hundred dollars."

This was the cue for Samuel Bacon, who advanced across the sawdust, awkward and grinning and embarrassed, and apparently was helped up to the stage by the extended hand of Collins.

"Is your life insured?" Collins demanded.

Sam shook his head and grinned.

"Then what are you tackling this for?"

"For the money," said Sam. "I jes' naturally needs it in my business."

"What is your business?"

"None of your business, mister." Here Sam grinned ingratiating apology for his impertinence and shuffled on his legs. "I might be investin' in lottery tickets, only I ain't. Do I get the money? that's our business."

"Sure you do," Collins replied. "When you earn it. Stand over there to one side and wait a moment. Ladies and gentlemen, if you will forgive the delay, I must ask for more volunteers. Any more takers? Fifty dollars for sixty seconds. Almost a dollar a second . . . if you win. Better! I'll make it a dollar a second. Sixty dollars to the boy, man, woman, or girl who sticks on Barney's back for one minute. Come on, ladies. Remember this is the day of equal suffrage. Here's where you put it over on your husbands, brothers, sons, fathers, and grandfathers. Age is no limit. Grandma, do I get you?" he uttered directly to what must have been a very elderly lady in a near front row. "You see," (to the prospective buyer), "I've got the entire patter for you. You could do it with two rehearsals, and you can do them right here, free of charge, part of the purchase."

The next two tumblers crossed the sawdust and were helped by Collins up to the imaginary stage.

"You can change the patter according to the cities you're in," he explained to the Frenchman. "It's easy to find out the names of the most despised and toughest neighbourhoods or villages, and have the boys hail from them."

Continuing the patter, Collins put the performance on. Sam's first attempt was brief. He was not half on when he was flung to the ground. Half a dozen attempts, quickly repeated, were scarcely better, the last one permitting him to remain on Barney's back nearly ten seconds, and culminating in a ludicrous fall over Barney's head. Sam withdrew from the ring, shaking his head dubiously and holding his side as if in pain. The other lads followed. Expert tumblers, they executed most amazing and side-splitting fails. Sam recovered and came back. Toward the last, all three made a combined attack on Barney, striving to mount him simultaneously from different slants of approach. They were scattered and flung like chaff, sometimes falling heaped together. Once, the two white boys, standing apart as if recovering breath, were mowed down by Sam's flying body.

"Remember, this is a real mule," Collins told the man with the waxed moustaches. "If any outsiders butt in for a hack at the money, all the better. They'll get theirs quick. The man don't live who can stay on his back a minute . . . if you keep him rehearsed with the spike. He must live in fear of the spike. Never let him slow up on it. Never let him forget it. If you lay off any time for a few days, rehearse him with the spike a couple of times just before you begin again, or else he might forget it and queer the turn by ambling around with the first outside rube that mounts him.

"And just suppose some rube, all hooks of arms and legs and hands, is managing to stick on anyway, and the minute is getting near up. Just have Sam here, or any of your three, slide in and spike him from the palm. That'll be good night for Mr. Rube. You can't lose, and the audience'll laugh its fool head off.

"Now for the climax! Watch! This always brings the house down. Get busy you two! Sam! Ready!"

While the white boys threatened to mount Barney from either side and kept his attention engaged, Sam, from outside, in a sudden fit of rage and desperation, made a flying dive across the ropes and from in front locked arms and legs about Barney's neck, tucking his own head close against Barney's head. And Barney reared up on his hind legs, as he had long since learned from the many palm-spikings he had received on head and neck.

"It's a corker," Collins announced, as Barney, on his hind legs, striking vainly with his fore, struggled about the ring. "There's no danger. He'll never fall over backwards. He's a mule, and he's too wise. Besides, even if he does, all Sam has to do is let go and fall clear."

The turn over, Barney gladly accepted the halter and was led out of the square ring and up to the Frenchman.

"Long life there, look him over," Collins continued to sell. "It's a full turn, including yourself, four performers, besides the mule, and besides any suckers from the audience. It's all ready to put on the boards, and dirt cheap at five thousand."

The Frenchman winced at the sum.

"Listen to arithmetic," Collins went on. "You can sell at twelve hundred a week at least, and you can net eight hundred certain. Six weeks of the net pays for the turn, and you can book a hundred weeks right off the bat and have them yelling for more. Wish I was young and footloose. I'd take it out on the road myself and coin a fortune."

And Barney was sold, and passed out of the Cedarwild Animal School to the slavery of the spike and to be provocative of much joy and laughter in the pleasure-theatre of the world.

CHAPTER XXVII

"The thing is, Johnny, you can't love dogs into doing professional tricks, which is the difference between dogs and women," Collins told his assistant. "You know how it is with any dog. You love it up into lying down and rolling over and playing dead and all such dub tricks. And then one day you show him off to your friends, and the conditions are changed, and he gets all excited and foolish, and you can't get him to do a thing. Children are like that. Lose their heads in company, forget all their training, and throw you down."

"Now on the stage, they got real tricks to do, tricks they don't do, tricks they hate. And they mightn't be feeling good, got a touch of cold, or mange, or are sour-balled. What are you going to do? Apologize to the audience? Besides, on the stage, the programme runs like clockwork. Got to start performing on the tick of the clock, and anywhere from one to seven turns a day, all depending what kind of time you've got. The point is, your dogs have got to get right up and perform. No loving them, no begging them, no waiting on them. And there's only the one way. They've got to know when you start, you mean it."

"And dogs ain't fools," Johnny opined. "They know when you mean anything, an' when you don't."

"Sure thing," Collins nodded approbation. "The moment you slack up on them is the moment they slack up in their work. You get soft, and see how quick they begin making mistakes in their tricks.

You've got to keep the fear of God over them. If you don't, they won't, and you'll find yourself begging for spotted time on the bush circuits."

Half an hour later, Michael heard, though he understood no word of it, the master-trainer laying another law down to another assistant.

"Cross-breds and mongrels are what's needed, Charles. Not one thoroughbred in ten makes good, unless he's got the heart of a coward, and that's just what distinguishes them from mongrels and cross-breds. Like race-horses, they're hot-blooded. They've got sensitiveness, and pride. Pride's the worst. You listen to me. I was born into the business and I've studied it all my life. I'm a success. There's only one reason I'm a success, I KNOW. Get that. I KNOW."

"Another thing is that cross-breds and mongrels are cheap. You needn't be afraid of losing them or working them out. You can always get more, and cheap. And they ain't the trouble in teaching. You can throw the fear of God into them. That's what's the matter with the thoroughbreds. You can't throw the fear of God into them."

"Give a mongrel a real licking, and what's he do? He'll kiss your hand, and be obedient, and crawl on his belly to do what you want him to do. They're slave dogs, that's what mongrels are. They ain't got courage, and you don't want courage in a performing dog. You want fear. Now you give a thoroughbred a licking and see what happens. Sometimes they die. I've known them to die. And if they don't die, what do they do? Either they go stubborn, or vicious, or both. Sometimes they just go to biting and foaming. You can kill them, but you can't keep them from biting and foaming. Or they'll go straight stubborn. They're the worst. They're the passive resisters, that's what I call them. They won't fight back. You can flog them to death, but it won't buy you anything. They're like those Christians that used to be burned at the stake or boiled in oil. They've got their opinions, and nothing you can do will change them. They'll die first. . . . And they do. I've had them. I was learning myself . . . and I learned to leave the thoroughbred alone. They beat you out. They get your goat. You never get theirs. And they're time- wasters, and patience-wasters, and they're expensive."

"Take this terrier here." Collins nodded at Michael, who stood several feet back of him, morosely regarding the various activities of the arena. "He's both kinds of a thoroughbred, and therefore no good. I've never given him a real licking, and I never will. It would be a waste of time. He'll fight if you press him too hard. And he'll die fighting you. He's too sensible to fight if you don't press him too hard. And if you don't press him too hard, he'll just stay as he is, and refuse to learn anything. I'd chuck him right now, except Del Mar couldn't make a mistake. Poor Harry knew he had a specially, and a crackerjack, and it's up to me to find it."

"Wonder if he's a lion dog," Charles suggested.

"He's the kind that ain't afraid of lions," Collins concurred. "But what sort of a specially trick could he do with lions? Stick his head in their mouths? I never heard of a dog doing that, and it's an idea. But we can try him. We've tried him at 'most everything else."

"There's old Hannibal," said Charles. "He used to take a woman's head in his mouth with the old Sales-Sinker shows."

"But old Hannibal's getting cranky," Collins objected. "I've been watching him and trying to get rid of him. Any animal is liable to go off its nut any time, especially wild ones. You see, the life ain't natural. And when they do, it's good night. You lose your investment, and, if you don't know your business, maybe your life."

And Michael might well have been tried out on Hannibal and have lost his head inside that animal's huge mouth, had not the good fortune of apropos- ness intervened. For, the next moment, Collins was listening to the hasty report of his lion-and-tiger keeper. The man who reported was possibly forty years of age, although he looked half as old again. He was a withered-faced man, whose face-lines, deep and vertical, looked as if they had been clawed there by some beast other than himself.

"Old Hannibal is going crazy," was the burden of his report.

"Nonsense," said Harris Collins. "It's you that's getting old. He's got your goat, that's all. I'll show it to you. Come on along, all of you. We'll take fifteen minutes off of the work, and I'll show you a show never seen in the show-ring. It'd be worth ten thousand a week anywhere . . . only it wouldn't last. Old Hannibal would turn up his toes out of sheer hurt feelings. Come on everybody! All hands! Fifteen minutes recess!"

And Michael followed at the heels of his latest and most terrible master, the twain leading the procession of employees and visiting professional animal men who trooped along behind. As was well known, when Harris Collins performed he performed only for the elite, for the hoi-polloi of the trained-animal world.

The lion-and-tiger man, who had clawed his own face with the beast-claws of his nature, whimpered protest when he saw his employer's preparation to enter Hannibal's cage; for the preparation consisted merely in equipping himself with a broom-handle.

Hannibal was old, but he was reputed the largest lion in captivity, and he had not lost his teeth. He was pacing up and down the length of his cage, heavily and swaying, after the manner of captive animals, when the unexpected audience erupted into the space before his cage. Yet he took no notice whatever, merely continuing his pacing, swinging his head from side to side, turning lithely at each end of his cage, with all the air of being bent on some determined purpose.

"That's the way he's been goin' on for two days," whimpered his keeper. "An' when you go near 'm, he just reaches for you. Look what he done to me." The man held up his right arm, the shirt and undershirt ripped to shreds, and red parallel grooves, slightly clotted with blood, showing where the claws had broken the skin. "An' I wasn't inside. He did it through the bars, with one swipe, when I was startin' to clean his cage. Now if he'd only roar, or something. But he never makes a sound, just keeps on goin' up an' down."

"Where's the key?" Collins demanded. "Good. Now let me in. And lock it afterward and take the key out. Lose it, forget it, throw it away. I'll have all the time in the world to wait for you to find it to let me out."

And Harris Collins, a sliver of a less than a light-weight man, who lived in mortal fear that at table the mother of his children would crown him with a plate of hot soup, went into the cage, before the critical audience of his employees and professional visitors, armed only with a broom-handle. Further, the door was locked behind him, and, the moment he was in, keeping a casual but alert eye on the pacing Hannibal, he reiterated his order to lock the door and remove the key.

Half a dozen times the lion paced up and down, declining to take any notice of the intruder. And then, when his back was turned as he went down the cage, Collins stepped directly in the way of his return path and stood still. Coming back and finding his way blocked, Hannibal did not roar. His muscular movements sliding each into the next like so much silk of tawny hide, he struck at the obstacle that confronted his way. But Collins, knowing ahead of the lion what the lion was going to do, struck first, with the broom-handle rapping the beast on its tender nose. Hannibal recoiled with a flash of snarl and flashed back a second sweeping stroke of his mighty paw. Again he was anticipated, and the rap on his nose sent him into recoil.

"Got to keep his head down, that way lies safety," the master-trainer muttered in a low, tense voice.

"Ah, would you? Take it, then."

Hannibal, in wrath, crouching for a spring, had lifted his head. The consequent blow on his nose forced his head down to the floor, and the king of beasts, nose still to floor, backed away with mouth-snarls and throat-and-chest noises.

"Follow up," Collins enunciated, himself following, rapping the nose again sharply and accelerating the lion's backward retreat.

"Man is the boss because he's got the head that thinks," Collins preached the lesson; "and he's just got to make his head boss his body, that's all, so that he can think one thought ahead of the animal, and act one act ahead. Watch me get his goat. He ain't the hard case he's trying to make himself believe he is. And that idea, which he's just starting, has got to be taken out of him. The broomstick will do it. Watch."

He backed the animal down the length of the cage, continually rapping at the nose and keeping it down to the floor.

"Now I'm going to pile him into the corner."

And Hannibal, snarling, growling, and spitting, ducking his head and with short paw-strokes trying to ward off the insistent broomstick, backed obediently into the corner, crumpled up his hind-parts, and tried to withdraw his corporeal body within itself in a pain-urged effort to make it smaller. And always he kept his nose down and himself harmless for a spring. In the thick of it he slowly raised his nose and yawned. Nor, because it came up slowly, and because Collins had anticipated the yawn by being one thought ahead of Hannibal in Hannibal's own brain, was the nose rapped.

"That's the goat," Collins announced, for the first time speaking in a hearty voice in which was no vibration of strain. "When a lion yawns in the thick of a fight, you know he ain't crazy. He's sensible. He's got to be sensible, or he'd be springing or lashing out instead of yawning. He knows he's licked, and that yawn of his merely says: 'I quit. For the I love of Mike leave me alone. My nose is awful sore. I'd like to get you, but I can't. I'll do anything you want, and I'll be dreadful good, but don't hit my poor sore nose.'

"But man is the boss, and he can't afford to be so easy. Drive the lesson home that you're boss. Rub it in. Don't stop when he quits. Make him swallow the medicine and lick the spoon. Make him kiss your foot on his neck holding him down in the dirt. Make him kiss the stick that's beaten him. Watch!"

And Hannibal, the largest lion in captivity, with all his teeth, captured out of the jungle after he was full-grown, a veritable king of beasts, before the menacing broomstick in the hand of a sliver of a man, backed deeper and more crumpled together into the corner. His back was bowed up, the very opposite muscular position to that for a spring, while he drew his head more and more down and under his chest in utter abjectness, resting his weight on his elbows and shielding his poor nose with his massive paws, a single stroke of which could have ripped the life of Collins quivering from his body.

"Now he might be tricky," Collins announced, "but he's got to kiss my foot and the stick just the same. Watch!"

He lifted and advanced his left foot, not tentatively and hesitantly, but quickly and firmly, bringing it to rest on the lion's neck. The stick was poised to strike, one act ahead of the lion's next possible act, as Collins's mind was one thought ahead of the lion's next thought.

And Hannibal did the forecasted and predestined. His head flashed up, huge jaws distended, fangs gleaming, to sink into the slender, silken- hosed ankle above the tan low-cut shoes. But the fangs never sank. They were scarcely started a fifth of the way of the distance, when the waiting broomstick rapped on his nose and made him sink it in the floor under his chest and cover it again with his paws.

"He ain't crazy," said Collins. "He knows, from the little he knows, that I know more than him and that I've got him licked to a fare-you-well. If he was crazy, he wouldn't know, and I wouldn't know his mind either, and I wouldn't be that one jump ahead of him, and he'd get me and mess the whole cage up with my insides."

He prodded Hannibal with the end of the broom-handle, after each prod poising it for a stroke. And the great lion lay and roared in helplessness, and at each prod exposed his nose more and lifted it higher, until, at the end, his red tongue ran out between his fangs and licked the boot resting none too gently on his neck, and, after that, licked the broomstick that had administered all the punishment.

"Going to be a good lion now?" Collins demanded, roughly rubbing his foot back and forth on Hannibal's neck.

Hannibal could not refrain from growling his hatred.

"Going to be a good lion?" Collins repeated, rubbing his foot back and forth still more roughly.

And Hannibal exposed his nose and with his red tongue licked again the tan shoe and the slender, tan-silken ankle that he could have destroyed with one crunch.

CHAPTER XXVIII

One friend Michael made among the many animals he encountered in the Cedarwild School, and a strange, sad friendship it was. Sara she was called, a small, green monkey from South America, who seemed to have been born hysterical and indignant, and with no appreciation of humour. Sometimes, following Collins about the arena, Michael would meet her while she waited to be tried out on some new turn. For, unable or unwilling to try, she was for ever being tried out on turns, or, with little herself to do, as a filler-in for more important performers.

But she always caused confusion, either chattering and squealing with fright or bickering at the other animals. Whenever they attempted to make her do anything, she protested indignantly; and if they tried force, her squalls and cries excited all the animals in the arena and set the work back.

"Never mind," said Collins finally. "She'll go into the next monkey band we make up."

This was the last and most horrible fate that could befall a monkey on the stage, to be a helpless marionette, compelled by unseen sticks and wires, poked and jerked by concealed men, to move and act throughout an entire turn.

But it was before this doom was passed upon her that Michael made her acquaintance. Their first meeting, she sprang suddenly at him, a screaming, chattering little demon, threatening him with nails and teeth. And Michael, already deep-sunk in habitual moroseness merely looked at her calmly, not a ripple to his neck-hair nor a prick to his ears. The next moment, her fuss and fury quite ignored, she saw him turn his head away. This gave her pause. Had he sprung at her, or snarled, or shown any anger or resentment such as did the other dogs when so treated by her, she would have screamed and screeched and raised a hubbub of expostulation, crying for help and calling all men to witness how she was being unwarrantably attacked.

As it was, Michael's unusual behaviour seemed to fascinate her. She approached him tentatively, without further racket; and the boy who had her in charge slacked the thin chain that held her.

"Hope he breaks her back for her," was his unholy wish; for he hated Sara intensely, desiring to be with the lions or elephants rather than dancing attendance on a cantankerous female monkey there was no reasoning with.

And because Michael took no notice of her, she made up to him. It was not long before she had her hands on him, and, quickly after that, an arm around his neck and her head snuggled against his. Then began her interminable tale. Day after day, catching him at odd times in the ring, she would cling closely to him and in a low voice, running on and on, never pausing for breath, tell him, for all he knew, the story of her life. At any rate, it sounded like the story of her woes and of all the indignities which had been wreaked upon her. It was one long complaint, and some of it might have been about her health, for she sniffed and coughed a great deal and her chest seemed always to hurt her from the way she had of continually and gingerly pressing the palm of her hand to it. Sometimes, however, she would cease her complaining, and love and mother him, uttering occasional series of gentle mellow sounds that were like croonings.

Hers was the only hand of affection that was laid on him at Cedarwild, and she was ever gentle, never pinching him, never pulling his ears. By the same token, he was the only friend she had; and he came to look forward to meeting her in the course of the morning work, and this, despite that every meeting always concluded in a scene, when she fought with her keeper against being taken away. Her cries and protests would give way to whimperings and wailings, while the men about laughed at the strangeness of the love-affair between her and the Irish terrier.

But Harris Collins tolerated, even encouraged, their friendship.

"The two sour-balls get along best together," he said. "And it does them good. Gives them something to live for, and that way lies health. But some day, mark my words, she'll turn on him and give him what for, and their friendship will get a terrible smash."

And half of it he spoke with the voice of prophecy, and, though she never turned on Michael, the day in the world was written when their friendship would truly receive a terrible smash.

"Now seals are too wise," Collins explained one day, in a sort of extempore lecture to several of his apprentice trainers. "You've just got to toss fish to them when they perform. If you don't, they won't, and there's an end of it. But you can't depend on feeding dainties to dogs, for instance, though you can make a young, untrained pig perform creditably by means of a nursing bottle hidden up your sleeve."

"All you have to do is think it over. Do you think you can make those greyhounds extend themselves with the promise of a bite of meat? It's the whip that makes them extend. Look over there at Billy Green. There ain't another way to teach that dog that trick. You can't love her into doing it. You can't pay her to do it. There's only one way, and that's make her."

Billy Green, at the moment, was training a tiny, nondescript, frizzly- haired dog. Always, on the stage, he made a hit by drawing from his pocket a tiny dog that would do this particular trick. The last one had died from a wrenched back, and he was now breaking in a new one. He was catching the little mite by the hind-legs and tossing it up in the air, where, making a half-flip and descending head first, it was supposed to alight with its forefeet on his hand and there balance itself, its hind feet and body above it in the air. Again and again he stooped, caught her hind-legs and flung her up into the half-turn. Almost frozen with fear, she vainly strove to effect the trick. Time after time, and every time, she failed to make the balance. Sometimes she fell crumpled; several times she all but struck the ground: and once, she did strike, on her side and so hard as to knock the breath out of her. Her master, taking advantage of the moment to wipe the sweat from his streaming face, nudged her about with his toe till she staggered weakly to her feet.

"The dog was never born that'd learn that trick for the promise of a bit of meat," Collins went on. "Any more than was the dog ever born that'd walk on its forelegs without having its hind-legs rapped up in the air with the stick a thousand times. Yet you take that trick there. It's always a winner, especially with the women, so cunning, you know, so adorable cute, to be yanked out of its beloved master's pocket and to have such trust and confidence in him as to allow herself to be tossed around that way. Trust and confidence hell! He's put the fear of God into her, that's what."

"Just the same, to dig a dainty out of your pocket once in a while and give an animal a nibble, always makes a hit with the audience. That's about all it's good for, yet it's a good stunt. Audiences like to believe that the animals enjoy doing their tricks, and that they are treated like pampered darlings, and that they just love their masters to death. But God help all of us and our meal tickets if the audiences could see behind the scenes. Every trained-animal turn would be taken off the stage instanter, and we'd be all hunting for a job."

"Yes, and there's rough stuff no end pulled off on the stage right before the audience's eyes. The best fooler I ever saw was Lottie's. She had a bunch of trained cats. She loved them to death right before everybody, especially if a trick wasn't going good. What'd she do? She'd take that cat right up in her arms and kiss it. And when she put it down it'd perform the trick all right all right, while the audience applauded its silly head off for the kindness and humaneness she'd shown. Kiss it? Did she? I'll tell you what she did. She bit its nose."

"Eleanor Pavalo learned the trick from Lottie, and used it herself on her toy dogs. And many a dog works on the stage in a spiked collar, and a clever man can twist a dog's nose and nobody in the audience any the wiser. But it's the fear that counts. It's what the dog knows he'll get afterward when the turn's over that keeps most of them straight."

"Remember Captain Roberts and his great Danes. They weren't pure-breds, though. He must have had a dozen of them, toughest bunch of brutes I ever saw. He boarded them here twice. You couldn't go among them without a club in your hand. I had a Mexican lad laid up by them. He was a tough one, too. But they got him down and nearly ate him. The doctors took over forty stitches in him and shot him full of that Pasteur dope for hydrophobia. And he always will limp with his right leg from what the dogs did to him. I tell you, they were the limit. And yet, every time the curtain went up, Captain Roberts brought the house down with the first stunt. Those dogs just flocked all over him, loving him to death, from the looks of it. And were they loving him? They hated him. I've seen him, right here in the cage at Cedarwild, wade into them with a club and whale the stuffing impartially out of all of them. Sure, they loved him not. Just a bit of the same old aniseed was what he used. He'd soak small pieces of meat in aniseed oil and stick them in his pockets. But that stunt would only work with a bunch of giant dogs like his. It was their size that got it across. Had they been a lot of ordinary dogs it would have looked silly. And, besides, they didn't do their regular tricks for aniseed. They did it for Captain Roberts's club. He was a tough bird himself."

"He used to say that the art of training animals was the art of inspiring them with fear. One of his assistants told me a nasty one about him afterwards. They had an off month in Los Angeles, and Captain Roberts got it into his head he was going to make a dog balance a silver dollar on the neck of a champagne bottle. Now just think that over and try to see yourself loving a dog into doing it. The assistant said he wore out about as many sticks as dogs, and that he wore out half a dozen dogs. He used to get them from the public pound at two and a half apiece, and every time one died he had another ready and waiting. And he succeeded with the seventh dog. I'm telling you, it learned to balance a dollar on the neck of a bottle. And it died from the effects of the learning within a week after he put it on the stage. Abscesses in the lungs, from the stick."

"There was an Englishman came over when I was a youngster. He had ponies, monkeys, and dogs. He bit the monkey's ears, so that, on the stage, all he had to do was to make a move as if he was going to bite and they'd quit their fooling and be good. He had a big chimpanzee that was a winner. It could turn four somersaults as fast as you could count on the back of a galloping pony, and he used to have to give it a real licking about twice a week. And sometimes the lickings were too stiff, and the monkey'd get sick and have to lay off. But the owner solved the problem. He got to giving him a little licking, a mere taste of the stick, regular, just before the turn came on. And that did it in his case, though with some other case the monkey most likely would have got sullen and not acted at all."

It was on that day that Harris Collins sold a valuable bit of information to a lion man who needed it. It was off time for him, and his three lions were boarding at Cedarwild. Their turn was an exciting and even terrifying one, when viewed from the audience; for, jumping about and roaring, they were made to appear as if about to destroy the slender little lady who performed with them and seemed to hold them in subjection only by her indomitable courage and a small riding-switch in her hand.

"The trouble is they're getting too used to it," the man complained. "Isadora can't prod them up any more. They just won't make a showing."

"I know them," Collins nodded. "They're pretty old now, and they're spirit-broken besides. Take old Sark there. He's had so many blank cartridges fired into his ears that he's stone deaf. And Selim, he lost his heart with his teeth. A Portuguese fellow who was handling him for the Barnum and Bailey show did that for him. You've heard?"

"I've often wondered," the man shook his head. "It must have been a smash."

"It was. The Portuguese did it with an iron bar. Selim was sulky and took a swipe at him with his paw, and he whopped it to him full in the mouth just as he opened it to let out a roar. He told me about it himself. Said Selim's teeth rattled on the floor like dominoes. But he shouldn't have done it. It was destroying valuable property. Anyway, they fired him for it."

"Well, all three of them ain't worth much to me now," said their owner. "They won't play up to Isadora in that roaring and rampaging at the end. It really made the turn. It was our finale, and we always got a great hand for it. Say, what am I going to do about it anyway? Ditch it? Or get some young lions?"

"Isadora would be safer with the old ones," Collins said.

"Too safe," Isadora's husband objected. "Of course, with younger lions, the work and responsibility piles up on me. But we've got to make our living, and this turn's about busted."

Harris Collins shook his head.

"What d'ye mean? what's the idea?" the man demanded eagerly.

"They'll live for years yet, seeing how captivity has agreed with them," Collins elucidated. "If you invest in young lions you run the risk of having them pass out on you. And you can go right on pulling the trick off with what you've got. All you've got to do is to take my advice . . . "

The master-trainer paused, and the lion man opened his mouth to speak.

"Which will cost you," Collins went on deliberately, "say three hundred dollars."

"Just for some advice?" the other asked quickly.

"Which I guarantee will work. What would you have to pay for three new lions? Here's where you make money at three hundred. And it's the simplest of advice. I can tell it to you in three words, which is at the rate of a hundred dollars a word, and one of the words is 'the.'"

"Too steep for me," the other objected. "I've got a make a living."

"So have I," Collins assured him. "That's why I'm here. I'm a specialist, and you're paying a specialist's fee. You'll be as mad as a hornet when I tell you, it's that simple; and for the life of me I can't understand why you don't already know it."

"And if it don't work?" was the dubious query.

"If it don't work, you don't pay."

"Well, shoot it along," the lion man surrendered.

"Wire the cage," said Collins.

At first the man could not comprehend; then the light began to break on him.

"You mean . . . ?"

"Just that," Collins nodded. "And nobody need be the wiser. Dry batteries will do it beautifully. You can install them nicely under the cage floor. All Isadora has to do when she's ready is to step on the button; and when the electricity shoots through their feet, if they don't go up in the air and rampage and roar around to beat the band, not only can you keep the three hundred, but I'll give you three hundred more. I know. I've seen it done, and it never misses fire. It's just as though they were dancing on a red-hot stove. Up they go, and every time they come down they burn their feet again.

"But you'll have to put the juice into them slowly," Collins warned. "I'll show you how to do the wiring. Just a weak battery first, so as they can work up to it, and then stronger and stronger to the curtain. And they never get used to it. As long as they live they'll dance just as lively as the first time. What do you think of it?"

"It's worth three hundred all right," the man admitted. "I wish I could make my money that easy."

CHAPTER XXIX

"Guess I'll have to wash my hands of him," Collins told Johnny. "I know Del Mar must have been right when he said he was the limit, but I can't get a clue to it."

This followed upon a fight between Michael and Collins. Michael, more morose than ever, had become even crusty-tempered, and, scarcely with provocation at all, had attacked the man he hated, failing, as ever, to put his teeth into him, and receiving, in turn, a couple of smashing kicks under his jaw.

"He's like a gold-mine all right all right," Collins meditated, "but I'm hanged if I can crack it, and he's getting grouchier every day. Look at him. What'd he want to jump me for? I wasn't rough with him. He's piling up a sour-ball that'll make him fight a policeman some day."

A few minutes later, one of his patrons, a tow-headed young man who was boarding and rehearsing three performing leopards at Cedarwild, was asking Collins for the loan of an Airedale.

"I've only got one left now," he explained, "and I ain't safe without two."

"What's happened to the other one?" the master-trainer queried.

"Alphonso, that's the big buck leopard, got nasty this morning and settled his hash. I had to put him out of his misery. He was gutted like a horse in the bull-ring. But he saved me all right. If it hadn't been for him I'd have got a mauling. Alphonso gets these bad streaks just about every so often. That's the second dog he's killed for me."

Collins shook his head.

"Haven't got an Airedale," he said, and just then his eyes chanced to fall on Michael. "Try out the Irish terrier," he suggested. "They're like the Airedale in disposition. Pretty close cousins, at any rate."

"I pin my faith on the Airedale when it comes to lion dogs," the leopard man demurred.

"So's an Irish terrier a lion dog. Take that one there. Look at the size and weight of him. Also, take it from me, he's all spunk. He'll stand up to anything. Try him out. I'll lend him to you. If he makes good I'll sell him to you cheap. An Irish terrier for a leopard dog will be a novelty."

"If he gets fresh with them cats he'll find his finish," Johnny told Collins, as Michael was led away by the leopard man.

"Then, maybe, the stage will lose a star," Collins answered, with a shrug of shoulders. "But I'll have him off my chest anyway. When a dog gets a perpetual sour-ball like that he's finished. Never can do a thing with them. I've had them on my hands before."

And Michael went to make the acquaintance of Jack, the surviving Airedale, and to do his daily turn with the leopards. In the big spotted cats he recognized the hereditary enemy, and, even before he was thrust into the cage, his neck was all a-prickle as the skin nervously tightened and the hair uprose stiff-ended. It was a nervous moment for all concerned, the introduction of a new dog into the cage. The tow-headed leopard man, who was billed on the boards as Raoul Castlemon and was called Ralph by his intimates, was already in the cage. The Airedale was with him, while outside stood several men armed with iron bars and long steel forks. These weapons, ready for immediate use, were thrust between the bars as a menace to the leopards who were, very much against their wills, to be made to perform.

They resented Michael's intrusion on the instant, spitting, lashing their long tails, and crouching to spring. At the same instant the trainer spoke with sharp imperativeness and raised his whip, while the men on the outside lifted their irons and advanced them intimidatingly into the cage. And the leopards, bitter-wise of the taste of the iron, remained crouched, although they still spat and whipped their tails angrily.

Michael was no coward. He did not slink behind the man for protection. On the other hand, he was too sensible to rush to attack such formidable creatures. What he did do, with bristling neck-hair, was to stalk stiff- leggedly across the cage, turn about with his face toward the danger, and stalk stiffly back, coming to a pause alongside of Jack, who gave him a good-natured sniff of greeting.

"He's the stuff," the trainer muttered in a curiously tense voice. "They don't get his goat."

The situation was deservedly tense, and Ralph developed it with cautious care, making no abrupt movements, his eyes playing everywhere over dogs and leopards and the men outside with the prods and bars. He made the savage cats come out of their crouch and separate from one another. At his word of command, Jack walked about among them. Michael, on his own initiative, followed. And, like Jack, he walked very stiffly on his guard and very circumspectly.

One of them, Alphonso, spat suddenly at him. He did not startle, though his hair rippled erect and he bared his fangs in a silent snarl. At the same moment the nearest iron bar was shoved in threateningly close to Alphonso, who shifted his yellow eyes from Michael to the bar and back again and did not strike out.

The first day was the hardest. After that the leopards accepted Michael as they accepted Jack. No love was lost on either side, nor were friendly overtures ever offered. Michael was quick to realize that it was the men and dogs against the cats and that the men and does must stand together. Each day he spent from an hour to two hours in the cage, watching the rehearsing, with nothing for him and Jack to do save stand vigilantly on guard. Sometimes, when the leopards seemed better natured, Ralph even encouraged the two dogs to lie down. But, on bad mornings, he saw to it that they were ever ready to spring in between him and any possible attack.

For the rest of the time Michael shared his large pen with Jack. They were well cared for, as were all animals at Cedarwild, receiving frequent scrubbings and being kept clean of vermin. For a dog only three years old, Jack was very sedate. Either he had never learned to play or had already forgotten how. On the other hand, he was sweet-tempered and equable, and he did not resent the early shows of crustiness which Michael made. And Michael quickly ceased from being crusty and took pleasure in their quiet companionship. There were no demonstrations. They were content to lie awake by the hour, merely pleasantly aware of each other's proximity.

Occasionally, Michael could hear Sara making a distant scene or sending out calls which he knew were for him. Once she got away from her keeper and located Michael coming out of the leopard cage. With a shrill squeal of joy she was upon him, clinging to him and chattering the hysterical tale of all her woes since they had been parted. The leopard man looked on tolerantly and let her have her few minutes. It was her keeper who tore her away in the end, cling as she would to Michael, screaming all the while like a harridan. When her hold was broken, she sprang at the man in a fury, and, before he could throttle her to subjection, sank her teeth into his thumb and wrist. All of which was provocative of great hilarity to the onlookers, while her squalls and cries excited the leopards to spitting and leaping against their bars. And, as she was borne away, she set up a soft wailing like that of a heart-broken child.

Although Michael proved a success with the leopards, Raoul Castlemon never bought him from Collins. One morning, several days later, the arena was vexed by uproar and commotion from the animal cages. The excitement, starting with revolver shots, was communicated everywhere. The various lions raised a great roaring, and the many dogs barked frantically. All tricks in the arena stopped, the animals temporarily unstrung and unable to continue. Several men, among them Collins, ran in the direction of the cages. Sara's keeper dropped her chain in order to follow.

"It's Alphonso, shillings to pence it is," Collins called to one of his assistants who was running beside him. "He'll get Ralph yet."

The affair was all but over and leaping to its culmination when Collins arrived. Castlemon was just being dragged out, and as Collins ran he could see the two men drop him to the ground so that they might slam the cage-door shut. Inside, in so wildly struggling a tangle on the floor that it was difficult to discern what animals composed it, were Alphonso, Jack, and Michael looked together. Men danced about outside, thrusting in with iron bars and trying to separate them. In the far end of the cage were the other two leopards, nursing their wounds and snarling and striking at the iron rods that kept them out of the combat.

Sara's arrival and what followed was a matter of seconds. Trailing her chain behind her, the little green monkey, the tailed female who knew love and hysteria and was remote cousin to human women, flashed up to the narrow cage-bars and squeezed through. Simultaneously the tangle underwent a violent upheaval. Flung out with such force as to be smashed against the near end of the cage, Michael fell to the floor, tried to spring up, but crumpled and sank down, his right shoulder streaming blood from a terrible mauling and crushing. To him Sara leaped, throwing her arms around him and mothering him up to her flat little hairy breast. She uttered solicitous cries, and, as Michael strove to rise on his ruined foreleg, scolded him with sharp gentleness and with her arms tried to hold him away from the battle. Also, in an interval, her eyes malevolent in her rage, she chattered piercing curses at Alphonso.

A crowbar, shoved into his side, distracted the big leopard. He struck at the weapon with his paw, and, when it was poked into him again, flung himself upon it, biting the naked iron with his teeth.

With a second fling he was against the cage bars, with a single slash of paw ripping down the forearm of the man who had poked him. The crowbar was dropped as the man leaped away. Alphonso flung back on Jack, a sorry antagonist by this time, who could only pant and quiver where he lay in the welter of what was left of him.

Michael had managed to get up on his three legs and was striving to stumble forward against the restraining arms of Sara. The mad leopard was on the verge of springing upon them when deflected by another prod of the iron. This time he went straight at the man, fetching up against the cage-bars with such fierceness as to shake the structure.

More men began thrusting with more rods, but Alphonso was not to be balked. Sara saw him coming and screamed her shrillest and savagest at him. Collins snatched a revolver from one of the men.

"Don't kill him!" Castlemon cried, seizing Collins's arm.

The leopard man was in a bad way himself. One arm dangled helplessly at his side, while his eyes, filling with blood from a scalp wound, he wiped on the master-trainer's shoulder so that he might see.

"He's my property," he protested. "And he's worth a hundred sick monkeys and sour-balled terriers. Anyway, we'll get them out all right. Give me a chance. Somebody mop my eyes out, please. I can't see. I've used up my blank cartridges. Has anybody any blanks?"

One moment Sara would interpose her body between Michael and the leopard, which was still being delayed by the prodding irons; and the next moment she would turn to screech at the fanged cat is if by very advertisement of her malignancy she might intimidate him into keeping back.

Michael, dragging her with him, growling and bristling, staggered forward a couple of three-legged steps, gave at the ruined shoulder, and collapsed. And then Sara did the great deed. With one last scream of utmost fury, she sprang full into the face of the monstrous cat, tearing and scratching with hands and feet, her mouth buried into the roots of one of its stubby ears. The astounded leopard upreared, with his forepaws striking and ripping at the little demon that would not let go.

The fight and the life in the little green monkey lasted a short ten seconds. But this was sufficient for Collins to get the door ajar and with a quick clutch on Michael's hind-leg jerk him out and to the ground.

CHAPTER XXX

No rough-and-ready surgery of the Del Mar sort obtained at Cedarwild, else Michael would not have lived. A real surgeon, skilful and audacious, came very close to vivisecting him as he radically repaired the ruin of a shoulder, doing things he would not have dared with a human but which proved to be correct for Michael.

"He'll always be lame," the surgeon said, wiping his hands and gazing down at Michael, who lay, for the most part of him, a motionless prisoner set in plaster of Paris. "All the healing, and there's plenty of it, will have to be by first intention. If his temperature shoots up we'll have to put him out of his misery. What's he worth?"

"He has no tricks," Collins answered. "Possibly fifty dollars, and certainly not that now. Lame dogs are not worth teaching tricks to."

Time was to prove both men wrong. Michael was not destined to permanent lameness, although in after-years his shoulder was always tender, and, on occasion, when the weather was damp, he was compelled to ease it with a slight limp. On the other hand, he was destined to appreciate to a great price and to become the star performer Harry Del Mar had predicted of him.

In the meantime he lay for many weary days in the plaster and abstained from raising a dangerous temperature. The care taken of him was excellent. But not out of love and affection was it given. It was merely a part of the system at Cedarwild which made the institution such a success. When he was taken out of the plaster, he was still denied that instinctive pleasure which all animals take in licking their wounds, for shrewdly arranged bandages were wrapped and buckled on him. And when they were finally removed, there were no wounds to lick; though deep in the shoulder was a pain that required months in which to die out.

Harris Collins bothered him no more with trying to teach him tricks, and, one day, loaned him as a filler-in to a man and woman who had lost three of their dog-troupe by pneumonia.

"If he makes out you can have him for twenty dollars," Collins told the man, Wilton Davis.

"And if he croaks?" Davis queried.

Collins shrugged his shoulders. "I won't sit up nights worrying about him. He's unteachable."

And when Michael departed from Cedarwild in a crate on an express wagon, he might well have never returned, for Wilton Davis was notorious among trained-animal men for his cruelty to dogs. Some care he might take of a particular dog with a particularly valuable trick, but mere fillers-in came too cheaply. They cost from three to five dollars apiece. Worse than that, so far as he was concerned, Michael had cost nothing. And if he died it meant nothing to Davis except the trouble of finding another dog.

The first stage of Michael's new adventure involved no unusual hardship, despite the fact that he was so cramped in his crate that he could not stand up and that the jolting and handling of the crate sent countless twinges of pain shooting through his shoulder. The journey was only to Brooklyn, where he was duly delivered to a second-rate theatre, Wilton Davis being so indifferent a second-rate animal man that he could never succeed in getting time with the big circuits.

The hardship of the cramped crate began after Michael had been carried into a big room above the stage and deposited with nearly a score of similarly crated dogs. A sorry lot they were, all of them scrubs and most of them spirit-broken and miserable. Several had bad sores on their heads from being knocked about by Davis. No care was taken of these sores, and they were not improved by the whitening that was put on them for concealment whenever they performed. Some of them howled lamentably at times, and every little while, as if it were all that remained for them to do in their narrow cells, all of them would break out into barking.

Michael was the only one who did not join in these choruses. Long since, as one feature of his developing moroseness, he had ceased from barking. He had become too unsociable for any such demonstrations; nor did he pattern after the example of some of the sourer-tempered dogs in the room, who were for ever bickering and snarling through the slats of their cages. In fact, Michael's sourness of temper had become too profound even for quarrelling. All he desired was to be let alone, and of this he had a surfeit for the first forty-eight hours.

Wilton Davis had assembled his troupe ahead of time, so that the change of programme was five days away. Having taken advantage of this to go to see his wife's people over in New Jersey, he had hired one of the stage- hands to feed and water his dogs. This the stage-hand would have done, had he not had the misfortune to get into an altercation with a barkeeper which culminated in a fractured skull and an ambulance ride to the receiving hospital. To make the situation perfect for what followed, the theatre was closed for three days in order to make certain alterations demanded by the Fire Commissioners.

No one came near the room, and after several hours Michael grew aware of hunger and thirst. The time passed, and the desire for food was supplanted by the desire for water. By nightfall the barking and yelping became continuous, changing through the long night hours to whimpering and whining. Michael alone made no sound, suffering dumbly in the bedlam of misery.

Morning of the second day dawned; the slow hours dragged by to the second night; and the darkness of the second night drew down upon a scene behind the scenes, sufficient of itself to condemn all trained-animal acts in all theatres and show-tents of all the world. Whether Michael dreamed or was in semi-delirium, there is no telling; but, whichever it was, he lived most of his past life over again. Again he played as a puppy on the broad verandas of Mister Haggin's plantation bungalow at Meringe; or, with Jerry, stalked the edges of the jungle down by the river-bank to spy upon the crocodiles; or, learning from Mister Haggin and Bob, and patterning after Biddy and Terrence, to consider black men as lesser and despised gods who must for ever be kept strictly in their places.

On the schooner Eugenie he sailed with Captain Kellar, his second master, and on the beach at Tulagi lost his heart to Steward of the magic fingers and sailed away with him and Kwaque on the steamer Makambo. Steward was most in his visions, against a hazy background of vessels, and of individuals like the Ancient Mariner, Simon Nishikanta, Grimshaw, Captain Doane, and little old Ah Moy. Nor least of all did Scraps appear, and Cocky, the valiant-hearted little fluff of life gallantly bearing himself through his brief adventure in the sun. And it would seem to Michael that on one side, clinging to him, Cocky talked farrago in his ear, and on the other side Sara clung to him and chattered an interminable and incommunicable tale. And then, deep about the roots of his ears would seem to prod the magic, caressing fingers of Steward the beloved.

"I just don't I have no luck," Wilton Davis mourned, gazing about at his dogs, the air still vibrating with the string of oaths he had at first ripped out.

"That comes of trusting a drunken stage-hand," his wife remarked placidly. "I wouldn't be surprised if half of them died on us now."

"Well, this is no time for talk," Davis snarled, proceeding to take off his coat. "Get busy, my love, and learn the worst. Water's what they need. I'll give them a tub of it."

Bucketful by bucketful, from the tap at the sink in the corner, he filled a large galvanized-iron tub. At sound of the running water the dogs began whimpering and yelping and moaning. Some tried to lick his hands with their swollen tongues as he dragged them roughly out of their cages. The weaker ones crawled and bellied toward the tub, and were over-trod by the stronger ones. There was not room for all, and the stronger ones drank first, with much fighting and squabbling and slashing of fangs. Into the foremost of this was Michael, slashing and being slashed, but managing to get hasty gulps of the life-saving fluid. Davis danced about among them, kicking right and left, so that all might have a chance. His wife took a hand, laying about her with a mop. It was a pandemonium of pain, for, their parched throats softened by the water, they were again able to yelp and cry out loudly all their hurt and woe.

Several were too weak to get to the water, so it was carried to them and doused and splashed into their mouths. It seemed that they would never be satisfied. They lay in collapse all about the room, but every little while one or another would crawl over to the tub and try to drink more. In the meantime Davis had started a fire and filled a caldron with potatoes.

"The place stinks like a den of skunks," Mrs. Davis observed, pausing from dabbing the end of her nose with a powder-puff. "Dearest, we'll just have to wash them."

"All right, sweetheart," her husband agreed. "And the quicker the better. We can get through with it while the potatoes are boiling and cooling. I'll scrub them and you dry them. Remember that pneumonia, and do it thoroughly."

It was quick, rough bathing. Reaching out for the dogs nearest him, he flung them in turn into the tub from which they had drunk. When they were frightened, or when they objected in any way, he rapped them on the head with the scrubbing brush or the bar of yellow laundry soap with which he was lathering them. Several minutes sufficed for a dog.

"Drink, damn you, drink, have some more," he would say, as he shoved their heads down and under the dirty, soapy water.

He seemed to hold them responsible for their horrible condition, to look upon their filthiness as a personal affront.

Michael yielded to being flung into the tub. He recognized that baths were necessary and compulsory, although they were administered in much better fashion at Cedarwild, while Kwaque and Steward had made a sort of love function of it when they bathed him. So he did his best to endure the scrubbing, and all might have been well had not Davis soused him under. Michael jerked his head up with a warning growl. Davis suspended half-way the blow he was delivering with the heavy brush, and emitted a low whistle of surprise.

"Hello!" he said. "And look who's here! Lovey, this is the Irish terrier I got from Collins. He's no good. Collins said so. Just a fill- in. Get out!" he commanded Michael. "That's all you get now, Mr. Fresh Dog. But take it from me pretty soon you'll be getting it fast enough to make you dizzy."

While the potatoes were cooling, Mrs. Davis kept the hungry dogs warned away by sharp cries. Michael lay down sullenly to one side, and took no part in the rush for the trough when permission was given. Again Davis danced among them, kicking away the stronger and the more eager.

"If they get to fighting after all we've done for them, kick in their ribs, lovey," he told his wife.

"There! You would, would you?" -this to a large black dog, accompanied by a savage kick in the side. The animal yelped its pain as it fled away, and, from a safe distance, looked on piteously at the steaming food.

"Well, after this they can't say I don't never give my dogs a bath," Davis remarked from the sink, where he was rinsing his arms. "What d'ye say we call it a day's work, my dear?" Mrs. Davis nodded agreement. "We can rehearse them to-morrow and next day. That will be plenty of time. I'll run in to-night and boil them some bran. They'll need an extra meal after fasting two days."

The potatoes finished, the dogs were put back in their cages for another twenty-four hours of close confinement. Water was poured into their drinking-tins, and, in the evening, still in their cages, they were served liberally with boiled bran and dog-biscuit. This was Michael's first food, for he had sulkily refused to go near the potatoes.

The rehearsing took place on the stage, and for Michael trouble came at the very start. The drop-curtain was supposed to go up and reveal the twenty dogs seated on chairs in a semi-circle. Because, while they were being thus arranged, the preceding turn was taking place in front of the drop-curtain, it was imperative that rigid silence should be kept. Next, when the curtain rose on full stage, the dogs were trained to make a great barking.

As a filler-in, Michael had nothing to do but sit on a chair. But he had to get upon the chair, first, and when Davis so ordered him he accompanied the order with a clout on the side of the head. Michael growled warningly.

"Oh, ho, eh?" the man sneered. "It's Fresh Dog looking for trouble. Well, you might as well get it over with now so your name can be changed to Good Dog. My dear, just keep the rest of them in order while I teach Fresh Dog lesson number one."

Of the beating that followed, the least said the better. Michael put up a fight that was hopeless, and was thoroughly beaten in return. Bruised and bleeding, he sat on the chair, taking no part in the performance and only sullenly engendering a deeper and bitterer sourness. To keep silent before the curtain went up was no hardship for him. But when the curtain did go up, he declined to join the rest of the dogs in their frantic barking and yelping.

The dogs, sometimes alone and sometimes in couples and trios and groups, left their chairs at command and performed the conventional dog tricks such as walking on hind-legs, hopping, limping, waltzing, and throwing somersaults. Wilton Davis's temper was short and his hand heavy throughout the rehearsal, as the shrill yelps of pain from the lagging and stupid attested.

In all, during that day and the forenoon of the next, three long rehearsals took place. Michael's troubles ceased for the time being. At command, he silently got on the chair and silently sat there. "Which shows, dearest, what a bit of the stick will do," Davis bragged to his wife. Nor did the pair of them dream of the scandalizing part Michael was going to play in their first performance.

Behind the curtain all was ready on the full stage. The dogs sat on their chairs in abject silence with Davis and his wife menacing them to remain silent, while, in front of the curtain, Dick and Daisy Bell delighted the matinee audience with their singing and dancing. And all went well, and no one in the audience would have suspected the full stage of dogs behind the curtain had not Dick and Daisy, accompanied by the orchestra, begun to sing "Roll Me Down to Rio."

Michael could not help it. Even as Kwaque had long before mastered him by the jews' harp, and Steward by love, and Harry Del Mar by the harmonica, so now was he mastered by the strains of the orchestra and the voices of the man and woman lifting the old familiar rhythm, taught him by Steward, of "Roll Me Down to Rio." Despite himself, despite his sullenness, the forces compulsive opened his jaws and set all his throat vibrating in accompaniment.

From beyond the curtain came a titter of children and women that grew into a roar and drowned out the voices of Dick and Daisy. Wilton Davis cursed unbelievably as he sprang down the stage to Michael. But Michael howled on, and the audience laughed on. Michael was still howling when the short club smote him. The shock and hurt of it made him break off and yelp an involuntary cry of pain.

"Knock his block off, dearest," Mrs. Davis counselled.

And then ensued battle royal. Davis struck shrewd blows that could be heard, as were heard the snarls and growls of Michael. The audience, under the sway of the comic, ignored Dick and Daisy Bell. Their turn was spoiled. The Davis turn was "queered," as Wilton impressed it. Michael's block was knocked off within the meaning of the term. And the audience, on the other side of the curtain, was edified and delighted.

Dick and Daisy could not continue. The audience wanted what was behind the curtain, not in front of it. Michael was taken off stage thoroughly throttled by one of the stage-hands, and the curtain arose on the full set, full, save for the one empty chair. The boys in the audience first realized the connection between the empty chair and the previous uproar, and began clamouring for the absent dog. The audience took up the cry, the dogs barked more excitedly, and five minutes of hilarity delayed the turn which, when at last started, was marked by rustiness and erraticness on the part of the dogs and by great peevishness on the part of Wilton Davis.

"Never mind, honey," his imperturbable wife assured him in a stage whisper. "We'll just ditch that dog and get a regular one. And, anyway, we've put one over on that Daisy Bell. I ain't told you yet what she said about me, only last week, to some of my friends."

Several minutes later, still on the stage and handling his animals, the husband managed a chance to mutter to his wife: "It's the dog. It's him I'm after. I'm going to lay him out."

"Yes, dearest," she agreed.

The curtain down, with a gleeful audience in front and with the dogs back in the room over the stage, Wilton Davis descended to look for Michael, who, instead of cowering in some corner, stood between the legs of the stage-hand, quivering yet from his mishandling and threatening to fight as hard as ever if attacked. On his way, Davis encountered the song-and- dance couple. The woman was in a tearful rage, the man in a dry one.

"You're a peach of a dog man, you are," he announced belligerently. "Here's where you get yours."

"You keep away from me, or I'll lay you out," Wilton Davis responded desperately, brandishing a short iron bar in his right hand. "Besides, you just wait if you want to, and I'll lay you out afterward. But first of all I'm going to lay out that dog. Come on along and see, damn him! How was I to know? He was a new one. He never peeped in rehearsal. How was I to know he was going to yap when we arranged the set behind you?"

"You've raised hell," the manager of the theatre greeted Davis, as the latter, trailed by Dick Bell, came upon Michael bristling from between the legs of the stage-hand.

"Nothing to what I'm going to raise," Davis retorted, shortening his grip on the iron bar and raising it. "I'm going to kill 'm. I'm going to beat the life out of him. You just watch."

Michael snarled acknowledgment of the threat, crouched to spring, and kept his eyes on the iron weapon.

"I just guess you ain't goin' to do anything of the sort," the stage-hand assured Davis.

"It's my property," the latter asserted with an air of legal convincingness.

"And against it I'm goin' to stack up my common sense," was the stage-hand's reply. "You tap him once, and see what you'll get. Dogs is dogs, and men is men, but I'm damned if I know what you are. You can't pull off rough stuff on that dog. First time he was on a stage in his life, after being starved and thirsted for two days. Oh, I know, Mr. Manager."

"If you kill the dog it'll cost you a dollar to the garbage man to get rid of the carcass," the manager took up.

"I'll pay it gladly," Davis said, again lifting the iron bar. "I've got some come-back, ain't I?"

"You animal guys make me sick," the stage-hand uttered. "You just make me draw the line somewheres. And here it is: you tap him once with that baby crowbar, and I'll tap you hard enough to lose me my job and to send you to hospital."

"Now look here, Jackson . . . " the manager began threateningly.

"You can't say nothin' to me," was the retort. "My mind's made up. If that cheap guy lays a finger on that dog I'm just sure goin' to lose my job. I'm gettin tired anyway of seein' these skates beatin' up their animals. They've made me sick clean through."

The manager looked to Davis and shrugged his shoulders helplessly.

"There's no use pulling off a rough-house," he counselled. "I don't want to lose Jackson and he'll put you into hospital if he ever gets started. Send the dog back where you got him. Your wife's told me about him. Stick him into a box and send him back collect. Collins won't mind. He'll take the singing out of him and work him into something."

Davis, with another glance at the truculent Jackson, wavered.

"I'll tell you what," the manager went on persuasively. "Jackson will attend to the whole thing, box him up, ship him, everything, won't you, Jackson?"

The stage-hand nodded curtly, then reached down and gently caressed Michael's bruised head.

"Well," Davis gave in, turning on his heel, "they can make fools of themselves over dogs, them that wants to. But when they've been in the business as long as I have . . . "

CHAPTER XXXI

A post card from Davis to Collins explained the reasons for Michael's return. "He sings too much to suit my fancy," was Davis's way of putting it, thereby unwittingly giving the clue to what Collins had vainly sought, and which Collins as unwittingly failed to grasp. As he told Johnny:

"From the looks of the beatings he's got no wonder he's been singing. That's the trouble with these animal people. They don't know how to take care of their property. They hammer its head off and get grouched because it ain't an angel of obedience. Put him away, Johnny. Wash him clean, and put on the regular dressing wherever the skin's broken. I give him up myself, but I'll find some place for him in the next bunch of dogs."

Two weeks later, by sheerest accident, Harris Collins made the discovery for himself of what Michael was good for. In a spare moment in the arena, he had sent for him to be tried out by a dog man who needed several fillers-in. Beyond what he knew, such as at command to stand up, to lie down, to come here and go there, Michael had done nothing. He had refused to learn the most elementary things a show-dog should know, and Collins had left him to go over to another part of the arena where a monkey band, on a sort of mimic stage, was being arranged and broken in.

Frightened and mutinous, nevertheless the monkeys were compelled to perform by being tied to their seats and instruments and by being pulled and jerked from off stage by wires fastened to their bodies. The leader of the orchestra, an irascible elderly monkey, sat on a revolving stool to which he was securely attached. When poked from off the stage by means of long poles, he flew into ecstasies of rage. At the same time, by a rope arrangement, his chair was whirled around and around. To an audience the effect would be that he was angered by the blunders of his fellow-musicians. And to an audience such anger would be highly ludicrous. As Collins said:

"A monkey band is always a winner. It fetches the laugh, and the money's in the laugh. Humans just have to laugh at monkeys because they're so similar and because the human has the advantage and feels himself superior. Suppose we're walking along the street, you and me, and you slip and fall down. Of course I laugh. That's because I'm superior to you. I didn't fall down. Same thing if your hat blows off. I laugh while you chase it down the street. I'm superior. My hat's still on my head. Same thing with the monkey band. All the fool things of it make us feel so superior. We don't see ourselves as foolish. That's why we pay to see the monkeys behave foolish."

It was scarcely a matter of training the monkeys. Rather was it the training of the men who operated the concealed mechanisms that made the monkeys perform. To this Harris Collins was devoting his effort.

"There isn't any reason why you fellows can't make them play a real tune. It's up to you, just according to how you pull the wires. Come on. It's worth going in for. Let's try something you all know. And remember, the regular orchestra will always help you out. Now, what do you all know? Something simple, and something the audience'll know, too?"

He became absorbed in trying out the idea, and even borrowed a circus rider whose act was to play the violin while standing on the back of a galloping horse and to throw somersaults on such precarious platform while still playing the violin. This man he got merely to play simple airs in slow time, so that the assistants could keep the time and the air and pull the wires accordingly.

"Of course, if you make a howling mistake," Collins told them, "that's when you all pull the wires like mad and poke the leader and whirl him around. That always brings down the house. They think he's got a real musical ear and is mad at his orchestra for the discord."

In the midst of the work, Johnny and Michael came along.

"That guy says he wouldn't take him for a gift," Johnny reported to his employer.

"All right, all right, put him back in the kennels," Collins ordered hurriedly. "Now, you fellows, all ready! 'Home, Sweet Home!' Go to it, Fisher! Now keep the time the rest of you! . . . That's it. With a full orchestra you're making motions like the tune. Faster, you, Simmons. You drag behind all the time."

And the accident happened. Johnny, instead of immediately obeying the order and taking Michael back to the kennels, lingered in the hope of seeing the orchestra leader whirled chattering around on his stool. The violinist, within a yard of where Michael sat squatted on his haunches, played the notes of "Home, Sweet Home" with loud slow exactitude and emphasis.

And Michael could not help it. No more could he help it than could he help responding with a snarl when threatened by a club; no more could he help it than when he had spoiled the turn of Dick and Daisy Bell when swept by the strains of "Roll Me Down to Rio"; no more could he help it than could Jerry, on the deck of the Ariel, help singing when Villa Kennan put her arms around him, smothered him deliciously in her cloud of hair, and sang his memory back into time and the fellowship of the ancient pack. As with Jerry, was it with Michael. Music was a drug of dream. He, too, remembered the lost pack and sought it, seeing the bare hills of snow and the stars glimmering overhead through the frosty darkness of night, hearing the faint answering howls from other hills as the pack assembled. Lost the pack was, through the thousands of years Michael's ancestors had lived by the fires of men; yet remembered always it was when the magic of rhythm poured through him and flooded his being with visions and sensations of that Otherwhere which in his own life he had never known.

Compounded with the waking dream of Otherwhere, was the memory of Steward and the love of Steward, with whom he had learned to sing the very series of notes that now were being reproduced by the circus-rider violinist. And Michael's jaw dropped down, his throat vibrated, his forefeet made restless little movements as if in the body he were running, as truly he was running in the mind, back to Steward, back through all the ages to the lost pack, and with the shadowy lost pack itself across the snowy wastes and through the forest aisles in the hunt of the meat.

The spectral forms of the lost pack were all about him as he sang and ran in open-eyed dream; the violinist paused in surprise; the men poked the monkey leader of the monkey orchestra and whirled him about wildly raging on his revolving stool; and Johnny laughed. But Harris Collins took note. He had heard Michael accurately follow the air. He had heard him sing, not merely howl, but sing.

Silence fell. The monkey leader ceased revolving and chattering. The men who had poked him held poles and wires suspended in their hands. The rest of the monkey orchestra merely shivered in apprehension of what next atrocity should be perpetrated. The violinist stared. Johnny still heaved from his laughter. But Harris Collins pondered, scratched his head, and continued to ponder.

"You can't tell me . . . " he began vaguely. "I know it. I heard it. That dog carried the tune. Didn't he now? I leave it to all of you. Didn't he? The damned dog sang. I'll stake my life on it. Hold on, you fellows; rest the monkeys off. This is worth following up. Mr. Violinist, play that over again, now, 'Home, Sweet Home,', let her go. Press her strong, and loud, and slow. Now watch, all of you, and listen, and tell me if I'm crazy, or if that dog ain't carrying the tune. There! What d'ye call it? Ain't it?"

There was no discussion. Michael's jaw dropped and his forefeet began their restless lifting after several measures had been played. And Harris Collins stepped close to him and sang with him and in accord.

"Harry Del Mar was right when he said that dog was the limit and sold his troupe. He knew. The dog's a dog Caruso. No howling chorus of mutts such as Kingman used to carry around with him, but a real singer, a soloist. No wonder he wouldn't learn tricks. He had his specially all the time. And just to think of it! I as good as gave him away to that dog-killing Wilton Davis. Only he came back. Johnny, take extra care of him after this. Bring him up to the house this afternoon, and I'll give him a real try-out. My daughter plays the violin. We'll see what music he'll sing with her. There's a mint of money in him, take it from me."

Thus was Michael discovered. The afternoon's try-out was partially successful. After vainly attempting strange music on him, Collins found that he could sing, and would sing, "God Save the King" and "Sweet Bye and Bye." Many hours of many days were spent in the quest. Vainly he tried to teach Michael new airs. Michael put no heart of love in the effort and sullenly abstained. But whenever one of the songs he had learned from Steward was played, he responded. He could not help responding. The magic was stronger than he. In the end, Collins discovered five of the six songs he knew: "God Save the King," "Sweet Bye and Bye," "Lead, Kindly Light," "Home, Sweet Home," and "Roll Me Down to Rio." Michael never sang "Shenandoah," because Collins and Collins's daughter did not know the old sea-chanty and therefore were unable to suggest it to him.

"Five songs are enough, if he won't never learn another note," Collins concluded. "They'll make him a bill-topper anywhere. There's a mint in him. Hang me if I wouldn't take him out on the road myself if only I was young and footloose."

CHAPTER XXXII

And so Michael was ultimately sold to one Jacob Henderson for two thousand dollars. "And I'm giving him away to you at that," said Collins. "If you don't refuse five thousand for him before six months, I don't know anything about the show game. He'll skin that last arithmetic dog of yours to a finish and you won't have to show yourself and work every minute of the turn. And if you don't insure him for fifty thousand as soon as he's made good you'll be a fool. Why, I wouldn't ask anything better, if I was young and footloose, than to take him out on the road myself."

Henderson proved totally different from any master Michael had had. The man was a neutral sort of creature. He was neither good nor evil. He neither drank, smoked, nor swore; nor did he go to church or belong to the Y.M.C.A. He was a vegetarian without being a bigoted one, liked moving pictures when they were concerned with travel, and spent most of his spare time in reading Swedenborg. He had no temper whatever. Nobody had ever witnessed anger in him, and all said he had the patience of Job. He was even timid of policemen, freight agents, and conductors, though he was not afraid of them. He was not afraid of anything, any more than was he enamoured of anything save Swedenborg. He was as colourless of character as the neutral-coloured clothes he wore, as the neutral-coloured hair that sprawled upon his crown, as the neutral-coloured eyes with which he observed the world. Nor was he a fool any more than was he a wise man or a scholar. He gave little to life, asked little of life, and, in the show business, was a recluse in the very heart of life.

Michael neither liked nor disliked him, but, rather, merely accepted him. They travelled the United States over together, and they never had a quarrel. Not once did Henderson raise his voice sharply to Michael, and not once did Michael snarl a warning at him. They simply endured together, existed together, because the currents of life had drifted them together. Of course, there was no heart-bond between them. Henderson was master. Michael was Henderson's chattel. Michael was as dead to him as he was himself dead to all things.

Yet Jacob Henderson was fair and square, business-like and methodical. Once each day, when not travelling on the interminable trains, he gave Michael a thorough bath and thoroughly dried him afterward. He was never harsh nor hasty in the bathing. Michael never was aware whether he liked or disliked the bathing function. It was all one, part of his own fate in the world as it was part of Henderson's fate to bathe him every so often.

Michael's own work was tolerably easy, though monotonous. Leaving out the eternal travelling, the never-ending jumps from town to town and from city to city, he appeared on the stage once each night for seven nights in the week and for two afternoon performances in the week. The curtain went up, leaving him alone on the stage in the full set that befitted a bill-topper. Henderson stood in the wings, unseen by the audience, and looked on. The orchestra played four of the pieces Michael had been taught by Steward, and Michael sang them, for his modulated howling was truly singing. He never responded to more than one encore, which was always "Home, Sweet Home." After that, while the audience clapped and stamped its approval and delight of the dog Caruso, Jacob Henderson would appear on the stage, bowing and smiling in stereotyped gladness and gratefulness, rest his right hand on Michael's shoulders with a play-acted assumption of comradeliness, whereupon both Henderson and Michael would bow ere the final curtain went down.

And yet Michael was a prisoner, a life-prisoner. Fed well, bathed well, exercised well, he never knew a moment of freedom. When travelling, days and nights he spent in the cage, which, however, was generous enough to allow him to stand at full height and to turn around without too uncomfortable squirming. Sometimes, in hotels in country towns, out of the crate he shared Henderson's room with him. Otherwise, unless other animals were hewing on the same circuit time, he had, outside his cage, the freedom of the animal room attached to the particular theatre where he performed for from three days to a week.

But there was never a chance, never a moment, when he might run free of a cage about him, of the walls of a room restricting him, of a chain shackled to the collar about his throat. In good weather, in the afternoons, Henderson often took him for a walk. But always it was at the end of a chain. And almost always the way led to some park, where Henderson fastened the other end of the chain to the bench on which he sat and browsed Swedenborg. Not one act of free agency was left to Michael. Other dogs ran free, playing with one another, or behaving bellicosely. If they approached him for purposes of investigation or acquaintance, Henderson invariably ceased from his reading long enough to drive them away.

A life prisoner to a lifeless gaoler, life was all grey to Michael. His moroseness changed to a deep-seated melancholy. He ceased to be interested in life and in the freedom of life. Not that he regarded the play of life about him with a jaundiced eye, but, rather, that his eyes became unseeing. Debarred from life, he ignored life. He permitted himself to become a sheer puppet slave, eating, taking his baths, travelling in his cage, performing regularly, and sleeping much.

He had pride, the pride of the thoroughbred; the pride of the North American Indian enslaved on the plantations of the West Indies who died uncomplaining and unbroken. So Michael. He submitted to the cage and the iron of the chain because they were too strong for his muscles and teeth. He did his slave-task of performance and rendered obedience to Jacob Henderson; but he neither loved nor feared that master. And because of this his spirit turned in on itself. He slept much, brooded much, and suffered unprotestingly a great loneliness. Had Henderson made a bid for his heart, he would surely have responded; but Henderson had a heart only for the fantastic mental gyrations of Swedenborg, and merely made his living out of Michael.

Sometimes there were hardships. Michael accepted them. Especially hard did he find railroad travel in winter-time, when, on occasion, fresh from the last night's performance in a town, he remained for hours in his crate on a truck waiting for the train that would take him to the next town of performance. There was a night on a station platform in Minnesota, when two dogs of a troupe, on the next truck to his, froze to death. He was himself well frosted, and the cold bit abominably into his shoulder wounded by the leopard; but a better constitution and better general care of him enabled him to survive.

Compared with other show animals, he was well treated. And much of the ill-treatment accorded other animals on the same turn with him he did not comprehend or guess. One turn, with which he played for three months, was a scandal amongst all vaudeville performers. Even the hardiest of them heartily disliked the turn and the man, although Duckworth, and Duckworth's Trained Cats and Rats, were an invariable popular success.

"Trained cats!" sniffed dainty little Pearl La Pearle, the bicyclist. "Crushed cats, that's what they are. All the cat has been beaten out of their blood, and they've become rats. You can't tell me. I know."

"Trained rats!" Manuel Fonseca, the contortionist, exploded in the bar- room of the Hotel Annandale, after refusing to drink with Duckworth. "Doped rats, believe me. Why don't they jump off when they crawl along the tight rope with a cat in front and a cat behind? Because they ain't got the life in 'm to jump. They're doped, straight doped when they're fresh, and starved afterward so as to making a saving on the dope. They never are fed. You can't tell me. I know. Else why does he use up anywhere to forty or fifty rats a week! I know his express shipments, when he can't buy 'm in the towns."

"My Gawd!" protested Miss Merle Merryweather, the Accordion Girl, who looked like sixteen on the stage, but who, in private life among her grand-children, acknowledged forty-eight. "My Gawd, how the public can fall for it gets my honest-to-Gawd goat. I looked myself yesterday morning early. Out of thirty rats there were seven dead, starved to death. He never feeds them. They're dying rats, dying of starvation, when they crawl along that rope. That's why they crawl. If they had a bit of bread and cheese in their tummies they'd jump and run to get away from the cats. They're dying, they're dying right there on the rope, trying to crawl as a dying man would try to crawl away from a tiger that was eating him. And my Gawd! The bonehead audience sits there and applauds the show as an educational act!"

But the audience! "Wonderful things kindness will do with animals," said a member of one, a banker and a deacon. "Even human love can be taught to them by kindness. The cat and the rat have been enemies since the world began. Yet here, to-night, we have seen them doing highly trained feats together, and neither a cat committed one hostile or overt act against a rat, nor ever a rat showed it was afraid of a cat. Human kindness! The power of human kindness!"

"The lion and the lamb," said another. "We have it that when the millennium comes the lion and the lamb will lie down together, and outside each other, my dear, outside each other. And this is a forecast, a proving up, by man, ahead of the day. Cats and rats! Think of it. And it shows conclusively the power of kindness. I shall see to it at once that we get pets for our own children, our palm branches. They shall learn kindness early, to the dog, the cat, yes, even the rat, and the pretty linnet in its cage."

"But," said his dear, beside him, "you remember what Blake said:

"'A Robin Redbreast in a cage   Puts all heaven in a rage.'"

"Ah, but not when it is treated truly with kindness, my dear. I shall immediately order some rabbits, and a canary or two, and what sort of a dog would you prefer our dear little ones to have to play with, my sweet?"

And his dear looked at him in all his imperturbable, complacent self-consciousness of kindness, and saw herself the little rural school- teacher who, with Ella Wheeler Wilcox and Lord Byron as her idols, and with the dream of herself writing "Poems of Passion," had come up to Topeka Town to be beaten by the game into marrying the solid, substantial business man beside her, who enjoyed delight in the spectacle of cats and rats walking the tight-rope in amity, and who was blissfully unaware that she was the Robin Redbreast in a cage that put all heaven in a rage.

"The rats are bad enough," said Miss Merle Merryweather. "But look how he uses up the cats. He's had three die on him in the last two weeks to my certain knowledge. They're only alley-cats, but they've got feelings. It's that boxing match that does for them."

The boxing match, sure always of a great hand from the audience, invariably concluded Duckworth's turn. Two cats, with small boxing-gloves, were put on a table for a friendly bout. Naturally, the cats that performed with the rats were too cowed for this. It was the fresh cats he used, the ones with spunk and spirit . . . until they lost all spunk and spirit or sickened and died. To the audience it was a side- splitting, playful encounter between four-legged creatures who thus displayed a ridiculous resemblance to superior, two-legged man. But it was not playful to the cats. They were always excited into starting a real fight with each other off stage just before they were brought on. In the blows they struck were anger and pain and bewilderment and fear. And the gloves just would come off, so that they were ripping and tearing at each other, biting as well as making the fur fly, like furies, when the curtain went down. In the eyes of the audience this apparent impromptu was always the ultimate scream, and the laughter and applause would compel the curtain up again to reveal Duckworth and an assistant stage- hand, as if caught by surprise, fanning the two belligerents with towels.

But the cats themselves were so continually torn and scratched that the wounds never had a chance to heal and became infected until they were a mass of sores. On occasion they died, or, when they had become too abjectly spiritless to attack even a rat, were set to work on the tight- rope with the doped starved rats that were too near dead to run away from them. And, as Miss Merle Merryweather said: the bonehead audiences, tickled to death, applauded Duckworth's Trained Cats and Rats as an educational act!

A big chimpanzee that covered one of the circuits with Michael had an antipathy for clothes. Like a horse that fights the putting on of the bridle, and, after it is on, takes no further notice of it, so the big chimpanzee fought the putting on the clothes. Once on, it was ready to go out on the stage and through its turn. But the rub was in putting on the clothes. It took the owner and two stage-hands, pulling him up to a ring in the wall and throttling him, to dress him, and this, despite the fact that the owner had long since knocked out his incisors.

All this cruelty Michael sensed without knowing. And he accepted it as the way of life, as he accepted the daylight and the dark, the bite of the frost on bleak and windy station platforms, the mysterious land of Otherwhere that he knew in dreams and song, the equally mysterious

Nothingness into which had vanished Meringe Plantation and ships and oceans and men and Steward.

CHAPTER XXXIII

For two years Michael sang his way over the United States, to fame for himself and to fortune for Jacob Henderson. There was never any time off. So great was his success, that Henderson refused flattering offers to cross the Atlantic to show in Europe. But off-time did come to Michael when Henderson fell ill of typhoid in Chicago.

It was a three-months' vacation for Michael, who, well treated but still a prisoner, spent it in a caged kennel in Mulcachy's Animal Home. Mulcachy, one of Harris Collins's brightest graduates, had emulated his master by setting up in business in Chicago, where he ran everything with the same rigid cleanliness, sanitation, and scientific cruelty. Michael received nothing but the excellent food and the cleanliness; but, a solitary and brooding prisoner in his cage, he could not help but sense the atmosphere of pain and terror about him of the animals being broken for the delight of men.

Mulcachy had originated aphorisms of his own which he continually enunciated, among which were:

"Take it from me, when an animal won't give way to pain, it can't be broke. Pain is the only school-teacher."

"Just as you got to take the buck out of a broncho, you've got to take the bite out of a lion."

"You can't break animals with a feather duster. The thicker the skull the thicker the crowbar."

"They'll always beat you in argument. First thing is to club the argument out of them."

"Heart-bonds between trainers and animals! Son, that's dope for the newspaper interviewer. The only heart-bond I know is a stout stick with some iron on the end of it."

"Sure you can make 'm eat outa your hand. But the thing to watch out for is that they don't eat your hand. A blank cartridge in the nose just about that time is the best preventive I know."

There were days when all the air was vexed with roars and squalls of ferocity and agony from the arena, until the last animal in the cages was excited and ill at ease. In truth, since it was Mulcachy's boast that he could break the best animal living, no end of the hardest cases fell to his hand. He had built a reputation for succeeding where others failed, and, endowed with fearlessness, callousness, and cunning, he never let his reputation wane. There was nothing he dared not tackle, and, when he gave up an animal, the last word was said. For it, remained nothing but to be a cage-animal, in solitary confinement, pacing ever up and down, embittered with all the world of man and roaring its bitterness to the most delicious enthrillment of the pay-spectators.

During the three months spent by Michael in Mulcachy's Animal Home, occurred two especially hard cases. Of course, the daily chant of ordinary pain of training went on all the time through the working hours, such as of "good" bears and lions and tigers that were made amenable under stress, and of elephants derricked and gaffed into making the head- stand or into the beating of a bass drum. But the two cases that were exceptional, put a mood of depression and fear into all the listening animals, such as humans might experience in an ante-room of hell, listening to the flailing and the flaying of their fellows who had preceded them into the torture-chamber.

The first was of the big Indian tiger. Free-born in the jungle, and free all his days, master, according to his nature and prowess, of all other living creatures including his fellow-tigers, he had come to grief in the end; and, from the trap to the cramped cage, by elephant-back and railroad and steamship, ever in the cramped cage, he had journeyed across seas and continents to Mulcachy's Animal Home. Prospective buyers had examined but not dared to purchase. But Mulcachy had been undeterred. His own fighting blood leapt hot at sight of the magnificent striped cat. It was a challenge of the brute in him to excel. And, two weeks of hell, for the great tiger and for all the other animals, were required to teach him his first lesson.

Ben Bolt he had been named, and he arrived indomitable and irreconcilable, though almost paralysed from eight weeks of cramp in his narrow cage which had restricted all movement. Mulcachy should have undertaken the job immediately, but two weeks were lost by the fact that he had got married and honeymooned for that length of time. And in that time, in a large cage of concrete and iron, Ben Bolt had exercised and recovered the use of his muscles, and added to his hatred of the two-legged things, puny against him in themselves, who by trick and wile had so helplessly imprisoned him.

So, on this morning when hell yawned for him, he was ready and eager to meet all comers. They came, equipped with formulas, nooses, and forked iron bars. Five of them tossed nooses in through the bars upon the floor of his cage. He snarled and struck at the curling ropes, and for ten minutes was a grand and impossible wild creature, lacking in nothing save the wit and the patience possessed by the miserable two-legged things. And then, impatient and careless of the inanimate ropes, he paused, snarling at the men, with one hind foot resting inside a noose. The next moment, craftily lifted up about the girth of his leg by an iron fork, the noose tightened and the bite of it sank home into his flesh and pride. He leaped, he roared, he was a maniac of ferocity. Again and again, almost burning their palms, he tore the rope smoking through their hands. But ever they took in the slack and paid it out again, until, ere he was aware, a similar noose tightened on his foreleg. What he had done was nothing to what he now did. But he was stupid and impatient. The man-creatures were wise and patient, and a third leg and a fourth leg were finally noosed, so that, with many men tailing on to the ropes, he was dragged ignominiously on his side to the bars, and, ignominiously, through the bars were hauled his four legs, his chiefest weapons of offence after his terribly fanged jaws.

And then a puny man-creature, Mulcachy himself, dared openly and brazenly to enter the cage and approach him. He sprang to be at him, or, rather, strove so to spring, but was withstrained by his four legs through the bars which he could not draw back and get under him. And Mulcachy knelt beside him, dared kneel beside him, and helped the fifth noose over his head and round his neck. Then his head was drawn to the bars as helplessly as his legs had been drawn through. Next, Mulcachy laid hands on him, on his head, on his ears, on his very nose within an inch of his fangs; and he could do nothing but snarl and roar and pant for breath as the noose shut off his breathing.

Quivering, not with fear but with rage, Ben Bolt perforce endured the buckling around his throat of a thick, broad collar of leather to which was attached a very stout and a very long trailing rope. After that, when Mulcachy had left the cage, one by one the five nooses were artfully manipulated off his legs and his neck. Again, after this prodigious indignity, he was free, within his cage. He went up into the air. With returning breath he roared his rage. He struck at the trailing rope that offended his nerves, clawed at the trap of the collar that encased his neck, fell, rolled over, offended his body-nerves more and more by entangling contacts with the rope, and for half an hour exhausted himself in the futile battle with the inanimate thing. Thus tigers are broken.

At the last, wearied, even with sensations of sickness from the nervous strain put upon himself by his own anger, he lay down in the middle of the floor, lashing his tail, hating with his eyes, and accepting the clinging thing about his neck which he had learned he could not get rid of.

To his amazement, if such a thing be possible in the mental processes of a tiger, the rear door to his cage was thrown open and left open. He regarded the aperture with belligerent suspicion. No one and no threatening danger appeared in the doorway. But his suspicion grew. Always, among these man-animals, occurred what he did not know and could not comprehend. His preference was to remain where he was, but from behind, through the bars of the cage, came shouts and yells, the lash of whips, and the painful thrusts of the long iron forks. Dragging the rope behind him, with no thought of escape, but in the hope that he would get at his tormentors, he leaped into the rear passage that ran behind the circle of permanent cages. The passage way was deserted and dark, but ahead he saw light. With great leaps and roars, he rushed in that direction, arousing a pandemonium of roars and screams from the animals in the cages.

He bounded through the light, and into the light, dazzled by the brightness of it, and crouched down, with long, lashing tail, to orient himself to the situation. But it was only another and larger cage that he was in, a very large cage, a big, bright performing-arena that was all cage. Save for himself, the arena was deserted, although, overhead, suspended from the roof-bars, were block-and-tackle and seven strong iron chairs that drew his instant suspicion and caused him to roar at them.

For half an hour he roamed the arena, which was the greatest area of restricted freedom he had known in the ten weeks of his captivity. Then, a hooked iron rod, thrust through the bars, caught and drew the bight of his trailing rope into the hands of the men outside. Immediately ten of them had hold of it, and he would have charged up to the bars at them had not, at that moment, Mulcachy entered the arena through a door on the opposite side. No bars stood between Ben Bolt and this creature, and Ben Bolt charged him. Even as he charged he was aware of suspicion in that the small, fragile man-creature before him did not flee or crouch down, but stood awaiting him.

Ben Bolt never reached him. First, with an access of caution, he craftily ceased from his charge, and, crouching, with lashing tail, studied the man who seemed so easily his. Mulcachy was equipped with a long-lashed whip and a sharp-pronged fork of iron.

In his belt, loaded with blank cartridges, was a revolver.

Bellying closer to the ground, Ben Bolt advanced upon him, creeping slowly like a cat stalking a mouse. When he came to his next pause, which was within certain leaping distance, he crouched lower, gathered himself for the leap, then turned his head to regard the men at his back outside the cage. The trailing rope in their hands, to his neck, he had forgotten.

"Now you might as well be good, old man," Mulcachy addressed him in soft, caressing tones, taking a step toward him and holding in advance the iron fork.

This merely incensed the huge, magnificent creature. He rumbled a low, tense growl, flattened his ears back, and soared into the air, his paws spread so that the claws stood out like talons, his tail behind him as stiff and straight as a rod. Neither did the man crouch or flee, nor did the beast attain to him. At the height of his leap the rope tightened taut on his neck, causing him to describe a somersault and fall heavily to the floor on his side.

Before he could regain his feet, Mulcachy was upon him, shouting to his small audience: "Here's where we pound the argument out of him!" And pound he did, on the nose with the butt of the whip, and jab he did, with the iron fork to the ribs. He rained a hurricane of blows and jabs on the animal's most sensitive parts. Ever Ben Bolt leaped to retaliate, but was thrown by the ten men tailed on to the rope, and, each time, even as he struck the floor on his side, Mulcachy was upon him, pounding, smashing, jabbing. His pain was exquisite, especially that of his tender nose. And the creature who inflicted the pain was as fierce and terrible as he, even more so because he was more intelligent. In but few minutes, dazed by the pain, appalled by his inability to rend and destroy the man who inflicted it, Ben Bolt lost his courage. He fled ignominiously before the little, two-legged creature who was more terrible than himself who was a full-grown Royal Bengal tiger. He leaped high in the air in sheer panic; he ran here and there, with lowered head, to avoid the rain of pain. He even charged the sides of the arena, springing up and vainly trying to climb the slippery vertical bars.

Ever, like an avenging devil, Mulcachy pursued and smashed and jabbed, gritting through his teeth: "You will argue, will you? I'll teach you what argument is! There! Take that! And that! And that!"

"Now I've got him afraid of me, and the rest ought to be easy," he announced, resting off and panting hard from his exertions, while the great tiger crouched and quivered and shrank back from him against the base of the arena-bars. "Take a five-minute spell, you fellows, and we'll got our breaths."

Lowering one of the iron chairs, and attaching it firmly in its place on the floor, Mulcachy prepared for the teaching of the first trick. Ben Bolt, jungle-born and jungle-reared, was to be compelled to sit in the chair in ludicrous and tragic imitation of man-creatures. But Mulcachy was not quite ready. The first lesson of fear of him must be reiterated and driven home.

Stepping to a near safe distance, he lashed Ben Bolt on the nose. He repeated it. He did it a score of times, and scores of times. Turn his head as he would, ever Ben Bolt received the bite of the whip on his fearfully bruised nose; for Mulcachy was as expert as a stage-driver in his manipulation of the whip, and unerringly the lash snapped and cracked and stung Ben Bolt's nose wherever Ben Bolt at the moment might have it.

When it became maddeningly unendurable, he sprang, only to be jerked back by the ten strong men who held the rope to his neck. And wrath, and ferocity, and intent to destroy, passed out utterly from the tiger's inflamed brain, until he knew fear, again and again, always fear and only fear, utter and abject fear, of this human mite who searched him with such pain.

Then the lesson of the first trick was taken up. Mulcachy tapped the chair sharply with the butt of the whip to draw the animal's attention to it, then flicked the whip-lash sharply on his nose. At the same moment, an attendant, through the bars behind, drove an iron fork into his ribs to force him away from the bars and toward the chair. He crouched forward, then shrank back against the side-bars. Again the chair was rapped, his nose was lashed, his ribs were jabbed, and he was forced by pain toward the chair. This went on interminably, for a quarter of an hour, for half an hour, for an hour; for the men-animals had the patience of gods while he was only a jungle-brute. Thus tigers are broken. And the verb means just what it means. A performing animal is broken. Something breaks in an animal of the wild ere such an animal submits to do tricks before pay-audiences.

Mulcachy ordered an assistant to enter the arena with him. Since he could not compel the tiger directly to sit in the chair, he must employ other means. The rope about Ben Bolt's neck was passed up through the bars and rove through the block-and-tackle. At signal from Mulcachy, the ten men hauled away. Snarling, struggling, choking, in a fresh madness of terror at this new outrage, Ben Bolt was slowly hoisted by his neck up from the floor, until, quite clear of it, whirling, squirming, battling, suspended by his neck like a man being hanged, his wind was shut off and he began to suffocate. He coiled and twisted, the splendid muscles of his body enabling him almost to tie knots in it.

The block-and-tackle, running like a trolley on the overhead track, made it possible for the assistant to seize his tail and drag him through the air till he was above the chair. His helpless body guided thus by the tail, his chest jabbed by the iron fork in Mulcachy's hands, the rope was suddenly lowered, and Ben Bolt, with swimming brain, found himself seated in the chair. On the instant he leaped for the floor, received a blow on the nose from the heavy whip-handle, and had a blank cartridge fired straight into his nostril. His madness of pain and fear was multiplied. He sprang away in flight, but Mulcachy's voice rang out, "Hoist him!" and he slowly rose in the air again, hanging by his neck, and began to strangle.

Once more he was swung into position by his tail, jabbed in the chest, and lowered suddenly on the run, but so suddenly, with a frantic twist of his body on his part, that he fell violently across the chair on his belly. What little wind was left him from the strangling, seemed to have been ruined out of him by the violence of the fall. The glare in his eyes was maniacal and swimming. He panted frightfully, and his head rolled back and forth. Slaver dripped from his mouth, blood ran from his nose.

"Hoist away!" Mulcachy shouted.

And again, struggling frantically as the tightening collar shut off his wind, Ben Bolt was slowly lifted into the air. So wildly did he struggle that, ere his hind feet were off the floor, he pranced back and forth, so that when he was heaved clear his body swung like a huge pendulum. Over the chair, he was dropped, and for a fraction of a second the posture was his of a man sitting in a chair. Then he uttered a terrible cry and sprang.

It was neither snarl, nor growl, nor roar, that cry, but a sheer scream, as if something had broken inside of him. He missed Mulcachy by inches, as another blank cartridge exploded up his other nostril and as the men with the rope snapped him back so abruptly as almost to break his neck.

This time, lowered quickly, he sank into the chair like a half-empty sack of meal, and continued so to sink, until, crumpling at the middle, his great tawny head falling forward, he lay on the floor unconscious. His tongue, black and swollen, lolled out of his mouth. As buckets of water were poured on him he groaned and moaned. And here ended the first lesson.

"It's all right," Mulcachy said, day after day, as the teaching went on. "Patience and hard work will pull off the trick. I've got his goat. He's afraid of me. All that's required is time, and time adds to value with an animal like him."

Not on that first day, nor on the second, nor on the third, did the requisite something really break inside Ben Bolt. But at the end of a fortnight it did break. For the day came when Mulcachy rapped the chair with his whip-butt, when the attendant through the bars jabbed the iron fork into Ben Bolt's ribs, and when Ben Bolt, anything but royal, slinking like a beaten alley-cat, in pitiable terror, crawled over to the chair and sat down in it like a man. He now was an "educated" tiger. The sight of him, so sitting, tragically travestying man, has been considered, and is considered, "educative" by multitudinous audiences.

The second case, that of St. Elias, was a harder one, and it was marked down against Mulcachy as one of his rare failures, though all admitted that it was an unavoidable failure. St. Elias was a huge monster of an Alaskan bear, who was good-natured and even facetious and humorous after the way of bears. But he had a will of his own that was correspondingly as stubborn as his bulk. He could be persuaded to do things, but he would not tolerate being compelled to do things. And in the trained-animal world, where turns must go off like clockwork, is little or no space for persuasion. An animal must do its turn, and do it promptly. Audiences will not brook the delay of waiting while a trainer tries to persuade a crusty or roguish beast to do what the audience has paid to see it do.

So St. Elias received his first lesson in compulsion. It was also his last lesson, and it never progressed so far as the training-arena, for it took place in his own cage.

Noosed in the customary way, his four legs dragged through the bars, and his head, by means of a "choke" collar, drawn against the bars, he was first of all manicured. Each one of his great claws was cut off flush with his flesh. The men outside did this. Then Mulcachy, on the inside, punched his nose. Not lightly as it sounds was this operation. The punch was a perforation. Thrusting the instrument into the huge bear's nostril, Mulcachy cut a clean round chunk of living meat out of one side of it. Mulcachy knew the bear business. At all times, to make an untrained bear obey, one must be fast to some sensitive portion of the bear. The ears, the nose, and the eyes are the accessible sensitive parts, and, the eyes being out of the question, remain the nose and the ears as the parts to which to make fast.

Through the perforation Mulcachy immediately clamped a metal ring. To the ring he fastened a long "lunge"-rope, which was well named. Any unruly lunge, at any time during all the subsequent life of St. Elias, could thus be checked by the man who held the lunge-rope. His destiny was patent and ordained. For ever, as long as he lived and breathed, would he be a prisoner and slave to the rope in the ring in his nostril.

The nooses were slipped, and St. Elias was at liberty, within the confines of his cage, to get acquainted with the ring in his nose. With his powerful forepaws, standing erect and roaring, he proceeded to get acquainted with the ring. It certainly was not a thing persuasible. It was living fire. And he tore at it with his paws as he would have torn at the stings of bees when raiding a honey-tree. He tore the thing out, ripping the ring clear through the flesh and transforming the round perforation into a ragged chasm of pain.

Mulcachy cursed. "Here's where hell coughs," he said. The nooses were introduced again. Again St. Elias, helpless on his side against and partly through the bars, had his nose punched. This time it was the other nostril. And hell coughed. As before, the moment he was released, he tore the ring out through his flesh.

Mulcachy was disgusted. "Listen to reason, won't you?" he objurgated, as, this time, the reason he referred to was the introduction of the ring clear through both nostrils, higher up, and through the central dividing wall of cartilage. But St. Elias was unreasonable. Unlike Ben Bolt, there was nothing inside of him weak enough, or nervous enough, or high- strung enough, to break. The moment he was free he ripped the ring away with half of his nose along with it. Mulcachy punched St. Elias's right ear. St. Elias tore his right ear to shreds. Mulcachy punched his left ear. He tore his left ear to shreds. And Mulcachy gave in. He had to. As he said plaintively:

"We're beaten. There ain't nothing left to make fast to."

Later, when St. Elias was condemned to be a "cage-animal" all his days, Mulcachy was wont to grumble:

"He was the most unreasonable animal! Couldn't do a thing with him. Couldn't ever get anything to make fast to."

CHAPTER XXXIV

It was in the Orpheum Theatre, of Oakland, California; and Harley Kennan was in the act of reaching under his seat for his hat, when his wife said:

"Why, this isn't the interval. There's one more turn yet."

"A dog turn," he answered, and thereby explained; for it was his practice to leave a theatre during the period of the performance of an animal-act.

Villa Kennan glanced hastily at the programme.

"Of course," she said, then added: "But it's a singing dog. A dog Caruso. And it points out that there is no one on the stage with the dog. Let us stay for once, and see how he compares with Jerry."

"Some poor brute tormented into howling," Harley grumbled.

"But it has the stage to itself," Villa urged. "Besides, if it is painful, then we can go out. I'll go out with you. But I just would like to see how much better Jerry sings than does he. And it says an Irish terrier, too."

So Harley Kennan remained. The two burnt-cork comedians finished their turn and their three encores, and the curtain behind them went up on a full set of an empty stage. A rough-coated Irish terrier entered at a sedate walk, sedately walked forward to the centre, nearly to the footlights, and faced the leader of the orchestra. As the programme had stated, he had the stage to himself.

The orchestra played the opening strains of "Sweet Bye and Bye." The dog yawned and sat down. But the orchestra was thoroughly instructed to play the opening strains over and over, until the dog responded, and then to follow on with him. By the third time, the dog opened his mouth and began. It was not a mere howling. For that matter, it was too mellow to be classified as a howl at all. Nor was it merely rhythmic. The notes the dog sang were of the air, and they were correct.

But Villa Kennan scarcely heard.

"He has Jerry beaten a mile," Harley muttered to her.

"Listen," she replied, in tense whispers. "Did you ever see that dog before?"

Harley shook his head.

"You have seen him before," she insisted. "Look at that crinkled ear. Think! Think back! Remember!"

Still her husband shook his head.

"Remember the Solomons," she pressed. "Remember the Ariel. Remember when we came back from Malaita, where we picked Jerry up, to Tulagi, that he had a brother there, a nigger-chaser on a schooner."

"And his name was Michael, go on."

"And he had that self-same crinkled ear," she hurried. "And he was rough- coated. And he was full brother to Jerry. And their father and mother were Terrence and Biddy of Meringe. And Jerry is our Sing Song Silly. And this dog sings. And he has a crinkled ear. And his name is Michael."

"Impossible," said Harley.

"It is when the impossible comes true that life proves worth while," she retorted. "And this is one of those worth-whiles of impossibles. I know it."

Still the man of him said impossible, and still the woman of her insisted that this was an impossible come true. By this time the dog on the stage was singing "God Save the King."

"That shows I am right," Villa contended. "No American, in America, would teach a dog 'God Save the King.' An Englishman originally owned that dog and taught it. The Solomons are British."

"That's a far cry," he smiled. "But what gets me is that ear. I remember it now. I remember the day when we were on the beach at Tulagi with Jerry, and when his brother came ashore from the Eugenie in a whaleboat. And his brother had that self-same, loppy, crinkled ear."

"And more," Villa argued. "How many singing dogs have we ever known! Only one, Jerry. Evidently such a type occurs rarely. The same family would more likely produce similar types than different families. The family of Terrence and Biddy produced Jerry. And this is Michael."

"He was rough-coated, along with a crinkly ear," Harley meditated back. "I see him distinctly as he stood up in the bow of the whaleboat and as he ran along the beach side by side with Jerry."

"If Jerry should to-morrow run side by side with him you would be convinced?" she queried.

"It was their trick, and the trick of Terrence and Biddy before them," he agreed. "But it's a far cry from the Solomons to the United States."

"Jerry is such a far cry," she replied. "And if Jerry won from the Solomons to California, then is there anything more remarkable in Michael so winning? Oh, listen!"

For the dog on the stage, now responding to its one encore, was singing "Home, Sweet Home." This finished, Jacob Henderson, to tumultuous applause, came on the stage from the wings and joined the dog in bowing. Villa and Harley sat in silence for a moment. Then Villa said, apropos of nothing:

"I have been sitting here and feeling very grateful for one particular thing."

He waited.

"It is that we are so abominably wealthy," she concluded.

"Which means that you want the dog, must have him, and are going to got him, just because I can afford to do it for you," he teased.

"Because you can't afford not to," she answered. "You must know he is Jerry's brother. At least, you must have a sneaking suspicion . . . ?"

"I have," he nodded. "The thing that can't sometimes does, and there is a chance that this may be one of those times. Of course, it isn't Michael; but, on the other hand, what's to prevent it from being Michael? Let us go behind and find out."

"More agents of the Society for the Prevention of Cruelty to Animals," was Jacob Henderson's thought, as the man and woman, accompanied by the manager of the theatre, were shown into his tiny dressing-room. Michael, on a chair and half asleep, took no notice of them. While Harley talked with Henderson, Villa investigated Michael; and Michael scarcely opened his eyes ere he closed them again. Too sour on the human world, and too glum in his own soured nature, he was anything save his old courtly self to chance humans who broke in upon him to pat his head, and say silly things, and go their way never to be seen by him again.

Villa Kennan, with a pang of disappointment at such rebuff, forwent her overtures for the moment, and listened to what tale Jacob Henderson could tell of his dog. Harry Del Mar, a trained-animal man, had picked the dog up somewhere on the Pacific Coast, most probably in San Francisco, she learned; but, having taken the dog east with him, Harry Del Mar had died by accident in New York before telling anybody anything about the animal. That was all, except that Henderson had paid two thousand dollars to one Harris Collins, and had found the investment the finest he had ever made.

Villa turned back to the dog.

"Michael," she called, caressingly, almost in a whisper.

And Michael's eyes partly opened, the base-muscles of his ears stiffened, and his body quivered.

"Michael," she repeated.

This time raising his head, the eyes open and the ears stiffly erect, Michael looked at her. Not since on the beach at Tulagi had he heard that name uttered. Across the years and the seas the word came to him out of the past. Its effect was electrical, for on the instant all the connotations of "Michael" flooded his consciousness. He saw again Captain Kellar, of the Eugenie, who had last called him it, and Mister Haggin, and Derby, and Bob of Meringe Plantation, and Biddy and Terrence, and, not least among these shades of the vanished past, his brother Jerry.

But was it the vanished past? The name which had ceased for years, had come back. It had entered the room along with this man and woman. All this he did not reason; but indubitably, as if he had so reasoned, he acted upon it.

He jumped from the chair and ran to the woman. He smelled her hand, and smelled her as she patted him. Then, as he recognized her, he went wild. He sprang away, dashing around and around the room, sniffing under the washstand and smelling out the corners. As in a frenzy he was back to the woman, whimpering eagerly as she strove to pet him. The next moment, stiff in a frenzy, he was away again, scurrying about the room and still whimpering.

Jacob Henderson looked on with mild disapproval.

"He never cuts up that way," he said. "He is a very quiet dog. Maybe it is a fit he is going to have, though he never has fits."

No one understood, not even Villa Kennan. But Michael understood. He was looking for that vanished world which had rushed back upon him at sound of his old-time name. If this name could come to him out of the Nothingness, as this woman had whom once he had seen treading the beach at Tulagi, then could all other things of Tulagi and the Nothingness come to him. As she was there, before him in the living flesh, uttering his name, so might Captain Kellar, and Mister Haggin, and Jerry be there, somewhere in the very room or just outside the door.

He ran to the door, whimpering as he scratched at it.

"Maybe he thinks there is something outside," said Jacob Henderson, opening the door for him.

And Michael did so think. As a matter of course, through that open door, he was prepared to have the South-Pacific Ocean flow in, bearing on its bosom schooners and ships, islands and reefs, and all men and animals and things he once had known and still remembered.

But no past flowed in through the door. Outside was the usual present. He came back dejectedly to the woman, who still called him Michael as she petted him. She, at any rate, was real. Next he carefully smelled and identified the man with the beach of Tulagi and the deck of the Ariel, and again his excitement began to mount.

"Oh, Harley, I know it is he!" Villa cried. "Can't you test him? Can't you prove him?"

"But how?" Harley pondered. "He seems to recognize his name. It excites him. And though he never knew us very well, he seems to remember us and to be excited by us, too. If only he could talk . . ."

"Oh, talk! Talk!" Villa pleaded with Michael, catching both sides of his head and jaws in her hands and swaying him back and forth.

"Be careful, madam," Jacob Henderson warned. "He is a very sour dog; and he don't let people take such liberties."

"He does me," she laughed, half-hysterically. "Because he knows me. . . . Harley!" She broke off as the great idea dawned on her. "I have a test. Listen! Remember, Jerry was a nigger-chaser before we got him. And Michael was a nigger-chaser. You talk in beche-de-mer. Appear angry with some black boy, and see how it will affect him."

"I'll have to remember hard to resurrect any beche-de-mer," Harley said, nodding approval of the suggestion.

"At the same time I'll distract him," she rushed on.

Sitting down and bending forward to Michael so that his head was buried in her arms and breast, she began swaying him and crooning to him as was her wont with Jerry. Nor did he resent the liberty she took, and, like Jerry, he yielded to her crooning and softly began to croon with her. She signalled Harley with her eyes.

"My word!" he began in tones of wrath. "What name you fella boy stop 'm along this fella place? You make 'm me cross along you any amount!"

And at the words Michael bristled, dragged himself clear of the woman's detaining hands, and, with a snarl, whirled about to get a look at the black boy who must have just then entered the room and aroused the white god's ire. But there was no black boy. He looked on, still bristling, to the door. Harley transferred his own gaze to the door, and Michael knew, beyond all doubt, that outside the door was standing a Solomons nigger.

"Hey! Michael!" Harley shouted. "Chase 'm that black fella boy overside!"

With a roaring snarl, Michael flung himself at the door. Such was the fury and weight of his onslaught that the latch flew loose and the door swung open. The emptiness of the space which he had expected to see occupied, was appalling, and he shrank down, sick and dizzy with the baffling apparitional past that thus vexed his consciousness.

"And now," said Harley to Jacob Henderson, "we will talk business . . . "

CHAPTER XXXV

When the train arrived at Glen Ellen, in the Valley of the Moon, it was Harley Kennan himself, at the side-door of the baggage-car, who caught hold of Michael and swung him to the ground. For the first time Michael had performed a railroad journey uncrated. Merely with collar and chain had he travelled up from Oakland. In the waiting automobile he found Villa Kennan, and, chain removed, sat beside her and between her and Harley

As the machine purred along the two miles of road that wound up the side of Sonoma Mountain, Michael scarcely looked at the forest-trees and vistas of wandering glades. He had been in the United States three years, during which time he had been kept a close prisoner. Cage and crate and chain had been his portion, and narrow rooms, baggage cars, and station platforms. The nearest he had come to the country was when chained to benches in the various parks while Jacob Henderson studied Swedenborg. So that trees and hills and fields had ceased to mean anything. They were something inaccessible, as inaccessible as the blue of the sky or the drifting cloud-fleeces. Thus did he regard the trees and hills and fields, if the negative act of not regarding a thing at all can be considered a state of mind.

"Don't seem to be enthusiastic over the ranch, eh, Michael?" Harley remarked.

He looked up at sound of his old name, and made acknowledgment by flattening his ears a quivering trifle and by touching his nose against Harley's shoulder.

"Nor does he seem demonstrative," was Villa's judgment. "At least, nothing like Jerry,"

"Wait till they meet," Harley smiled in anticipation. "Jerry will furnish enough excitement for both of them."

"If they remember each other after all this time," said Villa. "I wonder if they will."

"They did at Tulagi," he reminded her. "And they were full grown and hadn't seen each other since they were puppies. Remember how they barked and scampered all about the beach. Michael was the hurly-burly one. At least he made twice as much noise."

"But he seems dreadfully grown-up and subdued now."

"Three years ought to have subdued him," Harley insisted.

But Villa shook her head.

As the machine drew up at the house and Kennan first stepped out, a dog's whimperingly joyous bark of welcome struck Michael as not altogether unfamiliar. The joyous bark turned to a suspicious and jealous snarl as Jerry scented the other dog's presence from Harley's caressing hand. The next moment he had traced the original source of the scent into the limousine and sprung in after it. With snarl and forward leap Michael met the snarling rush less than half-way, and was rolled over on the bottom of the car.

The Irish terrier, under all circumstances amenable to the control of the master as are few breeds of dogs, was instantly manifest in Jerry and Michael an Harley Kennan's voice rang out. They separated, and, despite the rumbling of low growling in their throats, refrained from attacking each other as they plunged out to the ground. The little set-to had occurred in so few seconds, or fractions of seconds, that they had not begun to betray recognition of each other until they were out of the machine. They were still comically stiff-legged and bristly as they aloofly sniffed noses.

"They know each other!" Villa cried. "Let's wait and see what they will do."

As for Michael, he accepted, without surprise, the indubitable fact that Jerry had come back out of the Nothingness. Things of this sort had begun to happen rapidly, but it was not the things themselves, but the connotations of them, that almost stunned him. If the man and woman, whom he had last seen at Tulagi, and, likewise, Jerry, had come back from the Nothingness, then could come, and might come at any moment, the beloved Steward.

Instead of responding to Jerry, Michael sniffed and glanced about in quest of Steward. Jerry's first expression of greeting and friendliness took the form of a desire to run. He barked invitation to his brother, scampered away half a dozen jumps, scampered back, and dabbed playfully at Michael with one forepaw in added emphasis of invitation ere he scampered away again.

For so many years had Michael not run with another dog, that at first Jerry's invitation had little meaning to him. Nevertheless, such running was an habitual expression of happiness and friendliness in dogdom, and especially strong had been his inheritance of it from Terrence and Biddy, the noted love-runners of the Solomons.

The next time Jerry dabbed at him with a paw, barked, and scurried away in an enticing semi-circle, Michael started involuntarily though slowly after him. But Michael did not bark; and, after half a dozen leaps, he came to a full stop and looked to Villa and Harley for permission.

"All right, Michael," Harley called heartily, deliberately turning his shoulder in the non-interest of consent as he extended his hand to help Villa from the machine.

Michael sprang away again, and was numbly aware of an ancient joy as he shouldered Jerry who shouldered against him as they ran side by side. But most of the joy was Jerry's, as was the wildest of the skurrying and the racing and the shouldering, of the body-wriggling, and ear-pricking, and yelping cries. Also, Jerry barked; and Michael did not bark.

"He used to bark," said Villa.

"Much more than Jerry," Harley supplemented.

"Then they have taken the bark out of him," she concluded. "He must have gone through terrible experiences to have lost his bark."

The green California spring merged into tawny summer, as Jerry, ever running afield, made Michael acquainted with the farthest and highest reaches of the Kennan ranch in the Valley of the Moon. The pageant of the wild flowers vanished until all that lingered on the burnt hillsides were orange poppies faded to palest gold, and Mariposa lilies, wind-blown on slender stems amidst the desiccated grasses, that smouldered like ornate spotted moths fluttering in rest for a space between flight and flight.

And Michael, a follower always where the exuberant Jerry led, sought throughout the passing year for what he could not find.

"Looking for something, looking for something," Harley would say to Villa. "It is not alive. It is not here. Now just what is it he is always looking for?"

Steward it was, and Michael never found him. The Nothingness held him and would not yield him up, although, could Michael have journeyed a ten- days' steamer-journey into the South Pacific to the Marquesas, Steward he would have found, and, along with him, Kwaque and the Ancient Mariner, all three living like lotus-eaters on the beach-paradise of Taiohae. Also, in and about their grass-thatched bungalow under the lofty avocado trees, Michael would have found other pet, cats, and kittens, and pigs, donkeys and ponies, a pair of love-birds, and a mischievous monkey or two; but never a dog and never a cockatoo. For Dag Daughtry, with violence of language, had laid a taboo upon dogs. After Killeny Boy, he averred, there should be no other dog. And Kwaque, without averring anything at all, resolutely refrained from possessing himself of the white cockatoos brought ashore by the sailors off the trading schooners.

But Michael was long in giving over his search for Steward, and, running the mountain trails or scrambling and sliding down into the deep canyons, was ever expectant and ready for Steward to step forth before him, or to pick up the unmistakable scent that would lead him to him.

"Looking for something, looking for something," Harley Kennan would chant curiously, as he rode beside Villa and observed Michael's unending search. "Now Jerry's after rabbits, and fox-trails; but you'll notice they don't interest Michael much. They're not what he's after. He behaves like one who has lost a great treasure and doesn't know where he lost it nor where to look for it."

Much Michael learned from Jerry of the varied life of the forest and fields. To run with Jerry seemed the one pleasure he took, for he never played. Play had passed out of him. He was not precisely morose or gloomy from his years on the trained-animal stage and in Harris Collins's college of pain, but he was sobered, subdued. The spring and the spontaneity had gone out of him. Just as the leopard had claw-marked his shoulder so that damp and frosty weather made the pain of the old wound come back, so was his mind marked by what he had gone through. He liked Jerry, was glad to be with him and to run with him; but it was Jerry who was ever in the lead, who ever raised the hue and cry of hunting pursuit, who barked indignation and eager yearning at a tree'd squirrel in refuge forty feet above the ground. Michael looked on and listened, but took no part in such antics of enthusiasm.

In the same way he looked on when Jerry fought fearful comic battles with Norman Chief, the great Percheron stallion. It was only play, for Jerry and Norman Chief were tried friends; and, though the huge horse, ears laid back, mouth open to bite, pursued Jerry in mad gyrations all about the paddock, it was with no thought of inflicting hurt, but merely to act up to his part in the sham battle. Yet no invitation of Jerry's could induce Michael to join in the fun. He contented himself with sitting down outside the rails and looking on.

"Why play?" might Michael have asked, who had had all play taken out of him.

But when it came to serious work, he was there even ahead of Jerry. On account of foot-and-mouth disease and of hog-cholera, strange dogs were taboo on the Kennan ranch. It did not take Michael long to learn this, and stray dogs got short shrift from him. With never a warning bark nor growl, in deadly silence, he rushed them, slashed and bit them, rolled them over and over in the dust, and drove them from the place. It was like nigger-chasing, a service to perform for the gods whom he loved and who willed such chasing.

No wild passion of love, such as he had had for Steward, did he bear Villa and Harley, but he did develop for them a great, sober love. He did not go out of his way to express it with overtures of wrigglings and squirmings and whimpering yelpings. Jerry could be depended upon for that. But he was always seriously glad to be with Villa and Harley and to receive recognition from them next after Jerry. Some of his deepest moments of content, before the fireplace, were to sit beside Villa or Harley and lean his head against a knee and have a hand, on occasion, drop down on his head or gently twist his crinkled ear.

Jerry was even guilty of playing with children who happened at times to be under the Kennan aegis. Michael endured children for as long as they left him alone. If they waxed familiar, he would warn them with a bristling of his neck-hair and a throaty rumbling and get up and stalk away.

"I can't understand it," Villa would say. "He was the fullest of play, and spirits, and all foolishness. He was much sillier and much more excitable than Jerry and certainly noisier. He must have some terrible story to tell, if only he could, of all that happened between Tulagi and the time we found him on the Orpheum stage."

"And that may be the least little hint of it," Harley would reply, pointing to Michael's shoulder where the leopard had scarred it on the day Jack, the Airedale, and Sara, the little green monkey, had died.

"He used to bark, I know he used to bark," Villa would continue. "Why doesn't he bark now?"

And Harley would point to the scarred shoulder and say, "That may account for it, and most possibly a hundred other things like it of which we cannot see the marks."

But the time was to come when they were to hear him bark again, not once, but twice. And both times were to be but an earnest of another and graver time when, without barking at all, he would express in action the measure of his love and worship of them who had taken him from the crate and the footlights and given him the freedom of the Valley of the Moon.

And in the meantime, running endlessly with Jerry over the ranch, he learned all the ways of it and all the life of it from the chickenyards and the duck-ponds to the highest pitch of Sonoma Mountain. He learned where the wild deer, in their season, were to be found; when they raided the prune-orchard, the vineyards, and the apple-trees; when they sought the deepest canyons and most secret coverts; and when they stamped out in open glades and on bare hillsides and crashed and clattered their antlers together in combat. Under Jerry's leadership, always running second and after on the narrow trails as a subdued dog should, he learned the ways and habits of the foxes, the coons, the weasels, and the ring-tail cats that seemed compounded of cat and coon and weasel. He came to know the ground-nesting birds and the difference between the customs of the valley quail, the mountain quail, and the pheasants. The traits and lairs of the domestic cats gone wild he also learned, as did he learn the wild loves of mountain farm-dogs with the free-roving coyotes.

He knew of the presence of the mountain lion, adrift down from Mendocino County, ere the first shorthorn calf was slain, and came home from the encounter, torn and bleeding, to attest what he had discovered and to be the cause of Harley Kennan riding trail next day with a rifle across his pommel. Likewise Michael came to know what Harley Kennan never did know and always denied as existing on his ranch, the one rocky outcrop, in the dense heart of the mountain forest, where a score of rattlesnakes denned through the winters and warmed themselves in the sun.

CHAPTER XXXVI

Winter came on in its delectable way in the Valley of the Moon. The last Mariposa lily vanished from the burnt grasses as the California Indian summer dreamed itself out in purple mists on the windless air. Soft rain- showers first broke the spell. Snow fell on the summit of Sonoma Mountain. At the ranch house the morning air was crisp and brittle, yet mid-day made the shade welcome, and in the open, under the winter sun, roses bloomed and oranges, grape-fruit, and lemons turned to golden yellow ripeness. Yet, a thousand feet beneath, on the floor of the valley, the mornings were white with frost.

And Michael barked twice. The first time was when Harley Kennan, astride a hot-blooded sorrel colt, tried to make it leap a narrow stream. Villa reined in her steed at the crest beyond, and, looking back into the little valley, waited for the colt to receive its lesson. Michael waited, too, but closer at hand. At first he lay down, panting from his run, by the stream-edge. But he did not know horses very well, and soon his anxiety for the welfare of Harley Kennan brought him to his feet.

Harley was gentle and persuasive and all patience as he strove to make the colt take the leap. The urge of voice and rein was of the mildest; but the animal balked the take-off each time, and the hot thoroughbredness in its veins made it sweat and lather. The velvet of young grass was torn up by its hoofs, and its terror of the stream was such, that, when fetched to the edge at a canter, it stiffened and crouched to an abrupt stop, then reared on its hind-legs. Which was too much for Michael.

He sprang at the horse's head as it came down with forefeet to earth, and as he sprang he barked. In his bark was censure and menace, and, as the horse reared again, he leaped into the air after it, his teeth clipping together as he just barely missed its nose.

Villa rode back down the slope to the opposite bank of the stream.

"Mercy!" she cried. "Listen to him! He's actually barking."

"He thinks the colt is trying to do some damage to me," Harley said. "That's his provocation. He hasn't forgotten how to bark. He's reading the colt a lecture."

"If he gets him by the nose it will be more than a lecture," Villa warned. "Be careful, Harley, or he will."

"Now, Michael, lie down and be good," Harley commanded. "It's all right, I tell you. It's an right. Lie down."

Michael sank down obediently, but protestingly; and he had eyes only for the horse's antics, while all his muscles were gathered tensely to spring in case the horse threatened injury to Harley again.

"I can't give in to him now, or he never will jump anything," Harley said to his wife, as he whirled about to gallop back to a distance. "Either I lift him over or I take a cropper."

He came back at full speed, and the colt, despite himself, unable to stop, lifted into the leap that would avoid the stream he feared, so that he cleared it with a good two yards to spare on the other side.

The next time Michael barked was when Harley, on the same hot-blood mount, strove to close a poorly hung gate on the steep pitch of a mountain wood-road. Michael endured the danger to his man-god as long as he could, then flew at the colt's head in a frenzy of barking.

"Anyway, his barking helped," Harley conceded, as he managed to close the gate. "Michael must certainly have told the colt that he'd give him what- for if he didn't behave."

"At any rate, he's not tongue-tied," Villa laughed, "even if he isn't very loquacious."

And Michael's loquacity never went farther. Only on these two occasions, when his master-god seemed to be in peril, was he known to bark. He never barked at the moon, nor at hillside echoes, nor at any prowling thing. A particular echo, to be heard directly from the ranch-house, was an unfailing source of exercise for Jerry's lungs. At such times that Jerry barked, Michael, with a bored expression, would lie down and wait until the duet was over. Nor did he bark when he attacked strange dogs that strayed upon the ranch.

"He fights like a veteran," Harley remarked, after witnessing one such encounter. "He's cold-blooded. There's no excitement in him."

"He's old before his time," Villa said. "There is no heart of play left in him, and no desire for speech. Just the same I know he loves me, and you -"

"Without having to be voluble about it," her husband completed for her.

"You can see it shining in those quiet eyes of his," she supplemented.

"Reminds me of one of the survivors of Lieutenant Greeley's Expedition I used to know," he agreed. "He was an enlisted soldier and one of the handful of survivors. He had been through so much that he was just as subdued as Michael and just as taciturn. He bored most people, who could not understand him. Of course, the truth was the other way around. They bored him. They knew so little of life that he knew the last word of. And one could scarcely get any word out of him. It was not that he had forgotten how to speak, but that he could not see any reason for speaking when nobody could understand. He was really crusty from too-bitter wise experience. But all you had to do was look at him in his tremendous repose and know that he had been through the thousand hells, including all the frozen ones. His eyes had the same quietness of Michael's. And they had the same wisdom. I'd give almost anything to know how he got his shoulder scarred. It must have been a tiger or a lion."

The man, like the mountain lion whom Michael had encountered up the mountain, had strayed down from the wilds of Mendocino County, following the ruggedest mountain stretches, and, at night, crossing the farmed valley spaces where the presence of man was a danger to him. Like the mountain lion, the man was an enemy to man, and all men were his enemies, seeking his life which he had forfeited in ways more terrible than the lion which had merely killed calves for food.

Like the mountain lion, the man was a killer. But, unlike the lion, his vague description and the narrative of his deeds was in all the newspapers, and mankind was a vast deal more interested in him than in the lion. The lion had slain calves in upland pastures. But the man, for purposes of robbery, had slain an entire family, the postmaster, his wife, and their three children, in the upstairs over the post office in the mountain village of Chisholm.

For two weeks the man had eluded and exceeded pursuit. His last crossing had been from the mountains of the Russian River, across wide-farmed Santa Rosa Valley, to Sonoma Mountain. For two days he had laired and rested, sleeping much, in the wildest and most inaccessible precincts of the Kennan Ranch. With him he had carried coffee stolen from the last house he had raided. One of Harley Kennan's angora goats had furnished him with meat. Four times he had slept the clock around from exhaustion, rousing on occasion, like any animal, to eat voraciously of the goat-meat, to drink large quantities of the coffee hot or cold, and to sink down into heavy but nightmare-ridden sleep.

And in the meantime civilization, with its efficient organization and intricate inventions, including electricity, had closed in on him. Electricity had surrounded him. The spoken word had located him in the wild canyons of Sonoma Mountain and fringed the mountain with posses of peace-officers and detachments of armed farmers. More terrible to them than any mountain lion was a man-killing man astray in their landscape. The telephone on the Kennan Ranch, and the telephones on all other ranches abutting on Sonoma Mountain, had rung often and transmitted purposeful conversations and arrangements.

So it happened, when the posses had begun to penetrate the mountain, and when the man was compelled to make a daylight dash down into the Valley of the Moon to cross over to the mountain fastnesses that lay between it and Napa Valley, that Harley Kennan rode out on the hot-blooded colt he was training. He was not in pursuit of the man who had slain the postmaster of Chisholm and his family. The mountain was alive with man- hunters, as he well knew, for a score had bedded and eaten at the ranch house the night before. So the meeting of Harley Kennan with the man was unplanned and eventful.

It was not the first meeting with men the man had had that day. During the preceding night he had noted the campfires of several posses. At dawn, attempting to break forth down the south-western slopes of the mountain toward Petaluma, he had encountered not less than five separate detachments of dairy-ranchers all armed with Winchesters and shotguns. Breaking back to cover, the chase hot on his heels, he had run full tilt into a party of village youths from Glen Ellen and Caliente. Their squirrel and deer rifles had missed him, but his back had been peppered with birdshot in a score of places, the leaden pellets penetrating maddeningly in a score of places just under the skin.

In the rush of his retreat down the canyon slope, he had plunged into a bunch of shorthorn steers, who, far more startled than he, had rolled him on the forest floor, trampled over him in their panic, and smashed his rifle under their hoofs. Weaponless, desperate, stinging and aching from his superficial wounds and bruises, he had circled the forest slopes along deer-paths, crossed two canyons, and begun to descend the horse- trail he found in the third canyon.

It was on this trail, going down, that he met the reporter coming up. The reporter was, well, just a reporter, from the city, knowing only city ways, who had never before engaged in a man-hunt. The livery horse he had rented down in the valley was a broken-kneed, jaded, and spiritless creature, that stood calmly while its rider was dragged from its back by the wild-looking and violently impetuous man who sprang out around a sharp turn of the trail. The reporter struck at his assailant once with his riding-whip. Then he received a beating, such as he had often written up about sailor-rows and saloon-frequenters in his cub-reporter days, but which for the first time it was his lot to experience.

To the man's disgust he found the reporter unarmed save for a pencil and a wad of copy paper. Out of his disappointment in not securing a weapon, he beat the reporter up some more, left him wailing among the ferns, and, astride the reporter's horse, urging it on with the reporter's whip, continued down the trail.

Jerry, ever keenest on the hunting, had ranged farther afield than Michael as the pair of them accompanied Harley Kennan on his early morning ride. Even so, Michael, at the heels of his master's horse, did not see nor understand the beginning of the catastrophe. For that matter, neither did Harley. Where a steep, eight-foot bank came down to the edge of the road along which he was riding, Harley and the hot-blood colt were startled by an eruption through the screen of manzanita bushes above. Looking up, he saw a reluctant horse and a forceful rider plunging in mid-air down upon him. In that flashing glimpse, even as he reined and spurred to make his own horse leap sidewise out from under, Harley Kennan observed the scratched skin and torn clothing, the wild-burning eyes, and the haggardness under the scraggly growth of beard, of the man-hunted man.

The livery horse was justifiably reluctant to make that leap out and down the bank. Too painfully aware of the penalty its broken knees and rheumatic joints must pay, it dug its hoofs into the steep slope of moss and only sprang out and clear in the air in order to avoid a fall. Even so, its shoulder impacted against the shoulder of the whirling colt below it, overthrowing the latter. Harley Kennan's leg, caught under against the earth, snapped, and the colt, twisted and twisting as it struck the ground, snapped its backbone.

To his utter disgust, the man, pursued by an armed countryside, found Harley Kennan, his latest victim, like the reporter, to be weaponless. Dismounted, he snarled in his rage and disappointment and deliberately kicked the helpless man in the side. He had drawn back his foot for the second kick, when Michael took a hand, or a leg, rather, sinking his teeth into the calf of the back-drawn leg about to administer the kick.

With a curse the man jerked his leg clear, Michael's teeth ribboning flesh and trousers.

"Good boy, Michael!" Harley applauded from where he lay helplessly pinioned under his horse. "Hey! Michael!" he continued, lapsing back into beche-de-mer, "chase 'm that white fella marster to hell outa here along bush!"

"I'll kick your head off for that," the man gritted at Harley through his teeth.

Savage as were his acts and utterance, the man was nearly ready to cry. The long pursuit, his hand against all mankind and all mankind against him, had begun to break his stamina. He was surrounded by enemies. Even youths had risen up and peppered his back with birdshot, and beef cattle had trod him underfoot and smashed his rifle. Everything conspired against him. And now it was a dog that had slashed down his leg. He was on the death-road. Never before had this impressed him with such clear certainty. Everything was against him. His desire to cry was hysterical, and hysteria, in a desperate man, is prone to express itself in terrible savage ways. Without rhyme or reason he was prepared to carry out his threat to kick Harley Kennan to death. Not that Kennan had done anything to him. On the contrary, it was he who had attacked Kennan, hurling him down on the road and breaking his leg under his horse. But Harley Kennan was a man, and all mankind was his enemy; and, in killing Kennan, in some vague way it appeared to him that he was avenging himself, at least in part, on mankind in general. Going down himself in death, he would drag what he could with him into the red ruin.

But ere he could kick the man on the ground, Michael was back upon him. His other calf and trousers' leg were ribboned as he tore clear. Then, catching Michael in mid-leap with a kick that reached him under the chest, he sent him flying through the air off the road and down the slope. As mischance would have it, Michael did not reach the ground. Crashing through a scrub manzanita bush, his body was caught and pinched in an acute fork a yard above the ground.

"Now," the man announced grimly to Harley, "I'm going to do what I said. I'm just going to kick your head clean off."

"And I haven't done a thing to you," Harley parleyed. "I don't so much mind being murdered, but I'd like to know what I'm being murdered for."

"Chasing me for my life," the man snarled, as he advanced. "I know your kind. You've all got it in for me, and I ain't got a chance except to give you yours. I'll take a whole lot of it out on you."

Kennan was thoroughly aware of the gravity of his peril. Helpless himself, a man-killing lunatic was about to kill him and to kill him most horribly. Michael, a prisoner in the bush, hanging head-downward in the manzanita from his loins squeezed in the fork, and struggling vainly, could not come to his defence.

The man's first kick, aimed at Harley's face, he blocked with his forearm; and, before the man could make a second kick, Jerry erupted on the scene. Nor did he need encouragement or direction from his love-master. He flashed at the man, sinking his teeth harmlessly into the slack of the man's trousers at the waist-band above the hip, but by his weight dragging him half down to the ground.

And upon Jerry the man turned with an increase of madness. In truth all the world was against him. The very landscape rained dogs upon him. But from above, from the slopes of Sonoma Mountain, the cries and calls of the trailing poses caught his ear, and deflected his intention. They were the pursuing death, and it was from them he must escape. With another kick at Jerry, hurling him clear, he leaped astride the reporter's horse which had continued to stand, without movement or excitement, in utter apathy, where he had dismounted from it.

The horse went into a reluctant and stiff-legged gallop, while Jerry followed, snarling and growling wrath at so high a pitch that almost he squalled.

"It's all right, Michael," Harley soothed. "Take it easy. Don't hurt yourself. The trouble's over. Anybody'll happen along any time now and get us out of this fix."

But the smaller branch of the two composing the fork broke, and Michael fell to the ground, landing in momentary confusion on his head and shoulders. The next moment he was on his feet and tearing down the road in the direction of Jerry's noisy pursuit. Jerry's noise broke in a sharp cry of pain that added wings to Michael's feet. Michael passed him rolling helplessly on the road. What had happened was that the livery horse, in its stiff-jointed, broken-kneed gallop, had stumbled, nearly fallen, and, in its sprawling recovery, had accidentally stepped on Jerry, bruising and breaking his foreleg.

And the man, looking back and seeing Michael close upon him, decided that it was still another dog attacking him. But he had no fear of dogs. It was men, with their rifles and shotguns, that might bring him to ultimate grief. Nevertheless, the pain of his bleeding legs, lacerated by Jerry and Michael, maintained his rage against dogs.

"More dogs," was his bitter thought, as he leaned out and brought his whip down across Michael's face.

To his surprise, the dog did not wince under the blow. Nor for that matter did he yelp or cry out from the pain. Nor did he bark or growl or snarl. He closed in as though he had not received the blow, and as though the whip was not brandished above him. As Michael leaped for his right leg he swung the whip down, striking him squarely on the muzzle midway between nose and eyes. Deflected by the blow, Michael dropped back to earth and ran on with his longest leaps to catch up and make his next spring.

But the man had noticed another thing. At such close range, bringing his whip down, he could not help noting that Michael had kept his eyes open under the blow. Neither had he winced nor blinked as the whip slashed down on him. The thing was uncanny. It was something new in the way of dogs. Michael sprang again, the man timed him again with the whip, and he saw the uncanny thing repeated. By neither wince nor blink had the dog acknowledged the blow.

And then an entirely new kind of fear came upon the man. Was this the end for him, after all he had gone through? Was this deadly silent, rough-coated terrier the thing destined to destroy him where men had failed? He did not even know that the dog was real. Might it not be some terrible avenger, out of the mystery beyond life, placed to beset him and finish him finally on this road that he was convinced was surely the death-road? The dog was not real. It could not be real. The dog did not live that could take a full-arm whip-slash without wince or flinch.

Twice again, as the dog sprang, he deflected it with accurately delivered blows. And the dog came on with the same surety and silence. The man surrendered to his terror, clapping heels to his horse's old ribs, beating it over the head and under the belly with the whip until it galloped as it had not galloped in years. Even on that apathetic steed the terror descended. It was not terror of the dog, which it knew to be only a dog, but terror of the rider. In the past its knees had been broken and its joints stiffened for ever, by drunken-mad riders who had hired him from the stables. And here was another such drunken-mad rider, for the horse sensed the man's terror, who ached his ribs with the weight of his heels and beat him cruelly over face and nose and ears.

The best speed of the horse was not very great, not great enough to out- distance Michael, although it was fast enough to give the latter only infrequent opportunities to spring for the man's leg. But each spring was met by the unvarying whip-blow that by its very weight deflected him in the air. Though his teeth each time clipped together perilously close to the man's leg, each time he fell back to earth he had to gather himself together and run at his own top speed in order to overtake the terror-stricken man on the crazy-galloping horse.

Enrico Piccolomini saw the chase and was himself in at the finish; and the affair, his one great adventure in the world, gave him wealth as well as material for conversation to the end of his days. Enrico Piccolomini was a wood-chopper on the Kennan Ranch. On a rounded knoll, overlooking the road, he had first heard the galloping hoofs of the horse and the crack of the whip-blows on its body. Next, he had seen the running battle of the man, the horse, and the dog. When directly beneath him, not twenty feet distant, he saw the dog leap, in its queer silent way, straight up and in to the down-smash of the whip, and sink its teeth in the rider's leg. He saw the dog, with its weight, as it fell back to earth, drag the man half out of the saddle. He saw the man, in an effort to recover his balance, put his own weight on the bridle-reins. And he saw the horse, half-rearing, half-tottering and stumbling, overthrow the last shred of the man's balance so that he followed the dog to the ground.

"And then they are like two dogs, like two beasts," Piccolomini was wont to tell in after-years over a glass of wine in his little hotel in Glen Ellen. "The dog lets go the man's leg and jumps for the man's throat. And the man, rolling over, is at the dog's throat. Both his hands, so he fastens about the throat of this dog. And the dog makes no sound. He never makes sound, before or after. After the two hands of the man stop his breath he can not make sound. But he is not that kind of a dog. He will not make sound anyway. And the horse stands and looks on, and the horse coughs. It is very strange all that I see.

"And the man is mad. Only a madman will do what I see him do. I see the man show his teeth like any dog, and bite the dog on the paw, on the nose, on the body. And when he bites the dog on the nose, the dog bites him on the check. And the man and the dog fight like hell, and the dog gets his hind legs up like a cat. And like a cat he tears the man's shirt away from his chest, and tears the skin of the chest with his claws till it is all red with bleeding. And the man yow-yowls, and makes noises like a wild mountain lion. And always he chokes the dog. It is a hell of a fight.

"And the dog is Mister Kennan's dog, a fine man, and I have worked for him two years. So I will not stand there and see Mister Kennan's dog all killed to pieces by the man who fights like a mountain lion. I run down the hill, but I am excited and forget my axe. I run down the hill, maybe from this door to that door, twenty feet or maybe thirty feet. And it is nearly all finished for the dog. His tongue is a long ways out, and his eyes like covered with cobwebs; but still he scratches the man's chest with his hind-feet and the man yow-yowls like a hen of the mountains.

"What can I do? I have forgotten the axe. The man will kill the dog. I look for a big rock. There are no rocks. I look for a club. I cannot find a club. And the man is killing the dog. I tell you what I do. I am no fool. I kick the man. My shoes are very heavy, not like shoes I wear now. They are the shoes of the wood-chopper, very thick on the sole with hard leather, with many iron nails. I kick the man on the side of the face, on the neck, right under the ear. I kick once. It is a good kick. It is enough. I know the place, right under the ear.

"And the man lets go of the dog. He shuts his eyes, and opens his mouth, and lies very still. And the dog begins once more to breathe. And with the breath comes the life, and right away he wants to kill the man. But I say 'No,' though I am very much afraid of the dog. And the man begins to become alive. He opens his eyes and he looks at me like a mountain lion. And his mouth makes a noise like a mountain lion. And I am afraid of him like I am afraid of the dog. What am I to do? I have forgotten the axe. I tell you what I do. I kick the man once again under the ear. Then I take my belt, and my bandana handkerchief, and I tie him. I tie his hands. I tie his legs, too. And all the time I am saying 'No,' to the dog, and that he must leave the man alone. And the dog looks. He knows I am his friend and am tying the man. And he does not bite me, though I am very much afraid. The dog is a terrible dog. Do I not know? Have I not seen him take a strong man out of the saddle? a man that is like a mountain lion?

"And then the men come. They all have guns-rifles, shotguns, revolvers, pistols. And I think, first, that justice is very quick in the United States. Only just now have I kicked a man in the head, and, one-two-three, just like that, men come with guns to take me to jail for kicking a man in the head. At first I do not understand. The many men are angry with me. They call me names, and say bad things; but they do not arrest me. Ah! I begin to understand! I hear them talk about three thousand dollars. I have robbed them of three thousand dollars. It is not true. I say so. I say never have I robbed a man of one cent. Then they laugh. And I feel better and I understand better. The three thousand dollars is the reward of the Government for this man I have tied up with my belt and my bandana. And the three thousand dollars is mine because I kicked the man in the head and tied his hands and his feet.

"So I do not work for Mister Kennan any more. I am a rich man. Three thousand dollars, all mine, from the Government, and Mister Kennan sees that it is paid to me by the Government and not robbed from me by the men with the guns. Just because I kicked the man in the head who was like a mountain lion! It is fortune. It is America. And I am glad that I have left Italy and come to chop wood on Mister Kennan's ranch. And I start this hotel in Glen Ellen with the three thousand dollars. I know there is large money in the hotel business. When I was a little boy, did not my father have a hotel in Napoli? I have now two daughters in high school. Also I own an automobile."

"Mercy me, the whole ranch is a hospital!" cried Villa Kennan, two days later, as she came out on the broad sleeping-porch and regarded Harley and Jerry stretched out, the one with his leg in splints, the other with his leg in a plaster cast. "Look at Michael," she continued. "You're not the only ones with broken bones. I've only just discovered that if his nose isn't broken, it ought to be, from the blow he must have received on it. I've had hot compresses on it for the last hour. Look at it!"

Michael, who had followed in at her invitation, betrayed a ridiculously swollen nose as he sniffed noses with Jerry, wagged his bobtail to Harley in greeting, and was greeted in turn with a blissful hand laid on his head.

"Must have got it in the fight," Harley said. "The fellow struck him with the whip many times, so Piccolomini says, and, naturally, it would be right across the nose when he jumped for him."

"And Piccolomini says he never cried out when he was struck, but went on running and jumping," Villa took up enthusiastically. "Think of it! A dog no bigger than Michael dragging out of the saddle a man-killing outlaw whom scores of officers could not catch!"

"So far as we are concerned, he did better than that," Harley commented quietly. "If it hadn't been for Michael, and for Jerry, too, if it hadn't been for the pair of them, I do verily believe that that lunatic would have kicked my head off as he promised."

"The blessed pair of them!" Villa cried, with shining eyes, as her hand flashed out to her husband's in a quick press of heart-thankfulness. "The last word has not been said upon the wonder of dogs," she added, as, with a quick winking of her eyelashes to overcome the impending moistness, she controlled her emotion.

"The last word of the wonder of dogs will never be said," Harley spoke, returning the pressure of her hand and releasing it in order to help her.

"And just for that were going to say something right now," she smiled. "Jerry, and Michael, and I. We've been practising it in secret for a surprise for you. You just lie there and listen. It's the Doxology. Don't Laugh. No pun intended."

She bent forward from the stool on which she sat, and drew Michael to her so that he sat between her knees, her two hands holding his head and jowls, his nose half-buried in her hair.

"Now Jerry!" she called sharply, as a singing teacher might call, so that Jerry turned his head in attention, looked at her, smiled understanding with his eyes, and waited.

It was Villa who started and pitched the Doxology, but quickly the two dogs joined with their own soft, mellow howling, if howling it may be called when it was so soft and mellow and true. And all that had vanished into the Nothingness was in the minds of the two dogs as they sang, and they sang back through the Nothingness to the land of Otherwhere, and ran once again with the Lost Pack, and yet were not entirely unaware of the present and of the indubitable two-legged god who was called Villa and who sang with them and loved them.

"No reason we shouldn't make a quartette of it," remarked Harley Kennan, as with his own voice he joined in.

Jack London - A Short Biography

John Griffith "Jack" London was born John Griffith Chaney on January 12th 1876, near Third and Brannan Streets in San Francisco. He was directly descended from a prominent engineering family in Pennsylvania and some of the early Puritan settlers in the Massachusetts Bay Colony. Flora moved to the Pacific Coast following the death of her father, where she taught music and worked as a spiritualist. London's relationship with his father was fraught. Though the fires which followed the 1906 San Francisco earthquake destroyed his birth certificate, it is believed that his father was the astrologist William Chaney since Chaney and London's mother were living together when she became pregnant. There is strong evidence in support of this, particularly in several instances in Chaney's memoirs in which he refers to Flora as his wife, and an advertisement of Flora's for her teaching in which she refers to herself as "Florence Wellman Chaney". The claim made by Flora that Chaney demanded she have an abortion is unsubstantiated, but that shortly afterward he disclaimed responsibility for the unborn child is certain. She attempted suicide by shooting herself, though she failed and the resulting injuries left her temporarily deranged such that, on giving birth, she gave the child to Virginia Prentiss, an ex-slave, who became a prominent maternal figure for the duration of London's life. In late 1876 Flora married John London and brought her baby John wither her. As a family they settled in Oakland where London completed grade school.

By 1885 London had become an avid reader and that year he came across a copy of Signa, a lengthy Victorian novel by Ouida, which he later considered the catalyst for his literary career. He began frequenting the Oakland public library where he met Ina Coolbrith, the librarian, who actively encouraged his reading and learning through her recommendations and discussion. Later she became California's first poet laureate. He continued with this self-education until 1889 when he started work at Hickmott's Cannery, where he would often work up to eighteen hours per day. He quickly became dissatisfied with this and so borrowed money from Virginia Prentiss to buy Razzle-Dazzle, a small single-sail vessel known as a 'sloop', from an oyster pirate who was known as French Frank. Later, in his memoirs, London claimed to have stolen French Frank's mistress Mamie. The sloop lasted mere months before it was damaged beyond repair, so London turned to the California Fish Patrol for employment who hired him as a member.

In 1893 he signed on with the sealing schooner Sophie Sutherland as it was headed for Japan for several months. He returned to find the country threatened by polio, and Oakland by civil unrest brought about by labour shortage and exploitation. He found arduous work in a street-railway power plant and in a jute mill before joining Kelly's Army, a protest march formed by unemployed labourers, who would eventually march on Washington D.C. in protest. During this time as a tramp he spent thirty days in the Erie County Penitentiary in Buffalo, New York, for vagrancy. Later, in The Road, he wrote of his experience there;

Man-handling was merely one of the very minor unprintable horrors of the Erie County Pen. I say 'unprintable'; and in justice I must also say undescribable. They were unthinkable to me until I saw them, and I was no spring chicken in the ways of the world and the awful abysses of human degradation. It would take a deep plummet to reach bottom in the Erie County Pen, and I do but skim lightly and facetiously the surface of things as I there saw them.

Having completed his outstanding responsibilities with the California Fish Patrol London returned to Oakland and attended the Oakland High School, contributing numerous articles to The Aegis, the school's magazine. The first of these was "Typhoon off the Coast of Japan", in which he recounted many of his sailing experiences. During his time as a student he would frequently study at Heinold's First and Last Chance Saloon, a bar on the port in Oakland. At the age of seventeen he confided in the proprietor, John Heinold, of his ambition to go to University. Heinold loaded London the money he needed for his tuition. He particularly wanted to go to the University of California, Berkeley, and was admitted in 1896. He continued to work at Heinold's bar and during this time was introduced to several of the adventurers and sailors who would pass through Oakland, many of whom influenced his writing career, particularly Alexander McLean, a notoriously cruel sea captain who include Wolf Larsen, the protagonist in The Sea-Wolf. He was twenty-one when he enrolled at the University of California, Berkeley, and during his time there he undertook a search for the newspaper accounts of his mother's suicide attempt wherein he found the name of his biological father who by then was living in Chicago. London wrote to him eagerly, though Chaney responded by claiming impotence and that therefore he could not possibly be London's father. Moreover, on acknowledging that he had known London's mother, Chaney breezily informed London that she had been in relations with several men and that the abortion claims were slander against him. This response crushed London, and months later he quit Berkeley and headed to join the Klondike Gold Rush in the Yukon.

His time in Klondike was difficult. He, like so many others, developed various health problems as a result of malnourishment and extreme weather conditions. London suffered from scurvy, was constantly bothered by joint problems and had scars on his body and face for the rest of his life as a result of injuries and sores sustained during this period. He had left Oakland with a passing interest in social issues and, having spent much of his camp time in the Yukon in good-natured debate of matters of social interest with the wealthy Republican mining investors, returned to Oakland with an active social conscience as a socialism activist. He had also picked up some of the Republicans' capitalist ideals, realising his own intelligence and writing were his assets and that they could be exploited and nurtured in a businesslike fashion. Once back in California he wrote specifically in pursuit of publication, later detailing this experience in his 1908 novel, Martin Eden. The first work he saw published following his gold rush years was the short story To The Man On The Trail which was picked up by The Overland Monthly, though they offered him merely five dollars and were late to pay. This, he wrote later, almost ended his career, which was saved "literally and literarily" by The Black Cat, another magazine which offered forty dollars for A Thousand Deaths. That forty dollars was the first money he ever received for his writing. He eventually received his five outstanding dollars sometime afterward.

London's writing career took off in conjunction with the development of new printing technology which allowed for low-cost mass-production of popular magazines, enabling an enormous rise in the readership and popularity of these publications. In 1900 London earned approximately $2,500 from his writing, roughly $71,000 when inflation-adjusted for 2014. On April 7th of that year London married Elizabeth "Bessie" Maddern. He had known her for several years through his circle of friends and had enjoyed a strong friendship with her for much of that time. They publicly acknowledged that their marriage was out of friendship and the surety that they would produce "sturdy" children, rather than love. They shared pet-names: his for her was "Mother-Girl" and hers for him was "Daddy-Boy". On 15th January 1901 they had their first child, Joan, and a second, Bessie, on October 20th 1902. By 1903 the couple were "extremely incompatible", though London remained kind and gentle towards his wife, though he would confide in his friends privately, saying

[Bessie] is devoted to purity. When I tell her morality is only evidence of low blood pressure, she hates me. She'd sell me and the children out for her damned purity. It's terrible. Every time I come back after being away from home for a night she won't let me be in the same room with her if she can help it.

It has been suggested that part of Bessie's concerns were based on a fear that London had been "away from home for a night" visiting whores and that one day he would return carrying venereal disease.

In early 1903 London sold The Call of the Wild to The Saturday Evening Post for $750, and later the book rights to Macmillan for a further $2,000. Macmillan conducted an efficient and effective marketing campaign which saw the book sell in huge numbers. It addressed London's belief that the behaviour of animals is a direct result of the treatment they receive by their handlers and owners, something he witnessed first hand in the relationships between humans and animals in the Yukon. On July 24th 1903 London told Bessie that he was moving out, and rented a villa on Lake Merritt in Oakland. Here he met the poet George Stirling and struck up an immediate friendship. In their correspondence London signed himself as "Wolf", perhaps indicating his affinity to the animal and its wildness. With this in mind his remarks on the treatment of animals by their handlers can be seen as parallel to his own experience of his father, and that his abandonment at birth, and later personal disownment, perhaps caused London's sense of kinship with the wolf's wild existence.

The San Francisco Examiner offered London an assignment covering the Russo-Japanese War and he arrived in Yokohama on the 25th January 1904. He was quickly arrested by Japanese authorities in Shimonoseki, but thanks to American Ambassador Lloyd Griscom's intervention was soon released. He then travelled to Korea where he was soon arrested again, this time for unacceptable unauthorised proximity to the Manchuria border, and was sent back to Seoul. Once granted permission to travel to the border with the Imperial Japanese Army to observe the battle of the Yalu he continued with his assignment, though considered himself too restricted and monitored. He applied to William Randolph Hearst, the owner of the Examiner, for permission for a transfer to the Imperial Russian Army where he hoped for increased journalistic freedom. During the arrangements for this he accused his Japanese chaperones of stealing his horse's fodder which resulted in violence and his third arrest in four months. This time his release was secured by the intervention of

President Theodore Roosevelt and London returned to America in June of the same year. On the 18th of August London and Stirling went to the Bohemian Grove where he was elected to honour membership of the Bohemian Club. During the whole of 1904 he and Bessie negotiated terms of a divorce which was granted on 11th November of that year.

London was introduced to Charmian Kittredge by the publisher George Platt Brett, Sr., while she was working as his secretary. They married on the 19th November 1905. Together they travelled extensively and several of their experiences would inspire his writing, particularly their time in Hawaii and Australia. London pet-named Charmian "Mate-Woman", indicating her uninhibited sexuality which was a complete contrast from his first wife Bessie. With Charmian they tried twice for a baby, suffering the death of the first at birth and the miscarriage of the second. In 1905 London bought a ranch in Glen Ellen, California, saying "next to my wife, the ranch is the dearest thing in the world to me." Though he was desperate for the ranch to be a commercial success to the extent that he considered his writing now simply a means of funding his enterprise ("I write for no other purpose than to add to the beauty that now belongs to me. I wrote a book for no other reason than to add three or four hundred acres to my magnificent estate"), it was an abject economic failure. Critics are divided over whether this is because his ranching techniques were ahead of their time (he owned the first concrete silo in California) or whether he was impaired by his alcoholism and grandiose attitude to being a ranch-owner ("London's workers laughed at his efforts to play big-time rancher [and considered] the operation a rich man's hobby"). He built an $81,000 ($2,100,000 in 2014) property named Wolf House with 26 bedrooms over 15,000 square feet which burnt down just two weeks before he and his wife were due to move in.

His literary legacy is broad, and his social legacy even broader. Accusations of racism have been levelled at him, particularly for his opinions on the increasing population and domesticity of Asia, which he detailed in a 1904 essay named "The Yellow Peril". However, he admits "it must be taken into consideration that the above postulate is itself a product of Western race-egotism, urged by our belief in our own righteousness and fostered by a faith in ourselves which may be as erroneous as are most fond race fancies." George Orwell recognised "his love of violence and physical strength, his belief in 'natural aristocracy', his animal-worship and exaltation of the primitive, he had in him what one might fairly call a Fascist strain". That 'natural aristocracy' and exaltation of the primitive can be found as a common theme throughout his life and is perhaps most informed by his childhood and relationship with his father.

London died on the 22nd of November, 1916, in the sleeping porch of one of his ranch's cottages. He had suffered several illnesses deriving from his time in the Klondike and at the time of his death had dysentery, uraemia and late stage alcoholism. He was taking morphine as pain relief and it is possible that his death was a result of an overdose. He was cremated according to his wishes and buried under a rock taken from the ruins of Wolf House.

Jack London – A Concise Bibliography

Novels
The Cruise of the Dazzler (1902)
A Daughter of the Snows (1902)
The Call of the Wild (1903)
The Kempton-Wace Letters (1903) (written with Anna Strunsky)
The Sea-Wolf (1904)
The Game (1905)

White Fang (1906)
Before Adam (1907)
The Iron Heel (1908)
Martin Eden (1909)
Burning Daylight (1910)
Adventure (1911)
The Scarlet Plague (1912)
A Son of the Sun (1912)
The Abysmal Brute (1913)
The Valley of the Moon (1913)
The Mutiny of the Elsinore (1914)
The Star Rover (1915) (published in England as The Jacket)
The Little Lady of the Big House (1916)
Jerry of the Islands (1917)
Michael, Brother of Jerry (1917)
Hearts of Three (1920) (novelization of a script by Charles Goddard)
The Assassination Bureau, Ltd (1963) (un-finished, completed by Robert L. Fish)

Short Story Collections
Son of the Wolf (1900)
Chris Farrington, Able Seaman (1901)
The God of His Fathers & Other Stories (1901)
Children of the Frost (1902)
The Faith of Men and Other Stories (1904)
Tales of the Fish Patrol (1906)
Moon-Face and Other Stories (1906)
Love of Life and Other Stories (1907)
Lost Face (1910)
South Sea Tales (1911)
When God Laughs and Other Stories (1911)
The House of Pride & Other Tales of Hawaii (1912)
Smoke Bellew (1912)
A Son of the Sun (1912)
The Night Born (1913)
The Strength of the Strong (1914)
The Turtles of Tasman (1916)
The Human Drift (1917)
The Red One (1918)
On the Makaloa Mat (1919)
Dutch Courage & Other Stories (1922)

Autobiographical Memoirs
The Road (1907)
The Cruise of the Snark (1911)
John Barleycorn (1913)

Non-Fiction & Essays
Through The Rapids On The Way To The Klondike (1899)
From Dawson To The Sea (1899)
What Communities Lose By The Competitive System (1900)
The Impossibility Of War (1900)

Phenomena Of Literary Evolution (1900)
A Letter To Houghton Mifflin Co. (1900)
Husky, Wolf Dog Of The North (1900)
Editorial Crimes – A Protest (1901)
Again The Literary Aspirant (1902)
The People of the Abyss (1903)
How I Became a Socialist (1903)[85]
The War of the Classes (1905)[84]
The Story Of An Eyewitness (1906)
A Letter To Woman's Home Companion (1906)
Revolution, and other Essays (1910)
Mexico's Army And Ours (1914)
Lawgivers (1914)
Our Adventures In Tampico (1914)
Stalking The Pestilence (1914)
The Red Game Of War (1914)
The Trouble Makers Of Mexico (1914)
With Funston's Men (1914)

Plays
"The Return of Ulysses – A Modern Version."
One-Act Play written in heroic couplets.
"The Great Interrogation." One-Act Play, written with Lee Bascom (1905)
"As It Was in the Beginning." A Four-Act Comedy, written with Lee Bascom (1905)
Scorn of Women (1906). A Three-Act Play.
"Gold." A Three-Act Play, written with Herbert Heron (1910)
"Billy the Kid." (1910)
Theft (1910). A Four-Act Play.
The First Poet (1911). A One-Act Play.
"War." A Drama of Peace in Three Acts, written with Joseph Noel. (1912. Unpublished)
"Babylonia," A Musical Comedy, written with C. P. Clement and Edward Gage (1913. Unpublished)
"Gold." A Three-Act Play, written with Herbert Heron. (1913)
"The Damascus Road." A Three-Act Play, written with Walter H. Nichols, first as "The Common Man,"
and revised as "The Damascus Road." (1913. Unpublished)
"Daughters of the Rich," One-Act Play. (1915)
The Acorn Planter. A Three-Act Play (1916)
The Birth Mark (1917). A One-Act Play.
A Wicked Woman (1917) A One-Act Play.

Poetry
A Heart
Abalone Song (1913)
And Some Night (1914)
Ballade Of The False Lover (1914)
Cupid's Deal (1913)
Daybreak (1901)
Effusion (1901)
George Sterling (1913)
Gold (1915)
He Chortled With Glee (1899)

He Never Tried Again (1912)
His Trip To Hades (1913)
Homeland (1914)
Hors De Saison (1913)
If I Were God (1899)
In A Year (1901)
In And Out (1911)
Je Ris En Espoir (1914)
Memory (1913)
Moods (1913)
My Confession (1912)
My Little Palmist (1914)
Of Man Of The Future (1915)
Oh You Everybody's Girl (19)
On The Face Of The Earth You Are The One (1915)
Rainbows End (1914)
Republican Rallying Song (1916)
Sonnet (1901)
The Gift Of God (1905)
The Klondyker's Dream (1914)
The Lover's Liturgy (1913)
The Mammon Worshippers (1911)
The Republican Battle-Hymn (1905)
The Return Of Ulysses (1915)
The Sea Sprite And The Shooting Star (1916)
The Socialist's Dream (1912)
The Song Of The Flames (1903)
The Way Of War (1906)
The Worker And The Tramp (1911)
Tick! Tick! Tick! (1915)
Too Late (1912)
Weasel Thieves (1913)
When All The World Shouted My Name (1905)
Where The Rainbow Fell (1902)
Your Kiss (1914)

Short Stories
An Old Soldier's Story (1894)
Who Believes in Ghosts! (1895)
And 'FRISCO Kid Came Back (1895)
Night's Swim In Yeddo Bay (1895)
One More Unfortunate (1895)
Sakaicho, Hona Asi And Hakadaki (1895)
A Klondike Christmas (1897)
Mahatma's Little Joke (1897)
O Haru (1897)
Plague Ship (1897)
The Strange Experience Of A Misogynist (1897)
Two Gold Bricks (1897)
The Devil's Dice Box (1898)
A Dream Image (1898)

The Test: A Clondyke Wooing (1898)
To the Man on Trail (1898)
In a Far Country (1899)
The King of Mazy May (1899)
The End Of The Chapter (1899)
The Grilling Of Loren Ellery (1899)
The Handsome Cabin Boy (1899)
In The Time Of Prince Charley (1899)
Old Baldy (1899)
The Men of Forty Mile (1899)
Pluck And Pertinacity (1899)
The Rejuvenation of Major Rathbone (1899)
The White Silence (1899)
A Thousand Deaths (1899)
Wisdom of the Trail (1899)
An Odyssey of the North (1900)
The Son of the Wolf (1900)
Even unto Death (1900)
The Man with the Gash (1900)
A Lesson In Heraldry (1900)
A Northland Miracle (1900)
Proper "GIRLIE" (1900)
Thanksgiving On Slav Creek (1900)
Their Alcove (1900)
Housekeeping In The Klondike (1900)
Dutch Courage (1900)
Where the Trail Forks (1900)
Hyperborean Brew (1901)
A Relic of the Pliocene (1901)
The Lost Poacher" (1901)
The God of His Fathers (1901)
FRISCO Kid's "Story" (1901)
The Law of Life (1901)
The Minions of Midas (1901)
In the Forests of the North (1902)
The "Fuzziness" of Hoockla-Heen (1902)
The Story of Keesh (1902)
Keesh, Son of Keesh (1902)
Nam-Bok, the Unveracious (1902)
Li Wan the Fair (1902)
Lost Face
Master of Mystery (1902)
The Sunlanders (1902)
The Death of Ligoun (1902)
Moon-Face (1902)
Diable—A Dog (1902), renamed Bâtard in 1904
To Build a Fire (1902, revised 1908)
The League of the Old Men (1902)
The Dominant Primordial Beast (1903)
The One Thousand Dozen (1903)
The Marriage of Lit-lit (1903)

The Shadow and the Flash (1903)
The Leopard Man's Story (1903)
Negore the Coward (1904)
All Gold Cañon (1905)
Love of Life" (1905)
The Sun-Dog Trail" (1905)
The Apostate (1906)
Up The Slide (1906)
Planchette (1906)
Brown Wolf (1906)
Make Westing (1907)
Chased By The Trail (1907)
Trust (1908)
A Curious Fragment (1908)
Aloha Oe (1908)
That Spot (1908)
The Enemy of All the World (1908)
The Heathen (1908)
The House of Mapuhi (1909)
Good-by, Jack (1909)
Samuel (1909)
South of the Slot (1909)
The Chinago (1909)
The Dream of Debs (1909)
The Madness of John Harned (1909)
The Seed of McCoy (1909)
A Piece of Steak (1909)
Mauki (1909)
Goliath (1910)
The Unparalleled Invasion (1910)
Told in the Drooling Ward (1910)
When the World was Young (1910)
The Terrible Solomons (1910)
The Inevitable White Man (1910)
Yah! Yah! Yah! (1910)
By the Turtles of Tasman (1911)
The Mexican (1911)
War (1911)
The Unmasking Of The Cad (1911)
The Scarlet Plague (1912)
The Captain Of The Susan Drew (1912)
The Sea-Farmer (1912)
The Feathers of the Sun (1912)
The Prodigal Father (1912)
Samuel (1913)
The Sea-Gangsters (1913)
The Strength of the Strong (1914)
Told in the Drooling Ward (1914)
The Hussy (1916)
Like Argus of the Ancient Times (1917)
Jerry of the Islands (1917)

The Red One (1918)
Shin-Bones (1918)
The Bones of Kahekili (1919)

www.ingramcontent.com/pod-product-compliance
Lightning Source LLC
Chambersburg PA
CBHW071007280626
47160CB00015B/1905